Blue Solace
New Bonus Content 2017 Edition

ANGELA DAWN STATEN

Copyright © 2013 by Angela Dawn Atchley
Special 2017 Edition © 2016 by Angela Dawn Staten
All rights reserved, including the right of reproduction in
whole or in part in any form.
https://angeladawnsword.wordpress.com

First published in October 2013.
Available from Amazon.com, CreateSpace.com, and other
retail outlets 2016. A very brief quotation of Move B***h
from the album Word of Mouf by Ludacris featuring Mystikal
and I-20. Free use. The Love Song of J. Alfred Prufrock
(1915) by T.S. Eliot. Public Domain.

Cover: Drop Dead Designs ©2016.

The characters and events portrayed in this book are fictitious.
Any references to historical events, real people, or real locales
are used fictitiously. Any similarity to real persons, living or
dead, is coincidental and not intended by the author.

Atchley (Staten), Angela Dawn, 1988–
Blue Solace: a novel / by Angela Dawn Atchley (Staten).
Summary: When Cousins Lucas Kale and Leon Carmany
travel to Hastings, Nebraska to track down a mysterious
woman from Leon's vision, they discover Vampires are the
least of their troubles. The young woman covered in blood and
prophesied to die, according to the seer's vision, is the only
one who can save them from the zombies.

ISBN-10: 1530575869
ISBN-13: 978-1530575862

This is for my mother Mary (May 1961-June 1999) for reading to me. And for my English teacher at Springfield High School (TN). RIP Frankye Holmes.

~

CONTENTS

Character Guide

Prologue 1

1. First Encounters 6
2. The Weeping Willow 18
3. Out of the Clear Blue Sky 36
4. Hope 50
5. Dreams and Visions 68
6. Friends and Enemies 84
7. All Connected 98
8. Road Trip 116
9. Hello and Goodbye 134
10. Kansas 150
11. Once in a Blue Moon 166
12. The Banish 186
13. Three Kinds of Dead 199
14. The Last Supper 214
15. X Marks the Spot 237
16. Deaths 255
17. Happy Birthday 270
18. The Bite 286
19. Seeing Red 308
20. Between the Devil and the Deep Blue Sea 331
21. Return 351

Epilogue 364

About the Author

Character Guide

KRONOS: Leader of the Vampires.
BLAYNE: Vampire child of Kronos.
AMATERASU "TOKYO": Japanese Female. Vampire child of Kronos.

LUCAS "LUKE" KALE: Related to Leon. Vampire Hunter. Likes women.
BRIGHTON LEON CARMANY: Vampire Hunter/Seer/Genius. Goes by Leon.
LOKI: Troublemaker. Friends with Cole and Lana Queen. Not fond of Raven.
LANA QUEEN: Lead Shadow.
COLE: Shadow. In love with Lana.
RAVEN: The Mystery Lady.
MOZART: Raven's dog.
GANESHA: Part of Raven's crew.
SHEBA: Part of Raven's crew.
JET: Part of Raven's crew.
CRICKET: A mute from Africa. Also with Raven's crew.

LEE: Zombie.
KIMBERLY: Lee's sister.
ALEC: Bad acne. Also not fond of Raven.
SILHOU (Like Silhouette): Blue-haired female.

Shadow (n): 1, A spy. 2, A phantom. –v.t.
1, Trail; stay near, -shadowy, adj.

Blue: A color with a variety of meanings

~~~

Prologue

May 9
Hastings, Nebraska.
August Cemetery. 9:00 p.m.

LEE / KRONOS / LANA / COLE

A NEFARIOUS VAMPIRE with shoulder length and midnight black hair drains the life out of his prey. The prey in charge of closing the cemetery—the name sewn onto the man's shirt reads *Lee*—happens to be at the right place at the wrong time.

Unfortunately, August Cemetery has to close and for now Lee's employment involves making sure everyone has left the area. Having no use for a burial ground, he highly hopes his father will pass the reigns down to his other progeny—Kimberly. Lee does not desire a future that consists of death, and relishing the cemetery's fresh air will never counteract that verity.

Lee starts to think about the recent proceedings that brought him to this terrifying moment in time. Him driving along, being snatched from his truck, and unnervingly thrown to the dirt of a fresh grave.

Precious blood is now being pulled from his twenty-eight year old body. Literally *pulled.* The petrified man concentrates on pain. Pain of every blood drop reluctantly leaving his robust heart, and none returning.

The man is forced to stand, as if he were a post in the ground, in front of the black-haired Vampire while white holes stalk from an omnipresent sky. What was their use in spying? Would they really grant him his life? Instead the stars cruelly wink farewell while blood flows out of the man's mouth, into the air like a stream, and through the parted lips of the ravenous Vampire who steals his necessity.

Lee tries to run, but the killer's hand that is held out somehow compels him to stand still. The dying man gags on his own blood.

Agony. It is beyond agony when something in Lee's brain snaps. The life force—his blood—has been partially forced out of his body and into the Vampire's mouth, but now the rest of the man's blood begins to exit out through all the orifices on his face: mouth, nose, ears, and eyes. Even slight gusts of wind cannot help, for they do not stop paths of coalescing, merging red surges of blood as they promptly enter the Vampire's mouth and nostrils.

Coming within reach of their expiration date, deprived respiratory organs demand attention from inside the man's chest, as if they will create holes with their shielding ribcage to obtain the oxygen they desperately seek. Trepidation tumbles into the defenseless victim. Lee can feel the precious heart all mammals need still thrashing inside of him. But in his spirit Lee knows it is ineffectual, for him.

With calamitous blood loss and lack of oxygen, the suffocating man is sure of one thing. The stupefying spectrum of vibrant colors. They move in waves of…ecstasy. Who knew death could be so friendly and pleasant?

Lee attempts to breathe and his world egresses in ebony.

The blood taker keeps the human's heart pumping long after Lee's departure from existence. The last drop of blood enters the Vampire's mouth, and Lee's carcass collapses to the dirt.

Abruptly, his enemy flips down over the whitish-gray cemented wall and the dead human's idling monochrome truck still parked on the paved trail with the driver door open. "Kronos," a firm female voice says.

The Vampire seizes a single step forward into the illumination casting out from the street lamp, unveiling the scars on his square face. There is a horizontal disfigurement on his left cheek approximately three inches long. Another scar runs diagonally through his right eyebrow. His ghastly, demoralizing appearance is worthy of recoiling.

The murderer smiles with glee. "Lana! I was going to grab something to go, but when I heard *you* I wondered" —his vindictive grin expands; the scar residing at the right corner of the Vampire's upturned lip continues underneath his earlobe—"well, it appears I eat faster than you run, Shadow."

Clasping a handcrafted form of execution, her wooden stake, Lana glances at the lifeless man lying on the cemetery ground.

"Oh, it's dead. I suppose that is another that dies on *your* time." The Vampire charges towards the vigilant tracker.

Due to Lana's small, diminutive body frame people and vamps tend to underestimate the girl's competency. But Kronos no longer questions his foe's abilities. He will enjoy his thirty-five-year-old-looking face a lot more when this eighteen year old is not around to mess it up—in other words dead.

The teenager swings her right arm to stake the taunting blood sucker. But Kronos grabs her wrist and squeezes her throat, making it difficult for the dark-haired girl to counterattack. The Vampire pins the girl against the vehicle door, having used her rear to slam it closed. Two noticeable scars run parallel through the top and bottom of the girl's tiny scarlet lips. There is a third smaller scar next to the two on her bottom lip.

"Let me see," the Vampire calmly says running his hand along her hairline to her ear.

The dexterous girl vigorously delivers a punch to his ribs. The Vampire retaliates with a vicious head butt. Her hair falls back revealing a hole the size of a dime missing from the summit of her left ear.

"Such a beauty." He proudly looks at the irreparable ear.

Suddenly, Kronos releases the teen. While in the

motion of dodging to his left, Lana—pulse accelerates due to a viciously spinning blur en route for her forehead—barely has time to drop down. Her palms scrape against the dark gray concrete as a red throwing axe shatters the truck's window behind her.

Lana looks up expecting to see another Shadow, her friend Cole. Having to split up to inspect their vicinity, Lana and Cole had been together hunting their most hated Vampire when they lost track of him.

"Lana," the teenage boy utters, and worriedly helps his friend of five years to her feet, loathing himself for agreeing to her idea to separate.

"Kronos—"

"We'll never catch him," he interjects grabbing her arm to a halt.

With the man's cadaver over his shoulder further down the way, Kronos leaps over a seven foot cemetery wall—intended for guarding the dead—and disappears into the dark spine-chilling woods.

"At least he didn't leave the body this time," Cole happily notes reaching through the busted window to retrieve his axe, shunning shards of glass that accompany it on an ugly brown seat. A previous encounter with their obsessive nemesis Kronos ended with the teenagers having to dispose of a disgusting mess the Vampire purposely left.

"Thanks," she replies graciously nodding at his axe. Lana peers down at her palms to see what has become of her scrapping them against the pavement. No cuts. No bruising. Nothing.

~~~

Chapter 1
First Encounters

May 10

LUCAS KALE & MYSTERY LADY

LUCAS KALE IS NOT only behind schedule, but feels inexcusable for hitting the snooze button *four* times. He casts a fleeting look at his cheap watch as his feet move swiftly on the footway. The third hand on the small clock is stuck on the number one. The time reads 12:10 pm.

Today is sunny and balmy in Hastings, Nebraska. Spring zeal dominates an enduring atmosphere on this intoxicating tenth day of May. Paper and plastic "On Sale" signs roughly publicize on every front of the towering shops. But Lucas doesn't care what they are for or even observes numerously diverse features crafting enthralling stores. Now is not browsing time, and onslaughts of dawdling people are threatening the rushed man's patience.

Noticing an immense silver banner about Mother's Day across the way, swaying with poise to the will of a zephyr, prompts the now upset man into full speed. Turning at the corner of a brick building, Lucas unexpectedly collides with a young woman. Her books plummet to the sidewalk, and of course the freshly made warm cup of coffee in her hand splashes down the front of his nicely-fitted denim jeans and favorite polo shirt that exposes his burly arms.

Before Lucas's brain can register the incident that just happened, the awe-inspiring beauty immediately takes her white napkins, only things remaining in her startled hands, and starts rubbing the bottom of his green shirt.

"Oh my god! Oh my god!" the woman repeats, an abnormal feeling quickly stirring inside of her... The twenty-four year old has his hands thrown up in the air first out of shock from the caffeinated beverage, but now he is thunderstruck by this brunette. "Whoa, whoa, uh..." he gives her a peculiar look, an unusual feeling tugging at him...

The curly-headed woman, Lucas guesses to be a little younger than him, continues cleaning the mess moving on to his denims, practically on top of his penis, not noticing the expression on his face. How is he supposed to make her stop? Lucas is not *entirely* sure if that is even a want.

The young man bends down to get her

hardbacks, sunlight reflecting off his short, blonde hair. His plan is to get this fine young woman moving as far away from him as possible. The number one priority for Lucas is getting to the restaurant Rolling Acres to meet his cousin Leon.

Two volumes have been mounded up by the time she joins in to help. Lucas Kale's concentration is instantly interrupted, coming to the unsettling realization that they both have reached for the last book, *Mozart*. They look at each other, their eye color is akin, hazel. But a look is only a second. Enough time is passing to be classified as riveting.

The woman doesn't know what to say. The usually attentive lady had been too distracted to pay attention to where she was walking; this fact deeply concerns her. One thing occurs to her though, an apology is due for the irresponsibility. She opens her mouth to speak but the clean-shaved man quickly shoves the three books about Beethoven, Bach, and Mozart into her arms.

"Maybe you could learn to watch where you're going, princess," he coldly suggests as he passes.

There is no way she is about to accept such a repugnant attitude. With eyes narrowing in anger, she clenches her books, stands up, pivots in his direction, and screams after him, "Excuse me!" Several passers-by on the sidewalk, upon hearing the affray, clench their bags of purchased merchandise and cease their conversations to cast chary stares.

Lucas accelerates his pace. Getting to the restaurant is imperative.

The woman vehemently catches up to him and

plants her feet in front of the ill-mannered gentleman. "Tell me who gave you the right to talk to people that way?"

"Not people. Just you," Lucas chimes gently placing his hands on her shoulders and impelling the furious girl out of his path.

"Douche."

He flashes a smirk over a strapping shoulder as he continues through the tapering crowd, leaving the attractive woman.

Wow. I really like that shirt, Lucas thinks about the beautiful female's close-fitting icy blue AC/DC top—his favorite band. And then he thinks about his own shirt, his favorite shirt. Hoping it isn't ruined, he looks down examining the damage. It is salvageable he concludes, and the damp outline near his penis creating the illusion that he urinated on himself isn't on his I-Care list.

LEON CARMANY & LUCAS KALE

"You had a girl practically all over you and you *didn't* get her number?" The younger man with medium brown hair chuckles causing a few strands to fall around his round face. He quickly ceases laughing. "That's not your usual behavior, Luke. What is wrong with you?"

"Me? HER! There's something wrong with her," Lucas childishly remarks, surveying his surroundings inside of the restaurant Rolling Acres. The vale that an artist had skillfully painted covers the entire wall behind his cousin Leon. It reminds him of home in Tennessee. Splurges of deep blue and green paint throw open shady hills and dark but comforting heavens into his welcoming eyes.

A young waitress no older than twenty, Leon Carmany judges by her mature features and fresh zest of freedom from parents attitude, comes to take his older cousin's order. Leon had ordered himself a house salad and water before Lucas's arrival; half of both linger in their dishes. Immediately, Lucas mentality notes that the slim waitress has decent sized breasts but she has not quite blossomed as much as the mystery lady he encounter only moments ago. He also notices her name tag reads: Tina.

The waitress quickly observes the coffee stains and smiles. "What can *I* do to *you?*"

Lucas raises his eyebrows, trying to decide if her provocative question was asked intentionally. He decides he doesn't care. He likes the query. Leon, however, rolls his sapphire blue eyes and chooses to finish his drink through this banal and predictable conversation. The ruddy head had been overly nice to him, but Leon knew that once the "chick magnet" arrived his existence would ebb.

The red head clears her throat, still jovial. "I mean, what can I get you?"

"You're cheapest beer will do." Lucas flashes her his flirtatious smile. "For now."

Leon holds up his vacant glass. "I could use—" Instead of paying attention to her customer, the server walks away from the small azure table. "—some *WATER,*" he finishes while glaring across the table.

"What?" Lucas tries to act innocent.

"She was nice until you came."

Suddenly recalling why they are at this particular eating place, Lucas frantically searches the jade green bar with his eyes. A fellow's butt crack occupying a matching barstool is not what he has in mind. "Where's the blonde?"

"She's not here."

"Okay… That is not normal."

"You know my visions have *never* been wrong," an extremely solemn Leon reminds him of his infallible visions; the ones that tell him whom to save from the evil and perilous creatures—Vampires. The longhaired young man with blue eyes sees the ginger girl slinking back and worriedly whispers, "I didn't know I *could* be wrong."

Their flamboyant waitress places a strawberry Smirnoff in front of Lucas, and Leon hysterically expresses amusement; knowing that his beer loving cousin and friend hates any alcoholic beverage with a fruit taste. "No," the blonde man chuckles. The server brings her right arm out from behind her and places a Bud Light on the flat top. Lucas had to admit he enjoyed this practical joke. "Funny. I like you."

"Will that be all?"

Leon nods. She hands them each a white slip of paper and returns to the kitchen. Lucas casually looks at his slip. "This my lil' cuz' is better than a check." He turns the sheet to Leon's angle. It reads: "TINA 555-555-0138". "I hate you," Leon simply says observing the bill in his hand. Lucas smiles and chugs his beer.

* * *

"I already told you. I saw *this* parking lot," Leon hand motions as they exit the diner. "Her walking into Rolling Acres. Sitting at that bar. Third stool from the right."

The restaurant is located a block from where the shops held their Mother's Day sales. This place seems to have one of the bigger parking lots in the area. Lucas Kale stands on the sidewalk racking his brain, trying to figure out what went wrong. "That is when everything went black and she was…"

"Lying in her own blood." The displeased young man knows why his truly concerned best friend had paused at the end of his sentence. Leon has been receiving visions for the past eleven months since his twenty-second birthday and not once had any included a person's corpse. The cause of death had always presented itself.

Leon cannot help but notice that his eyesight is getting blurry… "Oh, no!" the seer panics…

* * *

COLE & LANA
"I searched my half of the city, but… I'm sorry. I didn't find him," Cole dejectedly informs his comrade Lana. Her deep lustrous black tresses touch the apex of her bosom as disappointment captures her oval face. "Guess you didn't either?"

The teenagers have been searching within Hastings, Nebraska for about an hour, doubling back repeatedly with no hope in finding their nemesis Kronos. Their abnormal abilities delivered nothing. Frustrated and disconcerted, Lana walks left clear of a shiny silver advertisement with dark red letters that spell "Mother's Day Sale". "We must have missed something when we searched the woods last night."

"Maybe he moved on." The cracked sidewalk transients, no longer guiding them straight. He pushes the button for the crosswalk.

A small breeze lightly plays with Lana's hair but it's just enough to make her grab it all and drape it down one side of her neck, covering her left ear. The ear that lost part of its cartilage at the top, about the size of a dime, to Kronos. The teasing at school is one thing, but having to deal with the looks from strangers can be a bit much. "Cole, forget your logic. What does your *instinct* tell you?"

"You know that only works when there are Deaths." He unnervingly runs his fair fingers through his loose dark hair. The seventeen year old, having been a Shadow for one year, is not fond of fighting Deaths—a group of Vampires. Facing off with a solitary vamp equals an adrenaline rush. Two or more Vampires is when fear enters the equation. He would rather slay *one* Vampire than hunt *Deaths.*

"Forget that. *We* know Kronos." Disregarding the flashing "Don't Walk", the impatient raven-haired girl heedlessly moves across the crosswalk. She nonchalantly sights wet spots and a brown and white coffee container sticking out of an overflowing trash bin as they advance to the other sidewalk. "Did you or did you not feel his presence?"

They are steps away from the walkway when an

unsightly lime green station wagon madly honks them to move faster—like a train shouting at people on the railroad tracks. The traffic light alters to red just before the car rashly enters the junction, and its right turn signal is on despite the fact that it does not take that route.

The teenagers astoundingly eye the speeding vehicle. *That's right. Draw more attention to that ugly piece of*—Cole interrupts his thought to answer his comrade as they turn right on the sidewalk. "I did. Kronos was there. Saturday-morning-slash-afternoon-sale-madness must be terminating." Several signs have already disappeared along with the consumers.

"He still has to be…hiding. We stayed there till dawn," Lana says with spangles in her young eighteen year old eyes.

Cole smiles down at her, fully understanding. "You're right. He's trapped." There is a glint of hope in Cole's eyes for he knows there is no way Kronos would *want* to feel the sun on his face, or any part of him for that matter. They happily begin their run to the bone yard, barely inside city limits, where Kronos unremorsefully took a life last night.

LEON & LUCAS
The best place to receive insight into the future is not in any populace for two reasons.

One, it is embarrassing. Humans in general tend to panic. Leon Carmany does not like going through pain to come to the realization that he is surrounded by an onslaught of people. Second, he doesn't like elucidating afterwards that a physician is not necessary. Hopefully.

Lucas knows what is happening by the way his younger relative covers his eyes. Luke glances around the parking lot and spots their ultramarine blue 1970 Chevrolet Biscayne. "Come on." He places his hand on the middle of Leon's back guiding him.

A shrillness, Leon depicted on more than one occasion is like the high piercing noise of all the school bus brakes in the world suddenly going bad, escalates in his eardrums. The twenty-two year old commences moaning.

"Has the ringing started?" Lucas asks. His question is answered when an abashing Leon quickly slams his hands over his ears and groans louder, the noise persisting to amplify.

"Can only imagine what this is gonna look like," Lucas mutters to himself and grips Leon's gratifying hand. The prominent men holding hands run through the half full parking lot. Someone whistles at them as they near the car, and Lucas caught off guard, and Leon unable to see, stumble over each other's feet. They tumble in front of a party of four women. Embarrassed, Lucas immediately gets up and helps the semi-blind man to his feet.

"Please tell me you aren't gay. That's nasty," the shorter woman says.

With a plan in mind, Lucas takes Leon's hand and they begin walking. Just as they pass by the shorter woman, Lucas takes his free palm and backhands her ass. "Bad girl," he says and sprints to the car, pulling the seer. "Next time we walk," the taller ladies' man says opening the door for the tormented and then makes his way to the driver's seat.

Hastily, Lucas sympathetically hands his angst-ridden cousin a white wash cloth from the backseat. By the time Leon slams it in between his teeth tears have begun to scuttle along his cheeks. He grunts powerfully and intensely as he unendingly grinds into the rag while blood gushes from his nasal passages. The ringing dwindles, disappearing completely. Leon wholly loses his sight and hearing of the things around him.

At first everything is coal black. Slowly evolving into his focus is a raven-haired teenager with a fragment of her ear absent... She raucously screams while something violently bites into her left cheek... Daylight emerges from the obscurity. A streetlight accompanies a gate with the words "Rush Cemetery".

Leon's senses return to him, immediately ending the vision. A trickle of blood has emanated out of his aching ears. He flings open his door and vomits.

Lucas, knowing the next step—research, puts the key in the ignition of the old and sentimental vehicle. The car had been bequeathed to him and Leon by Lucas Kale's mother after her unexpected death.

On the way back to their motel room, Lucas reminisces about the numerous times his mother caught the two of them pretending to drive the car, and out of fear she began hiding the key. Then the day came when he turned nine and no matter where she chose to hide it, Lucas always found the silver key. She would find him and Leon in the field slowly cruising along without fear of punishment.

Early one morning after he arose to the smell of bacon and eggs, Lucas saw the keys dangling from the designated key area on the wall. He snatched them from their place, put the key in the ignition, turned it over, and much to his disappointment nothing happened. It was not until after the death of his parents that his Uncle Joe told him his mother had started removing the battery. That very day Lucas realized what he wanted to be when he "grew up". A mechanic.

~~~~

Chapter 2
The Weeping Willow

LANA QUEEN

THIS PLACE ALWAYS looks more inviting than the one I live across from.

To avoid the blinding light shining in her eyes, Lana looks down and left into green foliage that never seems to end. Mercifully, August Cemetery does not bestow a startling impression of gloom and doom amid day hours. The dazzling yellow sun omits creepy shadows and Vampires could not be found playing. The grave markers do not look prehistoric due to the fact that they are not. This cemetery is not shoe-smelling-new, but it is undeniably modern compared to other quantities in Hastings.

Lana and Cole slow to a walk. They have ran

nonstop through the congested city but loping in a burial place would be eye-catching. It is daytime and middling humans would likely be here visiting, laying a loved or hated someone to rest, or perhaps both.

Lana said goodbye to her grandparents six years ago due to diabetes and cancer. Her adored father, also a Shadow, was taken a year later at the hands of Kronos; that battle also resulted in the physical scarring of her lips. But the underestimation of the thirteen year old girl's strength is what lead to a far worse scarring for the Vampire.

The damage to her ear though, that is new. Trying to dodge flying acid was harder than Lana had anticipated. Nine months ago, sometime during the first week of school, it was her turn to relieve Cole from watch (hunting of Vampires) for a week. The raven-haired senior, finding no signs of bloodsuckers in the quiet night, thought it best to return home before she died of boredom.

The Shadow walked the bumpy back road—New Hope Road—next to August Cemetery. (It eventually intersects with the main road where the cemetery's entrance is located.) Then she had that feeling, the sixth sense—the sense that yells *Vampire!*

The girl with lustrous black tresses was walking on the potholed road, now recently paved, when she saw and heard a boy her age sitting on the freshly dewed grass crying next to one of the road's rare streetlights.

"What happened?" she asked.

"Are you, Lana?"

"Uh…yeah."

"He said you go in alone or he's gonna kill her."

Given the teenage boy with short brunette hair had called the Shadow by her name and referred to the Vampire as male, she knew it could only be the Vampire she was on a first name basis with—Kronos.

"He… I think he's a damn vampire. And not the lame kind. He's really gonna fucking kill my girlfriend."

Lana gazed up. The street lamp casted a small amount of light in the dark night. The Haunted House she had heard about, and passed by very little due to the lack of food in the area for Vampires, eerily stood a little ways back from the light. A nauseating feeling quickly ensued in the pit of her stomach. The only thing she knew about this derelict place was the lady haunting the house had brown hair and was supposed to be a *nice* ghost.

Nice ghost or not, the lot had been uninhabited for decades and Lana was not really looking forward to finding out—especially with a bloodsucker in there—if the woman catered disgusting brown faucet water or delicious cookies. Which you never hear about. *If a ghost can alter the water, why can't they manifest giant ass dough with chocolate chips?*

But it was (still is) her obligation to save people. Casper or no Casper. Lana looked down at the teenage boy already lamenting the death of his girlfriend. He clung to the hard pole, face wet with tears, as if at any moment it would turn into his girlfriend and everything would be fine.

"What's your name?"

"Blayne." He didn't bother looking up this time.

"She's going to be okay. He is *not* going to kill her," Lana reassured him, and took in a deep breath. Lana stepped forward onto the pebbled walkway leading through knee-high blades of grass, some had slumped over the path underneath her pointed toe boots with a low heel.

For the first time in several years, Lana's knees began to shake as she approached the abandoned house (save for the ghost in question). The shutters had fallen down over time, only one or two remained giving it that *spooky* vibe. The three floors towered above her, and she wondered if the top floor with the lifeless window was truly considered to be a third level. The area looked (still does) too small to be a third story.

The same sixth sense that alerts her of the close proximity of multiple Vampires—Deaths— developed into the same feeling that warns her about the presence of Kronos and she seriously hoped her *instincts* were right about there being *one* killer in the faded yellow house.

Still hearing the sobbing boy behind her, Lana nervously looked up from the foot of the stairs that separates the bushes surrounding the porch; the dark house seemed to have grown two stories taller. But the petite girl frozen in front of the Haunted House knew it was her imagination. Houses do not *grow*.

The door stood directly across from her. The Shadow gripped the stake. Sweat coated her palm and seeped into the wood. Realizing she had been holding her breath, Lana exhaled and placed a foot on the first step.

Instantaneously, yellow light shown through *all* the windows, as if there were numerous beings standing by all the light switches waiting for her. Lana vomited. Chunks of that night's dinner landed right there beside her foot.

The Shadow knew it was now or never. Lana sprang up the steps, across the small porch, and easily pushed open the rotted door.

She found nothing. No furniture. No invincible lady. No Kronos.

The lights had to have come on somehow.

Lana noticed the two doors to her left and right. Someone or something had spray painted black **X**'s across them. *Great. Kronos is playing. Through the maze I go.*

The vigilant eye of the Shadow shifted over the empty house while her feet carefully moved over the dust free floor—surely a house this old built in the 1920's, and unoccupied since before her birth would have some degree of dust bunnies. *He swept his footprints away.*

The CLONK CLONK of her boots against the hardwood floor made her even more on edge. *He's going to know where I'm at! Like it matters. He can hear the rhythm of my heart.* Lana knew it would be pointless to take her shoes off, a futile effort, but the extra noise was increasing her anxiety. She decided instead of removing them, she would hurry up and end yet another exasperating game hosted by Kronos.

Lana passed the marked doors and entered the next unfurnished room. Immediately to her right on the other side of the first room's wall were stairs that lead to the next floor. On the hazardous steps (termites had feed on several of the boards and were crawling about) a thickly painted black arrow pointed from the bottom up.

Her sixth sense confirmed this was the correct path.

The Shadow cringed with every step she took, the creaking of the ancient wood sounded just as loud as the noise made by her shoes. *At least there's light in here.* She sighed. The lighted bulbs in the antique chandeliers hanging from the ceiling would make it easier to see when she needed to fight off an attacker. *Or possibly fall down and kill me. Why would he even turn the electricity on?*

From the center of the stairs, Lana saw a door at the top that displayed a question mark painted with the same dark black as the arrow and **X**'s. She quickly saw this was not the only one; the room to the left of it and the door to her right (it faced the crooning wood that lead her up here and ran perpendicular with the room across from the stairs) both had the same punctuation marks.

Lana mentally named the door to the right, Number One, the one in the middle, Two, and the other a good ways down from it to the left, Number Three. There was one room left.

At the far end, facing her and Number Three, was another door frame that was rotted; the ceiling around it had apparently been leaking for some time and brown circles nearly covered it. She feared the whole structure would cave in and end her life *for* Kronos.

There was no **X** or **?**. Instead it had a red smiley face.

The Nebraskan Shadow felt her face become warmer from her increased blood pressure. *I bet Blayne's girlfriend is behind that one and Kronos in one of the others. Maybe. Who knows?*

For a moment Lana stood between the steps and Number Two contemplating checking the three rooms and squaring off with Kronos or whatever was in there. But then decided she should find out if there was even a person *to* find and save; for all she knew the girl was dead.

Lana turned left and began following the railing that lead from the stairs to the Smiley Face; looking over the side she could see the big empty room below her. The old hardwood under her boots made more noise than the stairs and previous floor combined. Lana prayed it did give way.

The CLUNK CLUNK of her low heel intensified as she passed Number Three, coming closer to the red spray paint. Her hand so tightly squeezing the stake she feared she might break it. That certainly would not help things.

Standing in front of the last door, the smell of the fresh paint combined with the musty odor of the house made her extremely nauseated. *Let's get this over with.* Lana touched the chipped knob, stake ready for a slaying, and pushed the decayed door…

Inside sat a girl with brown hair.

Lana nearly peed on herself, but then noticed the gray masking tape over the wiry brunette's lips in the niche of time. The girl was taped to a chair the same way the Shadow saw in movies—tape wrapped around her feet and gray strips ran underneath her bosom to the back of the chair.

Blayne's girlfriend had been crying for some time, her cheeks were soaked and red. Lana knew she must have stopped recently because she had not heard the sniffling that comes with the heavy flow of tears. But upon seeing her savior the girl resumed weeping.

The rescuer did not like the scenery. There were no windows; jumping from the second story was not an option. They would have to go back the way Lana had come, or go up the stairs that went right up through the ceiling behind the kidnapped girl. Bad idea.

A trap. This entire thing was a trap. Lana knew this all along. She was not stupid. Seeing the scissors purposely left beside the chair not only guaranteed something bad was about to happen, but it would be seconds from now when they were on their way back towards the black question marks. It felt ironic somehow. *What to do now? That was the question.*

The Shadow slowly peeled the sticky tape back from the girl's lips, not wanting to cause her further pain. Although sore lips was the least of their worries.

"Elp me," she said.

Lana could tell by the way she spoke this girl had been born deaf or partially deaf; she did not know which due to a lack of education on this...*condition?* Lana tried to conceal her surprise. She had not expected Blayne's girlfriend to have a disability; until now she figured from her own experience that all teenage boys except for Cole were harsh and insensitive creatures.

Then her surprise turned into anger. She snatched the blades up and cut the thick strips at the back of the chair. *How could Kronos do this to her…? Well he is a Vampire and she is a human.*

Lana stood up after cutting the ligature around the girl's hands and feet. *Now what? I don't know where Kr* —the Shadow froze mid thought, a deadly suspicion formed in her bones like osteoporosis.

Lana stared at the oddly placed stairs. Why would someone build a stairway in a room?

The deaf girl rose from the old-fashioned chair. Lana put a finger to her lips, signaling her to be silent. It would not matter to Kronos how much, or how little, noise they made, but the absence of vocal chords being used helps the adept tracker concentrate.

When she ascended the stairway with the painted arrow on it, she had known her nemesis was up here Lana recalled.

But that feeling had not changed.

Her ability was supposed to work (only with Kronos) in the way someone saying "warmer" or "colder" upon finding something.

It did not lessen or become stronger.

Eyes closed, the highly alert Shadow walked to the second stairway. She waited. Waited for the "colder" feeling. The girl with the permanent scars stood at the foot of the stairs and opened her eyes. The wooden stairwell was not lit. It was pitch-black and she could see nothing.

Lana ran.

She grabbed the deaf girl's hand and ran. Lana knew. She had known before ever coming through the front door of the "Haunted House". But what was she to do? She could not send out an alert through the Shadow Connection—a system Shadows often use to communicate with each other by telepathically sending out images of their locations—it would result in Kronos killing the poor girl. Besides, even if she wanted to Lana did not to how to do such a thing. The superhuman was older (slaying Vampires wise) than those of her kind she had met over the years. But she seemed to be the only one who has yet to master this critical power...

Lana stood at the foot of the lightless stairway and faced the truth. There would be no "colder". Deaths—more than one Vampire—were here. Lana left the room hand and hand with the bait, not having the faintest idea where her enemies patiently waited.

But it did not take long for one—the one—to present himself.

The two girls just barely made it out of the red Smiley Face room when Kronos rushed out from behind door Number Three holding a silver canister. It became clear why he turned on the electricity. The Vampire wanted to make sure the Shadow could read the canister's label. It was marked *Acid, Bitch.*

Lana quickly turned for the railing that ran alongside the small floor. She tucked her left hand inside her long leather sleeved jacket and raised the jacket up to shield the side of her face while she simultaneously placed her right boot on the rail—her free hand still clasped with Blayne's girlfriend's shaking palm.

Then the Shadow heard the sound of her own voice bouncing off the bare walls. Her ear was on fire.

Lana did not realize the other girl had not stepped up onto the railing. And instead of them jumping down together, the other girl's legs bumped against the railing when she screamed from the acid eating away at her ear. Their hands dissevered, becoming two again, and while Lana was in the motion of jumping she saw a mop of brown hair topple over the side.

The Shadow witnessed the girl land neck first on the hardwood floor. She heard bones break and knew she had failed. The sudden distractions, pain in her ear and the kidnapped girl's fall, caused Lana to land on her backside (fortunate the old floor did not collapse from the impact). She opened her eyes. Cole's worried face was centimeters from hers, and when she looked up at the railing Kronos had disappeared.

The next thing the Shadow knew she was in the emergency room with no memory of how she came to be there. Lana asked her friend if Blayne was still alive and how he was handling the news of his dead girlfriend. Cole told her he never saw the boy.

Later Lana realized she had never known the name of Blayne's girlfriend and finding out was unlikely. To her, the girl would always be referred to as Blayne's Girlfriend or the Deaf Girl.

A girl had died right before her eyes and Lana

did not even know her name.

The alumni snaps back to the present, still walking on the cemetery's gray pavement next to the boy with the birthmark on his Adam's apple.

After the death of her father she had expected Kronos to come after her unstinting, generous mother, but he never showed any signs of interest. She was, *is*, grateful. Not bothering to look at them, she shudders as she passes the grave markers of her departed relatives. All three of them—grandfather, grandmother, and father—were laid to rest side by side.

Now is not the time for emotions to tear me. The hunt has to come first...not the hurt. The Shadow pushes forward, thoughts plaguing her mind.

Her graduation was four days ago. That same night Kronos had lead her and Cole on a wild goose chase to other states. The Shadow was more than willing to pursue, in hopes that college and life in general would be better without contentiously having to look over her shoulder.

But now they are back home and she does not know why.

Upon approaching a golden suburban parked on the left side with heavily tinted windows, they spot some visitors up ahead in the cemetery. One of the suburban's windows slides down and a cute little boy with a yellow sponge on his white shirt perches up from the backseat. "I'm Devin," he waves and smiles bashfully. Lana gently waves back thus causing the fair-haired boy to giggle and shy away from the window before slouching down in the seat.

Lana smiles at a couple, not too much older than

her and Cole, standing in between the rows of grave markers. The tall and unadorned woman politely returns the sweet gesture with a wave before bending to place variegated flowers on the grave in front of her. Cole gives that friendly nod that most men tend to do nowadays, which in return the oddly short man reciprocates.

The Shadows leave the pair as they stride upwards, bound for the vast empty space at the rear of the cemetery. Turning left at the zenith of the hill, they obey the cement wall on the right steering them to awaiting land that hankers for more bodies.

Right smack in the middle of freshly mowed bluestem grass, wind lurches a pacifying aroma and the tallest weeping willow Lana has ever seen. Its talon like limbs cavort in every direction, screaming for souls to accompany the loneliness that invades its territory. The tepid air settles, sending a calming peace over the broken-hearted willow. She thought the whole scene to be appropriate; that is what most people first look and feel like when they not only come here but to any resting place.

Their feet briskly glide downhill through patches of cut grass continuing on with their search for the Vampire in hiding. When the fence meets another seven foot wall, the excited seekers steal glances up the high land and the small woods on the other side of the field. Seeing no sign of ordinary humans, or anyone for that matter, Lana and Cole readily jump and flip over the border leaving city limits.

* * *

LUCAS & LEON

Parked in front of their motel room, the shirtless twenty-four year old blonde intensely directs his crazy eye look at Leon.

"What?"

Lucas continues eyeing him like a mad man.

"What?"

Not only does Luke continue staring incredulously, but does not answer. This time the seer demands, *"WHAT?"*

"A zombie?" Lucas questions, raising his eyebrow in continued skepticism.

"Man, that's what it looked and acted like. And the smell was worse than that summer our dads gutted those two deer in Uncle Joe's barn."

"Yeah. That was on your eighth birthday when you made Rachel yack by trying to explain what a uterus was," the mechanic laughs, muscles flexing. Their cousin Rachel, Uncle Joe's daughter, was a month shy of turning five when Leon drew her a diagram of her internal plumbing. For Lucas and Leon it was one of the best summers ever.

"Hey, it was difficult being the only seven year old in *sixth grade.*" Leon opens the car door. "Not only was I young," he continues as they stride over to their room, "but I seemed *younger* due to my birthday being June thirteen."

"Difficult for *you? You stole all my chicks!*" Lucas declares unlocking the entrance. The front door of their motel room displays the number nineteen; it is the only number in red on the motel's doors…

"Seeing as how I graduated from high school at

thirteen I couldn't really date *college women!*" The genius retorts, passing through the threshold. Leon's intelligence helped him to become a veterinarian at age twenty. Early one morning when he was four his father accidentally ran over his puppy backing out of the driveway. After weeks of grieving Leon knew he wanted to help spare others the pain of losing their pets too soon.

Inside the motel Lucas opens the burgundy bathroom door, his backpack of clothes on the bathroom floor exactly where he left it at lunch time. He shuts the cheap flimsy door behind him, intending on taking care of personal matters and exchanging his dirty clothes for clean ones, leaving it up to his cousin to find the location of the cemetery.

In his crimson cotton t-shirt, Leon recalls the events from the restaurant. He had not particularly cared for their waitress, but she had showed an interest in him until the *magnificent Luke* arrived. "It's not like you have trouble getting women now," a slightly defensive genius mutters to himself while opening up his royal blue laptop.

"I heard that!" Lucas says from the bathroom.
"Yeah, yeah." Leon rolls his eyes.

THE MYSTERY LADY
Wearing an inky lettered AC/DC shirt, the eavesdropper pendulously awaits on the motel's side. Raven had followed the two men and watched them get out of the old car and enter a motel room. The woman retrieves a vibrating phone from her pants pocket.

"I know what it is and it starts here," she says, but with a different accent than the American tone she used previously with the rude American man on the sidewalk. "Olsen. Olsen cease talking," the furtive lady commands with a British accent. "They reside in room nineteen, but I have not received further directives on this matter." A 2009 Gemballa Mirage GT pulls into the parking lot. "Until I do, we will be in Kansas." With her mind made up, Raven terminates the conversation and espionage.

I'll be seeing you soon, Leon. Farewell, she thinks, and climbs into the yellow Mirage GT...

KIMBERLY & JIMMY (The oddly short man)
"It's one o' nine." The boney woman in August Cemetery looks away from her watch and down at the headstone. She and her boyfriend have been here awhile—even before their brief encounter with the nice teenage boy and girl. A star, the sun, casts off rays onto exposed rows of buried bones; no shade to cover the graves. The frequent breezes have come to a standstill; no longer do they roll down the flowerless hill in her father's cemetery. The nape of her neck is perspiring and leaving before the unpleasant liquid covers her is highly on Kimberly's mind. "Ah!" A scream echoes throughout the cemetery.

"Jimmy, is that your brother?" Kimberly asks nervously.

The short five-foot-four man looks up from the headstone to the golden suburban. He sighs, seeing nothing out of the ordinary. "You know he's probably playin' games again."

"Help me!" A child's scream beckons.

Kimberly and Jimmy sprint through her father's cemetery, and fear enters their minds without an invitation. Running around the left of the suburban, Jimmy sees to his horror Kimberly's father holding his eight year old brother up by the shoulders. "Joseph, what are—," Jimmy stops short noticing the blood on the man's white collared shirt, a bloody tear in the arm, and a rib peeking out from the fabric.

A terrified Devin punches the zombie's pale gray chin.

Arriving on Devin's other side, Kimberly witnesses her father lean in and bite the skin off of the tiny child's neck.

Jimmy tackles the assailant to the grass, and the tall woman catches the crying child. Several layers of his tender skin are gone, blood drizzling down from the bite.

Kimberly yanks off his adorable little shirt and ties it around his slender neck muscles. She quickly straps him in the back and hurries around to the driver's seat.

Jimmy, now standing, thrusts the older man before he can completely stand again and the crazy man tumbles down the hill. Jimmy hurriedly hops in next to his alarmed girlfriend.

LEON & LUCAS
The certified genius glances up at Lucas sporting dark denims and a shirt with white long sleeves and a light blue middle as he exits the tinier than tiny bathroom. "I found it."

"How far do we have to drive *this* time?" The blonde Vampire Hunter doesn't bother to conceal his annoyance. Since their home is in Tennessee they are pretty much guaranteed to drive an extremely long distance. Leon's visions tend to take them back and forth across the States. "I'm a little disappointed that our trip here was a dead end. And zombies dude? I don't know. That's just stupid. You better not be losing your touch," he points to his skull, and collapses down spine first on the twin bed.

"Luke, that cemetery is only five miles from here."

He springs up from the surprisingly comfortable mattress. "Huh?"

"Yeah. I get a vision of bar girl covered in blood, and now I see someone getting their face ripped off. *In the same town.*"

Leon's comments sound more like questions to Lucas. He snatches up his backpack of clothes from the bathroom floor and returns prepared to leave. "Think this is somehow connected?"

"There is no way in hell it can't be." The seer doesn't need any more unequivocal proof. Leon Carmany is convinced there is something seriously wrong with Hastings, Nebraska.

~~~

Chapter 3
Out of the Clear Blue Sky

COLE & LANA

WHEN SPRING HAD arrived the trees certainly did not waste any time putting their clothes on. Every single one carries some sort of foliage in a variation of sizes and colors, even the green leaves present different shades. Not knowing the names of these trees, Lana adores the purple ones, whereas Cole does know most of the old but amazing looking trees, leaving him with a preference for maple.

They both can clearly see and hear that the vegetation is not lonesome. Squirrels observe and carry on, woodpeckers continue with their echoing decibels, and an amalgamation of birds chirping and tweeting would make you think they were inebriated.

The sun plays the part of a slow moving disco ball. Overall Mother Nature is throwing a fabulous party.

Lana inhales deeply. *"I love that smell! Gosh! Seeing the woods and being in the woods are two different things!* Lana keeps her thoughts to herself, their speed decreasing to a walk.

"I think I'm starting to sweat now," Cole whispers, not wanting to alert anyone that might be in the woods.

Lana lets out a low laugh. "Yeah." She starts tugging at her shirt trying to get an air flow even though they do not sweat as much or as quick as most humans would.

It is quiet for a moment. Well *they* are anyways. Listening. Watching. Smelling. Tracking. Hunting. Conspiring to kill.

"I feel it more," the female leader eagerly whispers.

"The sweat?"

She smiles. "No. The feeling."

"It's like a pull."

"Let's separate this time. See where our sixth sense leads us," he nods taking the space to the right, and she branches to the left. Out of the corner of his eye he can see her but they are quickly going in opposite directions. While his path leads him slightly uphill, he comes to the conclusion that hers is downhill.

Cole is aware that back at August Cemetery Lana did not so much as consider a momentary glimpse at what was left of the deceased. This deeply vexes him. When it comes to Lana he hates worrying.

RAVEN
A slightly irritated brunette sighs into her cell phone. "I know you are worried about me, but it is not necessary... Olsen, please just do it and get safe... Ganesha drove me here. I am pressing end now," she says in her American accent. "Later."

Going through airfield security had been easy enough for the traveler; no luggage, not even a purse. The noticeable female sits solo watching a reporter on the airport's TV. Future passengers (a few with overindulging issues, one girl that has to be visiting the toilet after every meal, a man who smells like he took a bath in cologne, and another man who could stand to borrow some) gather around her, trying to hear what the woman standing in front of the hospital on the flat screen is saying:

"It is believed that a doctor was admitted earlier today. When nurses and doctors sought to treat him they were attacked. It is still unclear as to who has this busy hospital locked down and why. The question now is, are there any hostages?"

The traveler looks down at the plane ticket threatening to crumble in her hand. Knowing that it does not matter if the hospital is locked or unlocked makes Raven's decision...difficult.

She desires to stay. To help those people turning into monsters.

But that is not my mission.

Taking a deep breath, the five-foot-seven woman stands up to be the first in line. The lady attendant behind a computer screen glares at her with a baffled expression. A female voice booms overhead causing people to gather their belongings. The small crowd gathered in front of the flat screen is last to the two rows of waiting passengers.

Two male teens—one with a mole on his cheek—quietly chat about who has the best chance of getting away with "accidentally" rubbing up against her. Silently laughing at the absurdity, the flattered observer smiles maliciously in their direction, all the way at the end of the line. The boys tense upon Raven looking at them, and she turns putting them out of her mind.

In God I trust. Her last thought in the terminal.

LEON & LUCAS

Leon stares out the passenger window. It is easy to tell they are nearing the end of the city. Buildings not only dwindle in size, but the houses seem to grow bigger lawns.

A fast-paced leisure vehicle moving towards them adverts his attention.

The speed limit sign up ahead reads "forty-five". He glances at the speedometer in front of his uncharacteristically silent cousin. They themselves are moving ten over the legal limit. They curiously eye the woman in the golden suburban as she noticeably speeds by them…

After a few acres of unbroken silence and open space, Leon and Lucas pass a road—New Hope Road—and a graveyard on their left with very little appreciation for its beauty.

KIMBERLY & JIMMY

"Hospital."

"Hospital," Jimmy agrees with Kimberly on their next course of action.

Devin wipes the tears from his small eyes. "I saw him walking. I thought he got hurted in the place where animals play." He digs into the black seat with his baby-like nails. "But then he looks really scary so I only watch."

"What is your dad doin' in the woods?" Jimmy asks his girlfriend, turning away from his bleeding baby brother in the backseat.

"I-I don't know. He said he thought that when he was done mowing he saw Lee in the woods." Lee was supposed to close their dad's cemetery last night. But after dark her father called in a blind panic. Her brother's truck had been abandon inside August Cemetery. The driver side window busted out.

"Why would Lee be in there?"

"I don't know that he was! I just figured dad was getting drunk during the day again." Kimberly is used to her father drinking at odd hours, then going weeks without even a sip, but this... She has never seen her dad, or anyone, pick up a child and do what he did to Devin. "What's with him?"

"Don't know."

The scenery of hogs and cattle pass by in the rearview mirror.

LEON & LUCAS

The two cousins sit in front of Rush Cemetery. Its setting is just the way it appeared in Leon's vision.

Vines emergent on the iron rods. But one could still see tombstones on the other side. An eight foot gate that is made out of iron as well but does not have climbing plants towers at the entrance. He easily spots the streetlight; it is the only object that remains taller than the entrance.

One thing the seer had not seen in his vision is the open land to his right that is occupied by a descent size, well-kept white house several acres back from the road…

"This is the place. So far nothing unusual. Think we should drive through to see if we can find anything?"

Without a word, Lucas Kale puts the gears in drive. The lettering, RUSH, is easy to spot because it definitely stands out in the center of the clusters of bars to their left.

Judging by the conditions of the tombstones, he guesses that the black chipping barrier not only keeps vandals out at night, but also attracts curious folks during daytime hours.

"You've been quiet."

Lucas pretends to take interest in the aged markers.

"Not once did you turn on the radio."

"I don't like this, Brighton." Calling Leon by his forename usually means he is serious. "Why is your vision extremely different? You've only seen two things. Vampires and Potentials." The people they save have a latent possibility to become exalted and significant. "And Potentials do not find out about us and Vampires existing." His voice begins to rise. "Because we KILL the vamps before they strike!

Now she is going to find out about *US!*"

The small roadway forces Lucas to calm down and make a decision. Right or left?

Broken and cracked headstones along with dying grass await to the left. He chooses big ancient trees, above ground tombs, and creepy statues. "What else is going to change?"

"Guess I haven't thought about it that way."

"You're always charge then ask."

"You're not? I'm surprised you don't have penis funk."

"Hey, I wrap it!" Lucas defends himself.

"What happens when you don't have *anything to wrap?*"

"It's not like I do it *every day with everyone.* Why am I talking to you about this? Let's leave the weird-cousin-sex-talk to Rachel." Their youngest cousin has a way of purposefully making them uncomfortable. And it isn't like him and Leon never talk about the things they do with the ladies, because they do—Lucas more than Leon. It's just that Lucas desperately wishes this business in Nebraska to be finished so he can head back to his cousin Rachel and Uncle Joe in Tennessee, escaping this nervous tension building in his stomach like there is an atomic bomb about to be dropped on him.

JIMMY & KIMBERLY

"I need to calm down," Jimmy tells himself. He rubs his short and sweaty palms up and down his jeans. He may be been done fighting his girlfriend's father, but his adrenaline is not finished with him.

Jimmy turns the knob on the radio, and hears a male's voice. "It is official. The only hospital in Hastings is on lockdown. Police and reporters have surrounded the campus but why is unclear," the man announces through the speakers. "Unfortunately, if you or someone you know needs to be admitted to the ER it won't be in Hastings."

"Maybe we should just go to the police," the balding man in his twenties suggests. "I mean I don't even think your dad knew *us* or *himself.* And you just don't turn into a cannibal overnight unless you've been…turned into—"

"Sweetie you're babbling," she says touching the top of his hand with hers.

"I know. I just—"

Kimberly is in the middle of the crossroads before it occurs to her that her college sweetheart is not wearing a thin piece of material across his chest. The side of her suburban crunches against the side of a dump truck. Her freckled hand no longer clenches the smooth steering-wheel…

COLE

In all the time I have come to know her… I cannot help but notice the changes. The more Lana looks at Cole the more he notices the sparkle that he adores so much… *It is almost gone. But does Lana know? Know how much she is starting to obsess over Kronos? Or the fact that I even care? Do I care…? Yes. Yes, I care.*

Would he not speak up and tell her she is a danger to herself? He knows she would never physically harm herself, but her pulling away from all her friends and being alone… That can't be healthy.

But what am I supposed to say? Hey, yes Kronos is evil stop trying to end his existence? That would go over like a turd in a punch bowel. Wow, I can't believe I just thought about a turd in a bowel.

Cole laughs at himself while trudging through the woods.

* * *

LANA & COLE

"That's it!" Excitement rings not only in Lana's mind, but her adrenaline is moving at speeds she has long since forgotten.

There before her eyes stands her nemesis' hiding place. Surrounded by oversized tree trunks and huge branches is the entrance to a well-hidden cave. A squirrel had ran a straight path through at the bottom of the trees. Lana looked closely, saw something back there, and pushed her way through the tree limbs and discovered it.

I've been through here five, six, eight times in my life and I've never noticed this? Then again, why would I? Those times me, Cole, and Loki were hanging out around here we were doing just that, hanging out.

In one of the rare acres of trees, each one of them had come to the welcoming and calm atmosphere on weekends to forget life. For Lana it was obviously Kronos and the teasing at school. She openly knew her friend and neighbor, Loki, came to escape the consequences of her parents' divorce.

But now days, Loki liked going anywhere that was not her own house for good reasons, reasons

Lana tries to ignore. Cole came because that is where she and Loki went—being around them helped him cope with being adopted.

Cole's entire family died in a house fire on the night of Christmas when he was eleven. He woke up choking from smoke that had drifted down from the top of the stairs. He ran out of the basement door that was practically next to his bed and sat in the snow. He cried while he watched the flames spread from the first floor to the second.

Cole told Lana and Loki he had heard his sister and mother screaming. And Lana could see why he would want to forget that nightmare. *Who wouldn't...?*

Must find— It is as though he read her thoughts. On top what she had thought was a hill, but in actuality is an enormous cave, appears the dark-haired teenage boy.

Her presence clearly surprises Cole. "Why did we *both* end up *here*?"

She beckons him with her hand. He jumps down.

"I don't see..." Cole trails off looking past all the dull brown, radiant green, and popping white colors. "A non-small cave I have never seen before!" His enthusism pours out as he races her through the thick entanglement. He makes it inside first. But twenty-feet is not much of a race.

"Hey, do you think this is the exit to that cavern we played in a few years back?" she whispers hoping not to alert Kronos.

"I don't know. I mean the only thing I remember other than the fact it's behind August is that we got lost because we couldn't...see."

It dawns on him that they are pretty much in the same situation.

Granted, being a Shadow has a lot of advantages; running faster than an Olympic athlete, being physically stronger, hearing, and having a better sense of smell than their species. But no matter what, it takes a minimum of two Shadows to dismember a Vampire. They do not possess the strength of their predators, and no matter how quick one moves their feet the Vampire will win. And unfortunately their eyesight is that of a regular human—in the dark.

"So how many people does it take to get flashlights?" Cole jokes.

Lana rolls her apple green eyes. "I'll go," she volunteers since they both know her house is closer. But a familiar scent invades her nostrils. Blood. Human blood.

"I smell..." he inhales deeper. And then they know they are in trouble—their instincts intensifying to the extreme. The sudden change can only mean one thing.

"Run!" Lana shouts.

Lana and Cole know they have seconds. *Seconds* to escape into the sun...or *seconds* to be claimed by one or several unhappy Vampires. Well maybe happy depending on which way they choose to look at the situation. Angry their habitat is being disturbed, or happy two blind-in-the-dark humans imprudently strolled in.

The frantic trackers know that no matter how hard they listen in the dark, even as advanced as their skills are compared to others like them, it will not save them.

While Shadows cannot be Pushed—the Vampires feeding ability by standing at a distance and expelling a human's blood from them and into the mouth of the predator—more than three blood feigns would surely rip them to pieces.

A pair of feet from above smash into Lana's face, knocking the breath out of her as she lands on what feels like unleveled rock. Her own nose blood flows freely into her dry mouth.

Something wet slides down the side of Lana's neck.

A fist connects against Cole's cheek and then a foot hits him not once, not twice, but three times. He hears dirt sling about from its rapid spin kicks. Taunting laughter ensues in front of him unveiling the voice of a woman.

Lana knows she must act quickly. Even though there isn't much light there is enough shining through at the top of the egress to create a silhouette of the villain. A chunk of rock that had come loose underneath Lana's spine leaves her steady fingertips.

The Vampire's body bends backwards, avoiding the flying object. Cole, seizing the opportunity, drops down sideswiping the female Vampire's feet out from underneath her. But the Vampire quickly springs up into a back flip, filling the dark cave with more disturbing cackles.

The Shadows charge.

The night creature lands—bare feet packing down the earth—and four hands push her through the forestry and into the beaming rays of sunlight.

The Vampire woman's eyes fall upon them. They are the same colors as any vamp in its form; the sclera in both eyes are emerald green, and the pupils and irises are orange outlined heavily with violet. "Even the Goddess will not be able to save you," she cryptically says.

Touching the sunbeams, red blood seeps out from her old, wrinkly skin like meat that is being cooked on one side. A green flame—the same color as the attacker's sclera—ignites from those taunting eyeballs. Juddering, her long white hair waving up and down in the wind bursts into the same horrid blaze. The Old Lady Vampire's entire body explodes into huge flames of emerald green.

LUCAS & LEON
Putting on the brakes, Lucas and Leon stare with open mouths. Several yards in front of them verdant fire rises over the fence in Rush Cemetery. Climbing towards the sky, the green fire changes into snow white smoke and then disappears. "Wow!" the young, longhaired man booms, "*A Vampire in daylight?*" They have never seen anything like this; only heard stories.

"More importantly, who killed it?" The blonde-haired Vampire Hunter knows the human-killing creatures of the night will never willing step foot in front of *the* star. And no normal human can force them to do so.

"We have never seen a"—Leon air quotes—"*Tracker.*" They have heard rumors of supercharged humans possessing the ability to instinctively track Vampires.

"Never seen a"—Lucas air quotes—"*Zombie*, either."

"Point taken."

While exiting the old graveyard to ponder and wait, the Vampire Hunters notice two dark-headed teens in the field running along the gravel driveway towards the white house…

~~~

Chapter 4
Hope

KIMBERLY

THE SKY IS AT THE WRONG angle. Upside down. Kimberly unbuckles her seatbelt, and Devin appears next to her outside of the wreckage. The tiny cuts on her hands sting as she climbs out through the glassless window. Shocked eyes refuse their sight. Facing the way they had traveled, a body lies in the intersection. Jimmy's body.

An elderly couple get out of the small car behind her and Devin. An obese woman with multiple chins walks toward them from the right. A man with a gun strides away from his white four-door truck that had been behind the person in the dump truck who caused the accident.

The door of the dump truck is open…something deadly looking resembling that of a human falls down from it…

The heavy woman yells, "Thing! Thing! Kill it!"

Bang!

The halfway sitting up *thing* dies and slumps down again.

Pistol by his side, the man from the white truck addresses Devin. "How did you get that on your neck?"

"Why?" Kimberly defensively asks. The boy's shirt is now soiled with a red coloring.

"The radio said to watch out for people that looked like death."

"And for people that had excessive bleeding," adds Hefty.

"And excessive bleeding," he echoes and points his weapon at the child. Devin screams in terror, and a cloud mutes the sun.

LEON/LUCAS/LANA/COLE

"If zombies do start taking over we've got a bigger problem than trying to kill them."

Eyes bulging, the philanderer demands, "What's harder than that?"

"Luke, look around you. What do you see?"

Rush Cemetery stands to their right and the field of bluestem grass (more than likely used for hay) to the left. He takes a few seconds to think, running his fingers over his square chin. "Nothing."

"And the nearest city's forever away," Leon informs him.

"Are you telling me that any cities we find out there—"

"—Population does well to even get above seven

hundred. They're going to be less likely to be infected—"

"And when they hear about this they're gonna keep it that way," Lucas concludes.

"Locking and boarding up. *No one* gets in." The realist turns to the small rolling knolls. "Luke, there is nowhere to hide out there."

"Damn it!" He contemplates their options. And arrives at only one. "Okay. After we save this girl we are going home."

"Which girl?"

"The one that shows up."

"Okay. Since we're waiting let's go back. I forgot my book."

"Seriously?" Leon spends more time reading the poems of T.S. Eliot than the amount of hours Lucas uses watching busting Asians on the internet. "You have it memorized. Can't you just write it?" Leon's annoyance causes him to laugh in amusement. "Okay, okay." The car's engine awakens. "Here's to her not dying while we go on a book quest."

"That street light was on and the gate was closed," Leon recalls from his vision as the tires roll along the road.

"Didn't you say this happened before dark…?"

…Lana and Cole, flashlights in hand, near the end of her gravel and dirt driveway. They see a deep blue-colored car so waxed that it reflects the scenery as it disappears away from the cemetery entrance. While the car passes by Rush Cemetery, the street lamp—not knowing the time of day—stirs from its slumber…

* * *

"This can't be good," Lucas says as they draw near a four-way stop sign. A dump truck and a golden suburban block a great deal of the crossroad. Four wheels of the beat-up suburban point towards the darkened blue sky, and broken glass and pieces of metal cover the pavement.

"Hey! What the hell is that guy doing?!" Leon cannot see any reason why anyone would be aiming something deadly like gun at a kid. The car comes to a stop at the white line painted on the pavement. Lucas reaches into the glove compartment and pulls out his pistol. He then places it against his back, the barrel pointing down inside his pants. The two young men quickly hop out hurrying over to the people idly watching as a man threatens a child's life.

The young, light-haired boy wraps himself around the leg of the female adult next to him, tears streaming down his innocent face. "Please, help!" Kimberly begs of the newcomers. The man with the obviously dyed hair, way too dark for his age, lowers his firearm upon their presence.

"What's your name?" The seer calls out to the older man.

"Tyler."

"Tyler, I'm Leon." He notices the pale gray-skinned dead man by the dump truck, and then another man, bald and lying facedown. "What happened here?"

"Something...zombies—I think. This kid is one of them."

"No, I'm not!" Devin cries, and shouts to his

unmoving brother, "Jimmy! Jimmy, help!"

The twenty-two year old with sapphire blue eyes and brown hair down to his shoulders moves toward the wrecked car. Tyler stiffens. "I'm just going to check on Jimmy," Leon says hoping to calm the man. He bends down beside the man lying face down on the pavement and places two fingers on Jimmy's carotid artery; located on the side of his neck. Leon looks at the extremely thin lady standing next to the child. "What is Jimmy to you?" He asks her.

"My boyfriend. And Devin's brother."

The Vampire Hunter hesitates. "He's dead."

Shocked, Kimberly hangs onto Devin's little hand for fear she might faint right there in the open. Her brother is missing, there is something wrong with her dad, a stranger is pointing a gun at Devin, and now her boyfriend is dead.

"I'm sorry." Tyler tries to give his condolences. "But he has to be stopped." The man points his gun at the little boy. Devin hides behind Kimberly, pulling at her clothes and frantically screaming.

"Listen to yourself," the older Vampire Hunter speaks up. "You're talking about killing kids."

"He's infected," Hefty throws in her opinion.

"He's not," lies Kimberly.

Lucas sneers at the uncaring overweight lady. "So what if he is? There might be a cure."

Kimberly once again tries reassuring everyone. "Nothing touched him."

"We don't know that," says Hefty.

"Exactly!" Lucas snaps at the eager to kill woman.

"I can know," Leon says in a calm manner.

Tyler becomes curious. "How?"

"I work with wounds. May I have a look?"

"Go," he says waving his life stopper.

The veterinarian briskly walks over to the shaking, condemned boy and squats down in front of him. "Devin, it's okay." The certainty in the stranger's voice brings the little boy out of hiding. Leon unties the knot and slowly unwinds the shirt, feeling the tension radiating from the stringy-haired female with scratches on her hands.

"I'm eight. Everyone tells me I'm smart for my age. Are you smart for your age?"

"Yeah," Leon smiles, and then his heart momentarily stops. Bright purple skin dangles from the top of a wound the size of Devin's fist. The edges are spotted with green pus and the tiny veins surrounding it are white underneath the flesh with a brown outline.

Looking the eight year old in his fear-filled eyes, a lump like the size of a life threatening tumor forms at the back of Leon's throat.

"Please." Devin pleads, barely loud enough for him to hear. Innocent tears sparkle in the light of what feels like frozen time.

Kimberly's body blocks the view from the two quiet observers behind her. The overweight woman can't see over Leon, and he knows Tyler is unable see this side of the poor child's neck. Leon's mouth parts in anguish. Does he open his mouth and take indirect responsibility for ending the imaginative spirit behind those dark youthful child eyes that look into him? *Or do I try to lie in hopes of saving him?*

Leon Carmany will never walk in this world the same way he did when he woke up this morning. He will never forget the silence. The silence of little Devin motionless before the child's body sways towards Kimberly. She swoops down, catching her dead boyfriend's dead brother.

Leon, unable to move, stares at the air where Devin had once stood.

"I'm sorry," Tyler apologizes for killing the child, and climbs back in his truck.

Lucas feels chunks of food and stomach acid touch his tongue. He hunches over and regurgitation splashes on the scattered debris.

Tyler and the oversized woman cross the intersection, moving around the collision. The old man ushers his sobbing wife to their car.

"Let's go, Brighton," Lucas Kale says, practically pulling Leon up by his arms. "We're going back to Rush then we are getting the hell out of here! As for your book, I'll buy you a new one."

* * *

To clear his mind, Lucas rolls the window down and breathes in the calm, misleading air blowing in on their way back to the graveyard. *I hope she lives.* A welcoming image of intelligent eyes brighten behind his own. The smile in her trusting irises make nauseating gloom and darkness fall away like beautiful sparkling snow from a graceful cloud.

Odd. I don't even know her name.

Maybe if he hadn't been up until three in the morning watching reruns of women's MMA matches and listening to classic rock, then Lucas would not have shown such hostility towards her and he would know her name. He could help her; the girl who wore the shirt displaying his favorite band.

But if I had not been up in the early AM maybe I wouldn't have seen her.

"What… Are you okay, Lucas?"

"I'm just thinking."

"About…that kid?" Leon can't bring himself to say his name.

"Not that. Anything that isn't that. This day is about to take a turn that involves me feeling like I've been butt-raped isn't it?"

The young brunette places a hand over his stomach. "I got a bad feeling."

"Considering what just happened, well yeah."

"Pull over." Not waiting for a complete stop, Leon's feet carry him to the front of the vehicle. Breathing fast, he places his hands on the hood trying to concentrate.

"Leon?" Lucas gives him a sidelong glance as he shuts his door.

"Luke, I've got a bad feeling." Leon walks away from him.

"Yeah, you mentioned that. Now say something else, like are you having some traumatized attack?"

Fatigue claims the younger man. Leon looks down at the vibrating pavement. "That's not right." Patches of grass shift around, chasing each other as if they are trying to find the right spot to settle.

"Seriously, I'm already freaked the hell out!" Lucas yells, not far behind him. "Stop moving!"

Eyelids blink once. A single footstep trudges

forward on the open road. The seer's knees buckle...

...Why is the sky so far down? *Leon wonders. He has been falling for some time now.* There has to be a bottom. Right? *Water gently touches his smooth cheeks.* That must be from the cascade. Where is it going? *Wind violently pushes him upwards taking him into a lightless abyss...*

* * *

...Black.

"Wake up."

"Who is that? Why are you whispering?" Raven calmly asks.

"Wake up," the familiar voice urges.

The sound of an irregular heartbeat thumps loudly before being masked by incoherent babbling.

Orange rays—source unknown—burst onto Raven's tan face, like sunrise on a scorching summer day, blinding her. Clasping her fingers over confused squinty eyes, incoherent babbling escalates into shouting. The orange rays respond angrily, dividing into three darker ones thwarting around her skull. Two of the rays dig with great effort through her ear canals, scratching at the eardrum like a cockroach. The third, without hesitation, unkindly delivers itself up into the airless passageway of her nose.

The voices stop.

All is mute except for the sound of a heart beating implausibly slow...

Raven smells an unforgettable scent. Fear.

The traveler's eyes snap wide open. The seats to her left and right are vacant. Every passenger on the plane is gathered behind Raven, screaming in her direction. Lifting her head off the back of the seat in front of her, Raven's vision aligns with the dead glazed pupils of a zombie. His lips seem to curl up with elation. Bent over the padded seat, it leans forward avidly moaning.

The irises and pupils in the traveler's eyes are not typical colors... The white parts are blue... Her brown ringlets flatten and turn light yellow...

Putting her hands around the zombie's neck, its eyes instantly change from red to the same brilliant blue she had seen earlier today... Grabbing her by the shoulders, it suddenly morphs into Leon. "Raven, you have to wake up!"

Raven calmly awakes from the nightmare—a first—to bundled layers of fluffy clouds drifting under a bird that will remain to be the interloper in the sky. She had not meant to go to sleep, at first, but then the relaxed atmosphere took over her body. She certainly didn't expect to have a bad dream with so many hearts beating in the enclosed area. What Raven finds more surprising than her not waking to the sound of the screaming voices in her head that haunt her when she sleeps, is the sensation that someone on this flight is not well...

* * *

LEON & LUCAS
"Stop!" Leon splutters, choking on falling water.

A bottle of water drops from Luke's trembling hand to join the other four bottles on the side of the road. "Finally! Do you have any idea what I've just been through?!"

The seer rests his head against the car. "No. Why?"

"I've been splashing crap on you for the last five minutes!"

He notices the plastic containers. "Or drowning me." He climbs to his feet.

"What are you doing?"

"I'm getting in." Leon plops down on the car seat.

Lucas huffs and walks around to the other side of the car. "Well?" he says shutting the driver side door, waiting for an explanation.

"I don't know. I feel better. The word **raven** feels like it should mean something."

"You nearly hit your big head and made my spine turn into Forest Gump pulling your dorky guts off the road because you wanted to dream about Edgar Allen Poe!"

"Why are you yell—"

"—Because your wrong vision made us come here! I just saw a tiny boy get his tiny boy brains removed! And I don't want to fight evil bastards that are just as evil as the evil Vampires we already remove from this psychotic planet you and I call home!"

Leon doesn't have a response. Lucas uses the moment of silence to compose himself.

"If this thing gets out of control we're going to be seeing more than Devin," the damp-haired man says.

"That's what scares me, Leon."

The engine starts and they persevere with their journey to save the unsuspecting black-haired girl with scars on her lips and damaged ear cartilage.

LANA & COLE

Black shadows dance around cave rocks caused by hand held lights. Something drips onto Lana's nose… Her light shines upward to the cave's ceiling, followed by her friend's ring of light. Cole's usual cheery smile quickly twists into the upside down version of the Joker's memorable smile; his favorite villain.

As if she swallowed tacks, air sharply cuts into Lana's throat causing her to fumble over her words. "S-S-Someone's been trying t-to Push for a while." Some of the bodies with missing heads and teeth marks tell her a new Vampire is or has been in this tunnel. Fresh Vampires are the easiest to kill for they have not acquired what the older ones have learned. And since they do not have the ability to Push they must feed by physically holding and biting their prey.

Cole pries his now oversized eyeballs from the horrible display of strung up bodies. "They are meals *and* practice."

The revolted girl counts nineteen torso's jagged together with railroad spikes. Lana shines the light on the dead but still bleeding gray-haired man nailed to the rest of the bodies. "If he's bleeding how did she, or anyone get him?" It is unlikely the Old Lady Vampire kept him over night and late into the afternoon, not the style of their inimical opponents.

"Do you want to get backup?"

"No," she sighs, and moves farther into the darkness. "Kronos first. Then we will decide where the burials are going." She hates that; the fact that those people will always be classified as "missing". Their families would worry themselves to their own graves.

Cole doesn't know if or what he should say. Should he comfort her with words or be quiet in a place where Vampires reside? Instead of vocalizing, he places his fingertips in between her short, skinny fingers.

Pretending to take interest in the holes created in the rocks over time by falling water drops, Lana lightly squeezes their palms together; grateful for the reassurance.

The once orphaned boy holds his breath, afraid she will let go too soon.

RAVEN

There *are* other ways for Raven to get to her home in Kansas, but she wanted to fly. It is nice to have the clouds underneath her. Even the sun changes; its perfect circle now replaced by a bright blur.

What she loves most about this experience is not just the view, but the silence.

When would she have the time to shoot across the sky like this? While the walking dead are feasting on strangers? The two she eavesdropped on? Her friends? Olsen?

Distracting her mind, the same undesirable smell—its resemblance is that of fresh vomit mixed with warm cat urine—she experienced only momentarily ago causes her to terminate respiration. Unbuckling the safety belt and rising to her feet, she knows exactly where the stench flees and is not surprised that the other passengers do not notice. Raven has always been tuned into what members of society either refuse or simply do not know.

Leaving the first row, the two horny teenagers—one with a mole on his face—gawk as she calmly glides down the aisle to the restroom.

Raven stands inches away from the opening lavatory door.

With sweat on his face and purple bags underneath his eye sockets, a man with a great toupee, he had to have paid a fortune for it, jumps at the sight of the unexpected passenger. Raven keeps her voice low. "What happened to you?"

"N-N-Nothing," he stutters trying to move forward but the inquisitive girl blocks him.

"Who bit you?"

"Um…" he hesitates pulling on the cufflinks of his pressed suit. "A cop that was on the side of the road. Someone pulled him from a green wagon."

"Hastings?"

The distressed man nods, and she quickly jabs her fist against the side of his neck. His eyes close. The restroom door shuts behind them. The captains voice booms over the intercom. But there is no need for her to pay attention for she knows they are landing shortly.

The unconscious man… Raven snaps his fragile vertebrae…

LANA & COLE

The course of the tunnel changes, no longer curving downward, leveling out to a straight path. The temperature had drastically cooled as soon as they had gone a few yards, but now it is cold. Due to the excitement, it had not occurred to Lana to bring a jacket. She can feel a shiver building underneath her cool layers of skin. If she were a normal girl she would be well beyond her first chattering of the teeth. Lana grips her workmate's hand tightly, hoping that stealing his body heat will warm more than her skinny fingers for she doesn't want to be the reason their voyage ends prematurely.

Even with his battery operated light Cole can barely see what lies ahead of them. He knows the further underground they proceed that eventually their sources that pierce the darkness will be insignificant. *Is that...water?* He wonders having been distracted. Water is generally good and one needs it to survive. But at this moment it extinguishes the fireworks in their joyous candid eyes. He senses Lana's other hand patching tear duct eruptions.

Lana's tears hurts him like hundreds of paper cuts sliced around his mouth.

Where the cave floor should be up ahead, Lana's light casts out into what they assume is a river, while Cole's shows a rock wall on its other side. Their man-made objects search the abyss. And Lana lets go of the bitter air she has been concealing; the sound lost in the violent torrent. To determine how deep it is would be a futile effort; she knows it does not matter how far down the bottom is for Kronos has surely slipped into the abysmal water.

Kronos could be as far as the Gulf of Mexico by now or right below our feet for we all know. Either way we lose. The hand the teenage boy had been holding onto so dearly pulls away from his warm skin.

"He's gone," Lana admits in defeat. The heartless stalker had left, taking her hopes for a better future without him with him. *Misery.* "As always."

A new hatred for Kronos penetrates Cole's yearning soul.

LUCAS & LEON

Outside of Rush Cemetery, Lucas opens the trunk of the car. Spread out over a spare tire and mechanical tools are numerous materials used for hunting; stakes, crossbows, a rope, and a big wooden cross that takes up most of the trunk. Leon carefully places pointed light brown pieces of wood to the right as Lucas uncaringly tosses the necessities.

I had a gun and I didn't use it. Bearing the onus of the murder of little Devin, the ashamed blond Hunter flips up a corner of the fuzzy interior. Leon picks up a loaded shotgun and a single box of shells from the hidden section. Lucas takes the bullets to his pistol. "Brighton," he says, pushing down the trunk's lid, "the longer this waiting thing takes the more creepier this place gets."

"More creepier is not the right—"

"—I know, Leon. I know. And I realize you're trying to distract me." The twenty-four year old leans over the polished roof and looks his best friend in the eyes. "But Brighton...there will never be a distraction from this day."

The verity in Lucas Kale's words settle in the back of Leon Carmany's throat like blood-sucking worms slowly being wrenched off of his future baby-maker.

LANA & COLE

Sprinting through tapered groups of trees, Lana stops short beside the light gray barrier of August Cemetery. Cole, having passed her, backtracks.

"Leave me," she coldly tells him.

The attentive teenage boy senses the bitterness in her words. What she feels does not please him. "I want you to go my house. Yours. Whatever."

The warm light from the now cloudless sky shines all around them. Gazing down at her oval face, Cole realizes, *It's gone*; the soul that once radiated optimism to the world through apple green eyes. Cole demurs, "I don't think you should be alone—"

"Leave me," she interrupts, staring intensely at the petty hindrance.

The blood rushes to his face. Her words are on order. The eighteen year old has pulled rank on the lesser experienced Shadow. His only option is to depart.

But never before in his life has he ever felt such...dismissal.

LANA QUEEN

Lana does not care about Cole. At least not what he

thinks of her giving him orders at this present time. *She* is the leader.

The leader in running around and staking nothing, the emotionally wounded girl thinks. She jumps over the petty barrier and lands with a mad thud on the butchered grass. A mild breeze circles through the graveless land, ruffling the arms of the willow tree. The red flashlight—wishing to do the same to her enemy's heart—cracks against the lifeless wall. Batteries land in undetermined places, and shoes pound onerously up the hill.

* * *

COLE
I can't believe she did that!

Lana's words have infuriated Cole. The two of them usually coincide on choices of action. Giving one of her friends a directive is rare, and he resents her for doing so when she needs consolation instead of solitude.

But today she doesn't want a friend. She wants HIM—Kronos.

Cole not only loathes the Vampire, but he despises everything right now. He despises the way the trees never move from their fixed roots, but yet, as he darts past their picturesque colors they are forced behind him. He despises the two-legged winged animals that are perched pompously on the dark thick branches singing merrily.

"Stupid birds!"

She wants him more than she wants me.

That fact, he truly despises.

~~~~

Chapter 5
Dreams and Visions

Concordia, Kansas.
2:10 p.m.

RAVEN, ON FOOT, steadily paces through the expiring rush hour traffic; the shadows casting off from poles and buildings onto the sidewalk helps her calculate the time of day. A metallic black super car with dark tinted windows stops at the red light in front of her. The doors open by rising up in the air; butterfly style. Energetically she skips over and hops in on the left side of the three seat coupe; the driver in the center with two rear passenger seats to the left and right. The vehicle, only one waiting, accelerates underneath the changed light; now green.

"Jet—"

"I know. I don't listen," the driver seated in the middle of the McLaren F1 admits, smiling. She had told the young-looking man and her friends, Sheba and Cricket (not here), that picking her up at the airport wasn't necessary; Ganesha had dropped her off at the airport in Nebraska so she didn't have the option of picking her up here. Jet is the only one of the three not submitting to her will.

Out of all the vehicles Jet has owned, Raven knows that *this* is his favorite, and rarely misses an opportunity to put it on exhibition. Even though it was built in 1994 it reaches a top speed of two-hundred-and-forty miles per hour. Everything except the blue-shirted girl in the automobile matches the outside: black velvet seats, black carpet, ceiling, and even Jet's hair and the clothes on his massively thick muscled body.

Raven rests her head against the headrest, letting the dim atmosphere relax her.

"Do you know your plan yet?" he asks.

"Are Sheba and Cricket still sleeping?"

"Yeah."

The content girl opens her hazel eyes. "We will get firearms. When Cricket and Sheba wake up, and Ganesha when she arrives, can help us finish the downstairs."

Jet raises his eyebrows. "We're not saving anyone else?"

"I told Olsen. Our friends can deal with their families the way *they* see fit."

"I get it. Who else can we tell that would believe in the walking dead?" He abandons the view straight ahead to look at her. "They don't believe in

Vampires and—"

"—They have existed since The Blending."

The side of his lip turns up at the corner. "How is it that you always finish my sentences?"

"Silly, we have been together—" Taking the words from her, Jet exultantly says, "Practically forever." Having proved he knows her just as well, she smiles faintly. "Watch the road."

"What's going to happen if I don't?" he teases.

"Shut up," Raven playfully scoffs, and rests her eyes; her thoughts on Leon Carmany and Lucas Kale.

Hastings, Nebraska
Not speaking a word, the Vampire Hunters sit with the windows up just in case they get an unwelcoming surprise. Leon glances around the back, looking for strange things: zombies, green and white flames, anything really. Not seeing anything out of the ordinary, he turns back around. Just then a teenage boy hurries out of the small woodland next to the creepy graveyard carrying a flashlight…

"Suspicious," Leon says, planting his hands on the shotgun lying across his lap. As if the stranger heard him, the teenager casts an uninviting look and stalks towards the sitting chunk of metal.

"What's he doing?" Lucas asks trying not to moves his lips. "Coming over here." Leon tries to give him the "duh attitude" through his pressed teeth.

The heated pale-skinned boy gives them another nasty look before darting off to into the meadow.

"What's that freak's problem?"

Leon shrugs.

COLE
She'll be okay. And you're being crazy. Why would someone be after Lana?

When Cole left the vegetation he had seen on older model car parked a few yards down from the cemetery entrance, facing him. He recalled the car driving in the opposite direction not long ago. Cole had planned on confronting them, but then decided that if they were up to no good the chances of them telling the truth are the same as Lana telling him she likes him.

Ugh! His mind yells in frustration as he nears her home, gravel crunching underneath his worn out tennis shoes on the driveway, prairie grass growing on either side of him. The adopted teen scolds himself. *You are crazy for thinking someone wouldn't be after Lana; Kronos! Hello! Remember the beginning of Senior year?*

Months ago graphic images of Lana had flashed in his mind—images that told him his best friend was in danger at the so called Haunted House. Although given the event that happened last year, passing by it (the increased housing on New Hope Road forced them to do so) doesn't radiant relief and cheer. But a haunting memory.

Receiving telepathic pictures is typical of his kind. But the lead Shadow told him she didn't send him anything, and he believes her. Lana has spent years trying to send out an alert but so far she remains to be only a recipient. He has heard of inexplicable pictures mysteriously being sent, but

Cole never put much thought to it until it happened to him that night for the first and last time—that he is aware of.

Where do they come from? A heartbreaking memory surfaces—the girl he likes laid on the floor while acid ate her beautiful skin—immediately pushing the question to the back of his mind. The Senior boy (now alumni) didn't leave her side for the next two weeks except for the times she went to the bathroom, and his turns visiting the toilet and shower. But he would have busted out penis swinging if he had to.

The seventeen year old wants nothing but for Lana to say she has feelings for him. *But why would she? I have never admitted to likely her. UGH!* Frustrated, the dark-haired boy stomps up Lana's steps and walks the length of the deck. The front door bangs against the frame behind him as he enters the house.

LANA QUEEN
Years of fighting in the dark have gotten me what? A messed up face for people to gossip about. Relationships based on lies—the reason I only have two friends.

The world comes back to Lana, unaware of how long she has been staring at her father's grave in August Cemetery. Her cheeks are soaked, and a salty wetness slides over her grazed lips creating another path down her thin neck. Kronos may be gone for now, but ultimately her father's killer will return to stalk the dejected girl. *Is this what my life is going to be like forever? Always on guard?*

Stressed out? Few friends? Surrounded by judgmental gossipers? The same unintelligent humans I save from Vampires and the stalker that did this to me in the first place!?

Lana snatches the flowers from their holder on the marble headstone. Blue petals rip in between troubled fingertips before making their escape to friendlier elements. The soft blue petals suddenly trigger the night dreams that started two days ago— the soothing dreams of a female with extremely long blonde hair and electric blue in her eyes...

LEON/LUCAS/LANA/KIMBERLY

The window next to Leon rolls down, letting the hot air out of the smothering heat trap of a car. "I think"—he pauses, collecting his thoughts— "I think he was headed for that house after we witnessed that Vampire die."

Lucas looks at the white house and then up at the scrambled white fluffy clouds where the fiery light had previously shone. "Maybe he *is* a tracker."

"Yeah, still that doesn't explain why he looked pissed. We didn't do anything."

They can take it. Lana squeezes her palms around the black bar and easily pulls it to the middle of Rush's entryway. Doing the same to the matching right one, her troubles seem to slowly drift into the inanimate objects. She firmly grasps them and runs forward forcing a loud *CLANG* from the old gate. A new found happiness.

"That's her!" the seer shrieks.

"Leave it to you to save the issued ones," Lucas says witnessing the teenager's stint of madness.

"Whoa!"

"Overly defensive?"

"Look!" points Leon.

The girl diagonally advancing to the double lines abruptly stops and looks up from the hard track. Lana whirls around to the beaten path her and Cole have used several times to enter the small woods. What she sees disturbs her. The thing slash man unflatteringly expressing pain has a jawbone punctured through one of its cheeks.

"Now *I* feel defensive." Lucas pulls the hammer back on his pistol. He unlocks his door and Leon reaches out to stop him. "Wait!"

"Uh, okay. I haven't seen enough organs today," he sarcastically remarks.

"Sh!"

"Did you just tell me—"

"Get ready," the seer cuts in. The stumbling man is closing in on Leon's Potential.

Lucas shakes his handgun, making the point of having been ready.

"Um...um, stop." Lana tries speaking to the abnormal looking man, but he doesn't show any signs of deceleration. She can clearly see that the man needs help, but she does not know how to handle this foreign situation.

The scary man staggers forward and she notices the name sown into the charcoal gray shirt. *Lee!* She gasps. As if her breath galvanizes him, his arms reach forward and his dirty hands come within inches of her slim shoulders.

A popping sound echoes off the four cardinal points.

It is only when Lee's skull hits the bright yellow lines that she peeks over her shoulder. She not only finds herself taking interest in the four-door sedan but the two saviors shutting their doors. Lowering their guns, they calmly stride over to the short, thin girl.

Lana breathes in the fresh warm oxygen in hopes of soothing her jumping heart that thrashes wildly from the adrenaline rush. "Um...thanks, I think," she thanks the taller one with the square face; hard fibrous substances have always been her weapon of choice, but she knows he saved her for there is no way a shotgun would leave a small wound.

"You're welcome," Lucas responds taken aback. Him and Leon never receive gratifications because the people in their past do not know they are alive due to them.

"Did you know him? It sort of seemed like you might."

Lana gives the longhaired stranger her attention. "Uh, sort of. The last time I saw this...man he was dead. Last night."

"Him and others, lady," the blonde brusquely remarks.

"What my cousin, Lucas, means is you should listen to the radio...or watch the news."

"Someone's coming," she tells them.

The two men half turn to the direction from whence they came. Leon never had appendicitis, but at this very moment the aching in his side makes him wish he could punch in his belly button and rip out the pain. The sideways glance Lucas gives the vehicle doesn't bother him until the stiffness of

Leon's body forces him to take more than a glance. Recognizing the accelerating suburban, for Lucas, feels like the top layer of his skin is slowly being pulled off from foot to skull.

Standing in the middle of the street, Lana crosses back over to the cemetery side in fear of being caught underneath the wobbling tires. To her surprise they skid on the paved road coming to a rough halt in between her and the ones who had come to her rescue.

The four-door vehicle is in a horrendous condition: the passenger side has obviously been pushed in almost to the center, deep scratches extend in every direction, and all the glass is busted and missing.

The dented door opens, and the hysteria in the woman's face does not go undetected. If she had been wearing mascara it would be everywhere except the eyelashes that are buried behind extremely swollen eyelids. "May I stay with you?" She dolefully says, "They're dead. My mother, father—" she sees the man on the pavement with the name *Lee* sown into his shirt— "brother, and…" She trails off, too pained to accept his and the other two deaths.

Leon nods in remembrance of the unfortunate encounter.

"We aren't from this city or even this state. And *we* ain't staying," Lucas grits out, walking away from her. "Leon, let's go."

Lana gives her attention to the distressed lady. "What's your name?"

"Kimberly." A small flow of air ruffles her dull,

stringy hair.

"Kimberly, why is your family dead?"

Lucas's jaw locks and his smooth face turns the color of Santa's pants as he stands in front of his door. "Leon. Get. In."

"You should…check on yours," the defiant man recommends to the girl with multiple abrasions on her face. Lucas begins stomping heatedly towards the vehicle's front.

Lana eyes the long barreled gun. "I don't have weapons like that."

"Is that your house over there?" Leon's head bobs.

"Yes."

"Get in."

She starts to follow the young man in the crimson t-shirt but he halts, having nearly bumped into Lucas. "Um, no!" Lucas glowers down into Leon's eyes, like a king being forced to surrender his territory. "Brighton, I met by your damn self!"

"After her," he challenges. Swiftly, the seer throws his palm to his forehead and starts blinking rapidly. "No. No." He agitatedly moans for he knows what the next few moments hold for him as he swings the passenger door outward and places himself in a safer area.

"Backseat," Lucas points for the Potential to get in, and then references Kimberly. "I'm assumin' she can follow us?"

Maybe it is the way they look at her, or rather don't, that gives Lana a sense of ease. Neither of the two young but older men regard her in the way most strangers often do; avoid eye contact, shift uncomfortably, point, or make rude and undue comments—these are the most popular reactions on a long list. (This shaking woman and the short man had been too far away in the graveyard to really see the scars, and the kid, well, he must have been raised properly.)

Lana nods and Kimberly scrabbles onto her shredded seat; neither one of them knows what is happening.

Lucas slams his door. "Take that gun from him."

Leon doesn't object when his Potential reaches over the slick blue seat. Who knows what he could do in this blacking out state? He does not have a suicide wish, or a homicide one for that matter.

The car reverses and maneuvers to the gravel and dirt driveway.

"What's he doing?" It took little for Lana to notice their changes in behavior. And now the one with two identities rocks violently.

Lucas is uncertain about the countenance of the raven-haired girl in his rearview mirror. But there are no indications of fear, unlike the hazardous clunker that trails needlessly close as if any space will permanently separate the two. He does not want Kimberly to die, but he wishes she would just disappear.

Leon cover his ears and Lucas avoids Lana's question. "Will you hand me a rag, please?" There are two wash clothes on the smooth leather seat. She hands Lucas the first one her hand touches. He tries to give the yellowish green fabric to a slumped down Leon.

But he thrashes his head hard against the seat.

Lucas kicks the brake, tires slide and dig up the gravel and dirt. Kimberly screams and swerves the hazardous suburban left, nearly clipping the side of the Biscayne. Lana adverts her attention to the distraught driver. But Lucas's sight doesn't leave his family. "Hold him back," he says requiring her assistance. Whipping her fingers through soft thick hair, she pins Leon against the headrest and hopes the conscious one will not ruminate over her strength.

Lucas forces Leon's round jaw open and places the cloth in between his shaking teeth. "The first time this happened to him we didn't think his tongue would stop bleedin'."

Below her apprehensive hands, thin lines of blood escape Leon's small ears. *"What is happening?"*

Lucas knows that this is when things become quieter in the seer's mind, and his body is always inert. But blackish-red spurts of blood run down the pulsating veins nearly popping out of Leon's neck and his entire body shakes in its upright position.

Lucas stares incredulously.

"This isn't supposed to happen?" Lana judges by his befuddled expression.

Still seizing, Leon unintentionally flings forward; forehead aimed for the dashboard…

…Wrong. The silence. It is just…wrong. And the colors are definitely not right: black and white.

Light curly hair waves up and down. The girl's face anxiously fixed like it knows something horrible is going to happen but awaits anyway. The columns on either side of her contrast to a bright white as if it were underneath a huge black light.

The angle changes like a camera rotating behind the young female. She disappears. The sky is now light green and the grass a deep blue. As if peering down from above, Leon sees the girl lying on her back on a set of steps separating the snow colored columns. Her head rests against a porch while a silhouette feasts on her stomach.

She screams. But silence mutes the audio.

Slightly to the right of the two, an unseen sun—until now—quickly becomes eaten from the outside in by darkness, expelling rays of crimson.

The screaming girl dies.

Falling from the green sky—clouded by a mass of yellow hair—an assumed feminine body smashes without a sound into the unmoving blueness. Without hesitation, the earth surrounding her rots and webs of black expand outward from her body. The foundation underneath the dead girl with blonde curls and the feasting silhouette crumbles.

Like someone changing the television channel, a familiar picture of no-show-bar girl covered in blood awakens the seer…

* * *

GANESHA

Pop music plays inside Ganesha's yellow Gemballa Mirage GT. Her phone rings and the music ends as a composed voice sounds through the stereo speakers. "Ganesha, where are you?"

"Kansas. I am thirty minutes away from you, Ray." After she had dropped her friend off at the airport the dark-skinned eighteen year old had promptly left the Cornhusker State.

"Someone is not obeying the speed limit signs," Raven's voice sings. The speed racer should not be this close to Concordia.

Ganesha laughs guiltily, and pops a potato chip in her mouth from the bag in between her legs.

"How's the new system?"

"Great!" The enthusiastic girl had been given an extremely sophisticated radar detector that locates police officers on speed control as an early birthday present by the homemade maker herself. Raven. "It is my third fav gift from you, my third fav ever! No tickets girl!"

"What are the first two?"

"Second, this ride!"

The sleek yellow 09' carbon edition was her Christmas present this past season. She had heard there were only five of them in the world. *What are the chances that I would ever get a limited anything?* She shoves several crispy chips in her mouth.

"And you know the first, Ray," Ganesha says, chomping on the snack food and repelling memories from her old life of neglect and poverty.

LEON CARMANY / LANA QUEEN

Feeling the warm light on his face, Leon tries opening his sticky eyes. But they sting. And his arms are itchy. Sitting up, confusion dominates him as two worried expressions greet him. The third— the one standing directly above his feet— perpetuates annoyance.

"Why am I not in the car?" Leon's hands cling to

the grassy earth in the middle of the prairie field.

"You okay?" The voice that speaks is not the one he expects. Concerned, Lana places a hand on his shoulder. "What did your vision contain?"

He looks questionably up, the sun shining in his eyes, to the man in the long sleeve shirt. Obviously the composed girl had been informed while his eyes were closed to the world. *But how much?* Leon accepts Lucas's held out hand, helping him to his feet. At once, he realizes his wrists and ankles are peculiarly sore...

"Yours." Lucas puts the bloody rags in Leon's palm and stomps away fuming through the field.

"Now what?" Kimberly meagerly asks as the three of them head to the vehicles.

Leon ignores her and asks the new girl, "What happened?"

"You, um..." Lana gives him a sideways glance, unsure of how much she should tell him. "Had a seizure. The pain you're experiencing is from where we moved you by the feet and hands." That was the truth.

Inside the vehicle, Lana stares at the acre of scattered trees by the prairie. She feels bad for the light red marks on Leon's wrists and the unseen ones (he had not looked, but she knows they are there) on his ankles. The Shadow hopes the strangers do not suspect that she is not normal; Kimberly is too frenetic to even wonder why Leon has visions in the first place, so the chances of her discovering the Shadow's true identity are slim to none.

Lana does not want her secret exposed to the two

males for fear that they will be killed. If a Vampire suspects that a human has knowledge of the night creatures then they are eradicated from the human population; save for those like her mother who do not pose a threat.

She has an inkling that someone who sees—other than with his eyes—has to be important.

And how many Vampires will knowingly let someone as significant as Leon live? They will either kill him or exploit him for his gift just as regular humans, Normals, would for her skills.

The seer causes her to think about someone…the Goddess in her dreams—the one the white-haired Vampire mentioned before she fried in the sunlight and burst into emerald and white flames—someone only starring in Lana's dreams.

~~~~

Chapter 6
Friends and Enemies

I'VE NEVER BEEN LIKE THIS. Not even when I had my first fight. Lana loves her mother. Kronos has no use for her, but it is not until now that Lana finds that she may have taken him not killing her for granted. Her number one enemy may not want her only parent dead, but other things might. Things like that man Lee now lying dead on the road.

It doesn't even have to be that. Crazy people could take her away. If not that, then there is sickness.

Sick. That is what she feels in the pit of her stomach as she tautly stands on the deck that extends to the back of the house. Looking at Lucas's uneasy hand on the front knob makes stomach acid touch the back of her throat. She forces the burning liquid matter back down.

With the barrier being pushed open, the cool air from inside gently strokes Lucas Kale's apprehensive face. Lucas does well at predicting outcomes. But not now.

Today's encounters have shown new intimidations. Before, when he was only hunting Vampires, he knew what would happen as soon as he and Leon would show up for the elimination. Not only would they win, but they would live.

Lucas stands before the threshold. It offers no promises. He senses nothing. And that makes him hate this day even more.

"Mom?" Lana's shaking voice passes by him interrupting the silence in the sunlit room.

"Lana?"

The tiny girl brushes past him, the sounds of her feet join the pair making their way towards them. Leon scans the wide area as Lucas hurriedly follows after the impetuous girl. A gentle humming from an aquarium against the right wall is first to grab Leon's attention. The window above it casts a rectangle light onto a light blue oval rug that matches a blue leather couch against the back wall that would normally be the first object to be noticed if he were not on edge.

And normally Leon would be interested in the handmade bookshelf next to the long seat. He believes that what a person reads says a lot about them; the fact there are even books in this household tells him that someone here has to be somewhat intelligent.

But it only makes him remember T.S. Eliot and

the reason his book is sitting on a night stand back at the motel. *Devin.*

Aware of an upcoming opening on the left, Leon swiftly turns…an empty kitchen. The fresh scent of the recently mopped floor, it probably has not even dried yet, is the only thing to strike him. In the brief moment, the lemon smell pulls him back to his childhood; him voluntarily sweeping and mopping the numerous footprints and dirt tracked in by him and the other kids running in and out of Uncle Joe's house. The intelligent boy had sympathized with the widower. The kindhearted man was raising more kids than he had originally planned and he did it with a song in his heart and a dance in his eyes.

Lucas passes into a room that displays a small dining table placed on black and white linoleum. He places his finger on the trigger of his pistol just has a pair of arms emerge from an opening on the right—in front of Lana…

BLAYNE / KRONOS
"We're on our way." Enthusiastic lips kiss the phone. The light brown-haired boy is joyous that he receives a signal so far down in a cavern. Even though he had been told it would work, he remained skeptical.

"Hello, Blayne." A deep voice greets him from the side.

The eighteen year old boy knows the calm set of feet that softly glide through the freshwater; four lit torches light the cavern. They do not need them to see—being true creatures of the night. The way the flames pierce the blackness captivates them, similar to the way an owl will perch on a limb and intelligently watch the orange flames of a campfire rising in the middle of the night.

Blayne smiles the smile of a little boy about to tattle on his sister for an act that was committed by himself. "It worked. Whose plan?"

Kronos cocks his head. "Why do you ask questions that you already have an answer to?" The Vampire steps onto the dirt ground with such pride and sagacity that makes Blayne feel ashamed for a split second, that he could actually forget something of this importance. He dismisses the elder Vampire's question as being rhetorical and answers his own. "Father."

Kronos, dressed in wet, black pants and shirt, nods towards the uphill path and they take off through the ridged and narrow land tunnels. The elder Vampire hates holding back his true speed to avoid losing the newborn.

An ice truck with its rear doors open backs up to the cave's entrance. Kronos and Blayne hurry inside the truck, avoiding the bright light of death. The doors shut, and the two sit quietly while it pulls into the garage attached at the back of a house.

"What happened to—"

"God's star," Kronos says bitterly. "They threw her out into that bastard's hindrance. But she delivered the message." Blayne shakes his head. Death by the sun, he can't imagine a worse way for his kind to die. But as for the Shadows, he knows plenty of ways to make them suffer—but only his favorite comes to mind…

LANA/LEON/KIMBERLY/LUCAS

The woman with her arms around Lana expresses great emotion, but it is not threatening.

"Mom, I have to talk to you."

The blonde man nods, signaling Leon to the dining area. "It's okay," Leon confirms to Kimberly who lingers in the middle of the entrance, holding the front door open.

"Who are you?" Mrs. Queen addresses the strangers in her house as she holds her daughter tightly. The resemblance between the two is uncanny. Both petite frames are equal in height and have the same dark and lustrous tresses. Lana's apple green irises—a trait apparently passed down from her father—is the only distinguishable feature separating the two women. "They saved me," Lana tells her, pulling away from her mother's embrace.

Mrs. Queen cups her hands around her youngster's oval face. "From?"

The two young men hear someone shuffling around in the next room. They immediately tense up. The teenage boy they had seen not long before Lana's arrival leans against the wooden frame behind the worried mother. Lana looks from her mom to Cole, uncertain how to tell them about a new found existence. She decides to start with the truth. "I was attacked."

Cole straightens. "By one of those sick persons?"

"You know?" Leon asks, surprised.

"Yeah. We are supposed to stay inside," says the woman of the house.

"Until quarantine is over," adds Cole. "Anyone wishing to leave the city has thirty minutes."

"WHAT!" Leon and Lucas roar, eyes wide.

"Those S.O.B's are caging us in with the really screwed up version of I-wanna-be-a-real-boy," Lucas says cynically. "Take care," he waves. "I'm going home to zombie free Tennessee."

Leon tags behind his cousin through the orderly living room, but with different intentions; he can't simply leave. What about the bar-girl? The reason they are here in the first place. And that last vision of his? A teenage blonde girl dies, triggering some catastrophic event. If Leon leaves the state now he will be dooming all of them.

Kimberly, unsure of what her role should be in this situation, follows after the two men. "What should I do?" she whispers.

"Don't know. Not a babysitter," Lucas wisecracks. He hears footsteps on the deck… He raises his pistol…the door opens…

"That's her!" The seer does not conceal his surprise. "From last time!"

"Lana, why are there mental patients in your home?" Hand on her hip, the girl in the doorway disgustingly eyes the lowering pistol.

Lana speaks in haste, aware of the pressing time. "This is Leon and his cousin Lucas. He saved me, and he has visions," she points.

Cole laughs with disbelief, and the taller woman tries to pull her daughter behind her in a shielding manner. "Mom, stop." Lana easily resists, and asks Leon, "You saw Loki?"

"If that is Loki, then yes."

"He's lying," the girl with blonde ringlets shaped around her heart shaped face warns. "He's probably one of the sick." Lucas rolls his eyes in annoyance.

"I witnessed it. And that blood is the result." Lana nods at the blood spots in the dark matted hair around Leon's ears and the light red smears on his neck.

Lucas still does not see the point in staying. "They're both alive. I'm leaving." With a quickness he is out the ingress. "Wait," Leon chases after him, catching the screen door before it slams in his face. He turns right, hurrying across the long black deck. "We have to stay."

"No, we don't." Lucas takes the steps two by two.

The seer turns left at the bottom of the steps and grabs his older cousin's shoulder. "That girl is in trouble."

"Thirty minutes, Leon!" Lucas turns away from him and stares out across the field to nothing in particular. "I'm twenty-four. Our lives are not normal *and* they're crappy. But I'm not ready to give up my life."

"You and *I"* —the seer breathes in a sharp breath and then reveals what he has seen— "Are going to die anyway."

* * *

Concordia, Kansas
Ganesha parks her car on the slightly elevated driveway. She straps her purse on her shoulder and hops out carrying the empty potato chip bag and a half full bottle of water.

The neighbors are usually out tending their lawns on Saturdays, but today they are not.

She misses the sounds of the mowers and the smell of the neighbors' barbeques. It is not often that she gets the chance to join them for her new life demands more from her.

Ganesha does not mind though.

It was not until a little over a year ago on her seventeenth birthday, in this very spot, that she even saw and experienced a real life barbeque. That day was the turning point for Ganesha. Two hours before the sizzling hotdogs, cheeseburgers, and chicken with grill markings, she had been thrown down by three boys to an alley floor for refusing to show them her breasts. Her punishment was two broken ribs and a black eye.

But her reward has been far greater.

Not only did she get to watch their bladders empty themselves while Raven snatched the delinquents off her and made them cry as they waited for the police—but she received a best friend, a real family, and a real home.

Unpleasant memories from her previous life in her old house force themselves upon her. She refuses to call the place *home* because HOME should be a place where one feels safe and truly wanted. And Ganesha had never felt that there.

Age fifteen: A shovel to the head for flushing cocaine down the toilet and burning needles used for heroine.

Age thirteen: Asked for a Christmas tree. "Why?" Her mother responded. "We don't celebrate that stupid shit. Jesus was invented by white people."

Age eight: Told to stop eating like a pig (even though it had been nearly forty-eight hours since she had a meal) because the money was needed to pay the rent; the male landlord had been replaced by a female who did not sleep with women.

Age six: Her mother performed oral sex on a man while she sat in the same room.

All the abusive and neglectful acts in Ganesha's life were committed by the woman who gave birth to her. Ganesha knows nothing of her father; not even who he is or where he lives. Or if he's even alive. She doubts her mother knows, given the woman is a drug addict and a prostitute.

Ganesha shakes her head, quickly pulling herself from the recollection of the unfitted woman's parenting skills. Since the entire neighborhood has been warned by her best friend and her other friend, Jet, there are only two people outside today.

Facing Raven's log house, to her left a man transports lumber into his yellow home. Across the street a woman carrying groceries waves and smiles at the girl standing on the paved driveway. Ganesha knows they are preparing for the zombies and that they are the only ones staying in their houses. The other two families at the other end of Jet Road have abandoned their beloved homes. Granted the evidence of automobiles, swings, and kiddy pools suggests otherwise.

Ganesha, not feeling like smiling, waves. *Can anyone truly be happy when their scariest nightmares are forming into real life?* Raven. Raven—curly brown wig off— walks down the cedar steps directly in front of the house entry.

Everyone believes in her. Ganesha smiles at her best friend. *Raven is the only thing, other than God, worthy of putting trust in. And by putting my faith in her it might as well be with God itself.*

"See anything?" Raven embraces her.

"Actually, no. It is not spreading that fast. Yet." They break away, and Ganesha is compelled to say what is now on her mind. "Ray?"

"Yes?"

"I know you do not have orders to stay with the boy with that gift, but you did not receive any to leave either."

Raven knows this is her youngest friend's way of saying that if she wanted to stay and help them she should. "My friendship is with you, Ganesha."

"I am warm and fuzzy inside," she jokes. "Thanks Ray sista'." The blonde woman rolls her hazel eyes and moves her feet back the way she came. "I love you," Ganesha smiles and walks off the oil black pavement through the green grass.

"You also love unicorns," Raven throws out.

Ganesha stops at the bottom of the red steps, mouth open. "You said you wouldn't tell!" She pulls the chain out from under her white designer collar and presses her thumb and index finger on the purple unicorn.

Raven chuckles. "No one heard." She pauses on the top step, in between two hanging pots of flowers, and giggles. "Well, *someone* heard…"

* * *

Hastings, Nebraska

"We're going to die? Care to elaborate?" Lucas presses the issue.

Leon cannot take it anymore. How is it possible to be surrounded by an uncluttered atmosphere that expands in every direction and still find it difficult to breathe?

"I'm not big on words, but I'm sure elaborate doesn't mean to walk cryptically away!" Lucas follows after him.

Leon sets his large gun on the car and then puts his forehead in his hands massaging it. Lucas leans back against the warm Chevrolet Biscayne. "Does it hurt?"

Leon nods. The visions are taking their toll on him. The most he receives, prior to a few hours ago, is one a week.

"It was different this time," Lucas recalls the last time his cousin received a vision. "You looked—well, it's the only reason I'm letting you get away with this."

He rolls up his white sleeve and shows him a jaundice looking bruise the size of a tennis ball.

Leon is about to apologize for something he had no control over when his instincts take control. Where Rush begins on the opposite side of the smooth pavement, an acre of scattered trees in front of it ends meeting Lana's expansive land. Two slow functioning zombies enter the massive area.

"There is no way we can get the shot from here," states Lucas.

Leon becomes fearful. How many other times will he have to get closer than he desires? He gulps in air and talks really fast. "I believe the no-show-blonde was in my last scene. And Lana's blonde friend is going to die and if she dies then somehow the other blonde, bar-girl, goes too."

The genius sucks in another gulp. "And that's bad because then everything dies, so I suggest that we get Loki and Lana and leave." Leon doesn't necessarily need Lana, but he has a feeling she won't let her friend leave with a couple of strangers. Even if they did save her.

"I think Lana is a tracker," Lucas admits.

"Shadow," Lana corrects him. They have been oblivious to the others gathered on the roofless deck. "That's the term. I am a Shadow and Cole is, too." Lana eyes the two sickly trespassers at the end of the property heading for her house. The undaunted Vampire's words echo in her mind. *Even the goddess will not be able to save you.* "I will gladly go with you," the eighteen year old volunteers.

A wheezing sound, like mice being choked, erupts from Mrs. Queen—not wanting to part from her daughter. "Mom," she sternly says and the woman presses her lips back together.

"I will leave as well," Cole announces, his arms crossed and eyes fixed, clearly not taking no for answer. "There are guns at Loki's," he offers.

No one has asked the gray-eyed girl her plans, and Lana waits for her decision. "Loki?"

"Who can resist being a damsel when there is not *one* but *two* gorgeous rescuers?" the girl beams, running her hand down the black railing.

Knowing Loki and her...*different* approaches to

situations, Lana is fixed on the new arrivals, waiting for their reactions. She becomes stunned. Lucas's features hold... *Flattery? Why? Wouldn't someone who looks like that hear similar phrases?* A tiny smile cuts through her thought process. Lucas clearly does not mind Loki's words, but Leon's round face resembles that of someone having avoided the urination process for quite some time.

Loki hooks her arm around Leon's. "Not gonna open the door?"

"Forgive him." Lucas opens the backdoor. "He doesn't like females." The eyes of Leon irritatingly roll inside their sockets, and Kimberly, without being invited, gets in on the other side. "Lana needs a moment," Cole tells him, looking up at the two above them; Lana stands with her forehead pressed against her mother's.

Leon understands the situation. If he had a mother he would not want to leave her behind either. But he respects the girl's decision. She may be younger physically, but Lana's mentality is closer to his own. That fact alone is worthy of his respect, unlike her coquettish friend who sits grinning at him through the car window like a child fascinated with their first puppy. *This isn't a game,* he thinks.

The burly man in the red t-shirt hands his shotgun up to Lana and she blinks with confusion. "I know you can cause massive damage, but who wants to get that close?" Leon makes a point. She takes another look at the zombies and decides to take the weapon. "Thanks."

Leon gives her the ammo from his back pants

pocket and jogs to the idling vehicle. "Be back *quickly*," he calls over his shoulder.

The sunlight burns down upon them, heating the grassy plain. Lucas glances at his watch. He had not been told exactly when the thirty minutes had started. And the assumed twenty something remaining ones do not bring him assurance.

They speed forward with Loki guiding the way.

Chapter 7
All Connected

LEON CARMANY

LEON SAT IN THE same spot of the car he had practically been in for most of the day. He sat there and ignored everything Loki had to say. Almost everything. The first part of the conversation—the only part he heard—was about her dad living out of state and that she could leave with them because her mother was on a business trip.

That was when the side mirror reflected a look on Cole's face that said Loki was lying.

The seer decided he had done enough deciphering for one day. He listened less and watched more. The tires rotated speedily on the worn path through the field behind Lana's. Before they rolled down the steep incline, from the top of the hill there were only three things to be seen; a big dull white house located near the bottom—Loki's he had assumed for she pointed at it—a tree every other acre, and miles of the same tall grass that seemed lifeless until the wind forced them to sway in the same commanded direction then they returned to slumping over like they meant nothing to the world.

Nothing. Leon is smart, genius smart, yet in less than forty-eight hours he received not one, but three clips of the future, and he only guessed that putting duct tape over that talkative girl's mouth would unfortunately be a bad idea. *Nothing. That is what I know. Some help I am.*

Two white pillars burn a hole in disheartened eyes. In his vision a zombie had consumed Loki in this very spot. He does not know how or why her death ends the bar-girl's life. Or why the bar-girl smothered in blood is highly important. But what makes him truly mad is the fact that he does not have all the puzzle pieces. He is missing the critical one. *Where is she?*

"You should wash that off."

Leon blinks into reality. "Huh?" For a moment he forgot he had stayed outside while the others gathered more weaponry from Loki's house. He was supposed to be watching for signs of trouble. But why? Were plants going to attack them with their oxygen? And what if he did see something? What was *he* going to do? Slingshot those ugly pink flowers that surround the entire front of the place? Nothing. That is what he had felt like doing otherwise he would have objected to Luke's ludicrous idea of playing watch dog.

"Your blood." Cole exits outside carrying a rifle. The old house is more expensive than the other houses in Nebraska, but the exterior has been neglected for some time. Its white paint faded and several spots have begun to chip. The two-by-fours on the porch's floor could also use another coat or two of color. "I know it attracts Vampires and sharks. Neither of which I can see right now, but I don't think—"

"Want to know if it attracts *them*," Leon interrupts, catching a wet rag tossed by Loki. She slings a rifle over her shoulder. *Still wearing shorts and a tank top? I don't know about her, but I feel more comfortable with less exposed skin.*

Lucas totes a shotgun and small boxes of rifle and shotgun ammunition outside, Kimberly nearly on his heels. The reason she had gone inside was to use the bathroom. But Leon suspects it was to secretly fall to pieces.

They U-turn, leaving pillars of death.

Leon thinks about her; the girl he has seen twice—not the coquette female now bouncing around next to him and Lucas. *It is not about Loki. Not really.* They are chess pieces—he hates chess. Since the death of his father he has yet to lose at the game that he no longer finds challenging or entertaining. *Protect your king. It's that simple. And Loki is maybe a knight at best.*

Leon smiles for the first time since little Devin's death.

LANA QUEEN

Lana killed the zombies with the cousin's shotgun, and said goodbye to her mother. She feels sad for leaving her mother at such a vital time, but the vision Leon had of her awakens something within Lana that she had forgotten for years.

She is thinking about someone—and the name *Kronos* is not in her thoughts.

Lana exhales, putting the tall, thin hardback she retrieved from under her bed into her backpack. This was the first item she thought of, but it is the last to be placed in a separate pocket in the black bag; the bigger section storing stakes and a crossbow.

From the second floor, she sees out her window the ultramarine Biscayne racing through the tall grass that will be used for hay. Lana looks around the room, taking the past and present into her soul. Save for the bathroom near the top of the stairs, the whole second story is one bedroom. It used to be her parents' sleeping quarters, but her father gave it to her because she was having various friends over and thought his sociable daughter should have the commodious area.

He died that unforgettable night. And now Cole and Loki are the only ones staying the night. The only ones staying around her. Lana lets out a sigh of...relief. She twirls to the cheval glass to her right, the tall and round mirror fixed into the dark frame, its legs mashing in the slate blue carpet. Even though she changed from shorts and a short sleeve shirt into their opposites, she still cannot place what is different about herself. Regardless, glossy lips push soft cheeks upwards to twinkling eyes.

She snatches the backpack off the queen-size bed.

COLE
Trust. Does he trust them? The way the short-haired guy encourages Loki works against Cole's favor. Sure one of them saved his friend's life, but as of right now the only reason he does not question the recently bloody man's sanity is because of Lana's credence.

Just because one of them knows of 'might' happenings doesn't make them BOTH saints. Cole does not know Lucas and Leon. And they do not know him. *Lana can handle herself. But there is no way in hell I'm handing her over.* If Lana had not decided to go then he would not have either.

Orphaned at age eleven and eventually adopted does not mean he loves his new parents any less than his biological parents. He called them from Loki's house and told them he had to leave, to be safe, and he loved them very much. And there are only two justifications for why he would ever forsake them. Vampires and... *Lana...?* They pull up in front of the buoyant girl, and Cole is about to be chivalrous when unexpectedly his army men below the belt, due to delectation, want to know if swimming... Aroused, he decides to scoot over to the right next to Kimberly.

Lana gets in, and the car takes off faster than a chained dog chasing a female scent after the line has snapped.

* * *

One minute and thirty seconds.

The yellow numbers counting down on the big rectangle timers placed along their route leaving the terrorized city feel as surreal as a dream. The ride through Hastings, Nebraska has been a quiet one—especially now. No one makes a sound out of fear that even talking will somehow preclude them from skipping town.

129... 125... 115, Leon counts down in his head. It seems time is going faster and they are moving slower.

105... 93...

Lucas wants to take his death grip off the steering wheel and punch Leon in the groin; he can feel his eyes constantly shifting to the speedometer—needle points to the far right—expecting the car to magically sprout higher numbers.

84...

73...

A car pulls out from the short line of vehicles behind them and passes the old but classic car.

60...

Finally, they see it. Stretched out—for what seems to be the distance from California to North Carolina—are hundreds of military soldiers with hundreds of guns and several tanks expanding horizontally from both sides of the road; there is no "going around" or "breaking through".

50...

They zoom by a house.

40... 37...

They zoom by another house. "Lucky bastards," Lucas says under his breath, and Kimberly jumps at the sound of his voice. "Must have been real easy for them to leave."

The timer at the roadblock is getting bigger and bigger, letting the six passengers know if they do not beat the countdown to God only knows what happens, they are going to be the first ones to find out.

30... Almost! Almost there!

Lucas takes his foot off the gas and slowly presses the brake pedal, the needle begins pointing towards the left.

Twenty-three seconds. The tires stop in front of the barricade; the yellow number twenty-three is on the screen.

Several men—the kind of hulked out men nobody in their right mind messes with—surround the car and point long barreled guns and what looks similar to grocery store barcode scanners at them.

Unable to take his eyes off, Leon watches the timer flick down from twenty-three. To him, it seems to be moving in slow motion.

"Trunk," the soldier closest to Lucas orders. *Great. It's not a zombie I'm stowing away.*

Still watching the big yellow numbers, Leon—the only one watching—sees the color change from yellow to red when the number twenty flicks to nineteen. *Why nineteen? Why not ten? Or twenty even?*

Lucas opens the door and pops the trunk. Two soldiers stare down at the giant cross and stakes, and then glare questionably at the driver of the car. Lucas smiles pleasantly, not offering an explanation. The guy to his left closes the lid. "Go."

Lucas doesn't need to be told twice. The guards part, and Hastings is nothing but a reflection of cornfields in his mirrors.

BLAYNE / KRONOS

"She's left her house, but she isn't alone," Blayne Vandor needlessly says to the eight hundred and sixteen year old Vampire with the young but scarred face of a thirty-five year old.

"That credulous boy will always trail behind my Lana. Poor little orphan will never stop chasing after her. His readiness to believe he has a chance with her is going to prematurely end his pathetic life." Kronos lets out a contemptuous cackle.

"And there are new humans." The floorboards creak as the Novice paces, listening to the voice on the other side of the phone conversation.

"New pleasure," the elder leers, sitting up straight with his forearms resting on the arms of a chair.

"Not a problem," Blayne grins into the phone. "If they slip up you know Lana is the one Kronos wants burned alive." He shoves the phone into his pocket.

Kronos, having heard the entire conversation, smiles with delight. "Hastings is closed."

"Yes."

They become noiseless. Hearkening a scream outside the perimeter, their jubilant laughs echo in the undersized room. Blayne composes himself, his triangle face serious. "What if Lana can't make it? And I thought *you* personally wanted to kill her."

The young Vampire has only seen the Shadow one time—in another life. The memory is hazy, but he recalls being scared and angry when the girl found him. Then he was running through the freshly dewed grass; he just wanted to go home. Blayne was halfway to his destination when suddenly he couldn't move. He woke up in the underground of August and Rush Cemetery's cavern. The Novice woke up and he was *hungry*. And his older human brother was present…

A couple of weeks later his creator told him it was time to go home. And so he did. Blayne feed off of his blood relatives, some of them, the rest he had over the course of a few months in another sitting. His grandfather, however, devastated by the loss of his family, blew his own brains out one cloudy morning.

Every blood relative in Blayne's family is dead. He killed his younger cousins first. Kronos told him it was important to do so… With them out of the way, Blayne Vandor has nothing to fret over.

"When I have her where I want her," the elder Vampire hisses up at him. "I must say, you will not live to be as old as I."

Blayne frowns.

"Cheer up. Care for a little" —Kronos looks up at the cream colored ceiling—"Push?"

A girl, and a man with dyed black hair—the man had told them his name was Tyler as if it meant something—have chains around their wrists and ankles that connect with two fixed points; one in front and the other behind them.

"You know I can't do that."

"Duh! One would think you knew the theory of repetition."

There are times when his sire can make him feel just like a worthless human—now being one of those times. Blayne sucks it up and begins his lesson with the girl— females are the easiest to Push. So he has heard. He stretches his hand upwards and concentrates. Other than the girl desperately tugging at the chains and making them noisily rattle—nothing happens.

Doubting he will ever learn, the kid—compared to the raven-haired Vampire—picks up an out of placed dresser and swings it down to the floor. The broken drawers lay in disorderly piles about the room.

"Toddler, let's not have a temper tantrum. Take out your frustration in a truly satisfying way."

Blayne jumps up and wraps his legs around his victim, positioning himself underneath the frightened girl with mascara on her face. He reaches over and removes the gray tape over Tyler's mouth. Then the Novice swings his arm back, making a fist. BAM! BAM! The chained girl's nose and eye sockets cave in.

Blayne's long fangs puncture the human girl's artery.

The only sound to be heard, other than the two rapid heartbeats, is the sound of the blood stream disturbing the air while it flows out from Tyler's mouth to satisfy the voracious appetite of his sire.

LUCAS/LEON/LANA/LOKI/COLE/KIMBERLY

After the escape from zombie land, Lucas figured since they have two professional Vampire assassins in their car—it had once belonged to his mother and Uncle Jay, Leon's dad—he could tell everyone about Leon and him being Vampire Hunters.

What makes this awkward is that six strangers have been forced together under this roof to save another stranger which in turns saves us, Leon thinks, *And now we are wandering south to Tennessee; which we know is a false destination.*

Leaving the county, Leon breaks the uncomfortable silence. "Lana, uh, your mother, what—"

"Basement. Food. Big gun," she says before he can complete his sentence. "Thanks, by the way."

"I haven't really done anything to—"

"Why are you being modest?" Loki cuts in. "You saved a stranger. A girl stranger that's hot!" She lasciviously traces his biceps with her fingers, making him wonder if she is talking about herself. Startled by the girl's provocative nature, Leon lets out a nervous laugh. Not knowing what to do, he looks back at Lana for support.

"Kool-aid was invented here by Edwin E. Perkins. Well, not here, but in Hastings." That does nothing to distract the teenager, still running the tips of her fingers on his arm. "Sorry," she mouths.

"I stole some tampons from a girl," Cole blurts out.

"What?" asks Leon merely a split second before Lucas points out, "As opposed to taking them from a dude?"

"I stole a tampon."

"Yeah. We heard that," says Lucas, his voice almost harsh.

"This one time—"

"—At band camp." The hazel-eyed man laughs.

"Seriously, Luke? The *American Pie* joke—"

"—Okay, granny panties." The twenty-four year old moves his arm back and forth and overenthusiastically says, "Let's hear about some tampons!" The excessive enthusiasm tickles Lana and Loki; their girly laughter fills the confined space and Cole cannot help but laugh at them. Lucas looks over at Leon and smiles with satisfaction. "Cute," the genius says, not amused.

"Okay," Cole starts again after the subsiding laughter. "One time Lana was telling me about how disgusting the girls' bathroom was. Sometimes she would go in there and used toilet paper and tampons would be the floor.

"Well, one day in the lunch line, I heard a girl talking about how she purposely left out used female stuff. She got a kick out of seeing people's faces and was gonna do it again after lunch. So I thought, what a disgusting bitch, and I easily looked in her purse and stole the two unused ones. Then I had Lana take a used one from the bathroom—"

"I wrapped it in toilet paper," Lana clarifies. "And near the end of lunch period Loki put the nasty thing in the girl's purse."

"We followed her into the bathroom," Loki says. "She always smoked and texted in there during that time. She reached in for her phone and instead grabbed the tissue. And when she unrolled it the bloody thing fell in her hand." They laugh triumphantly.

"After she washed her hands," Lana recounts, "she went into the stall, and when she couldn't find her tampons she said, 'Someone stole my tampons!' and someone said, 'Yeah, they're pretty sneaky with pulling it out of your vagina and all!'"

Leon laughs so hard his shoulders shake. It feels good; laughter.

Lucas nudges Loki with his shoulder. "You put the lady thing in her purse?" She nods. "That's not a lady thing to do. In fact, it's sick and vindictive. But I like it," he smiles.

Everyone seems to find it humorous except Kimberly, Lana notices. The fragile woman stares blankly out the window. The reflection of her stringy brown hair and pale face stares back. No signs of life in her eyes. Lana recollects the way she looked at the man on the pavement after she rushed out of her wrecked suburban. "Was Lee your brother?"

Kimberly nods and rocks back and forth.

"It's going to be okay."

The inconsolable woman returns to her blank state as if the optimistic teenager had never spoken.

The verdant-eyed girl turns to the dull scenery out of her open window; Lana cannot bear to watch Kimberly's freckled hands intensely squeeze her own arms to the point where it has to be causing pain. The air flowing through the car tosses her tresses and several strands of the adopted teen's hair. She stares at the pavement. Lines... Lines... Car... Lines... Lines... Car... And more painted strips dividing the two lanes of traffic.

Everyone that is attentive had decided that it is a good idea to avoid the interstate, it seems like a great place for unwanted things to happen.

Lana drifts yet again to her dreams of the previous nights. They bring her comfort in this uncomfortable time.

"I feel guilty," confesses Loki.

"Why? It was funny," Lucas says thinking about the disgraceful bathroom girl.

"Not that. For lying to you and Leon."

"Huh?"

"Her parents," Leon presumes. He had caught the reaction on the younger boy's face when Loki told them her mother was on a business trip.

"Yeah…my mom is not on a business trip. The truth is I don't know where she is. She comes and goes at all hours. The last I heard from her was like two days ago. She was at a friend's house with Jack Daniels and Captain Morgan. I wasn't lying about Dad though. He lives in Georgia."

Mom lives in her own world, and dad might as well live on the moon, the genius translates. Leon Carmany refuses to have sympathy for the girl sitting next to him; he knows everyone else does—excluding Kimberly, not seeming to hear a word said in the car—including his cousin who will never say so or show it. It will not stop Luke from sleeping with her though, in fact, to Lucas, Loki is a sure thing. And much to Leon's distaste, statistics would agree. He does not like statistics, and Loki is the object of his aversion.

"So, weapons," Cole interjects. "How should

they be divided?"

"I don't want one." Lana pulls out a small crossbow from her backpack. "Got my own."

Cole takes one look at Kimberly and decides the inoperative woman shouldn't be handling firearms. "Loki, you have terrible aim. Take the shotgun and let Leon have the rifle. If that is okay with you, man?" Leon nods and accepts the rifle from him. "Thanks." Loki receives the shotgun from Lana over the blue seat, making Kimberly the only one without protection.

The distributed guns make Lana realize that she has been waiting for the right moment. And it has arrived. She takes today's unfortunate events seriously, but seeing the chambers that will fire at her altering and dying species makes her think about the momentous volume she packed. "I-I didn't realize how much things... I'm saying we need help."

Lucas shuts her down. "Don't know anyone."

"I do," she suggests. "Sort of."

Leon raises an eyebrow. "Whom?"

She unzips her satchel and places the old book on her lap. "I don't know, Lana," Cole dubiously says, understanding where she is going with this.

"She is the only one of her, uh, kind," Lana says dismissing his doubts. "Half human. Half Vampire."

Lucas makes an unconvinced face. "Like Blade?"

"No." Cole destroys the look of enthusiasm on Leon's face. "You know how they have the ability to live forever but we force them not to due to their two weaknesses?"

"Vitamin D and trees?" Lucas jokes, seeing nothing but oxygen producing plants and sunshine as his hand guides the wheel.

"Well," he proceeds to explain. "She doesn't just have the ability. *She is actually Immortal.*"

"The legend says that vamps have tried for centuries to do away with her," adds Loki.

Lana directs her attention at the older cousin's reflection in the rearview mirror. "The only one who lived long enough to tell anything about her powers said he cut her arm off while his friend staked her heart—"

"Not only did it not make her go up in black smoke," Cole interrupts, "but both wounds healed instantly."

"That doesn't happen with Vampires," Lana says mostly to herself.

Ill-informed, and listening to a conversation for the first time since Hastings, Kimberly asks, her voice small, "Why not?"

Not hearing the meager lady Cole picks up where he left off. "He ran and hid while the other stayed out of fear."

"The Vampire quickly followed her scent to her home," Lana tells them as the sweet smell of honeysuckles drifts in the car; their twining stems dance gracefully beside the six engrossed people. "When he and eighteen others, some were Shadows, planned their attack to dismember and burn the girl" —she pauses— "well, it was as if she already knew."

"She tranquilized the Shadows just before dawn.

Vamps figured they chickened out I guess and continued with their execution plan."

"She was sitting outside, and when they followed her into the house it exploded," Lana gesticulates, her hands waving in the air. "After our Similars awakened—what we Shadows call others like us—they went to the house to find her waiting for them."

"She hurt them badly," Loki comments, her voice disparaging.

What was she going to do? Let them beat her? Cole defensively thinks. "They then retreated. She let them be."

"No Shadow has seen her since then," Lana finishes.

If she helps humans... "What does she eat?" the young, medium brown-haired man asks.

"Rumor has it that she doesn't eat humans."

"Then what?" Lucas demands of the two mirror-reflected faces with questionable information. "Don't tell me she's pulling an Edward Cullen."

Cole answers in a deep steady voice. "Vampires."

"They hate her and our kind doesn't trust her," comments Loki.

"May we pull over, please?" Lana asks. Lucas steers them over to the side of the road. "Her name is *Raven*, but the night predators have a different name for her. They call her *Goddess.*" She flips open the bookmarked page of the Goddess starring in her dreams, and then hands the red and black hardback over to Lucas. "Somehow her picture ended up in this book."

Someone once asked Lucas Kale if he were to look back in time could he identify the moment that sent a ripple through his life? Back then he cared little. It had seemed stupid and pointless.

But gripping the withered book…

Chapter 8
Road Trip

"OH MY GOD," LUCAS WHISPERS. Staring back at him from the page is the most beautiful smile he has ever seen. The black and white picture dates back two centuries ago, yet he recognizes the young-looking girl. The hair is different. Blonde. But those eyes, colorless in the photo—no amount of trauma could make Lucas Kale forget them.

Her...coffee...books...AC/DC. *Beauty.* "She touched me," Lucas quietly says. Leon gives him a dirty look. "*With a hot liquid substance.*" Lucas reaches over Loki's lap and gives him the bounded pages.

"The girl from noon today?" Leon gazes down at the crinkled page to find someone he does not expect to see. "OH!" He jerks back. There it is in black and white, a clue to finding the final piece—

the important piece—to the warped version of chess, the king.

Lucas misconstrues his cousin's enthusiasm. "Leon, I know she looks good for a rude dead chick—"

"That's the girl from my vision!" he practically shouts.

"A buh?" Lucas asks baffled. When he would get confused as a child he would try to say "huh", but it would come out "a buh".

"She's the one you've been seeing!" Lana half tells half asks. She, too, has seen Raven—in her dreams.

The seer gasps. He throws the book into Loki's lap. There is no ringing this time. The seer clenches his fist against his burning chest while his voice box yells as if he really is on fire. "My lungs!"

Lana and Lucas fling their doors open and rush out of the parked car. "Where are you going!" shrieks Loki.

Moving around the front of the Chevrolet, Lucas wonders how much of this can he take. *How much can Leon take?* He opens the door to a screaming man, and Loki worriedly moving away from Leon.

"His eyes!" cries the Shadow, the two of them peer down at a pair of open eyeballs.

The agony stops abruptly. The seer turns to Lucas and Lana, his blue eyes glossed with blood.

He had seen everything while conscious; Raven's house, street, and a state sign.

"Kansas." Leon leans out and coughs up a brown substance like that of coffee grounds. They notice blood has seeped out from underneath his nail beds and scalp.

"Raven's in Kansas. Don't ask me questions." The young man in the crimson t-shirt shuts the door, opens the glove compartment, and yanks out a medicine bottle. He feels like he just got done climbing the Eiffel Tower, only he used his nails and banged his head a couple hundred times. The white label on the bottle says one pill every four hours. He takes six coated capsules; without water. The girl who had moved away from Leon now watches, as well as the three in the backseat, as he pulls out the bloody but dry washcloth and starts dabbing his forehead.

The blonde in the denim jeans and blue and white long sleeve shirt yanks the keys out of the ignition. Driving directions are an essential for arriving at the location of Leon's Potential. Loki starts, "Why did—" Lucas answers the question he knows she is about to ask. "Me and Leon have disposable cell phones. They do not have internet or Global Positioning System. That means GPS. That's one of Leon's *did-you-knows* that no one cares about."

A dog ferociously barks somewhere close by.

The five passengers jerk upright, wildly scanning the open road for the cause of the vicious dog; Kimberly remains gazing at the floor of the vehicle. The view ahead and behind them seems to be free of anything walking that shouldn't be in the flat and vast fields. The view to the sides blocked by honeysuckle bushes.

Getting out of the car to retrieve Leon's laptop is a must; no one else seems to have a cell phone.

Lucas throws his door open and runs to the trunk faster than that time he ran circles in the yard after cousin Rachel found out he had coitus with her best friend and started shooting BBs at him.

Another dog follows suit, and the loud echoes nearly cause Lucas Kale to piss on himself.

He does not like being out here by himself. In fact, the Hunter does not like being out here at all. He feels as if he is the most popular Christmas toy remaining on display and at any moment the greedy vultures are going to shred him in their savage fight.

Lucas snatches Leon's laptop bag from inside the trunk and slams the lid back down. He reaches his door, still open, and a firecracker pops. He makes a startled noise incapable of spelling; if the situation was different the people in the polished car would have laughed. Lucas quickly realizes why they had not. The popping sound does not belong to any firecracker.

Someone fires a pistol for the second time.

The longhaired seer takes the bag. And gravel from the side of the road clinks against the Biscayne's undercarriage. The wheels taking them closer to the state line.

"Are you okay?" Loki asks Leon even though he had specifically said not to ask him questions.

"No."

"On a scale of one—"

"Loki!" Lana says in a hushed tone.

Leon does not wish to even slightly think about the levels of agony he is in or even contemplate describing it. Because if he does so, then he will have to justify the other feeling he is having right now that makes the pain bearable…

The one about Raven. And that feeling is not natural.

* * *

Concordia, Kansas
After her Orders and her brief run-in with the Kale boy, Raven decided that to acquire any knowledge of the cousins would be wise. She sits in front of a computer screen, Jet by her side, looking up certain information on Kale and Carmany. Bored, Jet's dark round eyes wander around the room. It had been nicknamed the Comfy Room due to its remarkably different interior and soothing atmosphere that the rest of the house neglects for security purposes. His favorite thing isn't the air hockey table in the middle of the room or the soft cushion in his red and white swirl patterned chair, but the tasteful red carpet. Not necessarily the hue of red, rather it is the only soft floor in the entire place.

What Jet finds interesting, besides the fact that Leon Carmany has a scary IQ and owns multiple Veterinarian clinics, or that Lucas Kale owns his very own mechanic shop, but the lack of communication from his longtime friend. "Are you going to speak today?"

"You know I have."

"Other than when spoken to?"

"No."

The man with a little bit of hair stubble on his square face lets out a deep sigh. "I know you hear it, Raven. *I* hear it." She groans in annoyance as he continues. "The fear in our neighbors. The fear from our friends."

"I do not hear that from Cricket."

"That is different and you know it. Now stop playing with me, Raven."

"Fine!" She huffs and gives him her undivided attention. "We both have had our share of friends over the years, but *these* are my favorites."

"They are going to die eventually. You know that, too."

Whispering, she grits out, "You started dancing around the imaginary bush first instead of asking about my problem!" "Why am I the only one you go kinderyard on?" he asks, his voice low as he gently strokes the side of her soft, oblong face with his long fingers.

"We have liked each other the longest. And kinderyard is not a word!"

"Why are we whispering?"

"Do you *want* a group pep talk?" Raven throws at him as he plays with the ends of her long, yellow strands. If the others suspect that she is worried about their deaths they both will be hounded by words of encouragement and affection that will only make them feel worse. And who really believes that more bonding will save them from the walking dead?

Hearing footsteps approaching the door, he whispers with demanding eyes, "We will talk later."

"There might not be a later," she retorts. His jaw drops. Raven smiles triumphantly and turns to the screen.

"Is he the real deal?" Ganesha vibrantly enters.

"Leon is the one I need."

"Everything is in place," Ganesha states with her hips snapped to the left and her right foot cocked out with one hand on her waist and the other extended by her side.

Jet releases the thick, yellow hair spiraled around his fingers and rises to his feet; his head inches from the ceiling. "There is only one thing left…"

Raven pushes the black screen down. "We leave."

Nebraska
The car is lacking gas, and everyone has to use the restroom but no one wants to leave the guns. Entering the gas station with automatic weapons (or a loaded crossbow) is not a great idea, but what if they need them? The hazel-eyed blonde with white, tight-fitting long sleeves takes off his seatbelt and turns around to the two Shadows; the 1970 Chevrolet Biscayne rests next to a gas pump. "Is that stuff about Shadow's Clark-Kent-hearing ability true?"

Kimberly watches a tan station wagon pass by her window.

"Yeah, kind of. Our range is limited and the reception, if you will, involuntarily cuts off during the day. But it can be turned back on. It works better at night. Why? Oh, duh, you want me to listen for…uh…" Lana clears her throat. "People." She and the other dark-haired Shadow close their eyes. A few seconds pass, customers exit and enter the small store. The petite girl opens her eyes. "Nothing."

"Nada," Cole blinks.

"But we don't hear heartbeats and stuff like Vampires. Everyone talking sounds fine."

"But there are lots of voices and there is music playing in every ride."

"We can't be one hundred percent," Lana states.

"But it sounds like regular noise if that helps."

"Not really," Lucas shakes his head. "Let's think about this. Hastings is quarantined, whatever that means, and we are the width of double-D boobies away from that place. I apologize for talking about breasts in mixed company, but a girl with nice ones just walked by and that's the only analogy I could I think of. We haven't actually seen anything else—not talking about the nice lady bits—so the virus couldn't have spread ubber fast like in the movies. Realistically we should be okay."

"Realistically, you don't have a science degree in Zombie Virus," Leon says indignantly. He shoves the bag containing the laptop off his lap and next to his feet on the blue mat; having memorized the directions in case something separates them from the machine. Given the seer's foul mood, Loki, Lana, Cole, and Kimberly are a little surprised the door gently closes behind him. Lucas, however, is not the least bit stunned; Leon Carmany has never been the relative know for slamming and breaking objects.

"Looks like I'm pumping." Lucas climbs out.

LEON CARMANY

The bell over the convenience store rings. The longhaired brunette in the crimson red shirt and dark denims with a frown on his face scans the walls for the RESTROOM sign.

Leon doesn't care if there happens to be one of those things like Lee in here. *I have to urinate and anything that tries to stop me is going to get a fist full of my headache.*

He strolls pass the short line of paying customers and rows of shelved chips and candy. He turns left in front of the coolers lining the wall. The bell dings again. *That's annoying. How do the clerks put up with this ALL day?* Leon looks across the store to see Lana, Loki, and Kimberly. He pushes the smooth MENS door.

LUCAS KALE
"Man, do you really think this Vampire can help us?" Cole asks sitting on the trunk.

With his firm buttocks pressed against the side of the vehicle, Lucas watches the black numbers increase on the pump. "The idea thrills me about as much as a teenage boy sitting on my baby while he plays babysitter," he halfway lies; everything is true except the part about him not looking forward to Kansas.

"I thought it would help if I—"

"Look, tampon boy." Lucas rolls his sleeves up. "I understand your little body is filled with Buffy Summers juice, but I've been fighting Vampires before you knew they even existed. I can handle myself out here. Unless there is a shit ton. Then by all means unload the juice."

LANA QUEEN
Lana enters the WOMENS room, the two girls

ambling behind. The three of them stop dead in their tracks. A thick line of blood extends from the middle of the small, tiled floor to the handicapped stall. The beige handicapped door, bigger than the door next to it, is open. They unmistakably see a gray and bloody handrail and smeared red handprints on the wall. "What is this?" Lana, already knowing the answer, asks the store clerk with a mop and a yellow pushcart of pale red water.

"Some woman left bleedin'. Left a trail all the way outta' store. Couldn't stop her." The older woman, hair graying at the roots, does not advert her attention from the task at hand.

"Maybe she was a zombie thing," Loki casually suggests as if it's no big deal.

The female clerk, currently taking on the role of janitor, laughs and slaps the wet mop out of the bucket and rubs the bloody tiles. "Kids."

"Is it only that one?" Lana nods at the bloody stall; she would rather do her business in a risk free environment.

"Yeah."

Lana moves towards the other toilet. Then stops. She just can't bring herself to touch anything—let alone drop her pants. "On second thought," she waves her hand in front of the paper towel dispenser, "we'll use the men's room." The woman doesn't object to them using the other designated facility for some reason. Lana pulls on the door handle using the brown paper towel, because in order for the infected woman to have left she had to touch the handle. *I hope we can't get infected this way and that I'm just being paranoid.*

LEON

Leon feels a little better. The visions have sapped his energy. If he had known about the chaos that would be bestowed upon him—and everyone else—he would have ate something besides half a salad at lunchtime. And here the opportunity is right in front of his face (literally) to put some food in his stomach and Leon decides to walk away from the sandwiches displayed inside the gas station. *Why bother? I know it's not going to stay down. Think I'll get water. No, the Dr. Sugar is what I need. No. Water.*

The indecisive man sees a blonde, a brunette, and a black-headed girl enter the MENS room. This prompts him to pick the first beverage he lays his blue sapphire eyes on, *The Dr.*, and Leon nearly breaks into a jog up to the counter. The bell rings again. *Seriously, how can anyone deal with this?*

Cole comes in the store, and Leon sees a woman outside approaching Lucas. Her friend, Leon judges by their matching bright pink flip-flops and bathing suit strings peeking out of the top of their shirts, struts to the glass entry. Leon puts two dollars on the counter (Lucas had to have prepaid with his credit card otherwise he would not be getting gas for the car). "Keep the change."

He gets to the door that has children's hand prints on it before the woman in the pink flip-flops. The chivalrous man decides to hold the glass door open for her. Instantly feminine eyes checkout the tall and handsome brunette with soul-touching eyes from head to toe. "Thank you," the woman with a wet pony tail smiles up at him. "You have nice eyes." The compliment, which he receives a lot but never gets tired of hearing, is exactly what he needs. The gentleman smiles at her. "Thank you."

Before Leon walks out of the convenience store, he glances back to see what had become of Cole entering the same restroom as Lana, Loki, and Kimberly. The Shadow with the birthmark on his Adam's apple converses with the young, blonde girl whom the seer pegs for a troublemaker.

LUCAS

Lucas Kale tries to maintain eye contact but he cannot help his wandering eyes. The wet swim suit has soaked through the white t-shirt and he can see what color it is; black with pink swirls.

The aroused man tightens the gas cap and shuts the cover. "Yeah, it's my car." He doesn't feel the least bit guilty for telling the partial truth. Both he and Leon have been omitting that it's not entirely either one of theirs. Unless of course the woman is the type to find sharing a turn on; in which case most of the women typically want a threesome with the two men and neither he nor his cousin are into "sharing" in that scenario.

Lucas is suddenly pulled into a reverie of the one time he had a threesome. But the two females were sharing *him*. Then, when he was a teenager, it had felt amazing, but now for some reason he feels ashamed as the AC/DC girl pops up in his mind. He knows Brighton Leon Carmany has never had sex with more than one female at a time. And will never have more than one partner.

"I saw that your plates were Tennessee. You here on business or pleasure?" The woman flicks her lose damp hair back and leans her right side against the slick blue paint.

The chick magnet does the same with his left side, positioning his muscular arm on the hardtop and tilting his head into his palm so that they are facing each other. The small square that covers the gas cap is the length between them. "Business, but dull I am not," he charmingly smiles.

Neither one of them bats an eye when the other owner of the Biscayne gets in.

Lucas Kale's jeans and long sleeve shirt do not mesh well with the warm air. He can feel the heat on his light blonde hair and the perspiration on his legs and chest. He already has his sleeves pushed up, defeating the purpose of wearing them. *I wonder how warm those smooth legs are?*

"If you want, sometime when your car is dirty I can come over and wash it for ya'." She rubs the tips of her fingers down the side of the car leaving small streaks.

"Coat it too?"

"I will coat anything you want," the woman flirts, running her fingers along the skin where her belly meets her shorts.

His eyebrow raises, intrigued.

A hand squeezes his upper arm muscles. But it does not belong to the woman his age. "We found something. Ready?" Loki asks him. Lana walks round the car's rear and Lucas snaps back to the harsh reality of today. "Yeah. Yeah."

The wet t-shirt woman sees her girlfriend exiting

the store. "Well, it was nice meeting you."

"You, too," Lucas says turning around to his door. He waits for Loki to climb inside the fully fueled vehicle.

"What was that about?" the gray-eyed girl asks, taking her place in the middle of the flat seat.

"She offered to wash my car," Lucas beams with satisfaction.

Loki watches the two older females pull out onto the road. "Slut," she resorts to name-calling. Lana shakes her head at the jealous girl's epithet for the other girl.

"Hey, don't you have to pee?" Loki reminds Lucas. "Oh yeah." Lucas gets back out again.

* * *

LEON / LUCAS

Leon doesn't realize he has dozed off until the knock at his window.

"We need a timeout," Lucas tells him with frustration written all over his face. Leon meets him at the taillights, still parked in front of the pump. Lucas loses his cool. "Kill Vampires. What I do. Kill vamps! I despise them! Instead of going *home* we are now going to *Concordia, Kansas*! I'm driving to find—not kill—and ask it," he contemplates on the correct pronoun, "her, for help?"

"I could tell you were giddy about Raven—"

"—Whoa! Timeout in the timeout. I have never been *giddy*. I don't get *giddy*."

"Luke, are you sure you're not afraid she will hold a grudge for your discourteous behavior?"

He is. "Anyway, this is about you, too. You've

been seeing it." The older Vampire Hunter reverts back to the original two letter word. "Which means for some reason we are supposed to save it. *IT. A VAMPIRE!*"

"I'm okay with that part of her," Leon confesses. "She *is* a Potential. Which means she not only does good in the future, but there is an amelioration, improvement, in the world."

Lucas does not know what bothers him more. The fact that she *is* a Vampire, or the part of *him* that is okay with that. "Call Uncle Joe. Give him and Rachel the heads up. Zombies. Vampire-God-thingy. All of it." Lucas cannot be there to help his family, but he sure is not going to leave them in the dark.

Lucas sees a black Mustang in his side mirror as he strides towards the reflection. The vehicle stops a little ways behind them on the side of the road before the entrance to the gas station. A cell phone sticks out, pointed at the four door Chevrolet…

Leon finally joins Loki and Lucas on the front seat, and Kimberly says quietly to no one in particular, "He's still in the tan wagon…" She rocks herself again.

The relatives look to Lana and Cole in the backseat for an explanation. They shrug, unable to offer one.

THE SIX PASSENGERS

The six passengers head down a long steep hill, the open road stretching out before them. Black birds flock overhead. "Do you think those birdies will peck us to death like in those movies?" Cole asks.

"And since everything in them seems to be zombiefied, I wonder if lions or owls can be zombies? Or kangaroos?"

Lucas, Loki, Leon, Lana, and Cole chuckle, picturing zombie kangaroos hoping all over the place.

"Kangaroos are herbivores," Lana points out.

"Yes, but what if they ate a plant that had infected blood on it?"

"Then anything could be…"

"Cows. Turtles," Leon throws out. Zombie turtles gets them laughing like hyenas, except Kimberly who remains introverted and withdrawn.

"Ants," Loki says, and unintentionally kills the laughter.

"Ants? That's not terrifying or funny," Cole states.

"But ants can lift ten times their bodyweight so—"

"I can still stomp them," Leon concludes.

Lucas checks his rearview mirror.

"What?" Leon queries, suspicious; it is the third time Luke has done this since the previous county.

"That Mustang behind that so-called-truck has been behind us since the gas station."

Leon looks in his mirror to see for himself. The dark-colored vehicle tails closely behind a small truck that has a missing tailgate. "Maybe he's leaving, too."

"He pulled over at the gas station just to take our picture."

"After we stopped?" asks Loki.

"Obviously," Cole snaps. "In order for him or

whomever to take the picture while we were at the gas station it would have to have been *after* we stopped at the gas station, Loki." Sometimes his friend's lack of reasoning skills can really irritate him.

Loki twirls one of her curls around her finger and flashes her gray adolescent eyes up at Lucas. "Sorry." Her soft, unprotected leg brushes against his jeans. "I'm just trying to figure out why." He flirtatiously grins at the young seductress.

"He's doing it again," Lana announces, facing the back windshield. Rounding a curve, everyone except Lucas turns around in their seats. They see a hairy arm retreat back inside the Mustang, phone in hand. "That would creep me out if I had not seen Lee today." A man taking photographs means little to her now that she has seen a dead man walk—that isn't a Vampire.

"Lee?"

Cole's perplexed tone offends her. *How could he have forgotten so soon? Does he always forget about the dead ones?*

"The man our cold-blood Kronos took last night," Lana recollects. Cole winces at the name. "He's the one they saved me from."

The seer nearly spits out the dark colored soda he just took a swig of. "Kronos? You have had an altercation with the Leader of the Vampires?"

"Yeah," they both answer.

"We were starting to doubt his existence."

"Oh, he's around," she confirms. "Unfortunately."

Suddenly confound, Cole asks, "How are you

guys able to kill vamps? It usually takes like two Shadows to do that."

"It helps to have the advantage—visions. But there have been times when were are only able to escape with my Potential—victims with the ability in their future to do significant good to the world."

"Maybe he just likes the ride," Lucas, still thinking about the picture man, shrugs.

They accelerate through the path of flat lands, temporarily away from danger, and closer to the unknown—not a comforting thought. After all, the hours of May tenth are just starting.

~~~~

Chapter 9
Hello and Goodbye

THE SIX PASSENGERS (CONTINUED)

THEY ARE NEARING the Nebraska and Kansas border, but a radio DJ—one of the few left—has announced that their journey out of the plagued Nebraskan state is still on a schedule. But the passengers are not too worried. They are approximately five minutes from the Nebraska/Kansas state line.

Cole empathizes with Kimberly. He, too, at one time was without a family. "Uh, Kimberly, do you want to tell us about yourself?" He tries to distract her mind from all that she has lost.

"I'm...I'm...in college. I-I have a red and green color deficiency."

"That's highly unusual," Leon states. "Women tend to be carriers of that gene but do not express the trait. They inadvertently pass the color deficiency or color blindness to their sons. Your mom—"

"Once he goes he doesn't stop," Lucas tells Loki, and they chuckle.

Lana gives Kimberly a stake. It does not seem fair to deny the woman her right to defend herself. "You were in the cemetery," Kimberly says to her and Cole. "Yeah!" Lana says, eager for conversation with the grieving woman. "You were with…"

"My boyfriend and his little brother."

"Devin?" Lana witnesses Leon and Lucas tense up at the mentioning of the little boy's name.

"He…" the wretched woman shakes her head.

"Turned?" Cole asks, stunned.

When Kimberly had said they were all dead before, Lana had not thought that included the boy. "Um…sorry," she swallows.

Loki spins around in the front seat. "I didn't know you knew a Devin." Resting her arm on the top of the seat, she gazes up at Lucas. "Did you guys know him?"

Cole and Lana both have the uneasy feeling that the cousins were somehow involved; the Shadows simultaneously say Loki's name in a way that translates into *shut up*. Abashed, Loki's presses her back hard against the seat. "Okay! I just wanted to know about him. He's not here because he probably was an idiot and got turned into a freak," she impudently remarks rolling her eyes.

Everyone except Lucas stares at her, appalled. However, Kimberly feels something other than shock. Piqued by the girl's words she yells, "Only a child!" She vehemently yanks a hand full of curls, pulling Loki's skull back against the seat. Cole automatically grabs Kimberly's wrist in hopes of prying her fingers loose, but she uses her right hand to club the girl on top of the head with the stake.

"Lana!" Loki pleads for help.

The halting brakes give most of them whiplash. They halt to a stop blocking a semi-paved driveway. Lucas looks in his side mirror, remembering they are not the only ones in a vehicle. The tiny truck swerves to the left avoiding a collision. Brakes grind on the Mustang. But that does not stop it from rear ending Lucas and his passengers. Just when he is about to take off his seatbelt and die from the damage of his precious ride—and the delay to the state line—something bumps them forward again.

"Stay," orders Lucas.

Outside of the parked car, he sees a smoking radiator that belongs to a lime green station wagon that has rear-ended the Picture Man. The blonde Hunter gives his trunk rapturous kisses for it only has a scratch.

The Picture Man shouts at Lucas. "Look at my car!" The paint is severally chipped and the tail-end is damaged from the station wagon. "Don't you know what's goin' on? What's wrong with you?"

"Tailgating *is* a crime," Lucas smirks.

"I didn't do anything to you!"

He looks at his line of missing paint, rolls his eyes, and struts back towards the front. "Pay for this!" The man shouts after him. And when Lucas does not respond, he threatens, "I know people!"

Just after the lunatic man speaks the cool and unseen wind tugs at Lucas's sleeves and pulls at the tiny hairs below his hairline. The sun hides. *Not again!* Lucas sees a driver, a great distance from the roadblock, demanding assistance while she tries to get out of her minivan parked a couple of yards ahead of them. Her feet hit the road, only to be pulled down and back by her messy hair into the purple van. *Gun!* Lucas's mind screams and he squeezes the driver's silver handle as Lana's door swings open.

Outside, the concerned girl's pupils Split—two pupils become four with silver rings around them—magnifying the image inside the van. The victim kicks and thrusts her body about because the brain tells her that it might have a chance at survival.

It is wrong.

This is not right! Friends and family are turning into cannibals.

Blocking out the warnings from the military soldiers, Lana runs—crossbow ready, eyes reverting back to their original shape—to the desperate voice.

The lady in the long brown skirt from the minivan is not going to live. *She has been bitten. If you get bitten then you become…a danger.* Lana has gathered this much due to the tension surrounding the subject of little Devin…and horror films.

Lana knows zombies have entered her world. And she knows how to stop them just like most people know how to get rid of a Vampire—even though they fail due to lack of training.

But the Shadow does not know how to kill a human.

Can she even do that? If not, why go to the middle-aged woman? The savior has been running to the rescue for years. Why would that change now?

She really is going to die.

Standing in the open way of the van's door, Lana looks upon what use to be a person. It grinds its teeth against skin that separates the lady's hopeless eyes. The fearless girl places her crossbow on the roof to pry the woman from hungry grasps; Lana punches the creature, then with both hands she grips the victim's shoulders and slings her down against the pavement. The tuned out words from non-civilians spring into her ears:

"Stop!"

"Stop!"

"You shouldn't be doing that!"

Further ignoring the warnings, Lana reaches down to the transformed passenger slumped over onto the driver's seat. The valiant girl makes a fist, and with one swift motion her bawled up fingers connect upwards against its chin with such hostile speed and strength that the head tears off, ripping at the neck. The bloody head spins backwards with such force that the passenger window pays for it. The detached head rolls off the edge of the seat and lands on the floor.

Rearing back, Lana glances at the road block. Several men in uniform are running alongside the vehicles of fleeing people. A bad situation. There is no way it is possible for a woman—especially a girl of her small size—to physically dismember another person.

And what is she to do with the infected? Put an arrow in her? Though it is a theory of Lana's, she has not seen for herself what happens when you get bit, so would it not be a good idea to leave her with the ones that hopefully do know?

I've never left. Blayne's girlfriend, Lee, and the bodies she and Cole saw in the cave flood her mind; people she could not save. *I can't leave.* But the single crack on the passenger window provides a cogent argument. Troubled, the Shadow gets her crossbow and leaves the probably doomed woman in knowledgeable hands.

Then Lana realizes the shouting had not been for her alone, for the scenery is not the same. The uneasy stillness in the air unmasks the truth; *Vampires have lived on this planet approximately forever and have truly spared the human race.*

Two Asian men are in the motion of jumping from the bed of a new red truck while Lucas runs in their direction… The tailgating man slumps over against his tinted car… The two houses, each one on her left and right of the road have expelled their occupants; the ones that are not the sparing types… Loki is walking across the road to the house on her right to eliminate a rotting and limping old man…

Now standing outside the car, Leon aims his rifle while Cole, after climbing over Kimberly, exits to deal with three more zombies slowly but hungrily moving towards the line of food. Lana notices something disturbing.

Three of the four zombies look normal save for the extremely pale skin covered with blood and the absent-mindedness. The fourth…is more frightening. Her white skin is the same color as the others but her veins are visible.

At least Lana thinks they are blood veins. Instead of tiny blue spider webs—the skin that is visible through the torn fabrics and not caked by blood—the veins and thick arteries seem to be... *Brown?* Lana's four pupils do not lie. But it is not the snow face penciled with brown lines that makes the Shadow shiver.

The red eyes.

The red eyes and the way the girl moves churns Lana's stomach. The girl is walking slow but faster than the plain ones as if...resolute.

Leon shoots her. But it is not his shot that makes Lana jump. She turns to the sound of multiple rounds being fired. The unfortunate girl Lana left behind now lays face up with holes in her head. The military shot her from a few yards away, and the pickup that had swerved past them now maneuvers past the van to be the second in line.

With all the distractions, no one sees the small device being attached below the bumper of the blue Biscayne...

* * *

...Two Asian men have fled the big red truck and are pointing at Lucas and the two Asians standing on the bed of the automobile; one male, one female. They are trying to tell him something, but of course he does not speak Chinese. Although the two in the front seat look Americanized and probably could translate, they stay safely inside their aseptic area free of deadly bacteria.

What a lovely time for tourism! To Nebraska!

While the last China man tries to make his leap, the Asian lady wraps her arms around him and bites into his spine.

Wanting to put the tourist out of his misery, Lucas fires. The man's tiny muscles relax. The creature releases her hold and the man's stomach hits the bedside and lands skull first. Lucas feels guilty. Not because he killed a human, but how easy it now feels.

The girl hunches over and hisses wildly at Lucas. "I like Asian chicks. Stop ruining it!"

Then something he has never seen happens. Her face is...changing. It's like there is an unseen force drawing thin brown lines expanding away from her mouth with colored pencils. Closing her eyes, she suddenly positions herself up right as if snapping her spine in place. At least that is what it sounds like to Lucas. Lots of loud and strange popping sounds expel from her body. *What the hell? Her bones breaking? Is this an Asian thing?*

By now the two Asian Americans are standing beside their open doors curiously gaping at the thing standing in their truck. The strange popping stops. Every passageway of blood in her face, neck, arms, and hands have clearly been defined. Her eyes open and gaze down upon Lucas. He reads the expression in its intelligent red eyes; you are going to kill me, but will you stop my kind? For the first time in his life, Lucas Kale thinks about something he doesn't believe exists. The Devil.

The Hunter's round connects above her newly developed red eyes. Lucas's jaw drops open as she begins hissing and swings her leg over the side—

coming for *him*.

Another bullet forces its way into her forehead. Silence.

More soldiers pursue Lana.

"Ma'am!"

She knows this is her last chance to flee.

Walking back towards the civilians, she witnesses Cole diminishing the last of the six zombies, two having joined the others. And Loki, with an abnormally thin-looking boy, walking to the slumped over Picture Man. But…*What is Lucas looking at…?*

The extremely thin teen boy with bad acne next to Loki tells the Picture Man slumped over the car, "Mister, this isn't the best place—"

The girl with ringlets of blonde hair interrupts. "Is there a bite mark on you?"

"Huh?" The teenage boy gives her a funny look. They are both standing inches from the unresponsive man.

"When you let those losers touch you with"— she pauses trying to think—"their…mouth…" Staring at the middle-aged man is something she has not done…until now. Until this moment, the tiny black spots on the outer layer of the careless driver's skin have gone undetected by Loki.

Lifting his head from his forearms, chocolate eyes shift down upon her, glazing over like they have been blind for years. The former human swings his arms as Loki takes a step back; her feet and legs tangle with the pimpled-faced boy. The only two trees on either side of the two way street throw themselves furiously in the same direction. The strong moving, no longer calm, winds move towards the tree trunks like a suddenly frighten child taking in a deep breath stealing the air from the room. Landing on her side, Loki helplessly watches her shotgun spin to the edge of the pavement…

…Leon hears two noises; the sound of a military tank moving on the opposite side of the road, and his own vociferous voice shouting, "Lucas!" Unsure if he heard him, he and Cole abandon their positions for the blonde who just fell to a questionable death.

While curiosity tempts Leon to see what his cousin is pointing at, the image of Raven replays in his mind—over and over she falls from the sky, dying and taking the world with her. And anxiety rocks his soul like that of a hundred convicts awaiting the verdict of a possible death sentence.

Is Loki bitten? If not it won't take long.

The wind wraps itself around chunks of his long hair while he tries to wiggle his way through the small space separating the two cars. His body rumbles forward and Loki stares at him with an infatuation similar to that of an eleven-year-old girl after being saved by an attractive lifeguard.

Raven! The seer's mind races. He reaches the end of his bumper as Lana pulls the gray-eyed girl up by her forearms. Cole, now on the hood of the Mustang, grabs Leon and holds him back in case the bullet fired from a soldier's gun misses.

Luckily it does not. The grumpy, older Picture

Man from the Mustang bows backwards, ending his moment of terror.

...Lucas knows he will not make the shot that matters.

He is and has been frantically racing back, recurrently using his vocal chords— blocked out by a tank—to the gang hoping that it counts for something.

Seven soldiers pass the group standing in the middle of the road. And even they do not notice the still, standing girl with ripped green pants and a hole in her brain...

The people traveling with him and a new guy finally take notice of Lucas.

His arm extends, pointing. Five faces turn to the deep blue car...

...Biting her nails, Kimberly sits in the empty car watching out the back window. The others turn, facing her... The side glass breaks. Nails dig into Kimberly's neck and broken glass slashes the sides of her arms as something pulls her through the window.

Cole stares hatefully at the girl Leon had supposedly killed. *I knew it!* Green Pants kneels to the ground taking the raw meal with her. The five of them rush to the other side of the car.

Cole has suspected and thought he had confirmed that Lucas and Leon cannot be trusted, but he sees the rifle's entry wound as the walking dead girl eats from Kimberly's voice box.

Leon shoots her...again. "Anyone in favor of

dismemberment?"

"Sure," Cole volunteers, the five of them standing on the gravel of the semi-paved driveway. "But I'm not touching it." He kicks the mailbox post in half, and then stabs at the bones in her neck with the jagged end, eventually dissevering the head.

Leon raises his gun and shoots Kimberly. He closes his blue eyes. In Leon's mind Devin's small feet and small hands and wondrous eyes fall once more to the hard pavement. Will he ever be able to let Devin go?

On his way over, Lucas had no choice but to watch with apprehension. He irately shouts, "Damn it!" as a huge dark green tank crushes Loki's shotgun. Leon and Cole stride over to him. "We have to go," Lucas tells them.

Cole Splits in the tanks direction. Numerous bodies are advancing towards the short line of vehicles. "More zombies."

Lana does not waste time getting in the waxed ultramarine door closest to them.

Wanting to forget about everything, Lucas jingles the keys in front of Leon. "I'm riding in the back." He smiles at Loki.

"She's seventeen," Cole whispers.

He snatches the keys out of Leon's hand. "I have a pretty ass."

"May I ride with you?" the new kid with bad acne points to his smoking vehicle.

"You can take the Mustang," Leon declines.

The boy goes to the idling vehicle and pulls up on the handle. Locked. He looks down at the key pad. "You gonna have me drive around with a busted window by myself?" He will have to break the glass in order to get inside the secured vehicle.

"You and Lana sit next to and in front of that kid in case *he* is changing," Lucas tells Cole. Leon signals for Alec, and Lana takes Leon's original spot upfront forcing Loki behind Lucas and next to Cole.

"What is your name?" Leon asks the newbie while everyone buckles up.

"Alec."

"I'm Leon." He thinks about offering him his hand, but then decides against it just in case he does have something.

They are next in line. A soldier scans them with those grocery store looking barcode scanners—*may be checking our body temperatures,* Leon surmises—and flags them to continue through, granting them passage. The gateway out of the state closes behind them.

"I'm Lana."

"Whoa! What happened to your face?"

"I'm Cole. Why do you so many zits?" The shamefaced boy next to him turns his eyes to the window. The girl with a heart shape face and gray irises raises her hand. "Loki." There is silence from the driver. Leon nudges Lucas with his elbow to introduce himself. "Disturbed," Lucas Kale responds. "How many times did you shoot—"

"—That different..." Lana is still unable to say the word *zombie.*

"Yeah."

Leon looks away from the old, wide road to his

cousin. "She seemed to be officially dead after—"

"—The second hole? One mutated in front of me."

"What?" Cole shudders. *I can't image seeing someone change much less the already transformed transforming.*

"I'm just gonna use the word 'species'," Lana says, "cause I have no idea what to use, but that girl wasn't just another species. She is, was—"

"Evolved," Cole and Lana simultaneously say.

"Perfect! They just popped into existence today *and* evolve!" Lucas sarcastically remarks.

"Luke, they are not immune to death."

"I don't think you understand."

"She was noticeably faster than the rest," Lana explains, "and the concentration in her eyes wasn't like them."

"You saw her eyes?" The longhaired Vampire Hunter had seen the red color in the dead girl's eyes and the way she walked, but body language was not something he had thought about in the dangerous moment—just kill.

"We see better than you," Cole admits.

"They have the ability to think, not like us, but they know certain things," Lucas says with absolute certainty, reverting back to the former subject. "When I saw yours she was near the car standing still, too still. She only moved after those panicking scared idiots passed. And when the Asian woman changed she saw everyone but came at me."

"So?" The boy with numerous zits responds, his voice straddling the line of rudeness.

"No one else had a weapon."

The seer runs his hand over his smooth chin, coming to a conclusion. "They know danger."

"And we know not to get bit," Loki chimes from the backseat. "How could Kimberly just sit there not knowing a crazy person was there? Also, her quietness and constantly rocking back and forth was freaking me out."

Surprised by the white around Luke's knuckles—he feels ashamed for wishing Kimberly would disappear while she was following them through Lana's field—Leon turns and looks directly into Loki's unsympathetic eyes. "There *is* this thing called the grieving process."

"*We* obviously didn't notice her either," Lana reminds her friend. "And I saw how close you were to that man."

"*I'm* not bit."

"You lost the shotgun," Lucas throws out.

"Sorry," she apologizes.

Yeah, sorry the only attention she's getting is the wrong kind, the genius thinks.

Cole knows there can only be one ugly Volkswagen in Nebraska. He recalls the vehicle speeding by Lana and him earlier today when they were hunting their favorite Vampire. He turns to Alec, the wind nipping at their faces through the busted window. "Hey, I think you almost hit—"

"—I knew I recognized you two!"

Lana turns around in the front seat, as much as her seatbelt will allow. "Why were you—"

"Sorry 'bout almost runnin' over you," Alec apologizes. "Was taking my niece to the hospital. What did you mean you see better?" He asks the other teenage boy with the birthmark on his Adam's apple.

"Want to hear another horror story? It ties in to where we are going."

"Which you haven't asked about," the short girl points out.

"My families dead. I was going anywhere."

Lucas presses the gas petal to the floor, the numbers noticeably increase on the speedometer. He cannot leave the bad place behind fast enough.

A sign reads:

Now leaving Nebraska. Come back soon!!
Yeah right! Lucas thinks.

Chapter 10
Kansas

Afternoon May 10

LUCAS KALE HAS A certain odium for Vampires. But even in his hatred, they have never made him this nervous.

He and the five passengers enter Cloud County. The county in which the populous city, Concordia, is there destination. His palm begins to sweat. Lucas takes his hand off the steering wheel and replaces it with the other, rubbing his free and moistened hand against his jeans.

If it were not for the Goddess, Lucas would be fantasizing about the cute teenager with tight ringlets in his rearview mirror. Granted, he would not act on anything now that he knows her age. He is, however, thinking about a blonde. Lucas should be worried about going to find someone truly of another species, but he feels…excited. The sun suddenly bursts out, making the land appear less deathlike, and Lucas Kale smiles.

COLE
The only fact Cole knows about Cloud County—other than they are nearing the city of Concordia—is the Orphan Train Museum is here. Once having been an orphan himself he had done research on the topic of orphans. He found that between the mid 1800's to early 1900's orphans, some kids were not, were moved across the United States and Canada.

The Orphan Train Movement. I'm blessed. Not all of those kids had happy endings with their new parents.

Cole's mother, the alive one, accepts him for who he is. Even his abilities. *I know it was difficult for her when she found out. Even though she tried not to show it.*

His mom had confronted him about the changes in his behavior; dropping his extra-curricular activities, staying out late, blood on his clothes, and his weird habit of seeming to only sleep when it was daytime and only for a few hours. Cole lied and told her it was nothing but she confessed to knowing what he was, is, a Shadow. Her father in his old age told her stories of her great-grandmother. She, of course, did not believe him until her son's odd behavior. His educated mother knew there had to be a stake, or dozen, hidden somewhere on the property; she discovered them in his tree house.

Cole's secret is something he only shares with

one parent. Cole loves his father, but unfortunately he is the type of man who will want to expose the Vampires, not thinking the unveiling will be detrimental to the Shadows—although he would never have that chance. The Vampires would surely see the human man to his death.

Cloudy County. Cloud. To Cole, the name is a dire portent.

* * *

Once again Leon Carmany is not keeping up with the conversation. His mind has drifted to *her*.

Every time I see her...

The seer has never felt much of anything for his "visionettes" other than simply not wanting them to die. But no matter how much pain he has felt—that last image had left him with the urge to actually cry—after seeing Raven he feels...happy.

Why? Do I need to know why?

"Do you have a girlfriend?" Loki pulls him from his thoughts.

"Um...not a serious one for a year and a half."

"Why?" The seventeen year old ecstatically looks at the back of his head.

"She was murdered."

Sitting next to Leon, Lana looks away from the Kansas road and tenderly queries, "Vampire?"

"Human."

"What happened? If you don't mind me asking."

"Burglary...while she was in her apartment. I was supposed to be there, but I was late. I found her...dead. The two guys are currently in jail."

"How long were you dating?"

"We got together when I was nearly twenty," he

says nostalgically.

THE NEW SIX

Touching a soft, smooth leg, Lucas moves his other hand up underneath her black shirt with a fervent desire. *Whoa, Lucas! What are you doing?* He chides himself. *A Vampire? Not to mention she'll never go out with—*

"—Do *you* have a girlfriend?"

The man behind the wheel can feel the hot air from Loki's mouth as she leans forward, her face nearly presses against his own, pulling him from his reverie. "No," Lucas sings. "And definitely not looking for one today." He turns the black knob on the radio and presses play. The voices of AC/DC lightly sweep through the enclosed area of crammed seekers.

"A Vampire?" The composed but almost seductive grin charming Alec from the old page is not the image he has in mind. "She doesn't have fangs."

Leon glances over his shoulder at the teenager holding the Shadow's book, the tepid air blows through the glassless window, ruffling the old book's pages at the corners. He curiously wonders what prompted Loki to ask him and Lucas about significant others. "Only Novices have fangs. But that might be her human face."

"Novices?"

"Recently turned vamps," the oldest blonde explains. "Usually come into their full powers at the mark of a year."

"What are their powers?"

The flapping of the pages is not helping preserve the book's condition. Cole takes the red and black volume from Alec's lazy grip and returns it to its keeper. "Mostly what you hear about; speed, strength, hearing, and healing faster than normal. But they don't regenerate. As in if they lose an arm it won't grow back."

"Like the *Goddess's* wounds," Lana directs at Cole, triggering the moments when they ran through the entanglement of thick tree trunks, discovered mutilated bodies in the dark cave by a Novice that is or has recently been living close to Lana, and the sun burning the flesh and bones of the white-haired Vampire.

Even the Goddess will not be able to save you. Cole has been uncertain as to why the girl he has a crush on mentioned Raven. Cole, up until now, had forgotten about the Old Lady Vampire's cryptic message.

"They also have the power of Burning," adds the younger Vampire Hunter.

"Make you forget," Lucas elucidates over his shoulder. *Something I'd like to do.* "Unless you are between thirteen and sixteen, then the fun alternative is you become dead. Like some bitch's happy-blood-meal dead."

"How do they eat?" The boy with inflamed skin blemishes asks the expert next to him.

"Pushing," answers Cole, Leon, and Lana.

"If you're lucky and they are feeding, they only force your blood out through the thing you eat with and into their mouth. Then they Burn you." Lucas turns the little black knob to the left. His soul purpose for the music was to calm himself, but Alec's inquisitiveness has done the opposite. "When feasting, crap comes out of every hole on your head. And then you're dead."

"It's really gross." Loki's nose crinkles with repugnance.

"Unless they are new of course," Cole says. "Then they just bite into your veins."

"Still ewe," Alec agrees.

"And all Vampires have orange irises and pupils with purple around them. The sclera—the part of the eye that is white on us—is green on them."

"I don't think Raven has the power to Push," Lana says, thinking out loud. "She survives off *them.*"

Alec looks at the back of the girl's head with disfavor. "She eats off *Vampires*?"

"According to some that I've killed," Cole gloats.

Puzzled, the genius turns to Lucas for answers. "How does she accomplish that without fangs *and* without Pushing?"

Silence. No one had really given it much thought.

What are we getting into? The adopted teenager wonders as they enter Concordia—a place where they have traveled miles upon miles seeking help from someone, *something*, that doesn't even know they are coming.

* * *

"What do you guys do for a living?" Alec asks as they turn on Jet Road; the road where Raven's house is located. "Staking vamps can't possibly pay."

"I'm a mechanic."

"Veterinarian," answers Leon. Lucas mutters, "And certified genius."

"Wow." Loki perks up.

"That is impressive. Both of you," the girl with green eyes and black hair praises.

Lucas guides the automobile left, the road curving around a yellow house that has chunks of wood nailed to every possible entrance. The purple house across from it is boarded up as well. "Guess someone gave them the memo."

Suddenly they see it to their left—the logged, rectangle-shaped house they have traveled miles and miles to find. To their right and in front of the yard belonging to the vampiric woman from the seer's visions is Brother Street. Jet Road intersects with Brother Street and continues past two more neighbor approved lawns before it disappears around the second brick house.

"Don't know the proper parking place at a vamp-human home." Lucas parks the car underneath a dark green tree near the intersecting pavement. "So here's good."

"I'm taking wood just in case." Cole says, and Lana gives him and Loki each a stake. Cole passes his rifle to Lucas and the driver hands his pistol to Alec. Lana clenches her crossbow—alert for those like Lee—and throws her backpack containing the book with the Goddess's picture over her shoulder.

The six of them step out of the vehicle.

"Now what?" Alec gazes questionably up at the Vampire's lair. "Do we—"

"Do you hear that?" Leon looks back, heads pivot in the direction from which Lucas had driven them. A yellow car with double-rounded headlights emerges from around the corner.

"They're coming fast." Lucas tenses, ready to run.

Tires squeal against the curved pavement and their heads snap to the right. Another vehicle, a black car, speeds past the brick houses. The mechanic recognizes it as being one of the top five most expensive cars in the world.

Both cars speed faster than necessary, closing in on the group standing almost in the middle of the T-junction. Alec quivers. "Um, should we move?"

Another object on Brother Street diverts their attention. The Kansas visitors whip their bodies around, alarmed; the yellow car is now to their right, the black car the left. A third car, a vehicle Lucas knows *is* the most expensive street legal car on the planet, quickly approaches them.

Everyone with a firearm clenches it to their chests and prepares to shoot…or run.

Lana closes her hand around Loki's making it easier to pull the girl out of harms way if necessary.

The leftward and rightward sports cars come to a screeching halt, creating black tread marks as the uniquely designed third car, a Bugatti Veyron, veers vertical to the black car and stops.

A dark-skinned female hastily gets out of the yellow Mirage, the one nearest to Leon, sword in hand. Two males from the black McLaren F1, one noticeably taller than all of them and the other black as a moonless night, and a wavy haired brunette from the passenger side of the red and black Bugatti simultaneously hurry towards them.

Lucas, Leon, Alec, and Lana's crew position themselves slightly to the left to awkwardly stare at the four individuals who purposely stand side by side. Lucas, weapon placed across his muscled chest aiming at the sky, takes awareness of everyone's positions. Standing on his left, rifle aimed at the ground, is his cousin. Next to Leon is the lead Shadow but a space separates them waiting to be occupied by Cole. Behind Lana and next to her male back up is her boy-crazy friend Loki.

Alec looks out of place standing at the rear of the three friends.

The charcoal-looking young man and the exotic brunette with red lipstick (she having reached them first) stand in front of Lana. The other female and the looming male are positioned near Lana and Leon.

No one is standing in front of Lucas Kale. His arms twitch as a soft gasp of air escapes from Leon. Raven—now with extremely long and straight blonde hair—appears next to the intimating humans with flashy cars. But they do not hear the sound of a door closing until after she is standing next to the tall man dressed in black.

Raven points her sword at Leon—purple circles enclose her orange pupils and irises... But her scleras are blue... "What is your appellation?"

Appellation is a word Lucas does not keep in his vocabulary. "What's an app—"

"Leon Carmany," he answers the demanding Vampire. *Vampire* is a term Leon would rather not refer to her as, but the way her eyes burn into him like an iron being pressed against his skin reminds him she is not human. "This is Lucas Kale, my—"

"—Cousin." Her beautiful predatory eyes plunder up at Lucas. The two of them raise their eyebrows, surprised by her knowledge.

"Jet," a deep voice comes from the man next to her.

"Ganesha," the girl from the yellow car says.

"Sheba," the exotic girl in a plaid miniskirt and spaghetti strap shirt introduces herself, and then points her thumb, "Cricket is what he prefers to be called."

Lucas wonders why she answered for the young man with a shaved head.

The seer continues, "I get visions of" —he hesitates— "people." He had seen *her*, but what is the correct term? After all, *people*, do not have the ability to live forever.

Lana feels that she should mention the cousins' heroism. "They saved my life."

The seer breathes in deeply. "I've seen your death," he informs the woman still pointing her sword at him. He felt the need to tell her as soon as possible. What was the point in waiting?

To his amazement and everyone else's from the blue ultramarine car, Raven and her followers do not look shocked or the least bit perturbed. Instead she points her long sword down to the earth. "And I've seen yours, Brighton Leon Carmany."

"Say what?" Lucas exclaims in disbelief. "And why ask our names when you clearly know? What are you playing at?"

Leon stands there with a baffled expression on his face. What is he to make of her words?

"Uh." Lana interrupts the uncomfortable seconds of silence by speaking to the Goddess from her Shadow dreams. "Probably not a great time, not sure when though—"

"Zombies," Sheba interjects, relieving Lana and saving time.

"Good guess," she nods. *I should have known that they would know such a thing.*

Lucas wants to point out the obvious and find out how they came to the discovery of zombies. "That's not a guess." Unfortunately now is not the time and Raven firmly demands, "Silence." The tone in her voice sends a shiver up Lucas Kale's spine. He recalls when he had been rude to her previously; when she unintentionally dumped her coffee on his chest. And now there is a voice in his head that tells him he is slightly afraid.

"If you want my help then you have to accept I, a Vampire, am your leader. You do what I say when I say. The only opinions I accept come from my team."

"Just for clarification purposes, *you* are not the team," Ganesha points at the foreigners.

The seer's blue sapphire irises cannot help but to be mesmerized by the electric blue in Raven's eyes as she cocks her head to the side. "Do you accept?" she asks him.

"Yes." His vision—his calling—had lead him to *her*. Why on earth would he say no?

The three extraordinary colors that astound Leon Carmany's soul and tremble Lucas Kale's merge;

Raven's sclera's turn white and the iris becomes hazel as the colors seem to liquefy, draining into the pupil and turning it black—like that of a human.

The sunlight bounces off Raven's long, shiny hair as her exquisite and threatening face questions Lucas for an answer. He smiles and opens his mouth without thinking. "I like being told what to—" Lucas's lips slowly retreat back over his white teeth.

Leon's serene eyes have grown to the size of hen eggs as he glowers up at his cousin, wondering what on earth would make him say such an incongruous phrase.

The flirtatious man, fairly certain he has made some sort of pass at the blonde girl with the sword, digs his heel into the pavement. The words Lucas spoke to her generally were the ones he used before he and some random girl hooked up for the night. Or day.

Raven holds her hazel gaze on a regretful Lucas. She finds his "almost sentence" to be inappropriate. But she has come to discover that is the way some humans function.

Lucas clears his throat, and then smiles to mask his uneasiness as he gives her his word. "Yes."

Alec, hands in pockets, answers before being asked or looked at. "Sure."

"The rest of you?" Sheba impatiently questions the unanswered three.

Lana tilts her head to the right then left, addressing her crew. "Cole? Loki?" The lanky male Shadow and the curly blonde exchange glances. When Cole is unsure of a situation he usually bases his opinions on his friend, but she has not yet made her decision known.

"No." Loki shakes her head. "No way. We came for help. Not to be her" —Loki narrows her eyes at the new company— "*Slaves.*" She peers into the Vampire's eyes and hisses, "I do not take orders from wannabe Alice Cullens!"

The reactions Loki receives comes from unexpected sources.

Cricket rolls his eyes. *There are flesh eating beings prowling around and she wants to throw around 'slaves' to mask her trust issues. What did she expect? What an idiot! If my luscious lips was into talking I couldn't just give her a piece of my mind I would have to give her the organ in its entirety 'cause the talented Cricket knows she needs his entire brain to even remotely form a sense of logic.*

Sheba and Ganesha sigh heavily, the two of them sensing the anger radiating off Jet. The four of them cast sideways glances at each other, each experiencing the tension created by Loki like thick, dark waves rushing to the lands with the speed of a snake to devour those remaining in her announced path but yet have chosen not to flee.

Raven accepts the human's decision. She doesn't necessarily agree with it, but she does not really care why or how humans choose to kill themselves. In her eyes, Loki would rather die than accept her help. The living Vampire, whole-heartedly believing in natural selection, decides if Loki's ignorance ends her existence then so be it. Raven gives her attention to the short petite Shadow, hoping she has not made such an ill-fated choice.

There is a brief silence caused by Lana's contemplations. But in the end she decides there really is not much to ponder. Her hand extends out to the waiting Vampire.

Loki gasps in fury. "Lana!"

Raven reaches out to the former leader's hand and shakes it with honor. In all of her years she has discovered few leaders that were willing to follow.

"Where Lana goes as does my loyalty." Cole bows to his new leader.

This sends Loki into an outrage. "Oh, hell no!" She makes her way around Lana and tries to approach the Vampire. "If you think—"

Within a blink of an eye, not only has Jet knocked Loki to the ground but has morphed into a towering, dark blue canine beast. Loki's shrills are muffled as thick, pointed nine-inch teeth gnash centimeters from her face.

Cole raises the stake above his head and Lana points her crossbow at the Werewolf—simple arrows will not be enough to stop something so powerful, however, two simple shots through the eyes will slow it down.

But they do not attack.

Silver rings expose themselves around Cricket's and Sheba's eyes as they Split. They have their crossbows aimed for the opposing Shadows' hearts. Ganesha raises her sword preparing for a slaughter.

Jet's vibrating growls rumble in Loki's ears. His weight pins her to the earth.

While everyone's attention is on the Werewolf and Shadows, the device lights up under the older vehicle...

Leon and Lucas do not have the slightest clue as to what just happened and what is happening before their eyes.

Alec is looking up at the sky. One, it is daylight. Secondly, there is no full moon.

"Shadows?" Lana whispers.

"A *Werewolf!*" Cole is astounded and upset, his voice thin and strained over his anger. *"You're harboring a Werewolf!"*

In all of the cousins' years of hunting they have never crossed paths with a four- legged animal of this build. They find the situation to be rather...neat. "Cool!" they cheer like children seeing Santa Claus for the first time.

Jet continues to terrorize Loki. She trembles against what feels like strands of sandstone.

Lana holds her firm gaze on Raven. "Werewolves are forbidden to live."

Ganesha smiles. "Not this one."

"He is different," the preternatural Vampire assures. "Jet, up," she orders.

The beast stands up on his two hind legs and morphs, shrinking back into the naked skin of a human. The Kansas visitors try to advert their eyeballs elsewhere.

Lana and Cole, seeing the proof they need, cautiously lower their weapons. Their two Similars and the girl carrying the shorter sword demonstrate the same weariness.

Managing to stand, Loki tries to make eye contact with the former beast. "H-How do y-you—"

"Do you hear that, Jet?" Raven interrupts the

stammering girl. Jet listens. "Yes," he answers, his voice barely above a whisper. Their heads turn in the direction of Lucas Kale and Leon Carmany's car…

~~~

Chapter 11
Once in a Blue Moon

THE RIDE FROM Nebraska had been outlandish. And until now the seer had been excited to meet the woman from his visions. Sweat tickles the inside of his palms. What is happening now clearly demonstrates that Raven is no ordinary Vampire. When a creature of night first starts out running, Leon has always been able to see them, however, this moment in the sunlight makes him question himself. *Why was I sent here? How can she possibly die?*

His Potential now stands noticeably closer to him—no one had even seen her move—holding a thin, black rectangle object with a blinking red light. "Kronos," she grits through clenched teeth. Any scent there might have been is long gone, but Raven knows her enemy's work; even without the golden

K displayed on the object's side. The tracking device cracks in multiple places under the pressure of her fingers.

Has he been spying on us? Leon and Lucas... Cole jumps to conclusions.

Raven looks into Leon's confused, sapphire eyes. "Are you aware that this tracking mechanism was attached to the car you sat in to arrive at this destination?"

The younger Vampire Hunter has never met Kronos, but he knows that the well-known antagonist dominates most of the Deaths. And rumor has it that while Shadows hunt his kind, the lead Vampire only has two enemies that pose a threat. *She has to be one of them...* "No." Leon swallows.

"We need a plan. Every Vampire from surrounding time zones will be gathering at our house." Raven pivots in the direction of the red cedar house with a calmness and aplomb that frightens and intrigues Leon. The two Vampire Hunters watch her blonde hair, grown down to her squeezable butt, slightly sway while she moves. Their ardor would have enthralled anyone—other than Loki—that had been paying close attention. The desirous seventeen year old clenches her jaw. Jealousy rising faster than steam off a hot roof.

The tan naked man and Cricket move instantly from the crowd standing around on the road. Sheba is next to leave. The owners of the Biscayne finally trail behind Ganesha. "What happened to their eyes?" Alec asks the Shadows in front of him. "Split. Used for magnification and identifying our kind," Cole answers while they step over a ditch and start up a very small hill.

"It would be useful if we could see at night," Lana comments.

"You physically can't change your eyes?"

"Oh, we can," Cole clears up the misunderstanding. "It's like when your pupils get big in the dark but you can't really see crap."

"*Where* are *we* going?" Lucas and Leon hear Loki, the last in line beside Alec, snootily ask her friends.

"In the house. Duh," Sheba throws over her shoulder.

"*I'm* not going in *there*." Loki stops and points, nearly stomping her foot like a three year old.

"You can stay your ass out here," the dark-skinned girl snaps.

Loki's lips part like she is about to say something but then remembers the boarded up residences. She stares at the perimeter and the two handsome relatives. Giving in, Loki huffs before trudging her feet one in front of the other across the yard.

"Ganesha, Jet, and Cricket do not forget you owe Raven and I each a Benjamin," the girl starting up the steps in the plaid miniskirt reminds them. "What? I was here first!" Ganesha protests. "Yes, but you were last to reach our guests," Jet counters. The five of them had previously made a bet to see who could be the first to arrive back at the house.

Opening the unlocked door, Raven proceeds to flip up a light switch. Walking into a well-lit area, the half-human half-Vampire chooses a path to the left side of a big wooden table; Sheba is the only one of her friends to make the same choice.

Lucas and Leon enter through the threshold.

"GRRR!"

They jump back. "Whoa!" Lucas shouts. An angry bark forces him and Leon back into Lana and Cole. Moving towards them with its lips slightly pulled back, Leon recognizes the canine breed with its erect gray and white ears, threatening blue and green eyes, and its impressive size. The Siberian Husky doesn't approve their clearance.

"Mozart," Raven sternly says. Instantly, the dog quietly sits on his furry bottom. "Those two men we can trust. I cannot vouch for the other four humans." She talks to the Husky as though he understands her... "Please, find yourselves a seat," she offers the newcomers as she sits at the far end of table; the head.

Lucas and Leon observe crosses plastered an inch apart on every wall—they are even on the ceiling and floor. Choosing the bench to the left, the two cautiously move past Mozart. But the dog's focus is on the other strangers...

"I want all of you to feel comfortable," the Goddess tells her guests.

"Not likely," mutters Loki. Instantly, Mozart stands on all four legs and threatens her with another low growl, his face resembling a wild wolf. Loki screams. The screen door squeaks open and is forced to be a barrier between her and the set of baby blue and green eyes that calmly watch. Laughter ensues from Raven's crew.

KRONOS / BLAYNE

A phone in one hand, and a smile on his face. Nothing could make Kronos happier... Except death. Not his own of course because he is dead.

"Are you sure you got the signal?" the newborn asks. The elder Vampire's exultant smile vanishes and his soulless eyes make Blayne retreat his own dubious pair.

The fledgling yanks the two bodies his maker and he drained dry down from the ceiling, slings them over his shoulder, and walks into the next room. He tosses the bodies as if they are small chopped logs into the flames, breaking and contorting the bones to fit inside the fireplace.

The blinking dot on the elder Vampire's phone vanishes. Kronos exits out of the map of Kansas. "I think it's time we made a few calls and left this dead Nebraskan city." His cruel smile returns; the indentation at the corner of his lip turning up on his permanently thirty-five year old face. "Tonight, soul-bitch meets reaper."

Raven's House
Lana and Cole have introduced themselves, that is what lead to Loki sitting at the opposite end of the thick table in the center of the cross-filled room closest to the entry, or exit. On one of the longer sides of the table a wide gap separates Alec and Ganesha to Loki's right. "Zombies seem like a bigger problem than the undead," the curly-headed girl complains.

Annoyance flows off of the dark-skinned girl like a teacher trying to educate her most imprudent student. "Are you being serious? You roll with Shadows yet you act like you don't have a clue."

"You know, I get it. All the vamps are coming." Loki waves her hands around in the air.

"So you understand my kind will be here as well?" Sheba, on Raven's right, leans up against the table to make her presence visible.

"Why will they be here?" asks the pimpled-faced boy.

Cricket, sitting in the chair below an unlit candelabra against the wall behind and to the left of the living Vampire, boringly sighs and folds his arms over his chest.

"When a human becomes a Shadow it gets that natural enemy instinct when one is near," Raven patiently explains.

"The more Vampires there are in a group— Deaths—means more enemies are alerted." Jet— fully clothed in black again; the male guests appreciative—with one foot over the other and arms crossed, props his side against the bumpy wall forming a triangle with Cricket and Raven.

"Shadows wanting roasted undead, and bloodsuckers wanting blood," Lucas sums up from his spot next to Leon on the bench behind Lana and Cole. "And most want..." He looks up from the floor to the girl from his daydreams; a few more inches and her mane will be touching the seat of the chair. *Her. Maybe not all of the Shadows do...but her other folk...*

No one knows—not even the seer or the all-knowing Goddess—what is going to happen. But they know it is something terrible. Changing the subject, Raven addresses the young male next to Sheba. "Cole, you are seventeen. When were you called?"

Her knowledge of his age does not startle him. All Vampires know the time of life of every human they happen to smell. "Sixteen."

"Sixteen?" Alec repeats. "That seems young to have to venture out at night to hunt down immortals."

"The typical age is sixteen or seventeen," Leon says, recounting the myth about Shadows, which turns out isn't a myth.

"How do you know so much about this?"

Lucas answers the blemished boy. "My mother and her brother, Uncle Jay—"

"My dad," Leon clarifies.

"—Shared a common enemy. *Avy Sinanna.*"

"A Vampire got him. And after Avy was turned he killed them."

"But not before the bastard tortured and killed Leon's mom and my dad in front of their spouses." For a spilt second Lucas can almost recall both of their parents' soothing voices, but the horrible screams and pleading win.

"He was enjoying his reprisal to the extent that he did not hear you two when you discovered him," gathers Raven.

"You were not even thirteen." Sheba twists around in her chair, sympathizing.

Alec looks dumbfounded. How could she possibly know that?

"You have to be at least sixteen to be transformed into a Vampire. But I have yet to see someone that young," Jet states, shifting his weight to the other foot. He suspects it has something to with puberty. "And nothing twelve or younger can be killed."

"Why those ages? And what stops vamps from—"

"That is the way," Jet snaps, fed up with his interrogations.

"Ten," Lucas volunteers. "I was ten. And he was eight."

The seer leans forward, his forearms resting on his legs, cupping his hands together. "We do not know why he has chosen to let us continue living." Seventeen-year-olds and over can forget forever, but children are not like them. No matter how current the Burning it always ends at age thirteen.

"Weird," Cole admits.

"Maybe he just died," Alec proposes in a way that means he is the only one to think of this. He turns his head towards the entryway, impudently rolling his eyes. A deploring growl makes him jump back against his seat. The front legs of the chair raise up, and the teenage boy quickly grasps at the table avoiding an uncomfortable landing on his back and saving himself from further embarrassment. "I do not approve of uncouthly behavior" —Raven's suddenly glowing orange and blue eyes freeze Alec in place— "and humans that cannot follow instructions."

The blemished boy's eyes burn, oxygen lightly nipping at them, too afraid to shrink to their normal size in fear they might be ripped out of their sockets.

"Why are you surprised, boy?" Ganesha shakes her head. "You were informed that your opinions have no place here."

"One should refrain from talking about things in which they have no education," Sheba advises him as Raven's Vampire eyes liquefy, becoming human again.

"If Avy Sinanna died, then someone connected to him would have done what he, thankfully, failed to do." Loki looks past Lana to Lucas and sits up as straight as possible, hoping to draw his attention to her breasts. The coquettish girl smiles as Lucas's gaze drifts from Alec. Loki knows he is about to look at her and is overjoyed, for there is no way Lucas would reject her after he sees how perky her nipples are.

Lucas Kale's attention is unexpectedly intercepted. "Twelve," Lana says. "I was called when I was twelve." Raven's head snaps toward the raven-haired Shadow, and Alec practically whines at Leon, "But you just said—"

The hazel irises of the half-breed scan the people in her dining room, contemplating whether or not she should share her knowledge. "It's okay, Raven," Lana consents. "You can tell them."

"He gave you those scars."

The girl with the backpack next to her feet tucks her dark hair behind her ear, showing them the damaged cartilage. The vampiric woman is the only one to not display emotion over it. "You are a descended of Kronos."

"What?" Alec asks. "The Vampire?"

"My Uncle," Lana says. "Insert a lot of greats."

Maybe it has something to do with all the blood in his ears because Leon is having trouble believing them. How can a Vampire be related to a Shadow? In his years of fighting the undead he has never come across a bloodsucker that had a heartbeat in the family. "You are related to Kronos?"

"The only reason anyone would change before their time is if a Vampire relative is close. Perimeter wise." Cole runs his fingers through his black hair. It is not black like Lana's; his roots sometimes look like they have a light tint of brown.

"Sadly," Sheba says, "if a relative of yours is turned into a Vampire then they can kill you at any age."

Mozart climbs out from underneath the table. He arches his back pushing his gray bottom into the air. His belly nearly touches the floor as his white front paws press down on top of Cricket's covered feet. Cricket smiles tenderly at the dog.

Who wasn't murdered? Leon wonders. *It's been centuries since Kronos turned.* "How did your ancestors survive?"

Lana shrugs.

The four-legged animal makes his way into the kitchen directly across from the table's head and begins to pace.

"You are a descended of Malinda," Raven says in amazement.

"The niece of Kronos," Jet confirms.

"I saw Kronos in an Order—"

"—Is that what our visions are called?" Leon's inquisitiveness about the gift that saves others while physically hurting him in the process is apparent.

"Later," she defers the subject. "I stole a baby from his sister, Malinda. I did not keep her, obviously." Raven switches her focus from the group to Lana. "I brought it here to the United States of America. I honestly did not think that line would survive. Do you know how rare you are, being called?"

Lucas raises an eyebrow. "How rare?"

"There has only been one, and that was before my lifetime."

"How old are—"

"I am more than four-hundred years, but less than a thousand," the intimidating female says, not revealing her true age. She does not think it polite to know such things.

Lucas looks at Leon and softly laughs. "Yeah, I'd say that's rare."

"The older Vampires with the exception of Kronos have been killed by some Shadows, but mostly Jet and myself. I have more years on Kronos, but he is better than I at Hide-n-Seek."

Hide-n-Seek is a game Lana is all too familiar with, and the day Kronos ceases to exist cannot arrive fast enough for her. *College starts in approximately three months. I want to be able to look back and say not all of my youth sucked.*

Raven, no longer willing to ignore Mozart's pacing, pushes back her walnut brown chair. "I am leaving. I will return shortly." Leon, heart pounding, untwines his fingers. Lana's face contorts in confusion. "Where are you going?"

"I'm taking Mozart for a run."

"*Now?*" Alec bolts up disapprovingly.

The golden-haired woman starts walking to her right, and Mozart springs to the exit of the kitchen with the matching interior; numerous crosses on the walls and no windows. The only light shining into the kitchen is from the single glass door.

"Is it crazy to think we need a plan?" Loki asks with disfavor, and eagerly waits for Lucas to share the same belief. But Lucas and Leon are not as appalled as Loki and the pimpled-faced boy.

Lucas smiles. "How long can a run with a Vampire—"

The seer does not feel the woman helping them should be classified with the soulless and malevolent enemies. "Human—"

"—Goddess, take?"

The word Goddess covets through his cousin's lips in a way that makes Leon secretly chastise himself. *Raven heard him. I have a higher IQ and I couldn't take the one word I knew he would play on and turn it into a gallant ass compliment.*

Jet follows his best friend and favorite canine out the side door.

"We fight," Lana tells Loki. "That's the plan."

Lucas folds his brawny arms, and it reminds him they are not nearly as burly and broad as Jet's. "Why does it take two to walk a dog?"

JET/RAVEN/MOZART

Outside, Jet—after hearing Lucas—sings, "I smell jealousy." The small tree, having only reached half the size of the house near the porch's side, lightly waves as if in agreement. White clouds pass around the yellow sun that longs for someone to play in its warm light.

Raven laughs airily, and then appears beyond her house next to Mozart on the worn path leading into the green woods. The towering man with wide shoulders and thick muscles watches Raven and Mozart while he begins removing his articles of clothing. The rustling sound of leaves cease, accepting the two into the land of quietude.

The canine looks up at Raven. He loves running with his master. Unlike most dogs, he gets to run at full speed. There is never a leash or lack of physical endurance from a person holding him back.

"Come on, Mozart. Is that all you got?"

He speeds up—his legs extend back and forth, back and forth, back and forth—sounding heavily through the air. The blue and green-eyed family member loves feeling the air as it zooms through his multicolor fur. In all his years of running with Raven, the Husky has went beyond the average speed of any dog.

His master slows down, dodges left then right, pretending he is going to catch her. Mozart knows that he can never win on his own. But he enjoys the game. The game of freedom.

Raven's House
Sitting in the dining/living room, (there are no windows or pictures hanging on the walls; there isn't even a clock—all the things found in a regular house are seriously lacking here) they, excluding Raven and Jet, assimilate the facts:

Shadows Sheba and Cricket, a Normal (a regular human) Ganesha, and a Werewolf work and live with Raven.

A Vampire—Avy Sinanna—is responsible for Lucas "Luke" Kale and "Brighton" Leon Carmany living with their Uncle Joe and cousin Rachel until the age of eighteen. And the reason they are Vampire Hunters. Avy Sinanna is also alive and no one knows when, but he will surely come for the Hunters.

Lana is related to Kronos, the leader of the Vampires, who no doubt is currently gathering his army. Vampires, lots, will be here when the sun starts to shine on the opposite side of the world; thus causing Shadows to march their way here to Concordia, Kansas.

The Nebraskan Shadow is alive thanks to Raven—whom Leon Carmany has seen die in the future. The living Vampire has seen the seer's death as well.

"Don't forget the zombies," Cole adds.

"Perfect. This is the bestest freakin' day of spring ever," Lucas says sarcastically. "Well, it runs a close second to the time I got three BBs in my back and one in my adorable ass cheek. And I'm not implying the other one isn't. It's just as perky." The slightly smug twenty-four year old adds, "Yeah, don't ever sleep with your relative's friends. You're the one who gets hurt."

With her elbows on the table and hands tucked under her chin, Loki lets the words freely flow from her mouth. "Do you think you'll die, Leon?"

Seven pairs of eyes pass their judgment on her. Cricket, still positioned below the fireless candelabrum, continues with replacing a crossbow string, shaking his head.

"That's not how I meant it."

Sheba looks up from the disassembled M-16 she is currently in the process of cleaning; a jammed weapon would really bite. "How *did* you mean it?"

Cole rushes to Loki's defense. "I think she's trying to ask... I don't mean any harm by this. Not only has the Goddess seen your death, but you've seen hers and she doesn't seem to care."

Alec agrees. "She's more concerned about a mutt."

An arrow zooms by Alec's nose, a fraction of a centimeter away, nearly grazing his pointed, pimpled nose. Ganesha lowers her book *Beethoven*; reading is her favorite pastime. "You really should not speak ill of Mozart."

"Noted." He glares questionably at the dark-skinned Shadow who released the arrow. Cricket shrugs in return.

* * *

JET & MOZART
Jet trots down the wide path of bent stems. Luscious leaves brush up against his dark blue coat while he and Raven pace themselves with Mozart.

Running until *he* gets tired is something Mozart rarely experiences with humans. Sure he has ran with Jet and Shadows, but it is never the same as being with the human he loves. His paws press into the earth and he leaps forward off the bluff with a Werewolf and his Raven by his side. Her long hair brushes back against the sweet air.

Drawing his legs together and tucking his head under, the sparkling creek rushes closer. His intellectual eyes capture the base of the bluff, and fluffy white shapes like that of cotton candy signal him back to his horizontal position. The warm dirt and grass slide in between his claws.

Mozart is not an idiot. He knows that Jet and Raven are not entirely human. He knows that people do not change their entire shape into something that could be his cousin. He can smell his master's faint unpleasant copper smell that never goes away—that is what makes it unpleasant. But that is what it is, *faint.*

His master's humanity makes it difficult for him to accept the moments when she must leave him. The Husky knows it is for his own well-being; that the ones with the odor that burns his nostrils will do bad things to him because he belongs to Raven.

But knowing why does not make it a gratifying experience. It does not make the time apart painless. And understanding the look in his master's eyes before she darts off across the leveled ground leaving him with Jet does not stop Mozart from whining.

LEON/LOKI/GANESHA/SHEBA/LANA
"Out of curiosity, who is in charge now?" Leon glances around the room.

Sheba is at the head of the table, and for a second her nose ring catches the light as she turns to face him. Everyone else is in their same spots except for Lucas and him having filled the gap separating Alec and Ganesha.

Lana had told the Hunters and Alec that the oldest Shadow—experience wise—takes the reigns.

But he senses that is not the case in this situation.

Cricket raises his hand, signaling that he, himself, is the leader now.

"Really?" Loki glares at Ganesha remembering her first encounter outside with the older girl. "I figured it was the African American girl with the attitude problem."

"I prefer to just be called American. I was not born in Africa. Cricket is African American."

"Are you from the hood?" Loki snickers.

Ganesha remains silent.

"You *are*, aren't you? Another white girl, Vampire in this case, saved one of the black folk," she laughs triumphantly.

"Loki!" Lana gasps.

Instead of reaching over and pulling out every single bobbing curl and shoving them down Loki's throat—exactly what she wants to do—Ganesha prudently responds, "Anyone who is wise knows it is important to have goals and ambition. Living in the *hood* is not the best way to live."

"Living with a Vampire is?"

The air in the room feels as if it has gone stale, and hostility threatens to take the form of a tidal wave.

"Some people in this room risk their lives while you all ride in expensive cars next to that icky thing. And since we have a Jacob here," Loki challenges, "I might as well go find my Edward."

The heavy table in front of them lifts up, spins over their heads, and collides against the wall. Wavy brown hair cuts the air straight to Loki. A furious hand squeezes around her throat. "Bitch, this is not *Twilight*!" Sheba has pinned the weaker girl against the wall—hand still clasping her neck. "You do not coddle and cuddle with *Vampires*!"

"You seem to think so," Loki manages to say.

"You do not know what I am thinking" —Sheba leans closer— "so let me tell you. I am wondering why none of your pals are coming to the rescue." Sheba's face nearly brushes the peach fuzz on the girl's cheekbone as she brings her lustrous lips to the troublemaker's ear. "Are they afraid? Or is it because they are smarter than you, Loki?"

Lana stands up. "I want a word with my friend."

Sheba, satisfied, places the girl on the floor without a second thought. Cricket points down the hallway to his left.

Lana and Loki walk down the dim-lit hall. The lowercase T shapes covering the floor feel foreign against their tennis shoes. And for the first time, Lana realizes that the woman from her dreams must have more enemies than she imagined. Crosses that seem to be frozen in time greet them from every angle, creating a mysterious and threatening vibe—even for a Shadow.

Noticing that it eventually veers left, they stop at a door to their right. Lana drags Loki inside and demands, "Why are you suddenly acting like you—"

"I'm only causing problems because she embarrassed me, and I just think they like Raven."

"They?"

"Did you see Lucas checking me out? And Leon's face when he ran to save me?"

"Loki," she gently says turning her eyes away

from the red and white swirl pattered chair. "I think Leon was worried because of what he saw."

"I know that Lucas liked me. But since he saw *her*..." Loki clenches her teeth, her acrimony running bone deep.

"So what if he doesn't like you?" She grasps Loki's upper arms and lightly shakes her. "You just met him *today*! And you know vamps don't go with us!"

LUCAS KALE & LEON CARMANY

Lucas and Leon are at the corner of Jet Road and Brother Street standing by their car under the shade of a silent tree. Leon wonders where the houses are that classify it to be a street, a paved black one for that matter.

Lucas looks at the busted out window and shakes his head. "I don't like what we've..."

"Seen?"

"I'm afraid," he admits; not an easy thing for him to do. He leans against the hood, wishing he could just wake up in Tennessee. "That guy just... He killed a child." Lucas chokes up, his eyes become watery as a light breeze ruffles the tree overhead. "There are a lot of small...us's. I thought losing half our family was bad, but damn it Leon, this is the worst day of my life." His throat feels like it is swelling shut and his eyelashes become very moist. A few leaves float down, waiting to be whisked away from the car.

The longhaired man shakes his head in agreement, and looks away trying to hide his own tears. He thinks about death...his death. *If I die…this truly will be the worst day of his life.*

Leon and Lucas nearly jump out of their skin, startled by Raven's sudden presence in front of them. Normally the flirtatious man will not have a girl see him cry, but today is not normal. Lucas looks away from her, not knowing what to say and wipes at his square face with the end of his sleeve.

Leon, truly interested, asks, "Did you enjoy your walk?" The twenty-two year old finds himself wanting to reach out and stroke her hair. But Leon refrains from doing do so; that would be an awkward and unconventional situation.

"No. I was looking for something. I did not find it," she says blandly. "You are hungry. Come inside when you are ready."

The young man in the light blue and white shirt thinks back to Rolling Acres. *It is true. I haven't eaten today.* A bark nearly causes Lucas to jump, again. Raven appears at the kitchen door next to Mozart and a stark-naked Jet picking up his dark colored clothes from the grass. Lucas and Leon watch them disappear inside the red house.

~~~~

Chapter 12
The Banish

"BECAUSE WE'RE FOLLOWING you shouldn't I know whom it is I'm putting that word faith in?" Lucas asks Raven after him and Leon enter the kitchen threshold. It is a small kitchen. There is descent countertop space; a purse sits on one of them near the sink. There is no dishwasher. The only other requirements are a stove and refrigerator. A small trashcan sits next to the box of cold air: the refrigerator. In their house (the two cousins share a place on their Uncle's land in Tennessee) a microwave is a necessity; not the case here.

They see Mozart eating green turnips out of a doggie bowl. "Peculiar dog," observes Leon.

"What is your question, Kale?" She addresses him by his last name from the dining area; a first for him.

He hesitates, going back and forth between questions he needs answers to and the ones he wants. "What's your favorite color?"

"Blue." She pauses and then adds, "Different shades more than others."

Blue is his favorite color, too.

"How did you and Jet come to exist?" Leon asks a more momentous question.

"There is no short explanation." Raven sighs and props her buttocks on the back of the wooden chair, her feet planted in the cushioned seat. "Magic exists, or it use to before The Banish."

"What is The Banish?" Leon asks as he and Lucas stand to her right, not bothering to join the circle at the damaged table that someone has put back in its original place; more than likely Sheba since she moved it in the first place.

"Eight-hundred years ago," Jet pauses and corrects himself, "Longer than that I think. Real witches could be found everywhere—"

Ganesha, all too familiar with this story, interrupts. "But there was a bad witch of course. The most powerful to have ever existed," she jokingly adds.

"She made several dimensions overlap," Sheba stands with an earnest expression on her face, "thus causing Werewolves, Vampires, and—"

"Shadows," Lana whispers. The answers she has been searching for since before she was twelve are unveiling right in front of her.

"Wow," Cole looks at his best friend. "We live complex lives due to a witch." Ganesha remembers where Lana got her scars and drops her eyes to the floor, ashamed for taking the matter so lightly. He tries uplifting her sorrowful mood. "Do you think she got a house dropped on her?" The corner of Ganesha's lip arches, a knowingly half smile.

"With combined worlds it was easy for humans to fear death." Jet leans against the wall, crosses imprinting themselves into his back. "And easier for the first Vampires to make more but weaker versions of their kind. Lana, Cole," he addresses them. "Originally, when your kind's eyes Split they could see the colored essence Vampires left behind them. It made vamps easier to track and kill during the day while they had their siestas."

"But The Witch thought it was best if we could see after sunset," Sheba says.

"She was wrong and the Shadow's death rate increased." The unpleasant memories spin in Raven's mind. "A less powerful witch thought it wrong to have messed with their abilities in the first place. He decided to reverse what had been done to your kind."

"He was not strong enough and, well, you know what happened," Jet alludes. "No pretty colors for you."

"I was human at the time. I sought to destroy The Witch." In those days Raven worried about The Witch's limits; the older woman did not seem to care what happened to the world or the people in it. "The only thing impervious to human magic was the Vampire."

Leon is the first to come to the conclusion. "Your intention prevented the complete transformation. You did not became a full

Vampire."

"The Blending, what I call overlapping, happened when I was eighteen. I became half human at age nineteen and stopped her from…more destruction."

By her brief pause, the genius's intuition tells him there is more to the story…

"And magic was soon banished," Jet finishes.

Lucas waits for them to continue but they do not. "By?"

"Who else?" Jet looks right into his eyes, waiting for him to connect the dots. "God."

Alec rolls his eyes.

Raven ignores him. "Any spell that was cast before then was supposed to pass through. But one did not."

"We do not know why, but my kind no longer changed at the full of the moon."

"Werewolves began to plague the streets at all hours eating anything that could die." To this day, Raven can still hear the sound of bone grinding against bone and the screams similar to Loki's when Jet forced her to the ground.

Lana pictures monster size Werewolves running about during the day shredding humans with their long, think claws and teeth as long as her face. "Is that when we were forbidden to let them live?"

"Yes. That is when I received my first Order."

"Raven taught me how to change the two skins." Jet steps away from the wall and places his wide palm on her shoulder. "I am the only one left from my kind, and Ray is the only one of her kind."

Something nips at Brighton Leon Carmany's brain. *Nineteen.* "Raven, when did you stop aging?"

"Twenty-three."

The red 19 and the yellow 23; the timer in Hastings...

"Do you think you and Leon are Gods?" Alec asks, his tone mocking and condescending.

"I am not what the Vampires call me."

"But I thought only God" —he rolls his eyes again— "could see the future?"

"My Orders come from the Heavenly Creator." The twenty three-year-old-looking woman in the icy blue shirt turns to Leon. "As does your Preventions."

The veterinarian and the mechanic rock with laughter.

"You do not believe in Him? Her, it, whatever?" Ganesha, surprised, asks the cousins.

"We believe God exists, it's just..." The small knot now formed in Leon's throat blocks his words.

"We don't believe in prayer," Lucas finishes. "God isn't going to rearrange his plans to suit me." Raven gets the feeling Kale believes that more than Leon. "So," Lucas asks, "why would He give power to someone who doesn't talk to Him?"

Raven looks up at them with demanding eyes. "This subject is for a later time."

"There is one more thing you should know," Ganesha says. "You know all those stories you hear about—ghosts and spirits and demon possessions?" The Tennessee and Nebraskan natives quizzically shake their heads. "They are lies."

"What are you saying?" Lana asks with the Haunted House in mind; the place where Kronos threw acid on her.

"They are lies," Ganesha repeats, uncertain as to how she can make it any clearer. "But that stuff—possessions, poltergeists, spirits, what have you—was real before The Banish. They all had something to do with magic so, now, they do not exist."

"Do Vampires date humans?" Loki randomly blurts out.

Raven retorts, "Do you want to date Mozart?"

The Siberian Husky sits in the threshold between the kitchen and dining room licking his lips, getting off the remainder of his food.

Loki crinkles her nose in disgust.

Just then Lucas thinks about bestiality. His intestines tie themselves into a knot. *Wow. When she thinks of us, me, she wants to vomit.* He sighs. *Didn't see that coming.*

"Vampires are coming here. They want Shadows and me dead. But they need the Normals alive." If all the non-supercharged humans died, how would the Vampires live? "Cole, Alec, Leon, and Kale, you four stay here. Jet and Sheba will prepare a meal for you humans. Lana, Cricket, and Ganesha will accompany me to the hospital to get blood for the Vampires that are due for feeding and feasting."

"Should we maybe cover the windows?" Alec suggests.

"If doing so will comfort you. But you should know this house is in the path of a tornado that will arrive shortly," the longhaired blonde informs them.

"What?" The irascible boy bolts up from his seat. "You didn't think we needed to know—"

"What about me?" Loki interjects. In Ravens commands she had not included her.

No one saw her move from the chair but the half-breed pushes it under the table. "I do not care what your decisions are as long as they do not bring physical harm to others."

"You should. My death is important."

"You were saved," Raven says, now standing at the other end of the table next to Loki. "If you were to die at this exact moment your death would be of little importance to me."

How did she know about Loki? The young man who recently woke up in a field with bloody eyes and sore wrists and ankles wonders.

Loki's face turns angry-mean-drunk red and she moves out of the sitting circle.

Raven glares down at her. "You did not agree to my terms. What happens to you is your own doing. You are only here in hopes of seducing or being seduced by two cousins."

Loki spits in Raven's face.

Or tries.

Lana and Cole shout— "Loki!" —while the Goddess dodges the saliva and grabs Loki by the throat. Willful feet once again lift above carved crosses and Loki's body pushes quickly against the air. Raven has opened the front door, Loki dangling from her grip. "I was wrong. I do care." She places the impertinent, disrespectful girl on the porch. "You can stay out there."

"Zombies could be out here," Loki whines and rubs her voice box.

The seventeen year old human in front of her is the last person Raven wants to deal with on this stressful day. But Raven knows she cannot let her die. "Mozart." She says in Hungarian, "Vedelem." Meaning guard. Knowing that Jet can protect Loki while in her absence, does not stop Raven from calling upon the charming Siberian.

Mozart trots outside and sits on two hind legs in front of the troublemaker. Loki stiffens, afraid to move.

Leaving them, Raven finds Lana and Cole standing halfway between her and the table. "Do you wish to leave now?"

"Yes," Lana answers.

"Raven, may I have a word with you in private?" The young man with specs of blood still in his soft looking hair calls from the other side of the room. She likes the politeness in his voice. *And his eyes,* she thinks.

Before Leon follows her down the hall, Ganesha whispers in Raven's ear. "Let's take Loki with us." Raven's crooked smile is the response to the mischievous light in the Normal's brown eyes.

LEON & RAVEN
Leon and Raven are nearly in the same stance Lana and Loki had been in previously in the Comfy Room next to the dining/living area. The vent on the ceiling blows cool air on his smooth, round face.

"Our deaths," the seer starts. "Yours and mine. I see you—"

"—Lying in my blood. I know." The Immortal disregards the astonishment on his tan face. "You did not see me at the bar because if you had I would have hurt you. The Witch foretold of you being sent to me. Past humans have attempted to be The Preventer, so I suspect that is why I saw you seeing me."

"You *were* at the bar. You ran into Luke."

"That accident has changed my view on fortuity." Ambivalent about Lucas Kale, she quickly changes the subject. "On your way here I saw everything you have seen."

"I am a… Preventer. And my visions are called Preventions." He hopes saying the words will help him to understand. "How are you not a Preventer?"

"Leon, you are *The* Preventer. You only see the human, Normals, you are supposed to save from the Vampires, with today's exception of Lana, Loki, and myself. I, however, see future courses of action; Shadows, Vampires, Jet."

He recalls the story the Nebraskan Shadows told him and Lucas. *It was as if she already knew.* "When do I die? I mean, do you… What is the order?" Raven can't protect him if she is dead. Does she save him before she dies? Does he save her before *he* dies?

The bar-girl pulls her long fair mane to one side and drapes it over her breast exposing the side of her neck and unintentionally arousing the twenty-two year old. "I die after you. Leon, you die because…I kill you."

End of erection.

* * *

GANESHA / LANA

"Lana, they might be a minute." Ganesha beckons with her hand as she pushes the screen door open. Cricket ambles behind the two girls. The red roof shields them from the heat.

Mozart rises from his spot and stands on his two hind legs. Ganesha takes his front paws in her hands and they slowly start square dancing on the porch. His tail wags merrily from side to side, and Lana squeals with excitement.

The girl from Nebraska has wanted a dog for several years but knows Kronos will take it away from her like he did with her first pet. Lana came home one day from school to find her cat's tiny paws in the fish tank, and when she turned on the ceiling fan in her bedroom it slung his tiny guts and intestines about the room.

"Your girl is coming with," Ganesha tells the shorter, apple green-eyed girl. "Shoot! I am not supposed to end my sentences with prepositions while in the company of new folks." She lets the Husky's paws drop, and points at Loki. "Thanks to *you* I will be doing laps!"

The troublemaker's presence makes the girl who dropped Raven off at the airport in Nebraska before driving herself back to Kansas, once again wretchedly aware of the barren lawns and window coverings. Wishing they could forget this mess and throw a barbeque, Ganesha tugs at the strap of her purse she fetched from the kitchen. "Eventually."

LEON & RAVEN
"You become..."

"Zombie?" Leon cringes at the idea, but it does not last long for the thought is turned into another repulsive reality.

"Vampire; by a Japanese girl. And I…" None of the words streaming through the Immortal girl seem to fit. "End you." *I will do my best to see to it that this intelligent and sexy—respectful human will not become my foe.*

She stands just like a Goddess. That hair. Tan skin. The way she talks. Uh-oh. I bet she can tell I want to kiss her. AWKWARD.

"I have a confession, Brighton."

"Please," —he grins— "call me Leon. Luke is the only person who calls me Brighton, and he only does so when he is annoyed or serious."

"I am serious."

"O…kay."

"Vampires do not have intimate relationships with humans. You know this. I do not consider myself to be Vampire or Human. Over the centuries I have had relations with your kind. But I no longer continue to have serious partners because only one of them was truly capable of accepting old age and death.

"My confession is, if you had been born centuries earlier I would have considered staying with you, Brighton Leon Carmany, until death claimed you. I can tell by your direction of blood flow I have excited you. Again. However, I must reject your invitation. A simple 'fling' will complicate our future work together. When I say future, I am not referring to that of today. I am confident we will survive this war. You do understand your calling, your life, is forever intertwined with mine?"

Leon is momentarily speechless. *She tells me she likes me, but it doesn't matter? And why is she assuming I will stay with her? Well, I might. By now I guess she would be a great judge of character.* The genius is suddenly intimated by her wisdom.

"I wish I knew more about your—" he stops short when Raven quickly opens the door and exits. "Death," he finishes. *What the hell?*

The fact is The Preventer does not know more about either of their deaths. And to Raven that is that.

LANA & LOKI
Lana stands at the bottom of the steps with Loki while Cricket, Ganesha, and Mozart wait in the white van Ganesha has just driven out of the basement.

The front door opens just after Lana tells Loki that her behavior is making her uncomfortable; the impudent remarks about Devin and Ganesha, provoking the Similar, and her insolence towards their leader.

Raven steps outside and Loki's hand tightens around the crossbow that Lana has given her; Lana figured no one would ever give her a gun.

The woman from Leon's Preventions passes by them and Loki whispers to her friend, "You don't owe her anything." She refers to Raven saving her ancestor; thus the reason for the Shadow's existence.

Lana does not know if it is the heat being trapped

in her winter wear or her friend's lack of respect, or a combination of the two that is causing her exasperation. "Raven has three humans" —she holds her fingers up— "two who are Shadows, and a Werewolf that follow her lead. I don't owe her anything other than my common sense." The irritated girl storms off.

Loki looks down at the bolt; it is aimed for the Vampire's backside… The troublemaker does not think twice. She presses the trigger…

Loki knows it is a mistake as soon as the bolt is released.

The petite dark-haired girl has gained on the tall Goddess. *Raven may not refer to herself has being godly, but the creatures of the dark do and so will I,* the Shadow makes up her mind.

Lana moves to the right—directly in the path of Loki's arrow…

Chapter 13
Three Kinds of Dead

RAVEN HEARS THE SOUNDS of hearts beating, the buzzing of bees pollinating flowers, flapping of wings as birds take flight, and a snake slithering through the grass...

The Immortal twenty-three-year-old-looking girl whips around and catches the narrow wood in between her fingertips. Lana's eyes widen, realizing the point almost went through her own neck. Her face hardens.

"I will let you deal with *this* the way *you* see fit," Raven says and snaps the arrow in half. She appears next to the white van opening its door.

"I'm sorry," Loki apologizes to her friend.

"You are relentless. Do you *want* to die?"

"They're not going to—"

"I'm not finished," Lana speaks over her. "I was

talking about cannibals. The reason why we are here. *Here*. At *Raven's* house. Yes, she is invincible. But the rest of us aren't. I do not want to hear your excuses or contrite promises." She flat out tells her, "We've been friends since elementary, but me and Cole have a lot to deal with that sun goes down and I will not choose you over her."

Tears form in her friend's eyes, but Lana doesn't feel the least bit sorry.

JET/COLE/ALEC
"Your blonde friend is going to get herself killed," Jet tells Cole. "And possibly the unusually short Shadow."

"Loki would never hurt Lana."

"She almost killed her with a crossbow. Granted, it was *my* friend she was hoping to hurt."

Cole groans as Jet passes by him and enters the kitchen.

"I'm going outside," Alec announces, opening the front door, and forgetting the pistol…

The acned boy sees the opulent cars still parked on the road and thinks back to the guy with the black Mustang. If that guy wasn't driving like an idiot Alec would still have a car. And he wouldn't be stuck here.

Alec is deep in thought. He sits on the steps in between the spinning flower pots, oblivious to the two girls hiding behind the two trees on opposite ends of the roofed exterior…

The one to the right of the boy on the porch turns her head towards the greenery behind the cedar house, revealing dark colored lines on half of her scalp where patches of orange hair had been ripped out by their roots. Holding her palm up, the nearly bald-headed female signals for another girl wearing a very short and shredded skirt, emerging from the woods to stop advancing. Then with one of the two fingers left on her hand, the orange headed girl points to the side door—warning her.

LANA & CRICKET
Should I tell her I dreamt about her? And ask her how her picture ended up in the book of Vampires? Nah, it's not important right now. Since arriving here I haven't felt as emotionally distressed...

An older rap song that Lana recognizes, *Move Bitch* by Ludacris, Mystikal, and I-20 plays in the van. Ganesha and Raven turn around and sing a verse to Loki:

"I been thankin' of bustin' you upside ya motherfuckin' forehead."

Loki's jaw drops as they resume dancing to the song. Holding her hand over her mouth, Lana quickly turns to the window trying to hold back laughter. The offended girl turns to her for support but does not receive any.

The mute gentleman smiles at Lana as she tries to force down her tiny giggles. He laughs. The teenage girls in the backseat turn to him, stunned that he made a sound. And then Cricket and Lana join each other in mirthful bliss.

"What?" Loki finally asks them. They shake their heads and turn to their windows. "What?"

She is so beautiful. How could anyone raise a hand to that face? Kronos. He's the one that's going to die. Not my Ray, Cricket not only thinks, but knows.

* * *

Lucas stands in the kitchen watching Jet put hamburger meat in a black skillet.

Noodles with meat; a meal he helped his mother with before she died. She would let him add the water and milk; making it his favorite choice of meals to eat before his little league football games. Football was a sport his mother encouraged; a sport Lucas quit when he was ten.

In the room of a hundred crosses, where the blonde troublemaker insulted nearly everyone and severally disrespected the one he was sent to save by expelling her saliva, Leon asks Cole, "Does Loki normally behave so…"

"Irrational? Yes, but not like this. She, uh, doesn't have a lot of friends."

"I wonder why," Sheba says, her voice sardonic. She leaves the dining room and enters the kitchen. Lucas comments on her mini skirt and spaghetti strap shirt. "That's a bold outfit given today's extracurricular activities. You looking for a little zombie nookie?" he jokes. "What are we having?" Cole enters behind the older girl. The halting Shadow in the skirt retorts to Lucas, "Do you think cotton will stop teeth punctures?"

Lucas is about to tell her it could not hurt when she and Cole close their eyes and tilt their heads downward towards their feet…

The Preventer observes the odd behavior. "What is happening to them?"

"Deaths must be near Shadows," Jet says as he

towers over the stove. "They are receiving a message through their Connection with their Similars. Or it is God." He flips several strands of pinkish brown meat over with his spatula. "There are moments when we have not been certain. A message will contain information that no Shadow has witnessed."

* * *

Images of Vampires occur rapidly in the Shadows' minds. Sheba and Cole see humanlike figures dart inhumanly past cities brightly lit in the night...
New York City...
Tallahassee...
Chicago...
Baton Rouge...
Oklahoma City...

"What happens if I—"

"—No!" Jet is unable to stop him. Lucas pokes Sheba's shoulder; her and Cole still have their eyes closed, heads tilted toward the floor. His muscles contract and his entire body feels like it is about to snap. Lucas shakes violently before releasing himself from the electric current.

He collapses to the floor of crosses...

...Meanwhile, Alec buries his head in his lap and imprints the scenery to memory in case tonight's chaos leaves him running around by his lonesome, like a chicken with its head cut off.

The road across from him, Brother Street, divides the vast land in half and seems to be stretched out infinitely. The polished car with the busted window is parked under the tree at the junction of the two roads, and the other three cars near it is liable to make someone think an accident had occurred.

To the far left on the other side of Jet Road stand two brick houses and with the availability of land Alec does not see why the homes were built fairly close to each other. A purple house occupies the lot to the far right and across from it on this side of the blacktop is a house that has been painted yellow.

There are no people coming and going. All is quiet. A zephyr forces light music from the wind chime dangling down near the swing to his right at the end of the porch. The teenage boy finds it irritating but he enjoys the stirring of the warm air.

Zombie Orange Head winks to the other tree girl. The balding girl with patches of dyed hair gets on her knees and hands—what is left of them. She silently and hungrily slinks around the raised platform to get an unwary meal...

Alec, having an unsettling feeling, takes his gluteus maximus off the red step. It takes him less than a second to know his life is in jeopardy. Lungs feeling with air, he hurriedly turns to flee the slinking and gaining zombie.

His effort is met with a stick to the temple thrown by Tree Girl...

...Jet sniffs. He has never smelt anything that...dead.

Leon's back hits the wall as Jet barrels past. He sees Alec reach for the handle...and a wild haired zombie stepping up to his level. Leon's view becomes blocked by a man transforming as he leaps off the wobbling table.

Jet blasts through the wall above the wood and screen doors. Alec ducks to keep from being mauled over by the Werewolf. Debris from above threatens to fall on the crouched boy. With eyes tightly shut, he moves his legs forward as Jet, with the screen door underneath him, lands on Zombie Orange Head. The entire house shakes and the porch collapses…

Lucas tries to move. He tries to *breathe.*

He heard a LOUD crash like that of a tree falling on a house, the noise pulling him from long forgotten memories of his father and mother, and the silver banner he saw earlier today advertising Mother's Day, and knows it's nothing good.

Opening his eyes, a figure Lucas Kale does not want to see steps in front of the kitchen door…

…Leon and Alec rush to the front of the house to see the Werewolf leap out of the hole and over the intact steps, gaining on the retreating Tree Girl. His front paw lifts up off the grass and swipes once at her torso. Four of his five nails slice into the crazed cannibal's neck, above and below her bosom, and through her hip bones.

Cole and Sheba see dozens of dark figures plunge and inhumanly swim through deep waters. The faded image is a sign of the Connection ending soon.

Too weak to get up, Lucas Kale is limited to seeing in only one direction. He cannot help but notice the yellow underwear. The skin around those panties is the second thing he notices. The pigments look like they use to be dark, but have paled, and the veins are bright orange. One of the advanced dead.

"Some help would be nice!" He shouts. It takes everything in him just to kick it in the abdomen, forcing Skirt Girl backwards.

But within seconds she lunges for more...

Outside, eyes blink on a detached head and Jet can see himself bringing his foot down. The feeling of the small, round skull squishing underneath his mammoth size paw brings him great joy.

The last image to be shown to the Shadows is a grainy image of a torch. The pair of orange and verdant eyes passing by somewhere in the deep underground of a cavern belong to the face of a pretty Japanese girl—a smile more devilish than that of Kronos...

Lucas brings his leg back to his chest again and kicks at the vile, repulsive thing threatening his life. The monster in the shredded skirt catches his ankle. Without hesitation, her deadly infectious mouth opens...

Chunks of her head hit the refrigerator.

Leon shoots again, not taking chances. Lucas is his family and he is not going to let him die because he did not expel enough rounds.

The rest of the plague-ridden body tumbles backwards and joining the brains splattered on the once white refrigerator.

Lucas rests his head on the bumpy floor, and gives his cousin a thumbs up as he rolls onto his side wheezing.

"Some are moving. The rest will be shortly," Sheba says, no longer connected.

"You know where," Cole validates.

Sheba looks down at Lucas on the floor and the zombie lying against the cold box. Blood and bits of exploded brain matter slide down the refrigerator. "You are cleaning up that mess."

"You're welcome, lady," Lucas says, positive her and Cole were next on the list to be eaten. Leon helps him up off the hard floor. "Hey," Lucas says to his cousin, panting, "did you know Mother's Day is tomorrow?"

"Yeah, it's the second Sunday."

"What did you get Uncle Joe?"

"New clothes. You?"

"A date."

"Really?"

"Yeah. But I think that idea has gone to hell."

"I thought *Uncle* implied a man," the slightly mystified brunette with crimped strands says.

"Yeah, well," Lucas turns to her, "the man raised some annoying butt sores. He deserves two holidays."

The Hospital

"It's happening. Just like you said," Lana says to Raven. *I wonder if I will ever be able to send a signal through the Connection...*

Cricket nods in agreement.

Loki, having to sit on the carpet to avoid being shocked possibly to death, takes her original position in between her friend and the other Shadow.

"And here I thought fun-time had started." Ganesha rubs her dark fingers through Mozart's soft, long hair. The Husky on her lap props his front paws against the door and sticks his head out the window. He loves the feeling of air blowing in his nostrils. The different smells make him feel like he is dog of the world.

Raven parks the van at the back of the hospital. The parking lot is the typical parking area; rows and rows of vehicles.

"So you're just going to take blood from people who need it?" Loki narrows her eyes.

"Blood transfusions are not going to help humans today. Lana. Cricket. Will you get those boxes?" They reach around the seat and grab the two big brown cardboard boxes.

"I want to go, too," Loki whines and pushes against the door. It quickly reverts back against the pressure of Raven's hand. "If you want a ride back, you will do well to stay with Ganesha."

Loki climbs up to the front seat. She leans against it and huffs, watching Mozart lingering outside by the building after the others have disappeared. She turns the radio on to avoid being heard by supernatural ears, and whispers, "How can you be friends with her?"

Ganesha terminates the musical sound. "What does *Lana* see in *you*?"

"Did you do that so Raven could hear?" She nods at the radio.

"No. I did it so that I can escape the disturbing

mouth of death. Also known as ZOMBIES, you idiot! And if that arrow had nearly pierced *my body*, I would have beat you with it. Or try. My friends would have stopped me from beating your rude ass."

Ganesha, again, wonders why anyone would *want* to hang out with this girl. "Friends. You and I have them; the *only* thing we have in common. And the only weapon we have is a bow! So shut the hell up and look around!"

CRICKET/LANA/RAVEN

Cricket and Lana patiently wait in the basement of the hospital; clear packages of blood at their feet. Raven had stolen the donated blood, dropped it off, and has disappeared again.

"I didn't know hospitals had basements." Filing cabinets, clothes, stretchers, junk food wrappers, beds without wheels, and a desk take up three fourths of the lowest level. "My basement was almost this messy when my mom put my dad's stuff down there after he died."

Cricket, sitting next to her on the desk, takes a pencil to a sheet of paper.

"No need for you to be sorry," Lana responds to his handwritten message, "Kronos killed him, not you. He died when I was thirteen," she answers the second part written on the thin sheet. "I turned twelve and became a Shadow like my dad, lost my grandparents, and then I lost him a year later. I hope my mother is okay. I left her locked in the basement."

The benevolent man rubs her back with his hand.

"How old are you? Why do you live with Raven?"

Twenty is all the mute young man has time to scribble down. Raven's unseen entrance with Mozart in her arms takes Lana by surprise and she grabs the closest arm next to her. Cricket, finding it adorable, grins from ear to ear exposing his white teeth. He flexes. The girl with the scars on her lips squeezes his biceps again…

Mozart puts his belly against the cool concrete and watches the humans overturn the cardboard boxes, dumping plastic bottles.

"Tell me about Alec." The way the Goddess stares down at her gives Lana an unsettling feeling.

Leon's bar-girl, wearing her dark wig as a disguise, had secretly been at Rolling Acres dissecting the human's body language and emotions. Whatever suspicions the Immortal had disappeared on the airplane when The Preventer subconsciously warned her in a dream about the infected human.

The half-Vampire half-human woman knew Kale wasn't a threat as soon as their accidental meeting occurred. Later Raven saw Leon Carmany having Preventions of Lana and Loki; she knows enough about the girls to not have to worry about them posing a threat to her and her family. Raven had gotten a good read from the lanky male Shadow upon his arrival.

But the acned Normal…

* * *

GANESHA / LOKI

"Why did she take him?" Loki finally asks after

seeing the Vampire swoop up the dog in her arms taking him inside the facility. Ganesha does not really think they are susceptible to attack, although silence amongst them would be wise, but Loki will not shut up to save her life. "Mozart goes everywhere with Ray unless he will be in danger." She gets a cigarette from her purse and lights it.

The silence amongst them lasts the length it takes for the cigarette to burn halfway to the filter.

"That smells funny," the girl in the tank top and shorts comments. "And the smoke isn't like any I've seen."

"So?" Ganesha takes a puff.

Loki sees the chain around the girl's dark neck and pulls the rest of it out from underneath the designer shirt. The girl laughs at the one-horned horse. "A unicorn?"

Ganesha exhales the "funny" smoke out the open window. "What is your problem? Your parents not love you enough or something?" The girl invading her personal space drops the purple unicorn and it dangles against her chest.

"No," Loki admits, sitting back in her seat. "My dad lives in another state and I am convinced my mom loves alcohol more than me."

The teenager in the driver's seat takes another puff from the filter and lets the younger girl's words settle in. "Boo-who," Ganesha finally exhales. "I come from the vagina of a prostitute. Get over yourself." Ganesha turns around in her seat abandoning the view of empty cars to face Loki. "Now," her voice threatens, "you will not speak again until I see my friend."

* * *

…It does not take long for Ganesha to see her friend. Cricket and Lana load the boxes in the back of the van while the Vampire walking in daylight opens Loki's door and throws a pair of jeans at her.

"Why should I wear these? Sheba isn't wearing pants."

"Sheba is a Shadow. You are a Normal."

"Well in the movies people wearing pants still get bit."

The diminutive framed girl and the young man with the shaved head climb inside the van. Mozart curls up on the carpet.

"Let's say for arguments sake that one scratch can turn a human." Raven appears next to the driver's side.

"Fine," Loki huffs. "But I'm not putting long sleeves on."

"They did not have your size in the first place," she says opening the door.

Ganesha gets down from the seat. "I'm hungry."

"I figured," their leader smiles knowingly and gets behind the wheel.

"Where do I change?" asks Loki.

"Here."

The girl with blonde ringlets down to her shoulders grunts as she gets out, door still open, and climbs in the back to change her clothes.

"Why didn't you just leave it in those plastic things?" Loki doffs her shorts.

"Since Vampires prefer to drink from humans, tearing into those things would be like an insult. It's sort of just to make them happy so they are less likely to eat you and the others."

Ganesha plops down next to Cricket just as he retrieves a sketch pad and pencil from under the seat—a certain image in his mind; he has pencil and paper stowed in most of the vehicles he has rode in.

The woman in the AC/DC shirt looks back at Ganesha. "I had to make a call to Olsen. He faxed me some information."

"The bad kind?"

She nods. "I was originally going to let you all vote on a fast-food restaurant, but you will have to make due with the nearest one."

Ganesha and the other members of Raven's crew, after living off one-hundred percent real meats, have developed a strong distaste for most of the fast-food chains. No matter the time of day Raven and Jet make sure they are served a real home cooked meal (not noodles and seasoning from a box), but the sacrifices of May tenth have stolen the hours of time.

"Girl, I have been hungry since I dropped you off at the airport. I am not opposed the nearest gas station right now." The bag of potato chips had done very little for her.

Loki closes the backdoor, and with Ganesha having taken the seat next to Cricket and Lana she is forced to sit upfront next to the thing she loathes. Raven.

They begin pulling away from the increasing amount of vehicles entering the lot…

~~~

Chapter 14
The Last Supper

THE LAST SUPPER.

That is how the young blonde mechanic feels.

The man (sometimes Werewolf) that looks to be Lucas's age had taken care of the body and blood so as not to expose it anyone while he helped Sheba with the food preparations. Lucas and the provocatively dressed girl had done a little bit of flirting while they stood next to the stove.

"Usually, I like panties," he winked at her, reliving his paralyzing experience that caused him to see up a zombie's skirt.

Sheba leaned in close to him and rubbed her palm up and down his chest. "*My* panties are red." She seductively bit her lower lip.

Lucas pressed his thin lips against hers. Then he quickly pulled back and asked for her age, and when she said nineteen he went back to kissing her. But then he suddenly pulled back again. "Whoa. Sorry. Normally I would not do this, but I'm *not* getting naked with zombies running around." "What makes you think we were going to have sex?" She asked with a half-smile and strutted away from him.

And now forks scrape against matching orange plates; the color stands out in the dull room.

Lucas and the others sit in more uncomfortable silence. No one really knows how to have a conversation with impending doom lingering in the air, like the gatekeepers of Heaven having just announced they are no longer taking submissions.

A breeze enters through the massive hole stirring the air but doing little to bring down the increased temperature. They had been able to hear the hum of the air unit until Sheba switched it off.

"How do you explain to someone like Luke and me unexpected electrocution?" Leon inquires halfway through his meal.

Sheba shoves the last bite of her food in between her red lipstick lips. "Normals are rarely present."

"Some know," Cole admits. "A few family members and friends. Loki is the only friend that knows about me and Lana."

"If crucifixes scare off vamps, then why doesn't everyone wear 'em?" Alec interjects. With a significant portion of the wall missing, the sirens of a fire truck in the distance are easily heard.

"A peewee cross doesn't do much." Cole shoves his fork into the small pile of beef and noodles on his bright orange plate.

"One of ya said that Vampires tend to sleep in

and travel by rivers and oceans. Why not just bless it?"

"It? The ocean? A Kardashian ass of holy water?" Lucas laughs at Alec's absurdity. "You think there is a Priest that powerful? And you're the first puberty kid to think of a strategy that easy? What world are you livin' in, man?"

The faded sirens of the fire truck are now replaced with the *whoop whoop* of a police car. There is not a thought in the room that doesn't wonder if the emergency is zombie related.

"They are here," Jet randomly announces, and the silence once again ensues.

Cole wonders if Raven did anything to his friends; bite, torture them?

Lucas and Leon become nervous...

Cricket is the first one they hear stepping on the ruble through the noticeable hole in the cross-filled room. The young man with a smooth head and a smile like that of a baby walks over to Sheba and hands her the white piece of paper in his hands. She unfolds the thin sheet. "Ha! I like it. It tickles my soul!"

Cole becomes intrigued. "May I see?" The artist snatches the comical image of a bug-eyed Loki trapped underneath a Werewolf from Sheba's hands. "That means no," Sheba needlessly translates and reaches up to hug her friend.

"Secrets don't make friends," Lucas says.

Cricket shrugs him off and takes his seat under the candles mounted on the wall.

"He doesn't care."

"Thanks," Lucas says with false gratitude. "I've never seen a shoulder move up and down. What you can tell me is why the lack of vocalization and why *you* answer?"

"He is mute, Luke. I suspect they all answer for him."

It suddenly makes sense to Lucas and his mouth parts in disbelief. He looks to Leon for help. Realizing there is no way out of this, Lucas shakes his head at his own ignorance. "I'm a tool," he sighs.

Before now, Sheba use to think it did not take a high I.Q to figure out Cricket is not just a quiet, taciturn guy. "I guess it does take a genius," she snickers and crosses her exposed legs.

With his back to the newly made entryway, Lucas's embarrassment by his arrogance shoots straight up when he hears four individuals moving around on what use to be a porch. He instantly fears who heard what. *You've got to be kidding me!*

"Jet, remodeling is not your forte," Raven nods at the damage; Mozart by her side. Finished with his meal, the tallest man in the room stands, holding out his arms. "My favorite smart ass!"

Raven wraps her arms around his neck and Jet embraces her small, fine waist.

Leon quickly looks away and stabs a saucy noodle.

Lucas feels his ears becoming very warm, and he watches Jet's hands like a hawk. *Bigger muscles…expensive ride. Fuckface,* he secretly calls him. Lucas tugs at his warm earlobe.

Sheba stands up and puts her arms around Ganesha's neck. "It's like a G-rated orgy," Lucas bitterly remarks as Sheba and Jet switch hugging partners.

"Um, excuse me?" Ganesha pulls away from Jet. "We may not be blood related but we *are* family." Jet and Sheba rub the top of the Husky's head and scratch behind his ears. Then the Shadow in the miniskirt starts gathering the empty plates.

Cole whispers in his friend's ear, "Lana, are you—"

"Yes." She looks up at him knowing what has been on his mind. "She didn't eat us. Obviously."

"Are you hungry?"

"We ate on the way back."

"Aren't you gonna ask what happened, and if we're okay?" Alec whines the same way a spoiled child does who thinks they are earth's axis.

The way the Goddess looks at the teenage adult… For a moment the certified genius thinks he sees a dark spark of…hate. But then it quickly disappears, leaving Leon wondering if he imaged the whole thing…

"I can smell your okayness," Raven jokes.

Lucas is surprised by Raven's causerie. He never thought she would make up words. And now she seems…human. The mechanic shop owner sees the woman he saw earlier today. Lucas replays the moment where the awe-inspiring beauty rubbed her hands on his lower abdomen and practically on his penis. Lucas tugs at his earlobe again.

"We can see what happened," an insulted Ganesha snaps at Alec.

Lucas rises from the chair and pretends to stretch his arms while he slyly sticks out his firm, brawny chest. Leon locks his jaw and narrows his eyes up at his cousin.

Two or three flies have easily made their way inside the dining room. "We should cover the windows and that" —Raven points to what is left of her wall— "perforation."

Perforation? Sometimes I wish I had paid attention in school. Lucas, then, remembers all the fun times he had in the girl's bathroom. *Yeah, right. Give that up?* He leans down and whispers to Leon, "What's perforation?"

"A hole," the genius answers with irritation in his voice. "A hole made in something!"

"Did you make a perforation for your tampon?"

Sheba returns the dirty dishes to the kitchen while the others with supernatural hearing abilities turn to the cousins. Leon shakes his head, dismissing the insult. A helicopter suddenly flies overhead, rumbling the floor. The plates and cups in the sink and cabinets vibrate, clanking together.

They wait for the helicopter to pass.

"I know vamps are coming because of you." Lana sympathizes with Raven. She would be terrified if hundreds of *anything* were coming for her. "But wouldn't they help us with Normals being their food?"

"In theory. But in my experience anything with a mouth can lie and plot."

"Especially them," Lana agrees. "They are unpredictable."

A fly lands on Alec's shoulder as Jet and Cricket

exit into the hallway.

The girl with the nose ring whom Lucas previously kissed returns from the kitchen and puts her hands on the table. "Up." Everyone gets out of Sheba's way. She holds the heavy table up on one of its shorter sides. The remaining three legs that didn't break when Sheba hurled it against the wall begin cracking off, with little effort under Cole and Lana's fingertips.

"Tornado?" Alec reminds them, swatting at the fly on his shoulder.

"The future. Zombies in the present," Raven brings to his attention.

A cat meows somewhere near the damaged porch and Mozart's ears perk up, not having chased anything in a few days.

Sheba picks up the thick brown table by herself and slaps it over the massive hole—creating a vast empty space between the now standing group. A disappointed look captures the dog's face. "Sorry, boy," Ganesha pouts, sticking out her bottom lip.

Jet and Cricket return with hammers and nails.

"If the plan is to fight then why do we need nails?" asks Loki. "Is it just you and the Shadows that are fighting now or something?"

"Yes," Raven answers.

"Hell no!" Lucas immediately protests. The Hunter did not travel across the country just to sit inside someone's house. He does not desire facing more flesh eating zombies, but if Lucas wanted to stay in a box he would have kept on driving to his own rectangle house in Tennessee.

"You can't make that decision," Leon confronts

her.

"You have your free will," the half-Vampire undeniably says, her eyes speaking as if they hold all the galaxy's secrets, as if she knows more about free will and how it works than the humans among her. "I will be back for anyone choosing to stay."

Lucas is averse to the thought of him sitting out of a war for mankind while a woman, who is not entirely human, fights for *his* life. "I'm killing shit!"

"Me, too." Leon folds his arms, refusing to budge from his decision.

"I won't leave my friends," Loki sincerely says, much to Sheba and Cricket's surprise. They had pegged her as the type to abandon her friends when needed most.

The pimpled-faced boy shrugs, "I'll fight."

"Ganesha?" The sagacious leader questions the teenager in the sparkling white long-sleeved shirt. Raven loves this shirt. She thinks her friend looks beautiful in it.

"Do not go down this road with me, girl. You have been trying to convince me to hide since Nebraska."

Loud pounding sounds caused by Jet and Cricket hitting metal against wood advert the relatives' attention. "If no one is staying then what's with the *Night of the Living Dead* craftsmanship?" Lucas nods.

His awe-inspiring beauty in the icy blue shirt takes a deep breath. Raven knows she must tell them what they do not want to hear. "The Shadows have been given a target to eliminate." She takes several steps forward into the center of the circle, her heavy hair drapes down both sides of her slender neck. Raven looks Lucas dead in the eyes and does not withhold the truth. "Their Connections and my Orders may cause us to depart from you at any given time."

"Then why did we come here!" Alec shouts, his face pink.

The hammering noises cease and everyone, disarrayed by the unexpected outburst, remains still like a standing puddle of water that needs more than a languid breeze to get it moving.

Leon finally steps forward out of the circle, moving closer to Raven. "Because I saw her," he defends his decision to come to Concordia, Kansas.

"Oh, because you saw *her*," the teenage boy repeats with thick mockery in his tone. "Well news flash pal, *you saw her dead*." His palms form into tight fists. "And she is standing here telling you that *her* and *her* supercharged buds are leaving us to kill *Vampires* instead of *zombies* who are trying to kill *us*!" Alec yells at the top of his lungs.

With his arms still crossed, The Preventer glares down. "When did I become your pal?"

"You were not listening to what she said." Lucas, now sitting on the bench, leans forward and looks up at the ill-tempered boy. "Why would she come back for dead bodies? You could stay your uncontrollable-teenage-raged-ass tucked away inside a hidey-hole while the rest of the world is slaughtered. And when it's over the real men," he happens to glance at Raven's butt, "and woman—women can return to save you from a strong wind."

"I assume you have a backup place in mind?"

Leon asks the Goddess standing in front of him. She nods.

"I-I-I," Alec stutters. "Sorry." The glares from the others make him incredibly nervous. "Where is the bathroom?"

Raven, having stood with her back to the boy, now pivots and walks up to him. The vampiric woman stonily stares at him. "You are a guest in this house and I am the owner. I will leave whenever to do whatever I please."

The intimated recipient of hospitality feels his throat becoming very dry.

"Cricket, will you please show him to the owner's restroom? And take the pistol from him."

The eighteen-year-old boy is about to follow the quiet Shadow who took the pistol Lucas lent him when Raven calls his name. "Alec." He turns around to find himself no longer looking into the eyes of a human; fear causes him to hold his breath.

"I put one person in their place today," the living Vampire reminds him. Her intense eyes causing him to feel as if she is using them to rip his insides out from his boney body. "When you return I will put *you* in *your* place."

Alec gulps, and lets Cricket guide him down the hallway of wooden crosses.

Raven faces the group, eyes normal; hazel. "There is something you all have a right to know. You may want to take a seat."

Everyone except Jet and Sheba, who remain standing, arrange the chairs closer together to fill the wide empty space left behind by the dining room table.

"Are we goin' to wait for ballsy-pimples?" Lucas asks.

"Yes."

"I-I, um," Loki hesitates. "Don't want to be outside, but um—"

"Speak," Raven coaxes her.

"Vampires feed off us, and you feed on them. I feel that you are only helping us because you have to and not out of the goodness of your heart."

"Then you're not using your brain, sweetheart," Lucas says to the girl across from him.

Lucas speaking against her makes Loki feel as if she has been stabbed in the heart.

"Her cravings would be mad with them gone. But she can't die. I bet the Vampire inside would eventually turn to the human part." *She would drink her own blood*, Lucas tries not to think about the gross and twisted scenario.

"Without Vampire blood her powers would be limited," the genius explains, "but it wouldn't matter with us and the Vampires being dead. She would need what we need. Food. Which I suspect she consumes from time to time. And Animal blood couldn't hurt."

"Sucks to be severally weakened though," Lucas admits.

"What about your God?" Alec ridicules as he and Cricket return; the mute Shadow had stopped in the hallway to switch the cool air on.

"I would not be the first to disobey, and turn against man," Raven counters. "Do you concur, Alec?"

"Sure."

"Do you agree that you have turned against them?" she nods at the group in front of her.

"What are you talkin' about?"

"Kronos and his device you put on the cousins' car" —Raven turns to Lucas and Leon— "Which I love by the way." "Thanks," they say while grinning like two school girls receiving a compliment from a crush.

"How could I possibly know who that is when I just found out about Vampires?" Alec protests.

His words trigger an event for Leon. "Yes, how could you? What was the question you asked after Raven said, 'You are a descended of Kronos.'?"

"I know what he said." Ganesha quotes, " '*What? The Vampire?*' "

"I assumed he was a vamp. So what?"

"Two nights ago, I received a vision of Kronos meeting with the maker of their kind," Raven recounts to the others sitting down in the spacious room; with a great section of the floor being uncovered the crosses seem to have multiplied. "Kronos said, '*The extinction of Raven will be my greatest honor. Thank you, Father.*' I did not know what the object was that he was given…then."

Raven takes a deep breath, knowing what she is about to reveal next is truly horrific.

"What Kronos obtained is out there in those walking dead bodies."

Jet, Sheba, Ganesha, and Cricket knew of Raven's vision, but they would have never foreseen a Vampire being responsible for the eradication of the human race; their only means of survival.

Puzzled, Cole asks, "The zombies? Why would—"

"Please hold all questions," Jet raises his arm. "Let her finish."

"Lana said that when she encountered Kronos last night," Raven begins, "he was feasting—"

"Oh, my god!" Lana suddenly squeals. "He-he, Cole, Lee wasn't dead!"

The once orphaned Shadow looks from Lana to Raven for answers.

"No," confirms their leader. "He was the first to be injected. A test."

"There is no way she can know that!" Alec intervenes.

Cricket quickly and angrily places a hand over Alec's mouth and wraps his left arm around the interrupting mans mid torso, pinning Alec's forearms to his side forcing him to be stationary and soundless.

"Obviously it worked," she continues. "But Kronos needed a way for it to spread rapidly. And a way to me. Alec was, and is, that way." Raven spins a chair around and sits down with her chest against its backside facing the group. Her hair being pulled to one side, exposing her slim neck, arouses Lucas, Leon and Jet. "Lana, tell them about your first experience with Alec."

"He came close to hitting Cole and me with his station wagon. At the time we didn't know who he was, but when he got in the car with us at the border Alec admitted that the reason he was supposedly going so fast was because his relative needed a doctor."

"The person in that car *was* a doctor, an infected doctor Alec purposely delivered," Raven divulges. "Today when I was on an airplane I encountered a man who told me that he saw a police officer being pulled out of a green wagon. When he stopped to help the officer the man attacked. I believe Alec was to transport him to the police station but the change happened too soon.

"When Jet transformed earlier during Loki's yelling I heard a faint ring. Now I believe it to be Alec's phone ringing once, signaling our enemy. He may speak," Raven nods to Cricket.

Cricket releases Alec. The accused boy presses his teeth together. "That was my niece!! She needed a doctor!!"

Niece. Nephew. Devin. Kimberly... He's still in the tan wagon, Leon recalls the dead girl's words. *Red-green color deficiency.* "Kimberly saw you, Alec. The girl I had to kill. She saw you at the gas station."

"Wait a minute..." Lucas thinks back. "Yeah...she mumbled something about a tan wagon. She had this thing with colors. If she couldn't see green then..."

"Kimberly would have seen brown or tan depending on the shade of green."

What did my eyes look like from her perception? Lana immediately feels guilty for thinking about herself when her focus should be on Alec.

Raven pulls out folded sheets of paper from her back pocket. "Olsen faxed these to me at the hospital when we were on our blood-run." She tosses the dossier to the older cousin.

"Who is Olsen?" Leon asks. He had wanted to inquire earlier but hadn't the opportunity.

The messenger of deplorable information shakes her head causing her blonde strands to fall around her oblong face. "Not important right now."

"You haven't had family since your balls got bigger." Lucas looks up from the papers containing Alec's photo and background information. "And damn they must be the size of a Werewolf's paw, you shameless bastard. What do you get out of this deal? Kronos promise you immortality?"

"Cause guess what I got out of this!" The Hunter screams. "I got to watch my cousin watch a little boy have the life taken out of him!" Lucas stands and very heatedly throws his chair against the wall. Mozart lets out an alarmed bark as it bounces to the floor.

"This is happening because of you." Lucas makes a dash for Alec.

Leon stands up to stop him from beating the teenager to a bloody pulp but Raven has vanished from her seat and puts her hands against Lucas Kale's chest, preventing him from advancing. "People are dying out there!" he continues yelling at the teenage boy responsible for helping to eradicate his own kind—the reason an innocent little boy had to die.

"Kale," Raven calmly says his name. He looks down at her, madness and certitude dominating his young eyes. "If it wasn't him it would have easily been someone else."

Lucas's burning eyes of hate look directly into

Alec's timorous eyes. "I've done some messed up things. But I am positive there is a reserved spot for you in hell right next to Satan's fat dildo, you son of a bitch."

Raven turns around, facing her shameless houseguest. "I do not kill humans, so I cannot leave you outdoors. With Loki it was different. She *is* worthy of protection by a dog. For your safety I think it best you be moved to another room for the time being."

"I didn't do anything," Alec defends himself again. Cricket takes him by the arm, once again heading for the dark hall.

"Oh, and Alec," Raven adds. "Since Kronos failed to tell you that blood is not the only thing we can smell, well, he never had any plans to let you live forever. In case you do not comprehend let me clarify. It is impossible to lie to a Vampire."

"You're the liar! I had no part in this! She's a *Vampire*! She's going to betray you all!"

Cricket drags Alec away by his scrawny arm. Swallowing his sadness and resentment to maintain his loyalty to his best friend by not killing Alec where he stands, Cricket shoves the betrayer inside the Comfy Room.

"That disease is meant to kill what I protect. I imagine they will only rescue enough to subsist on, and the rest is my punishment for helping humans." Raven looks at Jet. "For choosing not to be with those more like myself."

Jet presses her narrow shoulders against his chest and abdomen and strokes her back. Every century or so their enemy tries to persuade the woman he deeply cares for to abandon the feeble species. In exchange, a Vampire would willingly sacrifice him or herself as a meal to the Goddess. She would be their leader—not Kronos.

"Three nights ago a Vampire came with a new message," the man dressed in all black tells the humans from Tennessee and Nebraska. "Either Raven would accept her place as the true Goddess of the world or she could watch the weaker species be just that. Weak."

Biting his nails, Leon takes a spot on the bench. Lucas, thinking about picking up one of the rifles they had placed next to them upon their first entrance into the windowless room and beating Alec, joins him.

"I do not know how or if it works on Shadows," Raven admits to Cricket as he returns to the intense atmosphere.

"Ray," Sheba says making her way past the others. "We can handle ourselves." She stands next to Cricket and they join forces in staring their friend down, daring Raven to challenge them.

The worried leader turns away and meets Ganesha brown eyes. *She is not a Shadow. She is a Normal. A human.*

"The comfy has three windows. Two tables," Ganesha states avoiding her best friend's concerns.

Raven knows her only option, aside from chaining Ganesha up, is to accept the decision her youngest but capable friend has made. "We will use the bathroom doors." She glances at her dining table that is being used to cover up Jet's indubitable exit. "Jet, get your other half. His senses are better."

* * *

There are two laptops, a couch, an air hockey table, and two pinball machines in The Comfy Room. The four walls are covered by thick, red curtains like at a movie theatre. When Lana had commented on the absences of crosses in the room, Raven lifted up a corner of the red carpet showing that it isn't attached and they had been standing on the same pattern of lowercase T shapes that cover the floors and walls of the kitchen, dining room, and hallway. Then Raven lifted back the curtain—more Vampire repellent.

The Comfy Room is the only room that shows signs of normality. And the only signs of life displayed in the five bedrooms is the hundreds of painted wooden crucifies; there are no pictures or even windows.

When Lucas and Sheba entered her room—left at the end of the hall, past the restroom and an unidentified room on the right, another left going up the hallway to the first room on the left side—he had asked why. Sheba told him that in their American house safety comes first, and personality is reserved for their real home with Ray and Olsen. She had not said where their real house was and he assumed overseas.

There are two pieces of furniture in the windowless room; a bed with a few articles of clothing on it and a small dresser with a mirror attached. "We do not stay here for a lengthy amount of time, so why have a view anyway? This place is only meant as a backup plan incase our home is discovered."

The younger girl also told him that when they pulled up (all three at the same time) they had come from Ganesha's grandmother's—the only one of them with family in North America; the Normal has a mother, but refuses to see the evil woman. Sheba had video chatted with her own parents.

They had taken separate cars in case something unforeseen happened; Raven saw Lucas and Leon and the others arriving here so they raced back. Raven and she, by being the passenger, had won. And since passengers are able to win they can lose as well, hence Ganesha, Jet, and Cricket owing then each a hundred dollars.

"You don't sound foreign."

"Es tut mir leid," the exotic girl said with a thick German accent. "I am sorry," she translated, and then she told him she was born in Germany but only her father comes from there. "It is easy for us to learn languages and change our accents. It helps us blend in."

The Shadow also told him that if he mentions to anyone about their home she would tie him up. But not in the way he would have liked.

Now, the exotic and seductively dressed teenager pulls the second door off the bathroom that her and Ganesha share; the first one was yanked from its hinges by Cricket in the restroom across from the Comfy Room, the one Alec previously used.

Sheba lays the door down resting it against her leg and picks up a necklace with thick red jewels from inside a small dresser drawer.

"Who gave you that necklace? Your boyfriend?"

"I've learned a lot from Ray, but I don't see myself giving up friends with benefits." Sheba touches the heavy necklace remembering what she has left behind in another country. "It is my mother's."

She turns to face the older man with the same hazel eye color as Raven. "I am highly experienced with sex, yes. Friends, not strangers. I have been doing it since I was seventeen. Contrary to popular theories—absentee father, needs attention, blah, blah—my parents are happily married and give me lots of attention. They are lovely people.

"I understand the name, Sheba, is associated with lust. But it is only a name. It is true, with my exotic skin I am the object of lust for most men. However, I do not lust over them. I simply have sex with my friends because it is human. Being a Shadow, fighting, in my case every day, you miss out on what the humans, the Normals, do. I *do* use sex to make myself feel better. It is the one thing I can participate in that everyone does at some point in time. And it feels great."

Sheba runs her fingers over the red jewels. "This necklace has been passed down by the women in my family from generation to generation. A month ago my mother was diagnosed with stage four breast cancer. I suspect she will die within a few days if not tonight."

"Why are you telling me this?"

"Mr. Kale—" that freaks him out— "you should know the world you have entered. What it means to be a Shadow; a Shadow following Ray. Even being a Normal such as Ganesha. Being friends with her…

"By accepting Ray's help you, yourself, have given something up. When you survive this zombie ordeal, my Similars and the Vampires here are never going to forget your face—Leon's, too. You are targets."

"Shadows can kill humans?"

"There are those that believe the penalty for aiding a Vampire is and should be death. These are the only cases Normals have died without our kind receiving punishment. If we kill an innocent, though, then the sentence is death."

The girl in the plaid skirt picks the door up, and kisses Lucas on the cheek leaving a light red lip print. "You seem genuinely interested, but at this point in time we aren't exactly friends—"

"Not looking for that," he interrupts. "Flashy smug muffin." When it comes to sexual relationships he draws the line at friends with benefits. Nothing good can come from that Lucas believes.

"Then Loki's your type." The seductive girl walks away with the door and adds over her shoulder, "Even though Raven stimulates you."

Did she really just say that?

* * *

There is less than an hour until sunset.

Leon Carmany anxiously sits with Raven and Ganesha at the square table brought from the game room to the dining area. The Werewolf lays on the lumpy floor next to Raven. His gigantic body is a foot taller than her head. Mozart is curled up into a ball next to his master's feet.

"I get a vision—Prevention—every week," Leon proudly says. Raven can tell that even though it physically hurts him Leon enjoys saving people. "How many Orders do you get?"

This has been the question she has been avoiding. The Vampire Goddess hesitates, sitting down the half disassembled rifle the newcomers brought that she has been cleaning. "Somewhere between nine and fifteen."

"A week?" he asks impressed. "Wow!"

"A day."

He briefly coughs, choking on his own spit.

Not only does she worry about Leon feeling like his job—his gift—is now somehow less important, but she feels bad that he is the only one in pain.

"What happens if I have more Preventions?" Leon secretly fears what will happen if he loses his senses amongst the terrifying creatures. And what it will mean not only for her but for his cousin and the rest of the world.

"You will not." Raven does not want to share her knowledge with him. *What good will it accomplish if he knows the truth?* But she knows Leon has a right to know, after all he did come in search of her. "Well," she intently looks into his blue sapphire eyes, "you should pray for that not to happen."

Leon's heart skips a beat. *What on earth is she talking about?*

"Your Preventions are momentarily causing Labyrinthine disease."

Ganesha stops carving the sharp, tan form of Vampire execution and gazes sympathetically at him.

"Since you are a Veterinarian and a genius you should know what that means," Raven softly finishes.

"Malfunction of the inner ear." *The after effects have gotten worse today.* He has had every symptom: deafness, tinnitus, vertigo, nausea, vomiting, and blurred vision. *I even fell...*

"I must warn you. By having one today or more than one on the same day will cause you to have Menier's disease."

"It might be years, but in the end there will be total destruction of my hearing…"

~~~

Chapter 15
X Marks the Spot

LUCAS, SHEBA, LANA, COLE, and Cricket are having some fun before facing the fight—the fight not only for their lives, but for those humans who have not yet become infected by the creatures that Kronos had a hand in making.

They are trying to forget that tomorrow is Mother's Day.

While the five assisted in covering the glass the part German girl, with Cricket's permission—the Tennessean saw Sheba whispering and the dark-skinned boy nodding in response—told them that although Cricket became a Shadow at the age of sixteen he has been living with Raven and Olsen since he was fifteen. Five years.

Sheba proceeded to tell them Cricket thinks parts of Africa, his birthplace, are very beautiful. But when they have missions there he does not travel to the continent.

Lucas does not know why Cricket suddenly felt the need to share. But he thought it was a good idea (even if it was not much and it was through someone else). The curious man wanted to ask Cricket why he profoundly refused to set foot on the land. But if the mute man had wanted them to know Lucas would have been informed and he wouldn't be wondering why in the first place.

"When did you move in?" Lucas asks the girl whom he had a brief kissing session with.

"Two years ago. Ganesha came a year later."

Sheba sends another black disc across the white table. Lucas is once again unable to stop it from entering his slot. Lucas knows he is going to lose the air hockey game. But the eye candy is still enjoyable; legs, miniskirt, boobs in a spaghetti-strap shirt—it is an easy distraction from his Uncle Joe and his daughter Rachel.

Uncle Joe had welcomed his siblings' kids into his home after Avy Sinanna killed them. It had meant a lot to Lucas and Leon; their aunt died from an infection after giving birth to Rachel. Their uncle has never remarried.

Along the wall Lana and Cricket eagerly move the joysticks around on the pinball machines. Lana watches Cricket with desire in her apple green eyes like a child having seen the stars in the night sky for the first time. Cricket looks away from his game and smiles delightfully at her. She smiles back.

Cole observes their zealous behavior. Jealousy shatters the buoyancy in his eyes, as if he was sitting on the smooth sands of the beach enjoying the light breeze ready to dive into the soothing and calm water but having waited too long; the breeze grew stronger, the colors in the sky shaded over the light glow, and the waters swayed to the rhythm of a different song.

Sitting in a red and white swirl patterned chair at the end of the table facing the covered windows, Alec writes on a yellow sticky note with a black sharpie:

Raven is crazy. Vampires need us. Why kill off their food source?

He slides the small multicolored square pad to the right.

Loki reads the dark inked words. She takes the top sticky note off and rips it into several pieces. Gripping the marker in between her fingers, she writes on the tiny slip of orange paper with her left hand:

When this is over no Vampire is going to tell us what to do.

* * *

"So, tell me something most people don't know about you," Lucas says as he sits down across from Raven, joining her, Leon, and the others in the dining room.

Raven loads the rifle she was previously cleaning. "I am O-Negative," she says, not really taking an interest in his way of starting a conversation, and Leon slyly smiles.

"Where are you from—originally?" the Veterinarian asks.

"Overseas. I do not fancy talking about my birthplace."

He frowns. He has been met with the same success as his cousin. *But hey, I doubt she told him he was husband material. Bond with that, Luke.*

The man with the small chickenpox scar above his eyebrow does not give up. "Do you sleep?"

Lucas strikes a nerve.

Raven places the rifle on the table, he can almost feel the heat radiating off from her eyes. "I sleep one day out of the month. Not an entire day, just eight hours. I hate it. I often wake up crying. For eight hours I am reminded that I belong nowhere and everywhere. I am not human. I am not Vampire. I belong to neither species, yet when I awake my destiny is to repeatedly travel the Earth favoring the humans while I kill the blood that helped make me what I am in the first place."

She wraps her golden hair down over her busty breasts. "Not the heartfelt story you were searching for, Kale? I have another one. In my teen years I had a brother. But thanks to the Blending, which lasted a long time, he became trapped in another dimension. When I was finally able to get him out before the Banish, someone, a human someone, decided he needed to die."

The Immortal Vampire leans closer to the table. "How's this for closeness? I nearly accepted the offer from the Vampire." Raven leans back in her chair. "Would it matter if I did? Sure I save Humans from vamps every day, but in the end do they not die? You know that God who you say will not rearrange his plans just to suit you? I do not give a crap what his plans are. My only hope is that I will soon be rewarded for helping carry them out."

She intertwines her fingers and places them in front of her on the table. "Some of your kind do not believe in God. Now, you should pray there is one and that His plans, original or rearranged, include my belief always in the Heavenly Creator." She leans forward again, their hazel eyes still locked. "Because if I think, even for one second, there might not be one… Well, what do you think will happen, Kale?"

Lucas contemplates this for a moment. "I think everything you say is going to turn me on."

Leon lets out an angry sigh and hopes Raven rips Luke apart (not literally). Instead, the girl from his Prevention smiles and says, "I think you are right."

The young man coveting quickly wants to stop whatever is happening between Luke and the girl who takes his breath away. "Who created the Vampires?"

The Werewolf snorts in what sounds like disgust. Raven stops smiling and sharply turns to the young man who saw her before he meet her. "They call him Father. I believe here in America you call him Satan. Or the Devil."

"Satan? And you said you saw Kronos meeting with him?"

"You know what the Devil looks like?" Lucas asks intrigued.

"I saw black energy. That is it."

Ganesha, having been silent, finally speaks. "Want to know something else? Today is her birthday *and* anniversary of becoming Immortal."

They do not know how to respond to that.

"What is Cricket's story?" The man who had one of his favorite shirts ruined today pries. "He's got the whole Silent Bob thing going on. Silent Cricket. Never heard of one of those." He laughs at his own joke.

No one joins in. The air in the sunless room becomes still and uneasy.

The ringing sound of a cell phone breaks the silence.

"Cricket has no problem communicating with me," Raven tells him while she retrieves the phone from her pocket. "Olsen. Yes, the American is a traitor," she says into the receiver with a British accent. She exits the room and Jet follows; in human form to avoid further damage to the house.

It has been a while since Lucas Kale had his foot in his mouth—especially in front of a girl he seeks more than just sex from—and admits to himself it is not a pleasant taste.

Satisfied that Luke's joke did not strike a big hit with Raven, Leon stands and watches the Vampire

Goddess and Jet disappear around the corner at the end of the hall. Leon opens the door to the Comfy Room, and Mozart, tail wagging, bounces in behind him.

"There *is* a reason why Cricket does not speak. I see what you are trying to do here. You are trying to get on her good side by being the funny man. I get it I do. But you won't be making her laugh at Cricket's expense." Ganesha sits down in Raven's former spot and hands Lucas a dark colored soft drink.

"Is Raven from Britain?"

"No. Ray just likes the accent."

"Who is Olsen and what does he want?"

"An update. And Ray's boyfriend."

"Nesha!" Sheba disapprovingly says her nickname, given by the Shadow herself, from the dim-lit hall.

The tall blonde takes a sip from his soft drink. "Boyfriend, huh? For how long?"

Ganesha leans over the table, closer to him. "Why? You jealous? Huh? Huh? Huh?" She pops her head from side to side. Sheba, standing between her friend and Lucas, laughs so hard that her body rocks. Lucas may have thought the scene to be funny if it were not him getting the third degree. "Uh, no," he answers, backing away from the interrogation.

"Liar," the girl in the long white sleeve shirt calls his bluff. "He is not her boyfriend," Ganesha suddenly confesses and then adds, "If you are going to worry your pretty little head, then you shouldn't waste time over Olsen. Ray would pick Jet before she would pick him."

Lucas looks back and forth at the two teenagers. "Listen. One, I don't know if that such a good thing. Secondly, yeah, I will absolutely admit that I am attracted to Raven. "Look," he leans forward, "you can be on the Lucas/Raven bandwagon—even though Vampires don't go with us—but for me today is about survival. I don't usually make *wise* decisions, but today just doesn't seem like a great day to start dating."

But Lucas Kale sure wants to.

* * *

"Cricket, we've been doing this for five minutes," Lana says grinning from ear to ear. The black disc shoots across the smooth surface only to be smacked back her direction.

"The first one to score wins," Cole grates, quite bored of the air hockey game and tired of Lana flirting with the other Shadow.

Cricket once again blocks Lana's shot from advancing into his slot.

How does he feel about my face? She pushes the thought away, and grins, "Cricket, it's time to accept your defeat." He takes his hand off the white stopper. "Wait! It isn't *winning* if you *let* me!" Suddenly the stopper is in his hands and the black circle slides in her unguarded slot.

Lana raises her hands up, accepting defeat. "Fine." The word *fine* instantly causes her to think about her mother inside their basement in Hastings, Nebraska. *I hope she's still there and FINE.*

"Did you do it?"

The three of them turn to Leon sitting at the table

with Loki and Alec; he had been allowed in the red curtain room on the terms of him promising to not kill the younger male.

"Do what?" Alec asks.

"You know what," Leon says sitting in the chair next to the scrawny boy.

Cricket pulls out the only available chair, next to Loki, at the four person table.

"What did you come over her for?" Alec asks the silent man. "To intimidate me into a false confession? How can I be afraid of someone who can't even speak?"

"You were scared of those girls," Leon reminds him of the zombies on the porch; the reason why Jet destroyed the house.

Alec ignores him. "You gonna turn and eat me Cricket? Nah. You seem a little gay to me. Is that what's wrong with your throat?"

In the dining room, Jet's head instantly rises from the floor. Raven quickly slaps her palm down on his neck and grabs a hand full of thick dark blue fur. "Let Cricket have his pride."

"She can hear you," whispers Loki, warning the insolent boy to the left of her in The Comfy Room.

"So? I don't think I care. Supposedly I'm responsible for a lot of dead people, and have they done anything to me?" Alec gloats.

Leon's face is bright red. His palms squeeze together as his elbows dig into the table. His temper rising. "You're getting close," Cole warns.

Lana looks at the crass boy, trying to understand. "How could you kill your friends, Alec?"

"You let people sling your *friend* Loki around so

don't talk to me about friends, you ugly bitch."

The table knocks Alec in the chest with a force that sends him landing on his backside.

The silent, reticent man stands over him. He snatches the Normal up by his arms and drags him away from the table. Cricket looks at Leon and nods at Alec's feet. The Shadow whistles for Mozart while the blue-eyed, brunette man restrains Alec's legs with his hands. Cricket makes an invisible X with his dark finger across the teenage boy's pimpled face.

"What are you doing!" the impudent boy screams, his free arm nearly strikes the older male in the face. Cricket quickly pins his wrist to the carpet.

And Mozart hikes up a leg.

" 'X' marks the spot," Leon smirks while warm, yellow urine hits Alec in the nose, eyes, and mouth before running down his neck and under the collar of his shirt.

* * *

With less than nineteen minutes (Leon looks at Luke's cheap watch; the hand that counts the seconds is still on number one) before sunset Raven opens the wood door to the formerly unidentified room at the beginning of the second hall to reveal a steel door. She punches in the security code and they walk inside the panic room.

"Mozart's button," Lucas reads on the left wall a sign above a small, black, and round object towards the bottom of the floor. "O…kay."

High end rifles, shotguns, and ammunition line the back wall across from the entrance. The M-16

Sheba had previously disassembled and cleaned, along with Ganesha's and Raven's swords, lay on a small light brown table in the middle of the square area.

Ganesha lends Lana her own sword and slings a rifle over her shoulder while Sheba hands a rifle to Cole. Cricket hands the pistol back over to its owner, and Lucas accepts not wanting to part from his preferred choice of weapon.

"I'll take one of the rifles *we* brought," Loki says not trusting the Vampire.

Raven gives a shotgun to The Preventer. Cricket takes a rifle for himself, and everyone in the room except Lana, Loki, and Alec drapes bandoliers of ammunition across their chests from one shoulder. The two male Shadows and Lana exit the cramped the room.

"What's that for?" Lucas nods at the door on the other side of the small area.

"Do not worry about it, Joe Hardy. Or are you more like Frank?" Ganesha raises her nose up in the air comparing the two. She addles his brain. "Who?" Lucas asks.

"Seriously, dude?" Leon looks at him. "The Hardy Boys? Kid detectives? There is only like fifty-nine or sixty stories about them written by—"

"—Franklin W. Dixon," Ganesha proudly shares her knowledge. "I read the first book as a child. *The only book* I got to read that was not required by the school. My mother said that reading books was for people who thought they were better than everyone else simply because they had money to buy them. I stole that book from a girl on the school bus."

"That's great. You're a thief," Loki shakes her head, passing through the entrance-slash-exit back out into the hallway.

On their way out of the steel and concrete room, Lucas and Leon observe the security cameras...

The only ones remaining in the room are Raven, Sheba, and Alec. Raven sees the artillery, the walls, her friend...and something else...

An image of Alec's head fills the room. He flashes from normal to bloody eyes and a bashed in skull. He swipes at her face... The picture disappears.

"Ray, what is it?" Sheba softly places her hand on the Goddess's shoulder.

Raven stares Alec dead in the eyes. "If you leave with us you will die. You will be the thing you helped distribute."

"Yeah right. I don't believe you, and I'm not staying here. Since you said I made a deal with a Vampire then he should be coming for me, right? I supposedly know of his existence. And according to you he isn't gonna turn me so that leaves the other option.

"So," Alec continues with his eyes on the back wall, "I'm not gonna need those guns or the safety of this stupid house from *zombies.*"

Raven stares blankly down at the table. *He refuses to stay. How can I kill him for something that has not happened, yet? I cannot protect him, Leon, my friends,* and *the other humans.*

Sheba knows what is at stake if her friend does not end the Normal's life. The Shadow also knows what will happen if Raven *does* kill Alec. *Loki will spout it off to every human that wants her dead... We can't have that... Raven will never wash her hands clean... I can't have that.* Sheba picks up the M-16 before Raven can stop her. Alec collapses to the concrete floor; dead. The sound of gunfire echoing wildly in the small space.

Loki is the first one to come rushing back in the room. "What did you do to him!" she demands.

"I saw him. He was a threat and he refused to heed warning," the half-Vampire tells the group gathering once again inside the small room.

"It had to be done," Sheba backs her up, weapon still in hand.

"Liars!" Loki's accusing voice fills the small room. "You just didn't like him!"

"Then why are *you* alive?" Sheba retorts.

"You killed a human so now the other Shadows have to kill *you!*" Loki points at the Shadow.

"We didn't see anything," Lana admits, and Cole adds, "And it doesn't look like any of us have a Connection. Lana and I *do* believe he helped Kronos. Let it go, Loki." Loki crosses her arms in defeat, angrily biting her lip.

"Pretend you do not know about Kronos's plan," their leader says, moving on to more important matters. "We can kill them after we are done using them. Also," Raven addresses the Shadows while she waits by the door for everyone to file out into the hall, "let's see where things take us before you eliminate the Jap. But if others saw her and pursue do not stop them."

Mozart is the last face to approach the entrance. "Stay," she orders him. The dog whines for he knows he is being separated from his family. "If you want to say goodbye to Mozart now is the time," Raven offers her friends.

Ganesha, Sheba, and Cricket huddle around the gray and white Husky. The dog wags his tail and licks their salty faces as they pet him farewell. Then they turn to leave him. Mozart slumps his head down and cuts his eyes upward and whines.

"Wow. That's actually really depressing," Lucas admits.

"Yeah," the Veterinarian agrees, having a soft spot for animals, and tries to cough away the sneaky lump in his throat.

A Werewolf's low howl sounds through the hallway. The dog howls back; their goodbye. Jet is fond of the smaller animal, over the years having acquired brotherly love for the intelligent canine, and understands that neither of them wishes to be separated from their pack.

Cricket walks away with misty eyes. He has left Mozart behind hundreds of times but today is different. Cricket knows—as well as his small four-legged buddy—that there is a chance he will never see their faces again.

Raven hugs her dog and kisses him in between his blue and green eyes. Then she slings Alec's corpse over her shoulder intending to bury the traitor and sadly closes the door. What little light shining in the hall-ways unexpectedly flickers off. Darkness. "Time to change into your party clothes."

The backup generator kicks in, and the residents of the cedar house and its guests mentally prepare for the road ahead of them.

* * *

Lucas and Leon could not be more amazed with the choices of handmade t-shirts.

Sheba displays the band *Citizen Cope*. Ganesha wears a picture of the comedian *Ralphie May*. The Irish band *Flogging Molly* is stretched across Cricket's black shirt in green letters. Raven with her long hair pulled back in to a ponytail wears the name and picture of the MMA fighter *Gina Carano* on her dark blue shirt.

The reason Lucas Kale was up late last night and running behind schedule around lunch today was due to him watching reruns of mixed martial arts fights. "What are you looking at?" Ganesha snaps at the cousins. "Your jaws serve no purpose on the floor," Sheba says passing by Lucas and Leon. She enters the kitchen and stares out the glass door. It will only be seconds before the soothing light abandons them.

Ganesha and Cricket join Sheba, the three of them accepting the possibility that this might be the last time they ever stand together in this spot, witnessing the world spin away from the sun, yet towards it—they are not fools.

The others begin to crowd behind the three of them. Raven turns off the dining room and kitchen lights, and lingers at the rear of the brave group. With the orange light quickly fading several thoughts emerge:

Dear Lord, Ganesha silently prays, *I thank you for the life you blessed me with. Not just the new, but the old life as well, because now I know that the world doesn't suck. Only the idiotic morons.*

Speaking of morons, I know you know I don't like Loki. I don't want her to become a zombie, but heaven forbid if I turn and she lives. Please see to it that that annoying white girl does not get to have sex with Lucas before Raven does. Thank you for this beautiful sunset. Amen.

Sheba does not know if it will be the last sunset she ever sees. But she takes comfort in her training and the lessons Raven taught her—not just the ones involving combat. Then she realizes her mission is the same as it always has been. *Kill or be killed.* The exotic girl smiles.

Dear God, Cricket here. You are the man. You already know what I need. I need to not become a zombie, unless of course that is in your plan. But I must say that sucks. No offense. I love you dearly. If we are to die, please God, don't let Raven blame herself. Please help my family in this room as well as these strangers—even that one I don't like. The light I am fortunate enough to see outside is beautiful. So is the creation standing behind me—Lana—not Cole, just so we are clear. I love you, God. Amen.

Dear God, I hope my mom is alright. I thank you for sending me to Raven. Tonight Kronos dies. Thank you. In Jesus name I pray. Amen. Lana smiles—the orange, yellow glow on the horizon is no match for the light of certitude in her eyes.

God, I don't see how sending us away from our home helps anything. So far the Vampire Goddess hasn't really done much. The only thing I can say for certain is how tired I am of cleaning up after Kronos. He will *pay for this. And after this crap is over I'm going to ask Lana out. God, please don't take her away from me,* Cole silently pleads.

Hey, God. We both know I don't believe in prayer. Life is what it is. But I would like to put in a request, not a prayer. I request that my geeky cousin not turn and I be the one who has to kill him. Also, this sunset is giving me a boner, and it is possible I have an unnatural thing for someone so I want to get to the part where I kill sh-stuff so that I don't turn into Bella Swan. Thanks.

God, it's me, Leon. I cannot recall the last time I watched the sunrise. I cannot recall the last time I told Lucas I love him, and now I can't because he'll think I'm saying goodbye. I also cannot recall the last time I asked you for something, or the last time I simply thanked you. If it is you sending me Preventions then I want to thank you for sending me here. I want to at least live long enough to see the sun rise again. I want Lucas and Raven to be by my side. But I know we can't always get what we want...

The Werewolf watches Raven from inside the dining room; in order for him to pass through the threshold to the kitchen he will have to break his frame into the human bones. *I'm glad she's not like them. She, Mozart, and I are the only ones guaranteed to live. Zombies and Vampires can't kill us. I'm glad you're with me Raven, if only you were with me...*

Loki stares strangely indifferent up at the horizon, the light on the verge of being consumed by darkness. Standing in the middle of Lana and Cole, the malevolent girl with blonde curls and gray eyes takes each of their hands in her own, and wishes death to the former humans. Not just the zombies, but the Vampires as well—including the one standing somewhere behind her.

Raven watches from behind the eight humans with her multicolored eyes a sunset; a sunset that does not look the same to her as it does for the humans or the Wolf. A sunset that tells the Immortal there is a long road ahead of her. *On the bright side, it is not one of those nights were I have to sleep.* Red and blue clouds vanish with the light. "Bring on the night."

~~~~

Chapter 16
Deaths

Night May 10

"WHAT IS THAT smell?" Jet asks with disgust after morphing into his human skin.

Raven waits for the smell to hit her. A few seconds later it does and the odor causes a tightness in the pit of her stomach. "That is…weird," she says, never having smelled a funk like this. "Jet, go outside and change."

"But I can't stand that stench, it makes me want to vomit," he argues. "So vomit," she says, unwilling to negotiate. Jet opens the glass door and the warm air swirling in reminds the Shadows and Normals they are truly in *the* battle for their lives.

The sounds of Jet's bones breaking and growing and his skin stretching are background noise in

Raven's ears to the sound of hundreds of pairs of feet horridly stomping against the ground.

The Werewolf with the dark blue fur coat vomits.

"Can you feel that?" Lana asks, excitement spreading to her bones. Cricket nods. "Power," the word superiorly comes out of the three Shadows' mouths as the four of them smile. "Must be nice," Lucas mutters while their doughty leader leads them outside to face what awaits in the dangerous night.

With only the white glow of the moon to light their path, the ten fighters march down the grass, over the ditch, and into the road. As if cued, Vampires and more Vampires eerily begin to arrive in front of them on Brother Street. Thirty, fifty, eighty, barefoot bloodsuckers cover the vast green land and the road behind their raven-haired leader—the only one wearing a cape—who strides with pride and exultation, as if he has won at something, towards the small group positioned near the parked cars on the blacktop.

The night stalkers that had been born with a fair complexion when they were once human look even more freighting now with the moon reflecting off their pallid skin and their predator eyes clearly defined in the dark.

The numbers keep increasing.

And so does the groups of Shadows running out of the woods and filling in the area behind the Vampire Goddess and those aiding her.

Several gasps erupt from the Shadows at the sight of the giant animal thought to have been extinct and forbidden to exist. Lana, Cole, Sheba, and Cricket Split—their silver rings send a wave of disbelief and angry whispers through the large crowd.

"Kronos," Raven says the leader's name as he comes to a stop at the T-junction. The murmurs from the unhappy crowd behind her cease.

"Raven!" Kronos extends his arms out in a hugging gesture, his dark cape outlined in gold draping down his backside. "It has been centuries."

"Decided to come out of hiding?"

Kronos laughs, dropping his arms to his sides. A young male with light brown hair and a Japanese girl—Lana, Cricket, Sheba, and Cole recognize her as being the one from their Connection—stand on either side of the Vampire with multiple scars on his face.

A green-haired Shadow, Leon assumes to be the leader on that side for she is closest to them, shouts, "Shut up! You!" she points at Raven. "Hell is walking and we deserted our families thanks to *VAMPIRES,*" the word slithers out of her mouth as if it is venom itself. "Do you want to *burn* after we kill your relatives or before we rip apart those traitors for protecting *you* and that *Wolf*?"

"Now, now," Kronos says in the way a father would tell his children to settle down. "Lana belongs to me." Next to the green-haired woman a Similar with a lip ring and thick black hair longer than Raven's sneers, "She betrayed us to help a Vampire. It seems poetic one should kill her."

The word 'poetic' causes the Veterinarian to shiver. *My book of poems... Devin.*

Lana ignores their belligerence. "Why are you

here Kronos?"

"To protect our food, of course."

The Japanese girl dressed in a shimmering, black miniskirt and a dark red shirt that exposes the tops of her small breasts stares at the young man with sapphire eyes and shoulder length hair, running her tongue over her white fangs.

"I cannot control other states, but you will not be feeding or feasting here," Raven warns. "There is blood in the garage."

"How thoughtful of you," Kronos smiles.

"And I am sure you know it is in your best interest all around *not* to hurt the Shadows."

"You may go," he gives his followers permission. At least forty vamps depart and begin making a path through the reluctant crowd of Shadows; enmity and hostility from both sides threatening war. Vampires hiss and snarl in the faces of teenagers, men, and women refusing to step aside. And once the Shadows comply, knowing it's best to have a temporary alliance, the gleaming and twisted smiles of their enemies madden them enough to consider spurning them, rejecting the alliance.

The undead return from the garage, inhumanly running but not near as fast as Raven. Kronos accepts a plastic bottle from the Japanese girl. He unscrews the cap and takes a gulp. "What a shame," he says disgusted with the cold, old blood and revolted by the Goddess's presence amongst the humans.

Lucas observes a bald Vampire standing behind Kronos and the Asian girl for he stands out amongst what Lucas guesses to be two hundred blood suckers... He figures at least that number of Shadows must be behind him.

"Tell me your plan for saving these people," Raven orders. The way she stands—a piousness unlike any other—makes Lucas, Leon, Lana, and Cole feel as if their leader as underestimated her own value. She looks just like a god with her stance and long blonde hair and eyes of colors only she possesses.

"It's simple," the brunette boy to the right of Kronos answers. "Put 'em in their houses or whatever and don't let them get bit." He grins at the irony.

"You remember Blayne?" The scarred leader smiles at his niece.

So he's what happened to Blayne, Lana sums up, keeping her attention on Kronos. He puts his arm around the Japanese girl's shoulders. "And this is—"

"—Amaterasu," she introduces herself and Lucas blurts out, "How in the hell am I supposed to remember—"

"Tokyo," Raven nicknames the girl for the American's benefit. "That is your new name," she smiles. The girl's eyes narrow with antipathy.

"Zombies!" someone at the rear of the human crowd shouts. "My creations will be in your group," Kronos volunteers his novices Blayne and Amaterasu. "Myself and the others will join the Shadows."

A bright orange flame lights the sky.

"Run!" Raven yells. The vamps and Shadows

scatter, not having to be told twice. Raven runs to the left. Lucas, Leon, Sheba, Ganesha, Cricket, Lana, Cole, Loki, Jet, and the Novices of Kronos follow her down Jet Road. A wing from an airplane crashes into the flatland and skids into the purple house demolishing it.

Ganesha recalls her neighbor carrying groceries into the home when she pulled up in the driveway after he drive from Nebraska. She is positive the woman is dead now.

"Down!" Raven, Blayne, and Amaterasu shout to the humans. An airplane wing slices past their heads and lands in the embankment flinging dirt in every direction, a great amount landing on them. Leon and Loki try rubbing away the specks in their eyes, and Lucas and Ganesha cough uncontrollably from the grains they accidently sucked down into their lungs.

But the preternatural beings know there is no time to spare. Cricket, Sheba, Lana, and Cole pull the four Normals up from the dirt and they continue fleeing from the objects falling from the sky. And from the increasing number of club members whose main activity is eating humans while they are still alive.

They near the set of brick houses to their right, and the humans jump at the BOOM behind them. Lucas, Leon, and Raven steal glances over their shoulders. Another part of a plane sits ignited on the land not far from the brick homes, too close to the group for Lucas Kale and Leon Carmany's comfort. The fire brightens the area; the houses, T-junction, and the cars on the street. Suddenly the door on the side of the airplane bursts outward and lands on the ground.

And out walk burning bodies.

"Zombies," Lucas chokes. Within a second, vamps lunge from the rooftops and begin tearing the passengers apart; moving with enough speed to avoid being burned. Another piece from an airplane loudly crashes into the woods behind the living Vampire's house. "Let's go!" Raven orders, satisfied that the Vampires seem to be keeping their word.

Debris and balls of fire land around them. The road veers right, past the last brick house, but they do not go the way Lucas expects. Instead of taking the curve to the right they run straight, stepping over the curb. City lights can be seen from the small hilltop; the part that has electricity—the far away part.

To Lucas the small circles of light feel like giant fireflies luring them in like children on summer nights, only they won't be putting the bugs in jars, rather the humans without special abilities are likely to be the ones captured. The sounds of gunshots and screaming seem to be coming from all directions as they jog down the hill.

A rectangle building stands at the bottom. They draw closer, and a woman runs around the corner of the dull structure. "Let me in! Let me in!" She bangs on one of the doors. Something resembling the unnatural movements of the man Lucas Kale killed in front of Rush Cemetery rounds the same edge of the building, arms horizontal and legs practically dragging across the ground. "Now, you shit!" the woman screams, her voice angry and desperate.

A creature of the night arrives next to the woman and the walking dead man. He bashes the man's brains against the wall. The woman screams as her savior pulls the door off its hinges and takes her away into the lightless building.

The blonde woman with orange, purple, and electric blue eyes has not seen the same scene as everyone else...

"I have been given a Prevention." She knows it is not one of her Orders because the moving pictures happened in her mind—not the way Raven receives her images. The young man with labyrinths disease is speechless—they all are—but he feels grateful. He feels closer to her in this moment than anyone he has ever met. "There is a young teen girl and two teenage boys that must be saved."

Blayne and Amaterasu exchange glances—glances that make Lucas and Leon wish they could break the coalition and stake them right now. They know the Vampires have an agenda.

"You are leaving now," Lucas states. Leon is the only one able to hear the melancholy in his voice.

"No," Raven responds to everyone's surprise. "There are too many dead things, even for me. *We* are going back." They start sprinting up the hill, each wondering what they are likely to witness on their journey to rescuing the three strangers.

Jet makes it to the top first. Ganesha and the owners of the Chevrolet Biscayne are the slowest runners of the group and have to be dragged up the inclined dirt and grass.

Amazingly the street is empty save for fire lit

debris, the Shadows and Vampires must have fought off or are still fighting the rotten and mobile dead, and whatever it was that landed in the middle of the woods has sent it a blaze.

"Sheba, you take Jet's car to the church out of the limits. I need the fifteen year old Jewish boy. Lana, Cole, and Loki you will go with her," Raven instructs. "Jet, Blayne, and Tokyo will play guard."

Not wanting to separate from Raven, Jet roars in protest; what would normally be considered a low roar seems to be extra loud tonight due to the intense life and death ambiance and the humans struggle not to be unnerved by the sound itself. "Do you see Vampires going in that church? Do it," she commands while the three Shadows and Loki get into the black three seat coupe—Loki having to sit on Lana's lap.

They are on their way to rescuing two of the three people. The third, the Immortal recognizes the boy with the mole on his cheek as being the one who started the bet that involved her at the terminal, would just have to wait. She does not want to further split the humans. "Meet you at the hospital," Raven tells Sheba and Jet.

If those ticks or Shadows do anything to her there is no forgiving myself. What they could do to Raven Jet is uncertain, after all he had come to think of her as indestructible. But before today he had also thought there were only two ways a human came back from death; a miracle from God or as Vampire—usually the latter. For millenniums there had been no exceptions. Jet angrily roars and stomps off into the night, Blayne and Tokyo taking the lead.

Ganesha and Cricket hop in the driver and passenger sides of the yellow Mirage. "Shouldn't you steer us?" Leon asks the Vampire Goddess, whose senses are sharper and keener then all of theirs.

"Not allowed to drive stick," she confesses taking out a rope from the trunk and closing the lid. Lucas raises an eyebrow. "Who tells *you* what—"

"—Olsen," she cuts in. Raven walks to the passenger side with one end of the rope tied around her ankle. "Playground," she says pointing towards Brother Street.

The man who is used to doing most of the driving across the United States and the young man that rides shotgun with him on their quests squeeze their way into the backseat. The golden-haired Vampire gets on the car's roof. Cricket's window slides down and Raven gives him the other end of the rope. "Don't try out one of your funny ideas tonight."

The silent man smiles innocently and hands her Ganesha's gun. If lives weren't at stake, Cricket would without a doubt let go of the rope. She had known he was a jokester the first time she met him; when he was six years old—before he stopped speaking to people. Raven saw him a few times after the *bad thing he never speaks of* that shocked him into a lifetime of silence right after his seventh birthday. But then years passed without them seeing one another. And then one day it was fourteen year old Cricket who unexpectedly approached *her*. He has been living with her and Olsen for five years now.

"Why is she not allowed to drive stick?" Lucas, unwilling to let the subject go, asks the owner of the car as tires leave their mark on the pavement.

"She gets too excited and breaks the damn shaft."

"Sounds kinda dirty to me."

* * *

For the first few minutes there is not a zombie, or a Shadow, or Deaths in sight.

Then they enter a neighborhood. While balancing on top of the slick yellow roof, hair flowing like a yellow cascade against the wind, the woman with the female MMA fighter on her shirt fires at a zombie up ahead on the narrow road.

To their right, a man with glowing eyes and a hairless head—they recognize him as being one of the night creatures standing behind Kronos—and shoves two humans inside a house. The two zombies near him instinctively turn away from the bald Vampire growling at them. And a like a true predator, the Vampire enjoys the chase after the bloody, brown veined monsters.

Cricket holds the rope that is intended to prevent his Ray from flying off the roof in one hand while the other points his weapon, shooting the beings, their intestines exposed, as they run from the vamp. "That a boy, Cricket," Raven praises. "Ruin his fun." The Sun-fearing vamp turns and hisses at them. The blonde Hunter in the backseat chuckles.

The car careens around a curve. Double-rounded headlights light up a street unveiling Shadows with crossbows, the walking dead, and Deaths at the houses on the sidelines.

Six advanced and resolute cannibals attack a parked car. Someone inside the vehicle tries to start the ignition while the starved, frightening, nightmarish monsters violently rip the skin off the passengers as they drag them out of the small car.

Eight Shadows, after arrows prove to be ineffective, run into the street.

Ganesha fears there is no way around the crowd and at this speed are likely to hit someone. And slowing down is not an option. "Raven, I can't—"

"—Keep going!" The vampiric female easily steadying herself on top of the roof aims and releases rounds; careful to miss the cavalry. Some of the preternatural humans kick off the heads of their wild opponents with piercing red eyes, and Cricket leans out the window and starts putting a bullet in the Normals being eaten alive.

The bodies blocking their path have thinned out. Ganesha maneuvers to the left of the road and passes the death trap of a car and sneering Shadows. The muscular mechanic points to the ceiling and silently mouths to his cousin, "I am so turned on."

"Me, too."

"Back off," he forms the words silently but clearly.

"You wish." Leon mouths.

Lucas punches Leon in the arm.

BLAYNE / AMATERASU (TOKYO)

A steeple points to the sky, and the moon reflects the light of God's star; the sun. A security light stands close behind the building; trees wrap around both of them to the sides of the country church. Blayne and his Vampire sister converse on the other side of the old lot—away from the House of God. There are no signs of the walking dead. They hear the beating of hearts inside only they don't care enough to count how many.

Vampires can physically enter the sanctuary, or so they have been told. But they fear what will happen when they do enter. The newborns feel the life-threatening danger like a God-fearing human in the house of Satan worshippers. And it isn't just the Christian churches, they have felt a *Holy presence* emanating from other sacred places.

"That Bitch is protecting the one I want," she tells Blayne as she adjusts the chopsticks in her hair.

"I can't believe you drank that crap," he laughs at the empty bottle of blood on the ground.

"It was cold. I want warmth. *I want friend.*"

"Then follow me dear child," a voice they have never heard before beckons them. The two with fangs turn away from the church. They have never met the young girl but they feel as if they have known the stranger forever. They can feel the superiority emanating from the new arrival. She is powerful—more powerful than Kronos… *So why is he the leader?* They suddenly wonder.

The Novices stand up straight and say her name with more respect than they show their own sire. "Silhou." Amaterasu looks into the woods hesitating, unsure if she should leave the American boy.

"Tell her, Blayne." The stranger says his name like they are old friends. Silhou steps out from the black shadows. The white light from above reflects off the silver streaks in her blue pixie hair.

"It doesn't take two to wait for this idiot," Blayne says. And that is all the young Vampire needs to hear.

LOKI/LANA/SHEBA/COLE

"I know vamps don't go into churches. That they're just there to scare. But why did she send *us* when Jet can just save him?" Loki asks sitting in Lana's lap.

"Those like me, Cole, and Sheba don't see Jet the way we do."

Sheba, sitting in the driver's seat which is in the middle of the McLaren adds, "And no doubt our natural enemies want him dead for the same reasons Nyquil-head and them now want Cricket, Ganesha, me, The Preventer, his cousin, and your friends."

"Raven," Loki blames through gritted teeth.

"Stop," the only male teen in the car says. "We knew the price." He holds his gun and the sword Ganesha temporarily lent Lana in his lap.

"How can you protect Jet when he is not here?" Loki finally takes notice of the silver rings. "He's purposely staying in your range," she concludes. She looks from Lana to Cole. "You never told me about Werewolves."

Cole seated to the right of the girl with the nose ring simply answers, "Didn't have to."

The ride so far has been good given the situation; the three from Nebraska somewhat relieved there isn't a busted out window. But now they come to the only crossroad on the journey, and it is blocked by abandon fire trucks, ambulances, campers, and other vehicles.

"There are bluffs on the other side," the girl formally dressed provocatively tells them. "We have to move these—" she sniffs.

Sheba, Lana, and Cole shout, "Gas!"

The doors open on a white car parked horizontally on the pavement. Two flames flicker, and their holders' smiles dance wildly. Two grill matches fall to join the flammable liquid underneath unsuspecting tires…

~~~

Chapter 17
Happy Birthday

VAMPIRES & SHADOWS

THE BALD VAMPIRE STANDS in front of a house located in the middle of a subdivision. A zombie sits on the porch gnawing on an ear. The vamp grabs him by the head.

"Raven is gone." Kronos grins. "Pretenses are not necessary."

The predator in the tan trench coat, face eternally a few years younger than his leader, takes his hands off the repulsive animal and kicks his foot back—the front door to the house collapses.

The Vampires leave the ear-eating carnivore to feast on those inside. More of the crawling and walking dead hungrily make their way towards the once safe home.

The Vampires—others besides Kronos and his personal minion—run and leap from house to house destroying the boarded up doors and windows. The eldest full-blooded vamp who runs on the Earth's lands and swims in the waters, drops one of the infected monsters down a chimney for sport, leaving the windows and doors untouched.

Screams and screams from those inside their homes ring in the nearby Shadow's ears.

Kronos sees from the humans' shingled roof the Shadow with leprechaun green hair. Carrying a crossbow, she arrives first to the implausible scene of her enemies deliberately letting the infected humans consume those they are both supposed to be protecting.

The leader of the Vampires jumps down from the high point, his cape billowing out, and lands on the street ten-feet away from her. "Hello," the night creature with scars on his face and cold, soulless eyes grins.

The young woman freezes in fear. Without the glow of the streetlights the superhuman relies on the moonlight to help her see the bloodsucker.

"I, the one responsible for this glorious tenth day of May, want to welcome you to the beginning of the end. The end of the Goddess, the end of the Shadows' reign, and the end of *you*."

A group of fifteen or so of her Similars arrive at the scene of the betrayal.

"Where's the other tongue that spoke negatively about my Lana?"

"Right here," the minion in the tan trench coat says from behind him. The hairless vamp snatches a longhaired girl wearing a lip ring by the throat preventing her attempt at stopping the crazed cannibals. Kronos keeps his eyes fixed straight ahead.

"*You did this?*" the young woman with dyed hair standing in front of Kronos asks.

"How? *Why?* You live off of humans. There are easier ways for your kind to commit suicide."

They laugh. The Vampires. All of them stop what they are doing to laugh as if she had just told them the best joke in the world.

The young woman tightly squeezes her crossbow, and looks at the gothic girl dressed in all black pinned against the Vampire's chest. The young woman tries to hide the fear in her eyes. She knows they are outnumbered, and it usually takes two of her kind to kill one of the undead.

"Toss her," Kronos orders his minion without taking his emerald green sclera's and orange irises outlined with purple off the girl directly in front of him. The amenable vamp does as he is told and throws the gothic girl with naturally long black hair into a pit of zombies.

The Shadows attack. And within seconds the drinkers of blood have swarmed in.

Like water streaming down a mountainside, Kronos effortlessly pries the crossbow out of the timorous girl's hand, pointing her own weapon at her abdomen. "If you should see the Goddess, tell her *happy birthday* and there is a *cure*." The eight-hundred-and-sixteen-year-old Vampire pulls the trigger.

With an arrow piercing her kidney, the last thing

the Shadow sees before she closes her eyes is her Similars dying at the hands of their natural nemeses and their new enemies…

* * *

Ganesha steers her passengers to a fenced in playground behind an elementary school. The street light puts an orange glow on the metal fence and a section of the playground equipment. They see a really young girl on the highest level of a wooden shaped castle—with at least fifty zombies below her.

"I don't know the reason for not doing this. But can't you just run, get her, and run back?" Leon asks as they stand outside the vehicle.

Raven's chest rises, taking in a deep breath. "Today when Mozart, Jet, and I went for a walk, I hunted and found nothing," she admits. "Using my abilities increases the thirst, and I already feel…*hungry*."

Ganesha knows this is not a good thing. If Raven feeds it will surely not please the Vampires currently helping them; it will break the coalition. But she also knows that if her friend does not feed things are going to take a turn for the worst.

"But won't they just walk away from you like they do with the Vampires?" Lucas asks.

"You mean like walk away from *me* to *you*? How fast are your creative thinking skills?"

The thirteen year old in the castle like tower quivers with trepidation. The monsters below hit the bottom of the structure and make noises that will forever live in her nightmares. One of the things with a human shape but lacks the characteristics of one as already made his way inside the maze and is at the pinnacle of the castle; there are no more levels to the tower.

"Scratch that idea. What's your plan?"

"It is obvious. Hop those buns up there and start shooting at the ten closest to us. They are due for an upgrade, know what I mean?"

"Have you been looking at my ass?" Lucas is elated and mystified.

Leon whispers, "*Seriously, dude?*"

Kale's muscular body parts have not gone unnoticed by Raven. In fact, everything about him from the moment they bumped into each other, sending her books for Ganesha falling to the sidewalk, imprinted in her mind; his hazel eyes, blonde hair, smooth face, his small chicken pox scar, and how hard his abs were when she tried to wipe her hot coffee off him. The way Lucas became angry because he immediately liked her and could not process why. Why he not only cared for someone so quickly, but why he cared deeply about anyone other than his family?

The vampiric woman had known Lucas Kale had feelings for her long before he discovered the truth.

Raven had confessed to The Preventer that she would practically have sex with him if it were not for the work they share. And now, she realizes the ambivalence about Lucas Kale has vanished. Raven is certain she likes them both—a terrible thing.

The opulent woman returns the rifle to her friend in the red *Ralphie May* shirt. "Watch their backs. I do not think anything is coming, but it's hard to tell with all the noise and decaying flesh."

Raven walks to the streetlamp. Cricket helps her pull the pole out of the dirt to conserve her strength. "Here is your weapon," she says smiling. "Have fun." Raven tells the two on the car roof, "If you shoot Cricket I am going to be *so pissed*."

Lucas and Leon start shooting from the roof of the Gemballa Mirage GT while Ganesha stands watch. Cricket swings the pole, sending several zombies flying while breaking others in half.

The Immortal makes a bee line for the crying thirteen year old on the playground. The zombies part like Moses and the Red Sea; stepping aside. But that does not calm her nerves. She may be impervious to the walking dead, but her friends are not…

* * *

JET'S CAR
The black car explodes; flames stretching, jumping up and down as if in a contest to see which one reaches the sky first.

Loki and the black-haired teenagers lay on the grass separated from Sheba. Cole had been the first out of the trap while Lana shoved Loki out the door. Then Sheba climbed out, without the M-16, just as the lead Shadow dragged Loki around the rear just in time to join Cole on the other side.

Six zombies—the attentive kind—come out of hiding.

The two clever ones from the white car join two others that have plans to devour the Nebraskan teenagers. Lana takes the rifle from Loki and nods towards the only tree in the area. "Get up there and stay!"

Cole leaves the sword on the grass and stands up ready to shoot.

The bright flames from Jet's burning car help guide four snarling mouths with pulsating ruby eyes. Moaning avidly, they hurry for a meal that waits unarmed, and by herself.

Sheba hears Jet running to their rescue. The steadfast stomping of his four legs thunder in her eardrums. "Go, Jet! It's only two miles!" She knows there is no time to spare.

Sheba's fast legs easily take her past the monsters they have seriously underestimated towards the collage of vehicles. The girl in the purple shirt stops at the first car her feet bring her to. Her fingertips pull up on the hood of a police car. The hood rips off and the girl from Germany flicks it like a Frisbee. Three skulls detach from their bodies.

Loki watches from a tree branch. Her best friends down below release four bullets into the brains of two *things*. One of them barely has any flesh around his throat. The other has visible ribs and one of her arms is bent the wrong way.

Two down on this side and three permanently dead on Sheba's side. Thinking that the three remaining dead-but-craving-flesh people cannot take on three Vampire killers, Loki climbs down the thick bumpy limbs. Undaunted, she jumps down from the last limb of bark; the first one closest to the grass.

Sheba jogs to the one with no arms. Balancing on one foot, she uses the other to push the woman into the broiling flames. "You can handle the rest!"

she says, then runs and leaps across the clutter of vehicles leaving her comrades behind in order to aid her friend.

The descendant of the leader of all the Deaths quickly picks up the sword; leaving the rifle on the grass to save bullets. Lana swings her arm back and then forward. Loki watches her force the sword up its chin and out the top of its head.

And someone watches Loki... Arms extend pulling itself out of the valley shaped hollow behind the tree...

The sword returns to Lana's side as the dark-headed boy sideswipes the last of the schemers in the legs with his foot. The female warrior raises the long bladed weapon...

Warm dirty hands grip tightly on Loki's thin lower leg. Teeth sink into her jeans and grind against meat that involuntary rips away...

Lana decapitates the thing in front of her and the boy who came with her to Concordia, Kansas.

"Lana!" Loki jogs towards the Shadows, pointing at the amputee crawling on the ground...

SILHOU & AMATERASU
Silhou and Amaterasu arrive behind a cluster of trees on the outer perimeter of a chain linked fence.

Silhou grabs a Shadow during the girl's fight with a zombie. At the touch of Silhou's pale hand, the girl goes limp, almost lifeless.

"The Goddess is going to hear and smell us!" Amaterasu yells in a whisper; as much as one can.

Silhou lets go of the Shadow. But before the girl has a chance to fall, the silver and blue-haired girl rams her hands into the human girl's sides and pulls. The Japanese girl gasps. The Shadow's skin slides to the ground—but her entire skeleton remains intact in her killer's fingers, gripping the ribcage. "The Goddess has become weak."

"How you do that to Shadow?"

"I'm not one of you, am I?" Silhou's eyes sparkle with supreme intelligence. Her silky blue cape outlined first with black then a shiny silver ruffles in the wind. She observes Raven and the humans killing the last of the zombies on the playground. "Which one?"

"Eyes blue. She protect him. His death bring her pain," Amaterasu's fists rub her oval eyes mockingly. "I laugh."

"*Turning* one would be more *effective*."

"I—"

"No abilities. What a shame. Can't think for oneself." The intellectual girl ignores the Novice's confused reaction. "I could do it. But tell me, is *he* the one? Can you not use your brain to figure out which one has been with her the longest?"

The girl's acumen and perceptivity cause Amaterasu to feel insulted and doubt her own self but she will never show it—not to the higher being, like she did when the Goddess affronted her by giving her an insulting nickname.

Amaterasu knows the Werewolf has been around for centuries but he cannot be changed and neither can their enemies. "That one." Her parti-colored eyes, emerald green and orange—purple is awarded to them when they learn how to Push—fix on the girl with olive skin getting into the expensive yellow vehicle.

"Confirm the suspicions to Kronos. Not that it matters now. Don't bother to tell him of my attendance, for my purpose here is almost complete. When you're finished why don't you use your head and be productive...?"

"But Kronos—"

"—Cares for you about as much as a father dog does for his puppies."

"Why you say this?"

"Do you know the names of the ones Raven protects? Besides the wolf and your Leader's niece?"

"No," Amaterasu shakes her head.

"There is Sheba. Associated with lust," the caped girl pulls apart the Shadow's bones that she still holds in her hands, counting off the names, "Ganesha, the lord of obstacles, and Loki, my favorite—"

"I don't understand," the older-looking but younger girl interrupts her.

"Tell me, what is the meaning of Amaterasu?"

"Shining heaven," she proudly answers.

"The Shinto Sun deity," adds Silhou casually twirling a femur bone, the main bone of the thigh, as if it were a baton. The other bones that had been connected to the skeleton by way of the thick bone landed softly on the grass. "I can assure you these names, these beings, have a purpose just as much as I can assure you that your sire chose you because of your meaning. Think about it, child. How funny is it that a sun goddess is reduced to an eternal life in darkness?"

The young girl looks deeply stricken. Forehead creasing, lips pursing over non-retractable fangs, and her predator eyes turn to their dark, human color. Although grateful for the gift, she does not find it *funny* in the least bit. "This cannot be truth."

"How much time does Kronos spend with you? Or a better question, young and naive Amaterasu, whom does your maker practice the art of Pushing with the most? You or the other one?"

The fledgling's small rounded eyes revert back with consuming malice.

"It can't be equal. And now that you are no longer under the delusion you were created because you were *special*, do as I said."

* * *

There is not enough room in the Mirage to accommodate another person. They had searched for another vehicle and didn't have to look far. The small pickup is the only other vehicle in the vacant parking lot of the playground.

It seemed to Lucas that all of Raven's friends have skills—even the dog acted and obeyed as if he understood the words that people spoke. The truck will not properly start and this is the mechanic's opportunity to show that although he does not have the highest IQ he *can* be useful. Lucas knows a lot about that which most people have very little knowledge of, and although he is positive Raven could have done it, the mechanic puts the truck's belt back on track. *I did it!* Lucas thinks, slamming the hood down.

"There is only room in the truck for three." Raven turns away from the land of zombie limbs and carcasses. Blood and guts cover the grass and mulch of the playground. "Kale, I know you do not want to do this…but Leon is riding with us."

"You and the girl? Why? He came in the car why can't he go back in it?"

"To minimize the chances of my death, Luke," Leon reminds him of the Goddess's vision.

"Yeah, about that. Raven, what did you see?"

Wanting to leave this place, Leon impatiently asks, "Do you want to ride in the back?"

Lucas Kale does not want to be separated from his cousin, however, he doesn't fancy riding in the bed of the truck; too much open space for him. He unnervingly joins Ganesha and Cricket in Ganesha's car.

The Church

"They're coming!"

"Run!"

"Run faster!"

"Or die!"

Five terrified people, without weapons, sprint across the old faded lines of the parking lot to the glass doors of the white, country church.

Hearing fear behind the closing doors, Blayne snorts, "Humans." Then he smiles. "Here they come. Let's see what you think about those neatly painted windows now."

The starving people with gray faces and rotting flesh hit whatever remaining limbs they have against the glass door. Four of them have legs and feet but each are missing an arm; one with two legs but only one foot and no arms, the other one has all four arms and legs but no hands.

The tall and brown-eyed Vampire suddenly recalls why he is at this death trap. "How long does it take a stupid beast to get his fat—" he stops, deciding now is the time to look like he cares what happens to the humans. Blayne steps out of the shadows.

The flesh eating monsters do not have time to back away from the entrance. Blayne throws one, two, three, four, five of them like a baseball across the old lot; their skulls bounce off what is left of the pavement, some of it had been reduced to tiny gravel over the years, and their brains land with a splat on the lot.

Jet arrives in time to see a zombie being slammed four-feet underground, leaving a perfect outline of its body; head, feet, legs, and its one arm, looking just like a half-eaten gingerbread man cookie.

The Werewolf sniffs.

And then smashes his large, heavy body through the glass entrance of the church. Screaming ensues. And lots of tiny pellets from a preacher's shotgun tear into the Werewolf's hind leg.

The five unarmed humans inside the church scream in fear of the beast and the sick looking man who was here when they arrived. The man hunched over and glaring up at them with cold, piercing eyes has thin brown lines expanding away from his mouth. Suddenly, the infected man snaps into the upright position. Loud popping noises expel from his body.

Jet immediately understands why it takes two

bullets to the head to kill this kind. The brain has thickened its covering to protect itself. The two-thousand-pound giant slams his paw down, crushing the evolved man from head to feet. The humans just barely throw their hands up in time to shield their faces from the splattering blood.

The pews move and break as the Werewolf steps to the left of the aisle. He wraps his paw around a hyperventilating man and picks him up from the group of unarmed humans. The Werewolf takes one whiff of the human and smells the disease spreading inside the man. Jet drops him on his head, instantly killing the man.

The preacher fires his last shell at the animal's side. More of Jet's blood, blue in color, oozes from the tiny holes blasted in his body. The two men and the two women remaining from the group of five cover their ears, praying they do not go deaf from the dark blue giants roar or die from the shaking foundation.

Suddenly Jet smells it. An accustomed scent of a friend. He stops roaring and the miniature earthquake abruptly ends.

"Mr. Preacher, you would not know a savior if he turned into a Werewolf, stood before you, and smote the plague of death."

The people cast judging eyes on the nineteen-year-old girl in the purple *Citizen Cope* shirt.

"I am looking for someone. He is a Jew. You might have shot him, who knows with you people?"

No one answers.

"I get violent when I do not get what I want," Sheba threatens.

A flimsy looking door at the front left of the sanctuary opens. A dark-headed fifteen year old boy walks out. He takes one look at the towering beast with long claws and sharp looking teeth and says, "Well, at least it's not a moaning crazy person."

"*It* is a *Werewolf*. Would you like to ride him to a place that is not surrounded by painted glass and a gone-crazy-preacher with a gun?"

The boy does not make it a habit of running off with strangers, but everyone here is a stranger to him. Straining his neck to look up at the giant, he knows he doesn't really have a choice. "Um…sure."

* * *

Lisa, the thirteen-year-old with strawberry blonde hair and a birthmark in the shape of an L on her cheek, sits tranquilly next to the woman with inexplicable eye colors. "There is nobody out here," Leon says from behind the wheel of the pickup truck; his eyes on the country road and the car in front of them.

Raven, sitting in the middle, stares out at several bodies scattered in the houseless area. "They have either moved on or they are dead." She cannot see, smell, or hear any signs of human life. The only thing she can sense is the change in temperature. A storm is on its way… "God made a deal with the fallen angel sometime after I stopped ageing."

"God made a deal with the Devil?"

"It was Satan who devised it. One day if I was to die The Banish would cease. Magic and ghosts and other stuff would be allowed here. Also, the Devil's kind could walk on the third planet from the sun."

"What? Walk the Earth?" Leon asks. The girl from his Prevention looks at him, her circles of hazel meet his blue irises. "You're serious. Why? How do you know?"

WHACK!

Something rams against the truck's side flipping it over...

..."Oh god!" Ganesha yells at her rearview mirror. Cricket and Lucas immediately turn around in their seats. The truck with the three passengers is in the middle of a flip; four tires swing towards the sky.

Out of nowhere something hits Ganesha's car.

It flips once...twice... On the third flip the driver side smashes up against a tree...

...The pickup truck lands in the upright position. But it is about to collide against a heavy duty truck that has lumber hanging over the sides. And one of the pieces is aimed for Leon Carmany's head...

~~~~

Chapter 18
The Bite

THE WINDOW ON THE pickup truck breaks. Raven protectively grabs The Preventer's skull and forces it to her side. The two-by-four punctures her eye and half her skull. The girl next to her screams.

Raven very slowly pulls the board out of her head and face—the pain more intense and extreme than it should be; familiar with the degrees of physical pain over the centuries... She pushes the two-by-four out the window and across the field.

Leon raises up to see the eyeball inside Raven's skull spring upwards and position itself in the correct place. The orbital cracks and bends, forming to its perfect circle. The tissue, bones, and muscles on her face start growing, regenerating. The last to fix itself is her hair, slowly pushing itself through the healing scalp until it matches the length of the other long blonde strands.

The Vampire Goddess turns away from a stunned Leon to the wrecked car propped up against a tree trunk…

…"My side," Ganesha says in pain. There is thick red liquid leaking from her abdomen. Cricket rips a section of her clothing to better see the wound. Somehow the fabric of the seatbelt has torn and the metal that clicks into the buckle is sticking into Ganesha's right hip…

…Leon climbs out of the passenger side of the truck after the two females.

THUD! Something lands on the open tailgate.

Raven, Lisa, and Leon quickly turn to the rear of the truck. Standing on the tailgate is the green-haired Shadow—with red, luminous eyes and *black* veins and arteries…

"Hi, Raven," the thing says.

"*What the hell!*" Raven and Leon simultaneously curse.

The girl with black veins on her face grins. "Happy Birthday."

Leon shoots. But it ducks down, leaps off the truck, and *runs* to them with an unexpected speed, knocking Raven down and landing on top of her. Leon aims the shotgun and the thing grabs his ankle with one hand pulling his leg out from underneath him. Leon lands hard on his back; the wind knocked out of him.

With the speed and strength not possessed by any Shadow or zombie, the dead girl repeatedly punches Leon's Potential in the face. Weakened from lack of nutrition, combined with the monster's powerful fists, Leon guesses this has to be the most painful blow to the face Raven has ever felt. The woman he likes doesn't move and her face is smeared with blood.

The dead but-alive-and-punching girl stops pummeling the unresponsive half-blood. And violently tears into the woman from his visions... Teeth the color of old motor oil consume thick, long layers of skin dangling from its dark silver lips.

Three times Leon pulls the shotgun's trigger. Pieces of skin and brains and clotted blood splatter on the three of them.

"Raven!" The Preventer's panicking voice revives her from her weakened state. Through the stinging blood in her eyes, Raven sees a mass of black hair flapping in the wind—on the way to Ganesha's car...

...Cricket turns away from the younger girl who has a parent just as cruel and wicked as both of his and points his M-16 at the Vampire Hunter.

"Whoa!" Lucas defensively throws up his hands and slumps down in the seat.

Cricket fires.

The back windshield shatters, falling on the trunk and Lucas. Two pieces of metal connect with the gothic girl's head—Cricket recognizes her as being one of the Similars protesting against his family and Lana—but the bullets do nothing...

The infected girl with two bullets in her forehead jumps on the trunk causing the left side to level with the passenger side. Ganesha screams as the square piece of metal further tears her insides.

"Again! Again!" Lucas shouts for Cricket to fire his weapon.

Cricket fires off the last bullet in his rifle at the long black-haired *thing*; black spider web veins wrap around crimson, beady birdlike eyes and stretch in all directions across a pale face, expanding down the neck. It lets out a screech.

A screech so terrifying and familiar to Lucas that he tries climbing to the front of the car, but the dead *but very much alive* Shadow reaches inside the wide opening and grabs him by the shoulders, pulling him back against the seat.

Cricket fumbles with the bandolier of ammunition across his chest trying to reload the rifle.

The Hunter aims his pistol upwards underneath the girl's chin and expels two rounds.

"That tickles," the gothic girl says, smiling as she looks down at the horrified man.

"You're talking! Why are you talking, bitch!"

Five bullets, three from the forehead and two from its chin, fall out and roll down Lucas's shirt.

Dark silver lips part and a warm hand squeezes his throat…

* * *

AMATERASU & KRONOS

"It's true." Amaterasu acquaints her sire with the information. "The Goddess sees into the future."

"Not very well," Kronos laughs; an orange glow dances before them. The smell of burning flesh soothes his nostrils. The roof of an apartment building caves and twisting tongues of flame send more dark clouds of smoke into the night. The humans inside the living corridors were very much alive until Kronos wanted to play a game—Pick Your Death. Stay and burn? Or evacuate and be eaten alive?

Three humans choosing to flee their burning rooms from another apartment building across the street get thrown to the pit of snarling ex-Shadows; Shadow zombies. And the girl from Japan, and two dozen other Vampires including the Vampire in the tan trench coat, join their leader in menacing laughter.

Amaterasu's eyes drift from twisted face to twisted face searching for her new brother Blayne, but he is not among them. What *special* quest had their father sent him on and excluded her from yet again? The malice in her still burning strong, only hidden like burning charcoal underneath the lid of a grill, waiting for the opportune time to leave and carry out its destruction.

The Deaths have gathered several of their *uninfected* enemies and begin throwing them to the fire created right in the middle of the parking lot. The Shadows' screams bring them ecstasy of the highest kind.

The Vampires who hunt when the Earth rotates away from God's Star dance wildly around the fire, pushing those trying to flee the scorching flames back in—save for Kronos. Their leader's eight-hundred-and-sixteen-year-old eyes watch, burning with power and more malevolent and malign laughter than all of those surrounding him.

* * *

Arteries and veins resembling that of vines climb from animated fingers up ashen arms, and the foul smell of the warm but dead hand drifts up Lucas Kale's nostrils just before his airways crush together; stopping his breathing. The monster's dark hair falls down over him covering his upper body. Its face next to his throat.

Suddenly the stench enters his respiratory system again and the nightmarish face is pulled from his view.

Lucas Kale practically steps all over Cricket, throwing himself up front and scrambling out after him. In the cool air and under the snow-colored light of the moon, the two of them watch a bloody Raven firmly grasp hold of the monster's ankles, pick it up, and smack the devilish girl's torso against the trunk of a tree.

It giggles.

Jogging up beside Lucas and Cricket, Leon and Lisa stare in horror.

The woman whose hair is luminous yellow like the sun hits the hard tree trunk with the zombie's body again. And once again the girl giggles. Highly irritated, Raven drops the body.

Deformed arms and ribs that are protruding out begin to fix themselves...

Leon and Lucas, faces twisted in horror, turn to each other for answers. Raven rips the infected Shadow's head off and smashes it into the tree, and then wipes her bloody hands on her jeans. "Move the car," she tells Cricket, her breath shallow.

The unnaturally strong man gently slides the damaged sports car away from the tree, and easily opens the smashed in door. Raven carefully pulls her friend from the car and gently lays her down on the grass. Raven takes her shirt off, the one with the MMA fighter on it, revealing a silk undershirt, and ties it around Ganesha's waist.

"Ray, that is your favorite shirt," the girl protests.

"Save your breath," Raven says, and then looks up at the others. "She is going to bleed to death. I can fix her at my house."

"You go ahead," Lucas looks at her with sympathetic eyes. "One of these vehicles should still work."

SHEBA/JET/LANA/COLE/LOKI

The Jewish boy, Joshua, clings tightly to the woman's waist. Her ruby necklace bouncing up and down with the rhythm of the beast trotting underneath them. The air beats against their clothing, and heavy paws create cracks in the winding street dividing it into sections.

It is a sad time, but Jet has never felt so…free. Knowing that any minute someone could see him and it wouldn't mean anything of significance with everyone dying. The covert centuries of having to pass by in forests or while humans slept have been fun, but constricting. Jet has learned a lot and lost just as much. The few that had come to truly know him are deceased. And those that do know him come with an expiration date.

Raven is the exception.

She has been with him practically all his life. Raven is the one who knows him best—the one he loves.

The one that will never return those feelings.

But right now all he can think about is her well-being. "That's Lana!" Sheba distracts him.

Sure enough Lana sits behind the wheel of an ambulance; its one headlight desperately trying to light the way. After the crawling zombie was killed, the Shadows with speeds faster than Loki knew that she was going to slow them down. Lana and Cole decided to take the first vehicle that would start.

The Werewolf's massive feet slow on the asphalt.

"They found him!" Loki hears Lana.

While Loki was doing first aid on the bite above her ankle in the back of the emergency vehicle, she had lied and told her friends she scraped the skin while climbing down the tree. The apprehensive girl poured and rubbed anything she could find on the mouth size wound then bandaged the already budding infection.

Loki is not entirely sure how well a Werewolf can smell, but she is not willing to take chances. The anxious girl moves further away from the opening window. Loki hears the voice of the girl who flipped over the dining room table and pinned her against the wall. "We are taking him back and then going to the hospital for unknown reasons. I do not know what Raven wants you to do. You can go there or come back to the house."

"We should go back." Lana reasons, "This light isn't going to last much longer, and there isn't much gas."

LUCAS / CRICKET

Seeing Raven take her top off exposing her silky sky blue slip and matching bra straps should have turned Lucas on, and maybe it did, but there are no signs below the belt that denote anything of that nature.

Maybe it was Ganesha's blood or the image of the dead girl's smile forever engraved in his mind that stops his blood from rushing to his penis.

Or maybe it's because Leon cannot make this damn thing go fast enough.

Whatever the case, this is the first time today—the first time in his life—that Lucas Kale thinks about sex and does not get hard.

The truck bumps over another pothole in the wide road, too many to avoid, the light casting on puddles and streaks of blood. Lucas looks in the side mirror. There isn't enough room to fit the four of them in the front and they didn't want to further traumatize the girl of thirteen by having her sit on the lap of a stranger, so Cricket had decided to be the one to ride in the bed of the truck.

Ganesha's going to be fine. She's with Ray, Cricket reassures himself. *Jet isn't human, he's fine. But Sheba and Lana...*

Lucas cannot think of a scenario where it is possible for Cricket to disappear without them knowing, nevertheless, he fears that if he takes his eyes off of him—even for a few seconds—another one of Raven's friends could potentially die.

"It bit her."

"Huh?" Lucas looks away from the reflection of the countryside and the young mute man in the

Flogging Molly shirt.

"It told her happy birthday and..."

"*That's what happened to her throat?* Brighton, what the hell is going on here? We have dead people—not Vampire dead I guess 'cause those days weren't fun enough—and now they want to break the rules and go around singing lullabies! And, this my favorite part, it bit our Vampire!"

Lisa turns to the blonde-haired man. "At least you're not going through puberty."

"What an interesting perspective."

* * *

GANESHA & RAVEN
The stubborn eighteen-year-old insists on using her own two legs.

But Ganesha takes four steps inside the kitchen and it becomes evident she cannot support herself. She entwines her hands once again around Raven's neck; now healed. The half-Vampire carries her friend down the hallway, past the panic room, up the other hall, and into the girl's bedroom.

I don't feel...right... Raven gently lays Ganesha down and then leaves the bleeding, motionless girl on the bed. Raven walks out into the hallway—*rapidly breathing*—towards the steel and metal room to retrieve the first aid kit.

In her centuries of living, breathing has never been a problem... Nearly to her destination Raven stumbles into the wall.

Ganesha...regenerating and...weak...

In front of the panic room Raven's eyelids become heavy as if they were lifting weights, and

the crosses on the floor suddenly bid her goodnight.
Nesha...

MOZART

Watching the monitor inside the panic room, Mozart sees his owner lying motionless and begins to whine. The four-legged dog has never seen her like this; stumbling, falling down and not waking up.

Someone wearing a cape and dressed in sliver clothes enters his kitchen. His whines explode into low disapproving growls.

Silhou takes one look at the hundreds of crosses carved into the areas above, below, and beside her. She snickers, gliding down the hallway...

The girl stands over his Raven and the Siberian Husky growls viciously—his lips curl back and white foam seeps to the floor. Mozart has no idea what kind of being this girl is but he wants her heart in his pointy teeth.

She looks up at the camera and smiles. "So sweet. You can relax. I don't want *her*." The Husky barks furiously, hoping his master will stir. The girl starts walking towards the back of the second hallway, the direction of Ganesha's room, out of the camera's view. His view.

GANESHA

Feeling an ominous presence near her, Ganesha suddenly awakens, eyes wide and fearful. Standing over her is the most unusual looking girl approximately sixteen. The pallid skinned girl opens her mouth.

Fangs. Not white but coal black.

Ganesha screams bolting upright. The caped girl squeezes Ganesha's biceps. Bones snap. The girl wearing the purple unicorn necklace yells for Raven to save her.

"Raven is unconscious, and this is going to hurt. That is the truth." The Normal gets slammed back into her pillow.

"But…crosses…your eyes are black…"

The spiky blue-haired girl sticks her hand out over the weakened human and Ganesha loses control over her limbs. "If Raven wanted you to live she would have turned you. Don't you think? Really, what was the point in her putting you back together again?"

Ganesha's forehead begins to ache severally.

"So you can suffer through old age?" the girl continues. "Shitting on yourself and having her or someone else take your diaper off and wipe your ass like you're a baby. The only infant you are going to be is mine."

A tear slides from the corner of Ganesha's eye and down her cheek. Instantly blood flows out of Ganesha's nostrils and up the trespasser's nose. Ganesha soon feels as if she were left naked in the cold brutal depths of Antarctica.

Silhou stops taking the human's blood. The visitor opens her mouth and forces her blackish-red blood through the air and into Ganesha's voluntarily parting lips…

Time tricks the young adult; turning these seconds into days. Death and birth in the early stage of becoming one. After receiving all the blood

Silhou can spare, the poisoned girl slips into the dark corners of unconsciousness.

MOZART
Mozart watches the pixie, blue-haired girl glide past his master, up the other hall, and away from the perimeter.

He anxiously runs over to the wall and pushes the black button. His button. The panic room door opens and Mozart hurries out. He bites into the bottom of Raven's pants leg; her spaghetti strap shirt will not work. Maneuvering her legs around towards the door, Mozart tugs and pulls his family member inside the steel room.

* * *

The ambulance sits on the side of the road, gas tank empty, and its passengers now on foot in the dangerous night with no balls of light in the streetlamps lining the crooked sidewalk.

"Can't...run anymore," Loki pants, her lungs burning. But the bite above her ankle for some reason does not hurt as much anymore...

Abruptly, Lana and Cole snap their focus down the other side of the street. A silhouette moves on the balcony from one of the nearby homes. The figure steps into the moon's light casting on the rail and leaps down. Shimmering skirt. Chopsticks used as hair accessories. The two Shadows recognize the Vampire from their Connection; the torch in her hand penetrated the dark cavern walls as she moved and highlighted her baleful and menacing smile.

Tokyo. Also known as Amaterasu.

Thinking about the torch and seeing the house

stirs Cole's nearly suppressed memory of Christmas morning. The morning when he was eleven and had an immeasurable amount of happiness before and after shredding the wrapping paper that hid his Nerf gun. Toys and family, things couldn't have been better. But the moment didn't last. His head hit the soft fluffy pillow, and then he sat in the cold snow and watched the happiness die. Heard his mother and sister burn to their deaths.

While they watch the Vampire Novice force her way into another home, Loki bends down and pulls her pants leg up above her ankle. Loki nervously bites the inside of her lip, and her mouth immediately tastes like pennies. There are tiny black dots on the skin around her bandage. The last time the gray-eyed girl saw the ink-like dots was on the Picture Man right before his chocolate eyes glazed over at the border.

"Cole, you stay with Loki. Unless I need you." The eighteen year old steps off the sidewalk, slinks pass a car, and across a lawn through the moonlit night to the only house with a balcony. Sword drawn, Lana stands in the open entrance; the evidence suggests that it once had been enforced to keep the walking dead out but something had made it give way.

Tokyo.

Infuriated apple green eyes scan the first floor. An unsettling feeling tells her that when she takes a few steps inside, giving her eyes time to adjust to the dark, she will find a familiar and gruesome scene.

A white glow shines down on her raven hair and

through the open threshold, casting her shadow on a small section of the floorboards in front of her. Her right foot takes the lead, and Lana becomes frozen like a statue.

Her head slowly turns to the left. It is as she fears... Ten bodies—all without heads—lay lifelessly in odd directions on the furniture; the couch, the recliners, a piano. The place looks like an abattoir.

If Tokyo learns to Push... Lana runs at full speed away from the massacre, across the grass, up the walkway, and into the next house, hoping this one will not also resemble a slaughterhouse.

A backup generator providing the intense light vetoes her wish. A line of extremely fresh and bloody corpses lead away from the front door down the hall to her right. Blood soaks the white carpet, and the walls and ceiling are spotted and streaked in red. It is as if an artist had gone mad, flinging and tossing the color this way and that while dancing to the rhythm of sheer madness.

Walking down the hallway dodging falling blood drops, Lana counts the dead. *Two, four, six, nine.* Family photos hanging in frames, red splotches on some of their glass covers, reminds Lana once again of her mother sitting all alone in their basement. And of the depression eating away at those surviving. She shakes her head looking at a clump of hair matted to the light above her.

Suddenly, Lana raises the sword above her head. Ready to kill. *Warmer.* An expensive looking dining table with matching leather chairs stands at the end of the white and red hall. The room appears to open to the left. And the tracker is one hundred percent sure there is a Vampire on the other side of the dining room.

The Shadow steps out into the brightly lit area.

The nineteen year old in the black skirt and dark red shirt that stops at the top of her bellybutton stands underneath a chandelier. Draining blood, taking a life. But not from close contact with her victim....

The last wave of the younger girl's blood passes through the air and into Tokyo's mouth. The dead human girl falls to the carpet.

Tokyo turns around, facing Lana. Orange irises develop a purple ring.

Amaterasu smiles, fangs gone. No longer a Novice.

* * *

Raven's House
Sheba and Joshua turn left at the end of the cross-filled hallway, Jet impatiently guarding and waiting outside the house, and the door to the panic room opens. They walk in to find Raven pulling a first aid kit down from a small shelf.

Closing the entry, Sheba asks which one of them is hurt. "Who?"

"Ganesha. Shadows attacked us—the dead kind. Sheba, they can *run and talk.*"

Sheba types in the pass code to the other door. It swings inward almost soundlessly compared to the mechanisms of the wood and steal doors pulling and pushing upon opening and closing. The boy stares questionably at the wood stairs leading straight down in between two walls, the light bulb overhead making the path easily seen.

Joshua doesn't know what to expect when he sets foot at the bottom. But this place has to be safer than the one he was previously hiding in. Right? He has seen zombies, a Werewolf which he thought at first was Bigfoot, and then on the way here he saw creatures with weird eyes and could have sworn one of them had a pair of fangs...

Who knows what he actually saw? But then again this place *is* decorated with the Christian symbol associated with the crucifixion of Jesus...

"You will be safe down there," the hot girl with a mass of dark hair and a big red necklace reassures him though it is not necessary. After the Jewish boy begins stomping down the path she closes the door behind him. "I nearly got blown up by an advanced one," she says incredulously, grabbing a gun. "Ray, are you telling me—"

"—Yes. They are stronger and faster. Also, I have not made it to the hospital to get the last one. He is probably dead by now."

"Jet and I will get him. Description?"

"Teenage boy. Fifteen. Mole on his face. Blond hair. Meet you there."

Sheba runs out the door and through the house. The kitchen door swings out with a force that threatens to shatter it. "Hospital," she says leaping up onto Jet's back. They ride off underneath the disappearing and reappearing light of the moon; clouds rolling overhead.

* * *

Raven leaves her dog in the panic room, returning to Ganesha's side and omitting in her conversation with Sheba that she herself woke up in the panic room and is getting weaker by the minute.

Ganesha's brown eyes flutter open. "Ray... I am infected."

"They did not bite you." Raven places the white kit on the floor.

"My arms...broke... Forced me..."

She leans in close to Ganesha's moist dark lips. A meteor lands in the back of her throat. "N-n-n...no...

"Ray, take...me outside."

For someone who moves so fast Raven has never moved so slow in her entire life. Her palms slide underneath Ganesha, lifting her best friend from the bloody sheets. Time had never met much, but now it is everything as Raven walks the long, dark hallway that is guaranteed to lead to death.

Is Ganesha the only one? Or just the first?

Raven opens the kitchen door and gently lays the girl's unnaturally cold body on the grass...

Ganesha looks up the sky. Several stars manage to pierce through rolling gray clouds. "We have both seen hundreds of ways to die." Thinking about the numerous obstacles she overcame in her past, surviving a shovel to her head and overall dealing with her mother's drug usage and the woman soliciting herself to whoever would have her, Ganesha pauses and breathes in the crisp night air. "I would rather go like this, Ray. In the presence of a great friend."

Tears moisten Raven's hazel eyes. "You still

owe me three laps."

"Prepositions," the girl who lives in the same house with her overseas lets out a little laugh, "What a bitch." Then her smile fades becoming serious. "I had a great run, girl. But you gotta do this, Ray."

The wind begins to speed up. The gray clouds threatening to steal the promised light.

"You are human. You are Ganesha."

"Not for long. I am healing...and it is taking over my soul." The girl in the red shirt sobs. *"It hurts.* Please, Ray. Just do it."

Raven holds her family in her arms, tears pouring down both of their cheeks. "This is not right." By saving The Preventer Raven indirectly signed her close friend's death certificate. *What could possibly be right about this?*

"In God I trust," Ganesha says as she pulls out a one hundred dollar bill from her pocket. "You can have the Benjamin, but I still say I won the race here."

Quivering within herself, Raven places her hands on the girl's soft, dark face. Ganesha's young, brown eyes stare up at her. Wise for their age but the humanity in them will soon be replaced by a killer's darkness. "I love you, Raven." And with that her light does what every light eventually does, only the spark of God vanquishing with it, and brown eyelids close.

"I love you, Ganesha." Raven takes in a deep breath, and the wind chimes dangling down from the porch's ceiling explode into dark, angry tones, and dark clouds begin to circle the calm and beautiful light of the moon, quickly smothering it in a deep darkness.

The bones feel foreign in her best friend's neck, cracking as Raven twists them.

The circle that has been forming overhead starts spiraling down, and Raven heavily sobs holding a vacant shell. When the sun came up this morning who would have thought the first human she was going to kill was one she thought deserved to live? Ganesha lays dead in her arms while she sits on the grass, still no closer to finding a way to keep Cricket, Sheba, Lana, Cole, Lucas, Leon, Loki, and the other humans in the world from dying.

With all her lung power, Raven screams into the black night. The piercing wind carries the forming funnel to another place. But the Immortal knows the storm is only smoldering and when it flares back up its likely to be worse...

"Raven."

Her eyes open, turning her head towards her American house. Leon, Kale, Lisa, and Cricket stand like stick figures in between her and the tree next to her porch.

"Did you see me..." She cannot get her mouth to say *kill Ganesha.*

The mute man nods, a tear sliding down from his moist eye. "Lisa. Take her inside," she quietly tells him, her voice void of all emotion. The extremely young girl with the birthmark on her face follows Cricket into the cedar house.

"The Novice must have received her powers." Leon steps closer to Raven. "This is my fault. She wanted me."

"Tokyo," Lucas shakes his head with indignation. "I am going to kill that bitch!" He just clued in that his cousin was supposed to die by way of a bloodsucker, and now the woman he drove all the way from Tennessee to Nebraska to find is causing a knot in his throat. He wishes he could do something besides take up space.

Unexpectedly, the road separating the yellow home and the once standing purple house fills with ill-timed company; glowing crimson eyes easily spotting their prey.

Brighton Leon Carmany gently places his hand on Raven's small shoulder. "Raven, we have to move."

Suddenly hazel eyes change and with the change a peculiar bond forms. The concerned gentleman *feels* her loss; her sorrow, the immensity. The Preventer does not know how it is possible but he feels…her hatred. Her fury virtually burning Leon's bones and seeping into his soul.

Lightning momentarily rips through the darkness, highlighting the shrinking space between them and the dozens and dozens of dead people close to breaking out into a jog.

Raven climbs to her feet. Gone. The vampiric woman stands, red gas can in hand, next to her car. Sometime tonight the tires had been slashed. The silent young man returns witnessing his best friend spreading gasoline over her red and black vehicle; the most expensive car in the world.

"You need your—" Leon is going to say strength, but by that time she had lit the Bugatti Veyron on fire, and now she *holds* the glowing car in her hands.

With the weight of the world on her shoulders, the woman who receives Orders throws the giant car fire ball past the ultramarine blue Chevy. The car lands smack in the middle of the pugnacious and ravenous people eaters, taking down three fourths of them.

But the ones not burnt and pinned down by the car continue to move forward, unwavering, intrepid and valiant—as if they thought flying cars meant nothing and the one possessing the strength to pick them up could do nothing to stop them...

The car explodes catching the zombies on fire and catapulting their burning carcasses in various directions.

Cricket, Leon, Lucas stare at Raven. The three of them had thought themselves to be the obvious food of choice. But while the crazed monsters had moved as fast as they could on the pavement towards them their eyes were clearly fixed on Raven...

An ocean falls out of the sky.

~~~~

Chapter 19
Seeing Red

A CHANDELIER HANGS above a dining table and leather chairs. Four long vertical windows to the right of the furniture show the sunless day outside. Next to the floor windows is a bleeding heart plant, the leafs are heart shaped with red vines. And Tokyo stands across from the giant plant in front of the second story stairs.

There are four ways out of this room; the hall from which Lana came, the windows that fat rain drops pelt against, the stairs, and the entrance straight ahead to another part of the house.

The Vampire launches.

The vigilant tracker dodges to the right and rolls across the rectangle table. She lands on her feet, grips the handle of the sword with both hands, and takes several steps back from the windows and furniture. Not a single piece of wood on this floor seems to have served as a barrier against the walking dead. *How were these people surviving? Maybe the owners of the house weren't here and the group broke in? Focus. Focus.*

"Blayne may be youngest by a year, but we both change on same day. I mastered power first." Her triumphant laughs echo off the walls. "I. Rank. Above. Him."

"First you should master the power of hearing." Cole steps out from the hall. The lanky boy rams his stake in her ear and the bloody point comes out of her other ear. The hands of the Vampire snatch him by the collar, flinging him through the air.

Cole has many skills, but stopping himself from crashing through two of the long windows is not one of them. The once orphaned boy lands on his side in a nearly waterless pool. Blood changes the color of the concrete. The collected rain flows towards the drain in the center of the pool.

Seizing the moment of diversion, Lana raises the pointed blade above her head. The sharp blade cuts the air on its way back down, slicing through the Vampire's upper arm severing it from her body. With her intact hand, Amaterasu slings the niece of her sire up into the hanging light. Glass breaks and light bulbs lose their spark. Amaterasu quickly flees; arm cut off and stake in her skull.

Falling with the broken glass, Lana lands backside on the hard dining table. She briskly bolts upright, bits of chandelier in her skin, searching for the Vampire. Convinced Tokyo is gone she snatches a flashlight from the table and hops down. Big shards of window glass crunch under her tennis shoes as she steps through the wide opening. "Cole, we have to get back to Loki." Lights beam around the outside pool area, and the wind tosses her hair around her face, stinging her eyes. The Nebraskan girl steps closer to the edge of the pool, and her heart beats faster than the wings of a hummingbird. Her friend doesn't move from the red puddle around his head.

Sword and flashlight in hand, Lana jumps down running and splashing through the water collecting at the bottom of the pool. Nearing him, she can see his chest slowly rising and following, and she lets a breath she didn't know she was holding. "Cole!" Lana loudly whispers shaking his legs. "Cole! Cole!"

"Mmm," he stirs.

"Get up! We have to go!"

"My…my head hurts."

"Do you think you can make it to the hospital?" Lana helps her comrade to his feet.

"Uh…yeah. It's not bad. The vamp?"

Lana shakes her head.

* * *

The Japanese Vampire speeds by single and doublewide trailers.

Positive the two most threatening Shadows are not hunting her, Amaterasu stops and leans back against the base of a tree; her arm oozing blood onto the thick, exposed roots. She groans, slowly pulling the stake from her ears and silently cursing herself for letting the American boy sneak up on her.

The Vampire knows her arm will not grow back, but what really distresses her is the fact the bleeding should have slowed by now... The girl with drenched hair tied around chopsticks does not know why her stomach burns with a fire greater than that of her freshly cut limb...

The Vampire closes her eyes and concentrates—she must find her sire. He will know what is wrong with her. Her new fully developed eyes snap open. Amaterasu climbs to her feet. But before she sets out to her destination, the one arm girl doubles over in agony. Her stomach feels like at any moment it will burst into flames.

LANA & COLE
With tiny scratches on her face from the glass, and with blood in his brownish black hair and on the side of his smooth face, Lana and Cole return to the streets. The wind pushes against them, the sound of their flapping garments lost in the cracking and ripping of objects being forced together in the far off distance. *Tornado* weighs heavily on their minds.

Never in a movie about zombies have they seen Mother Nature respond. *You never see the ocean come ashore and kill everyone.* Cole points out to himself. *Or baseball size hail raining down and knocking zombie brains out.*

Squinting from the stinging wind, they finally spot Loki sitting on the sidewalk. Her head slumped over her knees in the small circle of light beaming from the flashlight. Cole reaches her first. "Loki, let's—Ah!" He pushes her head away from his shin.

The illumination shines on Loki's face and he sees to his horror a thick piece of his meat dangling from her smiling bloodstained teeth.

Cole quickly moves away from his former friend. Disbelief hitting him like a ton of bricks. And their problems intensify. At least thirty members of the walking dead *RUN* down the street after them. Lana grabs Cole's hand and they run for their lives leaving their friend behind.

Lana has spent years fighting dead things; starting with roaming cemeteries with her father and then the two of them blending in with the nightlife of the cities, eventually leading up to the fight where they fought Kronos and the Vampire scarred her face and killed her father. But she has never felt this alarmed.

Heart hammering, Lana cannot decide which is worse. A death by these things, which seem to be evolving at a rapid rate or by Vampires? Not keen on finding out, Lana makes a last minute decision. She turns right pulling Cole into a narrow alleyway. "We had a head start. We'll be okay," she hears Cole say over the howling wind and the beating of the sideways rain.

At the end of the two buildings, Lana faces the right and rolls the flashlight down the sidewalk, lines of rain caught in the swirling light. Hoping her plan works, Cole and Lana turn and sprint like lightning across the street. Once on the other sidewalk they make a left. Unable to see ten feet in front of them, Cole runs his hand along the brick and glass of a building. It must be one of those chain malls or something because there doesn't seem to be an end to it, and Cole fears for Lana's safety. *I have to make sure she makes it before I...*

Air. Finally. They make a sharp right, Cole still squeezing Lana's hand. They continue running, listening for the fearful sounds of footsteps bringing death. Darkness in every direction. Water pours down from the sky, pounding the city like a giant with thousands of fists, and rushes wildly through the gutters, gushing out like blood from a deep wound.

After what seems like an eternity of fleeing and running through the pelting rain going in who knows what directions, towards more death bringers or a Kansas twister, Cole abruptly stops at an intersection. "You have to kill me," he bows over.

Lana looks down at him, the rain and wind let up making it easier to see. "I didn't kill Loki. What makes you think I can kill you?"

Cole laughs. The deep uncharacteristic sounds send a dark chill down her spine before freezing her bones. "You know what kills me, Lana?" He suddenly stands erect looking down at her. Veins the size of string and arteries bigger than yarn and the color of her hair spread up and down Cole's arms, and slither out of the top of his collar stretching up his neck. "The time I spent thinking of you, well, you spent it thinking of Kronos. *Gotta find Kronos. Must kill Kronos,*" he mocks.

Lana slowly takes several steps back, careful not to slip on the wet sidewalk, backing out into the street.

"He's here! And what are you doing?" he taunts her, his face now marked with the disease. "Errands for a Vampire. Eye raping Cricket when you think no one is looking." Green foam drips from the corners of his lips.

He growls and reaches for her throat.

With more like Cole likely on the way, Lana doesn't have time to cogitate whether or not she can kill someone who isn't a Vampire—like when she left the woman from the purple van on the pavement at the border forcing the military to deal with her. Lana closes her eyes and raises the sword.

The former Shadow's head detaches from his body.

The wind and the rain abruptly stop. Several stars twinkle in the sky; easily seen in the lightless city. Lana stands next to the sidewalk listening and watching the water falling over in the storm drain; the path so clearly defined. As is hers. The three of them, her, Loki, and Cole will never sit chatting together in the small woods next to Rush Cemetery. Those days are over. The past has come and it hurts, as it should, but now the future is calling. *Raven. My dreams...*

Concordia, Kansas has become a quiet place. Extremely quiet. So quiet one could hear a pin drop. Lana is familiar with this type of eerie silence. It is the stillness of the earth before another storm...

Suddenly, there is a sharp pain in Lana's wrist...

LUCAS/LEON/CRICKET
"Why are they turning on you?" Lucas had been waiting to inquire why the zombies had come after Raven, and now the ride to the hospital in his own car through the scattered debris on the streets seems

like an opportune time.

The rain had stopped pouring down after they ditched the truck; the little amount of gas in it would not get them to where they are going, and instead of leaving the gas Lucas siphoned it and put it in the Biscayne.

Raven does not answer.

Lucas observes her reflection in his rearview mirror. Her eyes are closed and she doesn't look well…

"She will be okay, Luke," Leon assures him.

"You were right. I don't have a degree in Zombie Virus. Brighton, how is this gonna affect her?"

The brunette shakes his head and looks out his window. To know what caused the damage to the houses, apartments, and buildings is indistinguishable from the Shadows, zombies, Vampires, and the tornado.

Cricket puts his best friend's head on his shoulder, her hair wet, and wraps his own soaked arm around her. The water from the sky had found its way in through the opening where a window had once been and dampened a portion of the smooth leather seat. If his bottom wasn't already wet it would have been when he plopped down on the probably ruined blue seat.

Lucas sees the nonverbal boy kiss the Goddess's forehead. He does not feel jealous like he did when Jet and Raven hugged. Lucas Kale does not know what to call his *feeling*, but he wishes he could help Raven—that is something he does know.

LANA QUEEN

He came out of nowhere.

The pain in the Shadow's wrist causes her to release her grip on the long bladed sword, and he pushes her down to the pavement. Lana lands on her forearms. She quickly checks her wrist. No teeth marks.

The Shadow starts to flip over and the Vampire forces her onto her back with his weight.

Kronos!

The Vampire grabs Lana's left arm, the same one he had nearly broken her wrist bones in when he came up behind her, and with his palm Kronos forces her fingers from the index to the pinky completely back against the top of her own hand. Before Lana can register the pain of her four broken fingers, Kronos rises to his feet yanking her up with him. Her arch nemesis snaps her left arm around and pins it against her shoulder blades. Something pops and Lana screams.

"Don't worry. My intentions are to spill as little of your blood as possible. Wouldn't want anyone else to have it." The bloodsucker with the three inch scar on his cheek yanks her damaged arm and tosses her like a paperboy flinging a newspaper.

Lana unintentionally spins sideways through the air before landing in a crouch; the entire time thinking she needs a weapon. She is certain Ganesha's sword is a good ways behind her somewhere next to her friend's body. But the girl with a broken hand knows there is no way she is getting to it.

Lana tries to recall the objects around her. A

great distance from her are two parked cars on opposite sides of the street; no good, running there would be futile. *Wood. Wood. Wood.* There are no trees nearby, however there is a street light with no illumination next to her. The Nebraskan Shadow could kick it down, but that will take time and she only has one usable arm; the pole is too thick for her to pick up. The library is fairly close; plenty of wooden objects. *Enclosed space. Maybe I should take my chances with the sword.* The green-eyed girl can feel Kronos nearly on her back. Contemplation over.

Lana knows her enemy expects her to retaliate using her good fist or possible side sweep him. The teenager does something he never expects. She stands up, rears her leg back, and kicks him in his penis. With her six years of anger and frustration Lana turns around and kicks him in his crotch again. And again and again; each time hoping his penis and balls will be forced up inside him.

Then, seeing beyond the Vampire for the first time, Lana realizes they have an audience. *YIKES!* Her mind yells. Her scream of pain just a moment ago has drawn the attention of three death bringers; their eyes reminding her of Loki and the ones that caused Jet's car to explode.

The split second distraction costs her.

Lana brought her leg up intending to kick the side of the bloodsucker's head, but her focus is not one hundred percent. The Shadow does not move fast enough—Lana is no match for her opponents speed. The sinister Vampire with scars on his face catches her shoe. Planning to use him as leverage, the girl with the summit of her ear missing brings her right leg up to do what her other leg had intended. Kronos catches that one, too. He spins the teenager around in a circle and throws her to the starless sky.

Lana tries to gain control of her body, but her wounded arm makes it impossible. She goes from looking at the black sky to the position of someone doing a belly flop off a cliff. She sees two more cannibals join the group just has Kronos meets her in the air. His dark boot collides with her head right above her ear. The pain forces her eyes shut.

The Shadow's gut, or the pain consuming her body, tells her she is in trouble. But Lana doesn't know how to signal out for backup with the Connection. The only time she has ever been alone for a long period of time with a Vampire, *Vampires*, was the night Kronos threw acid on her. Cole had shown up, but she knows for a fact it wasn't because of her doing.

The memory makes Lana think about her father. His death takes the Shadow back to August Cemetery today when she first thought about her dreams—her dreams about Raven and the electric blue parts of her eyes. The Shadow feels…tingling in her brain similar to her foot falling asleep…

Lana doesn't have to open her eyes to know what hit her, or rather what she hit. The sounds of denting metal and cracking glass tell her she will not be using this vehicle for transportation. *You have to get up,* her voice tells her. Her head feels like it has tripled in size. Her heart beats but no oxygen enters her pipes, and Lana is positive she has landed on her left side.

The Shadow slowly opens her eyes.

Her legs are propped up against a car's cracked back windshield. Lana has suspected her arm is broken and, now, rolling onto her back, the teenager has no doubt. Her shoulder and fingers are dead weight. The girl trying to catch her breath tilts her forehead back, her eyes searching for Kronos. Her blurred vision sees a black blob walking in her direction carrying what Lana assumes to be the long-bladed sword...

* * *

Cricket promptly hops on the other side of the smooth seat away from Raven.

He can feel the static coming, and normally it would not do anything to his best friend but he is not taking any risks.

"What's wrong?" Lucas panics.

Leon turns around in the blue seat. "Cricket's doing the freeze-tilt-head-thing."

A grainy image of a Vampire dressed in black with disfigurements on his face enters the mind of the young man with the shaved head. The leader of the Vampires breaks the fingers of a dark-headed Shadow that has scars around her lips...

Cricket awakens.

There is no need for clues has to Lana's whereabouts; after a signal through the Connection a Shadow's body naturally goes in the direction of the Similar needing backup.

Lucas has no idea what the young man saw, but Cricket practically throws his entire body over the seat and firmly presses his knee down—the car accelerates.

The weak woman in the silk top with her hair pulled up in ponytail whispers, "Lana…"

Dazed, Raven can hear Kronos's deep voice nearby: "You have put up a great fight. Lana, you have made me proud. But I have grown bored of this tedious game. I must take this opportunity while there is no one alive to come to your rescue."

* * *

The Shadow looks up at the Vampire's pale face. "I know something you don't," Lana smirks.

"You can thank Raven," Kronos ignores her. "If she had stayed out of my affairs you would not be alive to feel this." He leans down and whispers in the Shadow's ear, "You will never know how truly dangerous you were to me."

Then with the speed of a Vampire, Kronos drops the sword, rips Lana's wet clothing; her right sleeve and her left pants leg, and disappears only to very quickly return with a small container of charcoal fluid. After spraying it on the Shadow, he pulls out two lighters from his pants pocket and sets her exposed skin on fire.

Kronos sees headlights approaching and the Vampire hears more heartbeats than he likes. Lana—on fire—drops from the trunk and smacks against the pavement. She frantically rolls around trying to smother the flames. Kronos bends down to pick up the burning girl and three bullets from a rifle puncture the Vampire's heart.

The vehicle burns rubber, the brakes screeching to a halt. A door flings open. Kronos unhappily flees. With the Vampire gone the death bringers begin their march.

His heart beating faster than its normal rhythm, Cricket runs to Lana's side. "Cricket...it worked." He sweeps the burnt girl up off the street and into his arms and carries her back to the car, gently placing her on her feet while Leon quickly retrieves the sword; the stench of death drawing closer to the idling car.

Lana, fighting tears, gets in after Cricket. "I think I only have first degree burns. I can't use my left hand." The silent gentleman can see red spots and swelling on her right arm. When Cricket picked the Shadow up he saw her left leg was burnt as well.

Lucas presses the gas petal. The headlights of the cousins' car shine on a severed head. "Cole." Leon shakes his head. "Loki?"

"One of them. I didn't—" Lana notices the way the Goddess is slumped back against the seat. "Raven, what's wrong?" The intelligent dead people move out of the vehicle's way.

"She had to kill Ganesha thanks to the Jap," answers Lucas. The loather tightly grips the steering wheel, anger threatening to break it. Lucas takes a deep breath, momentarily taming his hatred for Vampires. "She hasn't feed in a long ass time. And out of rage she used most of her energy."

Lana reaches over Cricket and tenderly touches the blonde woman's arm; warm and sweaty to the touch. "Raven, you need to feed."

"If I do then they will feast," she responds, her voice dry and barely above a whisper.

"They already are."

Raven's eyes snap open.

"Think about it," the black-haired girl says. "If Tokyo did that to Ganesha then she would had to practice Pushing, which I witnessed before I chopped her arm off. And it can't just be Tokyo breaking the rules, she was a Novice which means—"

"She had to have permission," Leon pieces together.

"I can't think." The hungry Vampire rubs her head. Sharp pains shoot up and down her body like bolts of lightning. Her brain shouts—*Blood!*—over and over again like a flashing neon sign. "Neither can we," the genius admits in a low, sorrowful voice.

Cricket wraps his hand around Raven's, comforting her.

I do like Cricket, the burnt girl admits to herself looking out through the hole where the glass used to be before a cannibal punched it and pulled Kimberly from this very seat. The reality of never seeing her best friends hits her. The people Lana used to play with and hang out with will not being joining her freshman year of college. *Cole and Loki will not be doing anything. Ever. Mom...* Lana takes comfort in the words she spoke to Kronos before he pulled out his lighters to fulfill his plan of burning her alive. *I know something you don't...*

Hospital
Lucas finally pulls the car into the disastrous parking lot of the hospital where the exotic girl is waiting for them at the entrance.

"I can walk," Lana tells Cricket. "Help our

friend."

The ultramarine blue vehicle comes to a stop on the grass near the entrance, the only available area in the chaotic mess in the lot; cars and cars and dead bodies.

"There's food in there. I'm suddenly feeling a little bit peppy," Raven manages a tiny grin. Cricket squeezes her hand, smiling. The four doors open.

"The boy you sent me here for is dead. He was a zombie when we found him," Sheba informs them of the Potential's death. "Jet is with nineteen survivors on the top floor." Sheba's eyes grow wide, realizing Ganesha is not with them. "Ray, what happened to—"

"Ganesha…is dead. Vampire. Lana needs treatment," Raven changes the subject.

"Cole and Loki are…" Lana is unable to finish her sentence. Sheba gives an understanding nod.

"Zombies have turned on me. I need a Vampire," Raven quickly informs her; the fair-headed woman doesn't know how much longer she can even stand.

Sheba smiles vindictively. "We will gladly help."

Inside the fully lit area, the hospital's backup generator doing all the work, Sheba, Cricket, and Lana branch away to find aid for the Shadow and a meal for Raven.

"My senses are all over the place," whispers Lana, painfully holding the sword with her good hand but burnt arm. "Have been since sunset."

"Ditto."

"This isn't going to be easy."

Cricket nods. Weapons ready, the three Shadows

keep their eyes and ears alert for trouble, usable medical supplies, and a Vampire.

* * *

Raven walks with the cousins, Lucas and Leon on both sides of her, down a hallway that looks like a train came through; paper and needles scattered everywhere, carts and gurneys on their sides.

Her knees begin to feel like water and Raven crumples into Lucas and Leon; the two of them grabbing her arms and sliding their hands around her waist. They help her to the tiled floor, propping her against the wall. Raven's hearing becomes muffled like a human with an extremely bad ear infection. She hears one of them say along the lines of, "It oing kay."

Raven can feel it inside her; hunger—the thirst for power building at an extreme rate. Head rush. Everything moves, leaving traces of its former place. The ill woman closes her eyes and rocks back and forth. She can't think about anything except, *Warm sweet blood.* How powerful it feels to pierce cold skin and have its warm juice slide down her throat. The scent alone is...pacifying. Just thinking about the aroma makes her feel serene.

Raven opens her hazel eyes. The dizziness stops and the rocking ceases. She gets to her feet. Looking straight ahead, she sees three reflections in a square mirror. But her focus is on one. What Raven is considering is going to hurt tremendously. *But the reward will be great.* Her left hand twitches. Then the right. Raven loses all control. The hard, white wall gives in to Raven's demands as she plows through it, knocking Blayne to the hospital floor with her landing on top of him.

The young Vampire easily flings his severely weakened attacker halfway down the corridor. Raven lands on her face, and Blayne is instantly on his feet strutting towards the inert Goddess.

"Where do you think you're going?" Lucas steps through the hole with Leon behind him.

"What are *you* going to do?" Blayne twists on his heels with a grin so cocky that it reminds Lucas of Alec; rekindling his resentment and loathsomeness. "Something awful hunter-like, you little sh—"

The gray tiles underneath their shoes vibrate. Followed by the sound of claws scratching against the surface of the hospital floor. Where the hall veers to the right, a four-legged animal emerges.

"Blayne," heeds Kronos unexpectedly from behind them; three other Vampires at his side. The Novice takes several steps back, standing in between the humans and the Deaths at the opposite end of the corridor.

The Werewolf nuzzles the bleeding girl's face with his muzzle.

"She would have you believe she has never murdered a human," Kronos calls down the hall, his eyes on the Goddess but intended for the ears of Lucas and Leon. Feeling as if her bones have been crushed, Raven, face and arms severally bruised, holds on to a giant paw—half her body size—letting Jet pull her up. "But there are other ways to kill," he continues, "that do not involve *enjoying* their precious blood…"

The half-Vampire in the sky blue undershirt with

the long ponytail reaching down her back lets go of Jet's fur, using what energy she has to stand on her own. "I killed my mother... She was The Witch." The two Hunters stare, their mouths in an O shape. "My stepfather was the only family *I* had left after the deaths of my mom and brother." Raven sways back and forth, blood running down her skin. "My biological father, jealous of our relationship, stabbed him to death."

Steadying herself, Raven intently focuses her eyes on the two humans. "I was new, and it doesn't take a Leon to guess what happened." The Goddess takes a deep breath trying to maintain her balance. "Are we done bonding now?" she asks the mechanic and the certified genius.

"For now," Lucas Kale says. "Just so we are clear, I am mad at you. For killing the Bugatti Veyron. She was beautiful, and now I will never see her again." Lucas has put a tiny smile on the face of the woman whom he first met in Hastings, Nebraska; a smile no matter how big or small is still a smile, and Lucas's thin lips turn up quite pleased with himself.

Vampires, fifteen Leon counts, join Kronos, Blayne, and the other three.

"You all ate before you came here," Raven factually says to the Vampires. "Jet, that is what we were smelling. The overwhelming smell of fresh human blood in their dead bodies is what caused you to vomit." Raven blinks away the blood in her eyes. "We know you are responsible for this, Kronos."

The Vampires drank the bottles of blood and

pretended to help the humans just for appearances; a verisimilitude so cold Raven is angered beyond her years.

Unable to see any benefit from lying, Kronos admits, "Alex was very helpful. The boy even brought us meals."

"Alec," she corrects him with animalistic anger.

"Food is food"—the caped Vampire acknowledges the two humans for the first time—"no matter what they call each other." Neither Lucas nor Leon like the way he looks at them; heartless, vacant of all humanity.

Lucas whimsically remarks, "Dude, with an attitude like that you're never going to get a date."

Raven licks her lips at Blayne. Her eyes change and for the first time her fangs show themselves. "I want half."

"How about none?" Blayne replies.

"She's not going to kill you," Kronos rolls his eyes. "Anyways, we know what happens when *we* die." He grins at the Goddess. "Do you know what happens when *you* die?"

The Werewolf pushes Raven with his fury forepaw so fast that Blayne lands once again on his back with the enemy on his chest. Raven's sharp teeth punctures the smooth skin on his neck, sucking and sucking the blood from his young veins. The sweet taste of the liquid covering her tongue, sliding down the back of her throat; waves of pleasure passing through her body. Momentarily satisfied, she pulls away licking the leakage off her lips.

"Check out what we found," Lana smiles,

coming from around the corner and passing by Jet. Her arm is in a cast and bandages cover her burns. Behind Lana the girl Lucas kissed earlier carries the feet of a Vampire dressed in a dark red shirt and a shiny black skirt. Cricket holds Tokyo's only arm. The Shadows stop next to the Hunters.

When the Vampire arrived here to find her sire the Shadows jumped her. She wiggles around in their grasp, but Amaterasu knows she does not have the strength to overpower three enemies—even on a day when she had two arms and her body didn't feel like it was burning from the inside out.

"We were also looking for another, but I see you found him." Lana looks directly at the pinned boy on the white floor of the hospital. Their currently restored leader leaps backwards off of the brunette boy. The Vampire from Lana, Sheba, and Cricket's Connections screams for Kronos as the Goddess's fingernails scratch into her raw bleeding wound.

But her sire turns his back. Blayne leans on one of the Vampires for support and all twenty of them round the corner leaving the amputee.

The newly powered woman demands from Tokyo, "Did you make anything today?"

"No."

"Then we are going to do you a favor." Raven nods to Sheba and Cricket. They release her and Tokyo lands on her feet. Cricket pulls out his stake from the back pocket of his jeans and sheathes the stake into the Vampire's heart.

From the origin of Tokyo's heart, thick black smoke consumes her body and then disappears.

"I love roasted undead," Lucas smiles. "No ashes

and unpleasant smells."

"Get the survivors and stay at the house," Raven orders her remaining followers; Jet, Cricket, Sheba, Lucas, Leon, and Lana. "I am the only one that should be fighting now."

* * *

Naked, Jet leads the way down the stairwell from the top story of the hospital; he doesn't want to risk breaking the stairs in his animal form.

Side by side, Lucas and Leon stomp hurriedly down the metal stairs behind the nude man having to look at Jet's buttocks in order to avoid tumbling down the steps and possibly touching his naked body. Sheba guards the rear of the moving crowd while Lana and Cricket strategically stay in the middle of the nineteen survivors ranging from ages ten to forty-five.

The crowd of twenty five put the exit door to the tenth level behind them. Down and down they go.

Level seven…

Lana's broken arm will heal significantly faster than the average human and the burns will have healed by tomorrow more than likely, but the continuous movement down the stairs isn't a picnic. The white bandages rub against her tender skin with every step she takes and having to carry the sword with her blistered arm makes the weapon feel like it weighs more than it should. *Focus. Dead Shadows…? Vamps…? Nothing.*

Level four…

Level two…

Jet, the Normals, and the supercharged humans pass by the door to the second floor. And as soon as

Sheba turns her back to go down the stairs the exit door flings open…

They move faster than Sheba could have ever imaged. She only has time to make a halfway turn. Four fast hands with black spider-webbed veins stop her like a lion attacking a gazelle.

A pair of teeth sinks into Sheba's ear, ripping it from the side of her head.

The girl with the long wavy hair and ruby necklace pushes the two zombie Shadows backwards. But a dozen or so monsters take their place. The only people with guns—Cricket, Lucas, and Leon—do not even have the chance to turn around and put Sheba out of her misery.

For a man that does not speak, Cricket's eyes tell it all; a teardrop soundlessly cuts him. *Two down.* He is now the only human alive from Raven's side. *Lana—the only one from hers.*

Cricket and Lana run rhythmically down the stairwell. Both of them know the rear should be guarded, but they now know from the unfortunate experience that it takes more than one Shadow. And while they are aware that the life of one individual is not more important than the many, neither Cricket nor Lana is willing to drift further back from The Preventer.

"When need a plan," Leon suggests, finally on the ground floor of the hospital.

Chapter 20
Between the Devil and the Deep Blue Sea

TROTTING DOWN THE STREET, the deluge from the clouds above soaks the Werewolf's thick coat down to his skin. But the weight of the water flatting his fur doesn't make him look less like a giant. Just a BIG wet one.

Lucas and Leon straddle the back of the beast that they just found out today not only exists but is near extinction. They hang on tightly to the noose around Jet's neck; it would have been impossible to carry the humans without the braided rope. Jet's fine hairs are too slippery to grasp, especially with the powerful wind blowing against them.

The Hunters grasp the big wooden cross they retrieved, as well as the rope, from the Biscayne. Leon knew it would be tough enough trying to make it back to Raven's with the zombies after them let alone the bloodsuckers that started this battle.

On foot below them, the people run in fear of being eaten alive. And in fear of the swirling vortex off to their far right; another twister for the state of Kansas. The Normals run breathlessly on the broken path. Small flickering balls of light from the streetlamps cast eerie silhouettes in every direction, increasing their adrenaline and keeping them on edge.

Something leaps out at them unexpectedly from behind a bush.

The man with flesh and muscles torn and eaten from his thighs is the same type of monster Cricket shot in the street while he was holding the rope that was tied to Raven—when Ganesha was alive. Cricket aims and twice he pulls the trigger of his rifle, killing the zombie and releasing his own pain.

The flickering lights lose the fight to have their spark and all of Concordia is under a blanket of darkness.

With the cousins on his back, Jet passes under a power line. Suddenly the line snaps and the thick cable swings back and stings Lucas in the throat; causing him to let go of the wet rope, cross, and his pistol. He skins his knees, elbows, and forearms on the cracked pavement. Tiny rocks stick to his scraped flesh, but the abrasions do not hurt nearly as bad as the thick red mark on his jugular.

The Werewolf does a one eighty. The twister tosses a damaged singlewide onto his path. The scariest monsters come out of the trailer at full speed—*their skin pigments match the dark sky and their veins are whiteout white.*

Lucas Kale sprints.

The blonde Vampire Hunter hears Jet stomping the zombies like cockroaches, but Lucas knows the others are now less protected and the dark gray funnel is drawing near. "Save *them!*" Over the howling of the wind he faintly hears—"Luke!"—as his instincts take him away from danger, and away from his cousin.

* * *

After Raven left the others who were to see the survivors to safety, she started roaming the streets in hopes of finding more humans in the wild storm. She heard, smelled, and saw nothing.

Even the college campus excludes heartbeats. *This place is a ghost town,* she thinks. Her feet trudge through the litter scattered across the wet grass of the courtyard. Passing by a table and bench, Raven suddenly halts. Out of the four buildings built in a square around the courtyard her inhuman eardrums detect movement towards the top floors of three of the tall buildings.

Without warning, windows break and a dozen bodies leap out of the campus building behind her. Then like a chain reaction the windows on the higher levels of the two buildings to the right and in front of her shatter. Virus infected monsters pour down into the campus courtyard and within a few seconds they will have the drenched half-human surrounded.

Instead of yanking up bolted down benches and tables—for no apparent reason Raven can think of—she reaches around for her long blonde ponytail, bends over, and vomits…

The dead Shadows are nearly at her side.

Raven takes off, barely escaping what is left of their dead finger tips. Black faces with glowing white eyes and white-out veins haunt Raven as she runs down the street. They are hungrier than the others—the infected Shadows are voracious, requiring more human organs and flesh—and now the supply in Concordia, Kansas has severally thinned. The former Shadows' bodies are entering their version of the decomposition stage. They desperately chase after her—their need to feed at an all-time high.

This is the first time Raven has ever feared for her life. She spent centuries being the hunter. And now *she* is the prey. The vampiric woman in the silky sky blue undershirt speeds up, vanishing from the insatiable mob.

Half a mile away from them, Raven runs through a backyard occupied with a swing set and sandbox. She kicks in the backdoor of a three-story house. The half-blood expects the humans to have barricaded it, but to her surprise the single object flings open into a hallway. The door bangs against the plaster wall and its corners stick inside the hard surface from the extra push of energy.

Raven easily pries the door from the painted wall, but the damaged lock will not latch. She places her forearm on the useless panel closing it and leans forward, her head resting on her wrist. She sighs not knowing her next course of action. Should she find a way to fight? Or should she retreat to the red cedar house?

What if they all turn into...zombies? What if Olsen dies? Am I going to know what it truly feels like to be alone?

The half-blood used to watch zombie flicks and wonder what it would be like if they really did exist. Raven no longer needs to imagine. She knows exactly how it feels to run for your life from multiple putrid corpses while adrenaline pulsates through your veins.

No more imagining what their faces would really look like.

That is the third thing Raven will never forget—never forget how the humans look when they are dead and wanting her to join their...*extinction.* The disturbing moaning coming from the dead rises in her eardrums. Now that she is rejuvenated she can hear every sound of pain—that is second. Whenever she closes her eyes the sound of tearing flesh, screams, and limbs dragging across the dirt, and the inhuman hissing and screeching noises will be the new bedtime lullabies.

Raven knows that if she doesn't die she will always remember... Remember the feeling of having to kill her own friends and family—the number one thing forever imprinted into Raven's soul.

"Are you okay?"

Her head snaps to the left. Kale had been standing a few feet away and she hadn't even noticed him. Or the tears on her face.

"There are many definitions for the word blue," Raven answers. "For example, right now I am blue in the face."

"Stupid question," he admits.

"What happened to your neck? Why are you here?"

"Twister. Fugly bastards. Me ran fast." Lucas steps forward with a hammer and a thin strip of wood. "I should fix that door. And the windows."

She doesn't budge from her place, just stares at him.

"What?"

The woman who is centuries old stands there looking at his torn clothes and bloody scrapes. *If I die it will not matter if the humans survive the zombies because,* "I know what happens if I die." The Goddess finishes her thought aloud. It clicks. The Vampire's question at the hospital had not been rhetorical. *He knows what happens...the deal...*

"There is a cure." Raven grabs his wrist, forcing him to drop the objects as their feet hastily move down the hallway. The unlocked door behind them does nothing to stop the dead humans with luminous crimson eyes from filing inside the narrow hallway. "Where's Jet?"

"Not here," he answers. The sound of stomping footsteps along with a noxious smell fills the hall. Lucas nearly jumps out of skin when the window to their right shatters as they pass by it.

The hall veers to the left. Lucas and Raven approach the stairs to the second story and the side door next to it busts open; shards of wood nearly hit them. The first floor is about to be flooded with zombies.

Before Lucas can form a plan, Raven scoops him up in her arms. The young man doesn't have time to think about how ridiculous it looks with her speeding up the first set of steps with him in *her* arms.

Before they continue up the rest of the steps to the right, a zombie Shadow crashes in from a tree outside the window above the first flight of stairs. Lucas Kale is glad no guy is around to hear him give a high-pitched girl scream.

"This is the second floor!" He exclaims with amazement, which quickly dies. The two windows on the left and right of the hallway cave under the pressure of all things two more zombie Shadows with unflattering black veins. The dead Shadow closest to them, the one on the left, throws his arm out to punch the half-blood. Raven ducks down with Lucas still in her arms and with one swift motion she places him on the smooth floor, grabs the zombie's feet, and tosses the monster into the Shadow that has just arrived behind them at the top of the stairs. The two zombie Shadows fall back through the steps breaking the boards and creating a wide hole in the stairs.

The only zombie that stands in front of them is a wavy-haired brunette wearing a ruby jeweled necklace...

* * *

The soaking wet Werewolf crouches down on all four of his beastly legs. His passenger with the Vampire repellent, the over-sized cross, plants his own two feet on the slippery grass at Raven's Kansas house.

The scrutiny in Cricket's eyes concerns Leon Carmany. "Ganesha's body." Leon finally understands. The corpse is not where Raven left it, and from what he can tell the body is not in the yard… "I'm sorry."

The children and adults follow the dark-skinned young man inside the red cedar house that has porch damage. Leon and Lana linger back, waiting for Jet to quickly make the transformation from beast to a mammal with opposable thumbs; the braided rope falls in circles around him.

The strangers gape at the interior of the kitchen, the spacious and windowless dining room, and the dimly lit hall. Not a single one of them says a word. Each of them feeling oddly comfortable. Leon leaves the wooden cross in the room where Jet previously busted through the door frame and wall to save the boy who played a significant part in this terrifying chaos.

The door opens to the panic room. Mozart had seen them on the cameras and pressed his button. The young man originally from Africa bends down and wraps his arms around the Husky. Cricket rubs his face up and down the dog's soft fur. *We are five down.* Hoping for Raven's return, the canine's heartbeat gives him a sense of closure. Lana feels her throat beginning to swell up and she fights back tears. "She'll be here," she assures him. Apple green eyes look directly at Leon. "Lucas, too."

Jet opens the door at the other end of the small room and the nineteen survivors begin descending the stairs, joining Lisa and Joshua. Abruptly, Mozart breaks free of the mute Shadow's tender hold and runs out of the room. "No!" Lana shouts and chases after the dog.

The gray and white Siberian Husky stops in front of the second door on the right, Jet's room, barking at the open entrance. Lana halts in front of Cricket's bedroom located between the safe room and Jet's sleeping quarters. "I don't feel anything. Do you?" she asks the male Shadow standing beside her. Cricket shakes his head. "Not a Vampire," the raven-haired girl eliminates, raising Ganesha's sword. They stare down the hall of crosses.

Cricket raises his rifle, walks forward, and turns. The canine ceases barking. The Shadow stares into the pitch black room. The dim light from the hallway casts little light and Cricket hesitates at the idea of having to stick his hand in the room and flip up the light switch.

Lana takes a few steps away from Cricket's bedroom door and the unforeseen happens. Cricket's bedroom door swings open and hits her in the backside. The dead thing inside grabs the back of her shoulders. It growls in her ear just before Cricket yanks her forward by her forearms. The petite girl lands on her side on the rough floor. Lana sees the white-eyed monster dig into the side of Cricket's throat. Jet fires a gun multiple times from inside the panic room killing the monster. But Cricket is already infected...

* * *

What is left of Sheba's lips that haven't yet fixed themselves smile at Lucas and Raven. Confusion flashes across his face. *Is that a sexy stance?* Sheba stands in the center of the hall blocking their path to the last flight of stairs. "Ray, trying to save them is not working." Sheba breaks her pose, smiling crookedly. "Well, except for that one you had me shoot. I don't recall a thank you."

They both recall how Alec died.

Lucas hears the creaking of the stairs. It will not take long for the bringers of death to reach them. The young man looks down at Raven waiting for her to make a move. A tear slides down her cheek.

"You're not grateful either, bitch." Lucas recalls the former Sheba's reaction when her Connection ended and the girl came back to reality to find him on the kitchen floor and an infected dead girl lying against the refrigerator.

Flipping backwards in the air, Raven upper kicks Sheba knocking her entire jaw out of socket. The dislocated bones sticking out of Sheba's nose prevent her from speaking. "Zombies aren't supposed to talk. Let's keep it that way," Lucas smirks before Raven picks him up and bolts by another one of her dead friends. Lucas Kale feels a tug on his foot...

On the top floor, the half-human half-Vampire woman sets the Hunter on his feet and locks the door to the stairs. Lucas looks down at his foot...

"Bitch stole my shoe!"

"Do you want to go get it?" Raven retorts looking around the nearly bare room for something to smash out the single window.

"No. I *want* to be able to *run!*"

She spots a tricycle and throws it at the window located on the farthest side of the room.

"What Sheba said," he starts. "You know she wouldn't want to be thanked for taking a life."

She dismisses his attempt at comforting her.

"Hop on, Bella."

"What did you call me?"

A fist breaks through the door motivating him to climb on her back. They move across the carpet of the commodious area with Lucas piggybacking as zombies bust through the cream colored door. The woman he met in Nebraska leaps on the windowsill and jumps out into the starless night. Raven grabs the edge of the roof and flips up with an exhilarated Lucas and lands on top of the house.

The rain has altogether stopped Raven detects. Lucas looks over the edge of the roof. A hundred or so carcasses have gathered below them. In the distance several houses and vehicles burn deep oranges, blues, and purples, sending thick clouds of gray and black smoke above the loud atmosphere.

"Jet!" Raven desperately calls.

"Jet!" Lucas joins her.

She hopes her friend can hear her. More and more zombies with luminous white eyes and crayon white arteries and veins are coming for Kale. *And for her.*

"Why are they all the same now?" he asks curiously.

"Those are not the pale or advanced zombies. They are former Shadows and they are dying from starvation. The other kinds have moved on. Yet they stay."

Raven knows she cannot make it back to her house without leaving Lucas Kale; carrying a human for more than a few seconds, even at a slower speed than what she is used to, damages them. She refuses to do either. "Jet!"

"Thank you," Lucas sincerely says. Raven whirls around in confusion. "I see something in you that I have never seen in any human or Vampire. You don't need us. You don't need *me*, yet here you are standing...standing with someone lower than you. *Staying with me.*"

I want you, Raven thinks as she watches the tears angrily throw themselves from the corner of his telling eye. She knows the mechanic thinks that he is not worthy. That she should save herself. And that there is something else... Something that he wants to tell her...

The blood having rushed to her face, Raven quickly turns away from Lucas, breaking the lustful gaze and avoiding the subject Lucas Kale had for once in his life found the courage to discuss.

"*Jet!*" the golden-haired woman yells. Echoing in the night, her voice once again thrusts back her oldest friend's name. Raven closes her eyelids. She can feel Lucas Kale staring at her as if he did not want to move from this spot. As if he did not *need* to. *As if the place he loves is within me.*

Unable to forget their first encounter, Lucas thinks about how captivated he was when, *She saw more to me.* Smoke drifts up from below them. The house is on fire.

"He's not coming, and *you* can't stay up here much longer," Lucas tells her.

"The human is right." Kronos lands on the rooftop.

"JET!" Raven screams with a desperation that stings her throat. Kronos laughs at her.

But the Goddess hears it—the heart of a giant. It does not take long for the ground to rumble, for the roof to vibrate. Sprinting through the gray and black smoke of charred wood, vehicles, and who knows what else, is the one person she knows will always be there for her. The walking and running dead fearfully part as if the beast could single-handedly kill all of them.

Raven turns sharply. "I know where to find the antidote," she says to Kronos and then adds something Lucas does not understand. "You win." The long pony-tailed woman snatches a bruised and mentally exhausted Lucas Kale by the arm, and they leap off the torched house.

In midair, Raven pulls Lucas Kale to her and puts him in the position she had previously used to carry him. She lands on Jet's back with Lucas in her arms. The woman in the undershirt swings the young man around to her backside. Lucas holds on to her small waist. Becoming turned on, he briskly adjusts his penis.

Kronos watches the Werewolf take off with the human and the Goddess, away from the dying crowd below. Deaths join Kronos on the roof of the burning house. "She finally figured it out. It is almost done. Kill it," the Vampire with the disfigurement on his left cheek gives the order. The Bald Vampire next to him nods and leaps down. Several others follow suit into the clearing crowd. The leader of all the Deaths turns to Blayne. "Kill the infected Shadows. Starting with Sheba," Kronos orders.

* * *

Jet kneels once again beside his kitchen door. His lifelong friend and the man with a crush on her get off of his back. The Werewolf takes his fur coat off, and the rope falls around his human body again.

"There is something…" Jet swallows, not wanting to tell Raven.

Lucas panics. "Leon?"

"No. It's—"

Raven doesn't wait for Jet to finish. She vanishes inside. The girl with the broken hand and burnt skin looks up at the Goddess standing in the hallway in front of Cricket's bedroom. "He won't come out. He is waiting for us…for us to kill him." Mozart is curdled up in a ball on the floor. His blue and green eyes look up at his master. The depressed dog whines. "No one wants to go in there," Leon says, his voice low and cracking, as him and Lana rise from the two chairs outside of the Shadow's door. "But he should be coming out soon," he hints squeezing his hands around the shotgun.

"I'm sorry," a deep voice says. The three of them turn to Lucas standing outside of the bathroom Cricket had once escorted Alec to sometime before sunset.

"I can do it," Jet offers her beside him.

"I have the antidote," Raven joylessly announces. "Think about we know, Jet. Killing the humans is not their intention."

"It is to kill you," Jet admits lowering his eyes.

The blonde man folds his arms across his chest. "Care to clue the rest of us in?"

Raven keeps her human eyes on the tallest man in the hallway of crosses. "I have to do this." "*NO!*"

Jet screams, making everyone except her jump.

"Raven, what is going on?" Lucas eyes her curiously.

"Nothing! Leave!" Jet yells at the three humans. "All of you."

"It really has been about me this entire time," the Goddess unenthusiastically says as if Jets outburst didn't happen. "*I am the cure.*"

"Isn't that *good?*" asks Lucas.

"You don't understand," Jet says vehemently.

"Then explain."

"Lucifer and God made a deal," Leon intervenes, and Jet skeptically looks at The Preventer. "Raven told me."

"What kind of deal?" the blonde Hunter asks, even more on edge. "A JOB biblical kind of thing?"

"If he, Lucifer, kills the Goddess," Leon sadly explains, "then The Banish not only ends but Demons will be released from Hell."

"*Real* Demons?"

"Yes. Enemies of God."

"Are they pretty?"

"*Luke.*"

"What? Valid question, dude. From what I know they were once Angels that went bad. And supposedly Angels aren't ugly. So in films how do they go from heavenly sexiness to"—Lucas suddenly turns to Raven—"I don't get why you think *you're* the antidote and why you're going to bit the dust."

"The zombies aren't eating the Vampires because…?"

"They're…dead… Some of the Shadows know

you're different."

Lana shakes her head. "It doesn't matter what they know. Our senses are stronger. The dead Shadows can probably smell the humanity... But while we were waiting for you Raven, Leon said you were bitten. You seem fine and people are still... Cricket is—"

Leon looks at the floor, feeling responsible for his Potential get bit. "I shot her before anything else happened."

"Again I ask," Lucas continues. "Raven, how do you know you are—"

"—She *doesn't* know that." Jet stares his friend down.

"Yes, I do!" Raven's eyes burn into his and Jet's dark eyes return the same tension. "*You* know, *too*, Jet." She turns to Lucas, Leon, and Lana. "I can prove it. Cricket needs my help. I am helping."

"Your skin will not stay open long enough to make samples will it? They are going to have to...bite you," Leon gathers, his voice soft.

Raven turns the knob on Crickets door and pushes...

The light from the ceiling fan shines on the slumped over figure in a rocking chair. Cricket lifts his head. His lips are badly cracked and his eyes have a tint of crimson...

He holds up a sign:

KILL ME

Raven hates seeing him like this; sick and dying before his time. "I cannot do that," she whispers.

His hand reaches out to her and she takes the slip of paper from his fingers:

It is not your fault. I love you, Ray.

Raven kneels down in front of him. "I love you, Cricket." She strokes the side of his warm cheek. "I know you heard us, and that you don't want to, but you have—"

He shakes his head, refusing.

"Please, Cricket. You can't fight forever," her voice cracks and tears stream down her face. "Just do it."

Tear drops leave his brownish-red eyes. The veins around his pale neck wound begin to turn his original skin color before the infection lightened it. Cricket knows she is right; it is a miracle he was able to hold on this long.

Raven holds her wrist out, offering it to him. Cricket gently places his dark fingers around her forearm. The black colored infection is spreading up his chin. He looks into her eyes.

In this moment, Lucas Kale wishes he could be in a bar somewhere chatting up some hot female of twenty-two. He wishes Leon did not have any insight into the future and that they had never gone to Nebraska. But most all he desires to feel nothing at all.

"It's okay," Raven tenderly coaxes Cricket.

Cricket slowly opens his mouth…and lets go of his willpower. Jet violently digs his fingers into the lowercase T shapes on the wall, pulling them apart, and refusing to stop until Cricket stops helping kill the only thing in this world that makes him happy. Raven is the only woman, the only person, he was certain that death wouldn't claim. How can he live in a world where she does not exist? How can he wake up every single morning knowing that he is going to outlive everyone on the planet, as well as the ones who are not even born yet?

His mouth bloodstained, Cricket releases his friend's wrist. Raven lays her head in Crickets lap, her blonde hair touching the floor, waiting.

The last of the pried off wall chunks join the rest of the pieces scattered on the floor. The skin around Jet's nails torn, blood coating his hands, gravity pulling the red fluid down in small streams. Moments of silence pass giving the illusion of minutes which feel like hours ticking and ticking away on the invisible clock of life—of more than one.

Jet could die if he chose never to be the wolf again, but he wouldn't begin the ageing process until years from now, and since Werewolves are immune to disease his death would be a slow and agonizing one. And he knows for a fact that poor Mozart will soon die without his master…

Lucas, Leon, and Lana gasp. Raven slowly looks up at Cricket's face. The open wound on the Shadow's neck has closed. The Goddess's blood pumping through his veins feels like ice smothering a flame; never before has he experienced a feeling this calm and palliative.

The red infection leaves his eyes, returning them to their friendly light. His complexion and veins virus free.

Raven wipes way the wetness around her eyes and begins walking the hall's route to the dining room. "Do not let Mozart out there."

Jet angrily grabs her unbitten wrist, spinning her around facing him. "You are really going to do this?"

"You can hug *me* now or a *corpse* later."

Cricket throws himself on her. The young man gives her the kind of hug he can never give a human; he squeezes her so tight that for a second Raven reconsiders her heroism. But then she remembers... "I have been infected for a while," she tells Jet with Cricket's arms still around her. "It *is* killing me. I threw up for the first time in my nine hundred years of being neither Vampire nor human."

The Shadow gives her a peck on the cheek, and then Jet pulls her to him burying her head against his chest. He sniffs her blonde hair. Over the years he had learned that sweet divine scent. But now he fears he will forget. He forces her back and Raven feels his warm lips pressing against hers, his warm wet tongue slides inside her mouth. Jet gently massages her compliant tongue.

The corners of Lucas Kale's lips turn up haughtily. When the taller man with bigger muscles hugged Raven earlier Lucas had instantly burned with jealousy. But this time Lucas fantasizes about running his own hands down the spine of her back while kissing the nape of her soft neck.

He decides to let Jet have his amorous moment. But as soon as Jet pulls away Lucas moves in, putting his hands on Raven's shoulders. "I do not care who rapes your face, this isn't goodbye." Lucas cups her soft face in his hands. "I meant what I said on that rooftop."

Raven leans in and kisses him on the cheek. "The Preventer has not figured out a way to save me." She turns to Lana, Lucas, and Leon and warns, "Mozart *will* bite." Their doughty leader passes through the rest of the house and exits out the kitchen door.

The wind has stopped, but the Olympic dead are just arriving. And so does fear. Sure Raven has been afraid for the humans, and frightened by the mass that had chased her through the city. But now she must face her greatest fear. Face the fact that once the humans are back to their normal selves the planet that flows with clear waters and various species will suffer in Hell's unseen fire.

Chapter 21
Return

THE DAY HAD started out with such beauty. The star that brought morning had also brought promises and security with its happy light. But for Raven—standing in the mists of what used to be a simpler and quieter time—she knows that before dawn glorifies the hills and streams her own light will never shine. If she does not do this, offer herself, humans will be near extinction. But by giving her life she will be handing over thousands.

Why do this when she has the choice to walk away and leave the sorrows of today? "Because it is the right thing to do," Raven says aloud, convincing herself. *Life is out of offers for me. And nothing here last forever. I would rather go this way, with dignity and honor.*

Mother Nature is calm as if it, too, waits holding

its breath. Memorizing their features, the woman Lucas was crude to today looks away from the four mournful faces and the lost look in the dark eyes of the only Werewolf in the world. Raven had asked Jet centuries ago why he did not make himself a mate, and Jet had in return asked her the same question; they were both unwillingly to risk the consequences. Who knows how the human would turn out? Now with her gone Raven wonders if Jet will change his mind.

Raven cannot think about the future. Standing on the paved path she closes her eyes, blocking out the view of bloody corpses mixed in with the dying ex-Shadows that have instantly surrounded her, and prays the present will end shortly.

One bite…

Two bites…

Three…

The fourth tear sends her to the ground screaming. The ravenous ex-humans tear into her flesh; scratching, pulling, and ripping.

Leon, Lucas, Cricket, and Lana helplessly watch the one they were sent to get eaten alive right before their eyes. The girl with the summit of her ear missing heavily sobs. Cricket pulls Lana to his side, rubbing his hand up and down her arm.

"I can't watch this," Lucas chokes out, rubbing at his mouth and nose as a teardrop escapes his despondent eyes.

Suddenly, Mozart slams the kitchen door handle down and pushes against the rectangle glass. Lucas, the closest, reaches out to grab the canine's light blue collar. Sharp wolf-like teeth pierce his skin and blood immediately streams down his hand.

Mozart dodges Lana's attempt to catch him. But the familiar Cricket clamps his dark fingers over the protective dog's snout. Cricket picks Mozart up off the grass. Twisting and turning, the Husky digs his nails into the Shadow's strong arms. Realizing he won't be able to get loose, Mozart whimpers loudly at the sight in the night.

Is this my purpose? Jet hears Raven convulsing while the abominations shred her smooth skin. *Really? To watch the one thing that was supposed to be with me forever die?* Mozart cries next to him in Cricket's arms, and the wolf's blood boils. *This is too much!* Ululating howls of grief rip through the lightless atmosphere. *That's it! I've had enough!* The Werewolf throws his feet forward and leaps on to the road. Ten blurs slam into him, knocking Jet on his side. The Deaths ram their feet into his coat, shattering several of his thick ribs. Jet roars savagely.

Lana moves from her place to save the Werewolf but the cousins quickly grab her. "Don't," Lucas whispers in her ear. "We can't over power them. We need to stick as close to the panic room as possible."

Jet painfully gets to his feet. He slices his front claws into two of the Vampires and pulls out their hearts. The dead organs on his claws turn into maggots. The Vampires that had once been their hosts reduce to ashes.

Four Vampires dig their cold dead fingers into Jet's hind legs pulling them out from underneath him. The Werewolf lands on his face and Jet's steak knife teeth snap at a nearby ankle. A screaming bloodsucker retreats to the grass; his foot bitten off.

The Bald Vampire and another nightwalker pick up the Werewolf's head and easily force it *into* the hard asphalt.

Meanwhile, the strangest thing is happening…

The zombies that have fed off the Goddess begin staggering away from her…The other zombies violently attack the ones that now contain the half-human half-Vampire's blood…

Thunderclaps above them. "Jet!" Raven screams with despair; the image of her enemies breaking the bones in her lifelong friend's front legs scars her retinas. Exasperated, she breathes in the last air of hope. The exposed bones in the woman's arms swing against the vultures, but that only makes the pain worse. Her eyes refuse the heartbreaking scene. Weakened, her eyelids have no choice but to close.

The wind howls—the sound like that of a freight train stings the eardrums of the four humans. The frightening faces around Raven begin clearing out; each and every one of the reviving walking dead fall unconscious to the ground…

Death. Birth. Birthday… A stream of sentences and memories flow through the seer: *I became half-human at age nineteen… When did you stop ageing…? Twenty three… In Hastings we stopped at the roadblock on twenty three seconds. The yellow numbers flashed red at nineteen seconds. Our room number in Nebraska was nineteen… Nineteen people at the hospital… The green-haired woman biting Raven…*

"She had trouble breathing after killing the gothic looking—*I threw up for the first time in my nine hundred years of being...*" Lucas, Cricket, and Lana stare at the incoherent man. Leon Carmany sees his Potential's body positioned the way it had been in his first Prevention of her; on her side and bathed in blood... "Lana, I need your help," The Preventer says and rushes to the door—the three of them on his heels.

"Brighton,—"

"*—You only see the human,*" Leon continues rambling through the kitchen, *"Normals, you are supposed to save from the Vampires."* The door bangs shut against the frame behind Cricket; still restraining the upset dog.

In the capacious dining room Leon halts in front of the large cross. "Take it. You're faster," he points out to the raven-haired girl. Lana drops the sword and lifts the repellent off the floor. Leon snatches the teenage girl's crossbow off the table. "Get Raven," he tells Lucas as they head back out to the tainted world.

Nine more Vampires, Novices, have arrived—with silver spikes. The Novices stab the Werewolf repeatedly in his hind limb with the jagged spikes, weakening the wolf for their superiors. Finished with their mission, the young Vampires move out of the way. Deaths take Jet's back leg in their hands and yank, ripping it from his body. Blue blood squirts out and quickly covers the pavement while a wounded roar expressing immense pain echoes in the night. The pain is worse than a shark taking a human's leg.

Cricket and Mozart anxiously watch the Shadow and the Hunters running across the yard; the Hunters for Raven, and Lana for Jet. Lana draws closer with the crucifix held out in front of her. But Cricket fears she is too late.

Kronos jumps up on top of Jet holding a giant silver spike that is half his height. The Vampire in the black and gold cape raises the silver weapon above his head.

The Husky howls and Cricket buries the side of his face against Mozart's; using the dog's warmth for comfort.

Kronos brings the thick pointed spike down piercing Jet's hard outer core. Another rib breaks and the silver punctures the Werewolf's heart.

Mozart's fur dampens with Cricket's tears.

The silver in his heart forces Jet to return to his human skin, one legged, rendering him ultimately vulnerable. Feeling the bloodsucker's fingers close around his neck, Jet prays what he is certain is his last prayer. *God, please let Ray have a better outcome.*

Kronos breaks Jet's neck.

A green wave like that of a force field expels from the wooden cross and propels Kronos and the other Vampires through the air. Leon prepares to put an arrow in anything that approaches him and his cousin as Lucas sweeps up a bloody Raven in his arms. The wind snatches limbs from the nearby tree creating a new version of its life.

"Lana, let's go!" The Preventer shouts for her to retreat.

Leon, Lana, and Lucas with Raven in his

muscular arms approach the side door. Cricket is the first one in after Mozart. Not having the faintest idea when she will be back out here, Lana snatches up Ganesha's sword and the backpack containing the book of Vampires from the dining room floor.

On the way to the safe room, hope dominates four pairs of eyes. Cricket punches in the security code. Once inside the panic room the male Shadow opens the other door on the opposite side and they hurry down the lighted stairwell. The light bulb above them casting their silhouettes.

Leon's quick observation of the underground room reveals sleeping cots, a refrigerator, stove, canned goods on counters, people, and a cistern. The freshwater in the enormous tank and the supply of food is enough to at least last unit the crazed cannibals withered away from lack of human body parts; starvation.

Lucas gently sets the woman with barely any skin on her bones—literally—on the cold concrete floor.

"What's wrong with her?" someone asks.

With blood on his hands and on his white and blue shirt, Lucas looks up at his cousin. "What are we doing, Leon?"

The twenty-two year old genius kneels beside them. "You'll see."

An elderly man steps forward. "Is she...dead?"

"Yeah," Leon says. He looks at the old man and then at the other people. He recognizes Lisa and figures the boy next to her is Joshua. But there seems to be more people here than the nineteen they rescued... "Who are you people?"

"My...my..." a weak voice says from the concrete floor. Everyone in the room stares at the dead body...

"Raven?" The blonde man with the chickenpox scar above his eyebrow gapes as the bones in Raven's arms and legs miraculously join together. Her missing flesh closing up over them. Her body renewing itself. But that is not what causes them to gasp...

"Neighbors," Raven finishes.

"I told you this wasn't bye," Lucas flashes a smug smile.

"My heart..." She places her hand over her chest, astounded. "It...it's beating the way it used to before I... I'm... I think I'm...*human.*"

"You think that's neat? Got a mirror?"

Raven jumps up and hurries into the bathroom. "I'm..." she stares in shock at her reflection. She isn't looking at the reflection of a twenty three year old female. "Am I... nineteen?"

"So...this thing made you *completely* human?" Lucas raises his eyebrows intrigued. "And *younger?*"

Raven suddenly recalls why she is human. She rushes out of the bathroom. "Jet?" Cricket shakes his head and hugs her.

"The zom...zombie," Lana is finally able to say the word. "The zombie virus kills people and then brings them back to life. It killed the Vampire part of you—and now you're actually *alive*. You were the only one of your kind—half-human half-Vampire. And now there is no such thing. Raven, you technically died."

"You're dead because you are fully alive?" The elderly man rephrases. "I would say that doesn't make a shit ton of sense. But the concept of Werewolves, Vampires, and zombies has always been lost on me."

"If I had known… My friends," Raven looks at all the people in the underground room. "Our friends…"

"Don't." Leon wraps his brawny arms around her. "It had to happen a certain way. Think about it. In my Prevention, when Loki was to die in Hastings, you somehow died and the rest of us died as well. If our lives were not entangled with Loki's the Vampires would have killed you as soon as they realized you were human."

"I guess they think you don't exist anymore," Lana figures. "Like when *we* all die."

"You are right, Raven. I only see the *human* I am to save. My visionettes have the potential to do significant good in the future. From my point of view you have already done that, but clearly you just can't stop. Happy birthday, Benjamin Button!"

Familiar with the story about a man who reverts back from old age to infancy, Raven faintly smiles up at the certified genius. "Thank you. But I do not see how this is a good thing. Lucifer and Kronos got what they wanted. The Shadows numbers are down—and not just here. I'm not a threat, and this world is about to be, if not already, crawling with Demons, ghosts, and a lot of things you have no awareness of."

Lana grins. "At least we got what *we* wanted." The corners of Raven and Cricket's lips turn up and the three of them stand there smiling mysteriously.

"What do you three know that *I* don't know?" Leon asks.

"You'll see," Lana gloats.

* * *

KRONOS & THE OTHERS

The nefarious Vampire with midnight black hair can feel the fire stirring around in the pit of his old stomach. Burning him. Demolishing his insides.

At first Kronos thinks he is the only one in this agony, but then he sees more and more of his kind slumping over; hands on their stomachs. For the first time in his long existence, Kronos remembers what fear feels like.

The steel door to the panic room opens. Raven is the first to step out onto the rubble; her entire house has been torn apart by a Kansas tornado. The only thing remaining is the steel and concrete room she and the Hunters, each with a stake, Cricket and Lana, both sporting crossbows, and Mozart have come out from.

The path of the tornado is apparent. It came through the section of the woods that had burned due to the object that fell from the sky and landed there. The twister, after causing further damage to the trees, went straight through the cedar house. "The slope and ditch must have caused it to stop," Leon guesses. The moon has come out of hiding and Leon Carmany is unable to recall a time when it has shined this bright.

"I didn't kill Sheba. Maybe she will be here," the former Goddess says with a little optimism.

"What's up with them?" Lucas asks of the thirty

or so bloodsuckers moaning and falling down around the front perimeter of what use to be Raven's cedar house.

The two females march across the flattened house, the debris covering the entire lawn, and around the limbs scattered on the road over to Kronos perched under the tree at the corner of Jet Road and Brother Street. The leader of the Vampires stands waiting for their attack, lips curled back, spine arched like an injured and pissed off feline ready to pounce. A mad gleam in his eyes as if using the moon's light to scorch the two women.

"What's the matter Kronos?" the raven-haired girl taunts. "Drink something you shouldn't have?"

Raven picks up one of the plastic bottles of blood that more than likely had been left here by the storm. "With all those filthy smells gone and a clear head you should be able to tell me what this smells like." She tosses him the bottle.

Kronos sniffs, and sees Raven's canine standing in the middle of the road with the three humans. *"Dog."* Kronos closes his eyes anticipating the next words out of the daywalker's mouth.

"It covers the smell of Lana's and Cricket's blood quite well, wouldn't you agree?"

Kronos's legs begin to shake from the poison.

"Did you honestly think I didn't know that a Shadow's blood weakens Vampires?"

"But it won't *hurt* you, will it Kronos?" Lana takes a step closer. "It's going to *end* you. The blood of a Shadow who is your relative." She smiles. "I was able to kill you after all… *Uncle*."

"The hospital!" Leon concludes standing next to

Lucas in the middle of Jet Road. "That's the *real* reason you went!"

"Geniuses," Raven jokes with Lana. "So overrated."

"This here"—Kronos gestures—"is nothing, Shadow. Your kind is dying all over this continent," he snickers.

"Hey, dumbass," Lucas addresses the elder Vampire, interrupting his soulless laughter. "You wouldn't happen to know where I can find Avy Sinanna? He's about your height, hair more girly than his," he points to his cousin.

Kronos breaks off a small limb from the tree above him and Lana stops the nightwalker before he can impale himself. "Now, now. Kronos belongs to me," she mocks, and the caped Vampire screams in unbelievable agony as he kneels to the ground. "Move back," Raven cautions the Shadow, taking a few steps back herself.

"Reaper was going to claim you!" The dying Vampire digs his claws into the dirt. Kronos can feel it detaching... Moving around in his eight-hundred and sixteen year old ribcage... Tearing the pipe in his throat that is used for swallowing down the blood of his victims. His teeth scrape against it...

A black heart plops out on the damp grass. The night predator, unable to move, watches his heart explode into black dust.

Kronos looks up at the two human girls.

"It seems I have a little more pull with my God then you do yours. Farwell, trickster," Raven waves.

The Vampire with the scarred face screams as his eyes lose their colors, turning white, and then rolling back in his head. His eyeballs and the skin around them erodes down to the sockets. The erosion quickly spreads to his pale nose, lips, and hair leaving dark empty sockets and bare teeth, like a skull found at the bottom of an ocean, and continues on to the rest of the nightwalker's flesh and organs—becoming nothing more than an old skeleton under the light of the stars.

They stare at the Vampire's remains; even his followers that are bowed over and the ones forced to lie down from the toxic substance.

The leader of the nightwalkers is dead. Dead dead.

Lucas Kale and Leon Carmany cheer victoriously.

Lana Queen blinks several times, accepting a world free of her tormentor. She smiles at the human next to her who made this possible and gives her a hug like that of lifelong friends.

Worlds start to move; what is left of the dark clouds part and skies start to resemble what they were when the five of them were children.

Raven, Lana Queen, Lucas Kale, Leon Carmany, and Cricket happily run about staking the undead, having found some degree of the solace they each have sought for so long.

~~~~

Epilogue

WITH THE SHOTGUN next to her on the couch cushion, Mrs. Queen quietly sits in her basement waiting for her daughter to return. She has been awake since the absence of her only child. The electricity went out not long after Lana's departure. Luckily Mrs. Queen had thought to find the Christmas candles she stored down here in one of the boxes and a lighter before the lights left her in the lonely room. Some of the candles that reflected a beautiful array of slow dancing flame in the ceiling mirror had burnt down to their wick and she had to light new ones.

    There are no windows in the basement and Mrs. Queen has no idea whether dawn has come or not. Either way it does little help to know. The single mother has grown tired but she cannot truly rest until her daughter comes home. Mesmerized by the tiny flames flicking silhouettes on the walls from the small table next to the old couch, her long eyelashes gravitate towards her warm cheeks. The tired woman is near nodding off when a radiant white light shines before her. Startled, Mrs. Queen grabs the shotgun and leaps off the couch.

The bright light reflecting off the ceiling mirror temporarily blinds her. The white light quickly disappears behind a man with wrinkleless skin clothed in a white robe. The black-haired woman stands frozen, shotgun aimed at the man. "Do not be frightened, child," he speaks soothingly, his voice soft and beautiful like blooming meadow flowers. "My Father has sent me to ask for your permission."

"For? Are you an Angel?" She shakes nervously.

"To take over your vessel." His golden wings flutter. "Your life and your daughter's depends on your decision."

"Lana? I-I-I don't understand."

"Proverbs 3:5." The man quotes, "Trust in the lord with all your heart and do not lean upon your own understanding."

"Uh… Okay." She lowers the shotgun.

"Do I have your permission?"

"Yes." Mrs. Queen vigorously shakes her head. "I will do anything for Lana." Suddenly, Mrs. Queen feels like she is half awake, half asleep—as if a force has overcome her putting her in some weird dream-like state. Without thinking about it, just like breathing, she points the barrel of the shotgun at her abdomen and pulls the trigger. Tremendous pain, as if a volcano erupted from inside, explodes through her stomach.

Abruptly, Mrs. Queen's head snaps upwards and she is forced to watch her irises, reflected in the mirror, as they turn darker than the corners of the room. Black veins spread out from her black irises, covering the white parts of her eyes.

The Demon, now inside of Mrs. Queen, speaks with his vessel's voice. "*An Angel?* Humans are hilariously stupid." The body that had once belonged to Lana's mother begins walking up the basement stairs, running a hand along the railing and carrying the dangling intestines with the other. "You don't understand anything."

* * *

"She killed Kronos."

"Kronos was prideful. He had it coming," the Bald Vampire in the trench coat says as he washes zombie blood from his hands in the cavern's water. "I doubt his death means anything to Father. The Goddess is what mattered."

"When will your hair grow back?" Blayne asks lying down. His back on a hard, thick rock.

"In a few hours. The sun is almost here. We must rest now."

"You stood right in front of the blood cousins. How is it they didn't recognize you? Even without your hair, Avy?"

Avy Sinanna stands upright and smirks. "Lucas and Leon may not be Burned anymore, but their memories are that of a child." Then out of the blue he says, "You're in love with her."

"That's impossible," Blayne counters sitting up. The two torches on either side of the massive brown rock cast his silhouette on the cave wall. "You can't deny what we smelled after seeing what they did to my sire and the others. Raven is human now." A wicked grin flashes across the eighteen year old boy's face. "But what are the odds of her resisting the change *again?*" Their evil laughs of joy echo off the cave walls.

Blayne fiddles with the necklaces looped around his fingers—one with rubies, the other a purple unicorn... "The body—"

"It's fine..."

* * *

"Hi!"

Lana opens her apple green eyes. The sun's godly yellow light momentarily blinds her. Someone leans over her, blocking the bright light. "Loki!"

"I think I missed a lot," the girl with bobbing ringlets says, her friend embracing her in a tight hug. "Like why everyone's sleeping on the grass?" Cricket and Raven sit up next to Lana on the wet lawn. Loki gasps in shock at Raven's face.

On the other side of the nineteen year old, Leon raises up off the ground and wraps his arms around his bended knees. "Long night. Seeing the sunrise seemed like the thing to do."

Next to Leon, Lucas rolls over on his side facing Loki. "She's beautiful." For a moment Loki's heart leaps with excitement thinking Lucas is talking about her, but then she realizes he is looking up at the sky. Lucas takes his hazel eyes off the light and steals a glance at Raven. "But it hurts to look at her." He pulls himself away from the group. *Her friends are dead. I saw firsthand the pain she went through last night when Ganesha died. She's human. Raven has a lot to deal with. Funerals.*

Demons. I don't want to further ruin her life.

"It's Sunday," Lana realizes. "I feel like we owe God a visit."

"Yeah," Leon agrees.

"I didn't have time to get my mom a Mother's Day gift. But she's so gonna say I'm the only gift she wants."

"Where's Cole?" asks Loki.

"What do you remember?" Leon asks as he and the others under the warm sun rays begin to follow after Lucas.

"It's a blur really. Like I know people turned into freaks and we came to this bloodsuck—Raven's. What's up with her face? And where's our Cole at?"

"I had to—he's not coming back," Lana tells Loki, her voice low. "Can we change the subject?"

The mentioning of Cole's death freezes Raven in the middle of the debris scattered on the lawn. "Ganesha was bitten *after* I took her into the house," Raven recalls. "I was unconscious and when I came to…"

Lucas whirls around. Cricket, Leon, and Lana stop in their tracks.

Loki puts her hand on her hips. "What's the big deal? A flesh eating weirdo attacked her inside. So what?"

The petite girl with bandages covering her burns glares, her eyes like that of fire. "Can you say that one more time with even less of a heart?"

"That's not how I—" Suddenly Loki takes a blow to the eye.

"You will find I am not as tolerant as I use to

be," Raven tells the younger blonde girl. "If your brain cannot process this then your face will." She leaves the stunned girl holding her hand over her already bruising eye.

"The surveillance tapes," Raven explains, punching the code in to the safe room. The door slides open and everyone except Loki, who remains outside, hurries over to the monitors displaying black screens; the cameras had been damaged by the storm. Raven presses the rewind button below one of the screens. She cannot believe what pops up on the monitor. "No disc?" She presses the eject button. Nothing happens. "It's gone..." She presses the eject buttons under the other screens. "They're *all* gone. How is this possible?"

The survivors begin clearing out from the underground room. Some of them hug their savior, others hoot and holler on their way to the outside world. Lisa and Joshua give their thanks, and then Raven heads down the stairs.

"We will figure this out," Leon assures.

The concealed room has everything; electricity, food, a water tank, bathrooms, and entertainment. "If I had known all this was down here I would have stayed," Lucas lies. *She can't know I like her. It will only complicated things. I have to forget what I was feeling on that roof.*

"It is going to take some time for my blood—my old blood—to spread." Raven pulls out a CD binder from the dozens displayed on the case next to the stereo system. "I'm not in a hurry to go anywhere. I am going to sit here for an hour, maybe two. You guys are welcome to join Cricket and me." Raven puts a CD in the stereo. The five of them sit at a circled table listening to music and rummaging through binders of music.

"You owe me a book," Leon reminds his cousin.

"You owe me for the years and years of lady stealing, c-blocker."

Leon rolls his sapphire eyes.

"Hey, what nationality was Kronos?" Lana asks the long fair-haired woman who has done so much for the human race. "I've always assumed he was from America because he never used an accent."

"He was born in Ireland."

"Wow, I'm part Irish." Lana looks at the Irish band on Cricket's shirt. "I think you and I are going to be great friends." He grins wide, all of his white teeth exposed.

"How did you first find out about the zombies?" Leon asks Raven.

"Do you really want to know?"

"Yeah, what happened?" Lana closes the binder of CD's.

"Okay." Raven says to the pairs of enthusiastic eyes, "You may have a hard time believing this… Yesterday in Hastings, Nebraska, sometime before meeting Lucas and before my departure from the airport…"

Yesterday in Hastings, Nebraska

"…You know you don't like that white boy," Raven said as Ganesha parked the sleek yellow car on the side of New Hope Road.

"I think Eric Forman is cute, thank you very much! I would so sleep with him."

"Eric Forman isn't real," Raven laughed. The topic of today was *That 70's Show*.

Her friend pressed play on her I-pod and rap music sounded through the speakers. *"Eric Forman isn't real,"* Ganesha mimicked.

Raven smiled. "You're stupid."

"You're more stupid. And here's your birthday present from Cricket. He was gonna give it to you later but he wanted us to go ahead and have it." Ganesha pulled out a brown blunt from her purse.

"Oh my god!" Raven took it from her fingers. "Is this a homemade chocolate blunt?"

Ganesha smiled. "Yes. Yes it is. Now fire it up." She handed her a lighter, and they followed the puff puff pass rule while dancing to the music. The wonderful skunk aroma they enjoyed so much filled the car. "Do you think anyone's watching?" Ganesha asked.

Raven took a long drag, held it for a few seconds, and then answered; a small cloud of smoke escaped. "The only couple I hear are having sex."

"Glad I don't hear that shit. Anyways, which one would you do?"

"Hyde. Totally," she grinned, passing the brown shell. They laughed hysterically. The music filled their ears and the smoke thickened around them.

Something with a gray face and eyes glazed like a blind person's smacked its palms against the driver window. "Ahhhh!" Ganesha—high as a kite—screamed and put the car in drive. Raven, with half a blunt in between her two fingers, narrowed her eyes. "What the fuck is that?"

"Zombie!" her friend yelled and pushed the gas

pedal.

"Stop! Stop!"

Ganesha let off of the gas and pressed the break. "Why?"

"Don't I have to like"—Raven started laughing mid-sentence—"kill it or something?"

"Oh yeah," Ganesha started laughing, and then put the gears in reverse. "That's probably a good idea."

The back tires bumped as they rolled over the creature, then the backend went up again as the car moved forward over it. Ganesha took the chocolate flavored blunt. "I'll guard this." Raven opened the car door and a cloud of smoke rolled out.

Now

"You smoke *marijuana*?" Lucas adjust his pants, trying to hide his boner for what seems like the millionth time since meeting the attractive woman with long blonde hair. The song on the CD player ends.

"Well, I have to use the bathroom," Raven announces. The next song plays as she enters the huge bathroom closing the door behind her.

"You are human now," a male voice says.

Raven turns away from the door. A being resembling that of a naked man stands before her; it has no male genitals. Its skin is dark blue and its legs look like two legs morphed together. The face as no nose or ears, and where the eyes should be are empty holes darker than a cave. A thin blue aura shines around his body.

"Yes, sir," Raven respectfully answers.

"Your mission is still the same." Its blue tongue withers around as it speaks. "Deliver Loki to the Light Bearer."

"Do I dare disturb the universe? In a minute there is time for decisions and revisions which a minute will reverse. For I have known them all already, know them all—Have known the evenings, mornings, afternoons, I have measured out my life with coffee spoons," Raven quotes the words written by the poetic T.S. Eliot, *"I know the voices dying with a dying fall beneath the music from a farther room.*

"So how should I presume?"

TO BE CONTINUED...

~~~

</div>

Thank you for reading my book. Please take a moment to leave me a review.
I can't wait to hear your thoughts!
xoxo -*Angela*

P.S. Look for

HOME,

the chilling sequel to *Blue Solace*.

~~

ABOUT THE AUTHOR

Angela Dawn Staten (March 1988) wrote her very first novel at an early age. She was just twenty-five when Blue Solace was first published. This is her first novel in *The Blue Solace Series*. Angela was born in Georgia, and raised in Tennessee (USA). She was voted biggest bookworm by her classmates from Springfield High School (2006). Angela also has a background in modeling and acting.

*Check out my website for an updated list of books, interviews, and more!
https://angeladawnsworld.wordpress.com
Come say Hi on Facebook, Twitter, and Instagram!

CPSIA information can be obtained
at www.ICGtesting.com
Printed in the USA
BVOW04s1851140517
484112BV00001B/2/P